to the power of three

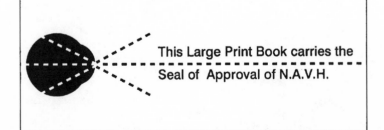

to the power of three

Laura Lippman

Published in 2005 by arrangement with William Morrow, an imprint of HarperCollins Publishers.

Wheeler Large Print Hardcover.

The text of this Large Print edition is unabridged.
Other aspects of the book may vary from the original edition.

Set in 16 pt. Plantin by Carleen Stearns.

Printed in the United States on permanent paper.

Library of Congress Cataloging-in-Publication Data

Lippman, Laura, 1959–
    To the power of three / by Laura Lippman.
      p. cm.
    ISBN 1-59722-106-6 (lg. print : hc : alk. paper)
    1. Police — Maryland — Baltimore — Fiction.
2. Teenage girls — Crimes against — Fiction.   3. Female friendship — Fiction.   4. Baltimore (Md.) — Fiction.
5. Teenage girls — Fiction.   6. Large type books. I. Title.
PS3562.I586T6 2005b
  813'.6—dc22   2005019891

For Nancy Goldman Greenberg

As the Founder/CEO of NAVH, the only national health agency solely devoted to those who, although not totally blind, have an eye disease which could lead to serious visual impairment, I am pleased to recognize Thorndike Press* as one of the leading publishers in the large print field.

Founded in 1954 in San Francisco to prepare large print textbooks for partially seeing children, NAVH became the pioneer and standard setting agency in the preparation of large type.

Today, those publishers who meet our standards carry the prestigious "Seal of Approval" indicating high quality large print. We are delighted that Thorndike Press is one of the publishers whose titles meet these standards. We are also pleased to recognize the significant contribution Thorndike Press is making in this important and growing field.

Lorraine H. Marchi, L.H.D.
Founder/CEO
NAVH

* Thorndike Press encompasses the following imprints: Thorndike, Wheeler, Walker and Large Print Press.

My Life had stood — a Loaded gun —
In Corners — till a Day
The Owner passed — identified —
And carried Me away —

. . .

Though I than He — may longer live
He longer must — than I —
For I have but the power to kill,
Without — the power to die
                    — Emily Dickinson

Three can keep a secret, if two are dead.
                    — Benjamin Franklin

Thursday

I

People would want to know what she was thinking, the night before. They always do, or think they do — but in her case they would have been disappointed. Because by the night before, the thinking was long over and she was preoccupied mainly with logistics. Planning, preparing, packing. Finding her old knapsack, an orange-and-black JanSport she hadn't used for months, not since Christmastime.

Knapsacks had gone out of fashion that spring at Glendale High School, at least among the stylish girls. The divas, as they were known — they had bestowed the name on themselves and considered it laudatory — had taken to carrying plastic totes in bright primary colors, see-through and flimsy. Even the name-brand versions, the ones that cost upwards of a hundred dollars, buckled under the weight the divas expected them to carry. But then it's a myth that more expensive things are better made — or so her father always said, whenever she expressed a desire for something trendy. At the mall she had seen diva mothers storm into Nordstrom or Hecht Co., proclaiming the totes defective. "What was she using it for?" skeptical salesladies inquired, examining the torn and stretched-out handles beneath the fluorescent lights. "The usual," lied the mothers. "Girl stuff."

In the end the salesladies didn't care if the mothers stretched the truth as far as those rubbery handles, because they always left with even more merchandise — not only a replacement tote or two but those hideous Louis Vuitton billfolds that were so unfathomably popular that spring, maybe a small cosmetic bag in the same distinctive-tacky pattern. They needed cosmetic bags because the totes had another design flaw. The not-quite-opaque plastic allowed the world to see whatever one carried. Forget trying to bring Tampax to school, or even a hairbrush. (She had always considered hairbrushes one of the more horrible secrets that regular purses kept — oily, matted with hair, shedding those strange little scales.) Yet perhaps that was the very source of the totes' cachet: To use one, you had to pretend you had no se-

crets, that your life was an open book —
or, more correctly, a see-through purse.
You couldn't put *anything* in those totes
that you didn't want other people to
glimpse.

Especially a gun, no matter how small.
Even a gun wrapped in a scarf, as hers
would be.

The problem was that she, too, had
abandoned her knapsack earlier that
school year, although she was not one to
follow the trends, quite the opposite. She
had different reasons for retiring her trusty
JanSport. *I am putting away childish
things,* she told herself in November,
having been reminded of that Bible verse
while rereading a favorite childhood novel.
Her mother had gotten a canvas bag at
Barnes & Noble, one with Emily Dickinson's face, and she had co-opted it for a
joke, just to test how ignorant everyone
was. ("Is that someone you know?" "Is that
you?" "A relative?") She hadn't planned to
use it every day, but then her parents
began to nag, said she was going to throw
her spine out of alignment or damage the
nerves in her shoulder. Then she *had* to
keep using it, if only to prove to them that
it was her spine, her nerves, her life.

Except the Emily Dickinson bag was forever falling over, scattering its contents. She couldn't afford such accidents or missteps, not on the day she took her gun to school.

She finally found her knapsack at the back of her closet, and it was a kind of relief to be reunited with her old, practical friend. She dampened a paper towel and ran it over the bag's insides, removing debris from last fall — cookie crumbs, specks of chocolate, a lone Brazil nut, which would have been there since September, when she tried to go vegan and lasted all of a week. She had carried this knapsack for four years, from fall of eighth grade to the fall of twelfth grade, and its surface — the names and former loyalties inked onto its orange nylon, the rips and tears — was a vivid reminder of how much she had changed. *You probably shouldn't get tattooed,* her mother always said. *You don't know who you're going to be when you're thirty.* But a tattoo can be concealed, or even removed with lasers. Piercings close up if you give them enough time. A knapsack covered with embarrassing sentiments in permanent ink could only be discarded or replaced. Her parents would have purchased her a new one if she had only explained her reasons, but that was one thing she hadn't dared to do. She was tired of explaining herself.

Once the bag was clean inside, she surveyed the things laid out on her bed. There was her notebook, the take-home test for Mrs. Downey, her independent study project for Ms. Cunningham. And there was the gun, wrapped in a silk scarf from the old dress-up chest.

The gun had been in her possession for almost a month, but the mere sight of it still shocked her. It was so like the toy six-shooter she had begged for when she was little, not even four. Why had she yearned for a gun, a holster, and a cowboy hat at such an age? She had wanted to be Calamity Jane or Annie Oakley, marching around the house singing "Anything You Can Do, I Can Do Better." Yes, it was queer, but then everyone was queer when little. And maybe she had wanted to shock her parents, who weren't hippies but were antiwar, even this current one, which a lot of Glendale parents had said was okay when it started.

Standing in her bedroom, a real gun in her hand, she finally understood how toddlers could pick up a weapon and fire, with no instruction or training. The gun she had taken was just like her old toy — six

chambers for six bullets, each one dis-
lodged by pressing the trigger. Or so she
assumed, because she hadn't dared to fire
it, not even once. There was no place she
wouldn't be overheard. Once Glendale had
had large tracts of woods, areas where a
kid could hide, escape the world for a little
while. But those spots had been mowed
down, leveled, replaced with strip malls
and parking lots, just like the song said.
She had really liked that song before her
parents told her it was a cover, that the
Counting Crows hadn't done it first, that
they had listened to it, too, when they were
even younger than she was now. Her parents meant well, but sometimes she wanted
something that was all for her. Was that so
much to ask?

The gun had come with four bullets,
which seemed an odd number to her, not
that she could ask how that came to be.
How many bullets are in the gun, Chino?
That was a line from *West Side Story*,
Maria's big moment at the end. She was
never the kind of girl who got to play
Maria, nor did she want to be. Namby-
pamby "I Feel Pretty" Maria, totally re-
active. It had been stealing, of course, to
take the gun, but then the people who
owned it had broken laws, too. It should

have been in a safe and equipped with a childproof lock. She had written a paper on state gun laws for history last year, arguing strenuously for a true ban on all firearms. The rednecks had been outraged, of course. Not that there were many rednecks in AP American history.

Before she'd wrapped the gun up in the scarf, she'd picked it up and held it next to her cheek, stroking herself, the way villains were always caressing women in spy movies. It didn't look the same. Maybe it was because she didn't have the right kind of face. Her mother always told her that her face was heart-shaped, but all she saw was that it was sharp in an almost witchy way — pointy chin, hollow cheeks. When an actor traced a line down an actress's face, the gesture was sexual and violent at the same time, or so Ms. Cunningham had said in her "Rhetoric of Images" class. She told the girls they had to learn to recognize such images and decode them, so they wouldn't be infected by them. It made no sense, though. She couldn't get why the gesture was sexual if it denoted rape, which everyone kept insisting wasn't about sex but violence. *Because the gun is a phallic symbol,* Ms. Cunningham explained. *Rape is an act of violence that happens to be expressed through sex.* "But you also said rape isn't about sex, that if boys force us to do anything we don't want to do, it's the same as assault." *Yes, and films confuse the message, suggesting that rape can be sexual, when it clearly isn't, setting you up to make poor choices. Don't you see?*

She was beginning to. She now saw how ideas that might appear to be at the opposite ends of a spectrum were really matched sets, yin and yang, eternally connected rings. No love without hate. No peace without war. "We had to destroy the village in order to save it." Mr. Blum, the history teacher, was always offering this as an example of the idiotic things said during the Vietnam War, that war being his big reference point, the proof that he had once cared about something larger than himself and his precious little sports car, which he buffed with a chamois cloth in good weather, out in the teachers' parking lot. It seemed silly to be so proud of a car, when half the kids at Glendale drove nicer ones. *You have to destroy the village in order to save it.* She no longer saw the paradox. Sometimes you do have to destroy things, even people, in order to save them.

Yet these thoughts, while appropriately

deep, did not figure into her last words. She had only so much time, so much space, and she was undeniably self-conscious, perhaps a bit too fixated on the effect of what she was doing. The letter she composed was factual, yet somehow false. Even her handwriting was false — florid, overdone, so she couldn't fit it all onto one sheet of paper as she had planned. She had lost the habit of expressing herself honestly, without irony and grandiose turns of phrase. She wrote about heaven and love, and called on old loyalties. She asked only that the truth be told. She wrote it just that way, in just those words: *"I ask only that the truth be told."*

After much chewing on the end of her pen, a bad habit she had never outgrown even though it often left her with blue lips, she crossed out the word "only." She knew that it was a lot to ask, perhaps the most a person can ask, under certain circumstances.

Part One

the lost tribe of the ka-pe-jos

Friday

2

When the shooting started, Alexa Cunningham was looking at Anita Whitehead's arms — her arms, then her underarms, because Anita threw her hands over her head and began to shriek. Later Alexa Cunningham would try to rewrite that memory in her head, replace it with something more portentous, but the image was stubborn: Anita's tremulous upper arms bursting into hives, then the tiny white mothballs of roll-on deodorant visible in the stubble of her underarms just before she threw the telephone down. Alexa even caught a whiff of something floral, antiperspirant or perfume, and found time to wonder why someone who claimed to suffer from multiple chemical sensitivities would use anything scented.

That troubled her, too — how one track of her mind detached, finding room for trivial observations in the midst of a crisis. Later she told herself that it was simply a citizen's duty to be prepared for the role of eyewitness, absorbing every detail of an unfolding tragedy, and one could not pick and choose what one noticed. Still, there was no getting around it — what Alexa saw, at the moment that everything changed, was Anita's arms, swaying like poorly staked hammocks; Anita's lips, puckered around the straw in her omnipresent Diet Vanilla Coke, then rounding into a scream; and Anita's eyebrows, too overplucked to register surprise. And what Alexa heard was a voice in her head, coolly narrating events. Why was that? Where did such a voice come from? But Alexa knew. If you lived to tell the story, then you *lived*. She had instinctively thought like a survivor, and there could be no shame in that.

When the shots came, I was picking up my mail in the office and listening to Anita complain about her imaginary symptoms.

"TGIF," Anita had said a few minutes earlier by way of greeting. "Tee-Gee-Eye-Eff."

"Hmmm," Alexa murmured, eyes on her mail so she would not stare at Anita's arms, left bare by a sleeveless knit top. Alexa's older brother, Evan, had once dressed as a woman for Halloween, donning a flesh-colored turtleneck beneath a muumuu, then stuffing the arms with tennis balls so they wobbled back and forth just the way Anita's arms shook whenever she moved them. Alexa, eight at the time, had laughed until she almost wet herself. Evan was imitating their own mother, who was a good sport about such things.

"You got big plans for the weekend, Lexy?"

Alexa had never been known by this nickname, which sounded a little soap-operaish to her ear.

"Uh-uh. You know how the work floods in, the last week for seniors. Have to make sure all my kids are ready to walk next Thursday."

"Supposed to be beautiful this weekend. I wish I could go somewhere. But even if we could get down the ocean" — she gave it the local pronunciation, *downy eauchin* — "my doctor says I really shouldn't."

"Hmmmm."

"Because of the sun."

Alexa made no reply, pretending absorption in Barbara Paulson's memo on senior pranks. Faculty and staff were to be reminded — that was her wording, *were to be reminded* — that any student participating in a stunt involving damage to property, no matter how small, would be banned from the graduation ceremony. As a relatively new school, Glendale did not have many entrenched traditions, but outgoing seniors did have a curious habit of setting off firecrackers in the woods just beyond the athletic fields. *We also take a strict view of injury,* Barbara had added, making bodily injury seem an afterthought to the more serious problem of vandalism. The memo was pure Barbara — bureaucratic, poorly written, unintentionally funny. But then Barbara was never funny on purpose.

"And the air." *Aaaaaah-er* in Anita's accent. "The very air makes my skin *sting*. My doctor says it's because of the salt in the breeze."

"Hmmmmm."

Anita's doctor was a topic to be avoided at all costs. Six months ago Anita had decided that her health problems — not only her hives but the headaches and chronic shortness of breath — were the fault of some toxin in the Glendale High School heating and cooling ducts. Or the carpet. Or the sealant used on the gymnasium floor. Three tests had been ordered so far, and three tests had come back with inconclusive results. Yet Anita was still threatening legal action, and when she tired of speaking of her doctor, she mulled out loud about which lawyer might represent her. All her options advertised on local television, although she sometimes glimpsed someone promising on Court TV. Otherwise she was waffling between the "Let's talk about it" guy and the firm endorsed by former Baltimore Colt Bubba Smith. Alexa, one of the few faculty members who accepted multiple chemical sensitivity as a legitimate medical condition, did not scoff at the science behind Anita's claim. She just didn't happen to believe that Anita suffered from anything other than her own bad choices.

"My girlfriend who used to work for social services?" Alexa did not take the bait, but Anita was not someone who considered a lack of response inimical to a conversation. In fact, silence only encouraged her. "They shut down the whole building because it was making people sick. Now she works in that old Caldor on York Road, across the street from a Panera Breads and a Giant Foods and a Starbucks. She says it's real convenient, especially since Blockbuster Videos went in."

So that's your plan, Alexa thought. Keep demanding tests until she was reassigned to a better location or Glendale High

School was rebuilt on a site more convenient to overstuffed sandwiches, grocery shopping, and movie rentals.

The irony was that there had been growing support to level Glendale and rebuild a new school before Anita began threatening legal action. Such an act, while drastic, would not be unprecedented. Nearby Howard County had recently blown up a windowless octagon built in the heyday of the open-space movement, replacing it with a more traditional rectangle of beige and glass bricks. But Anita Whitehead's complaints had forced the school board into a defensive posture. The school had no flaws, the Baltimore County school board and superintendent now maintained, a laughable contention at a school that had been obsolete and reviled from the day its doors had opened ten years earlier.

To begin with, Glendale was too small, a common enough problem in Maryland, where school construction seldom kept pace with growth. The best elementary schools were surrounded by portable classrooms, and some students spent their first five years in these nominally temporary settings. At the high-school level, unhampered by mandated student-teacher ratios, they simply crammed more bodies into existing buildings. Glendale, built for twelve hundred students, held almost fifteen hundred.

Yet while Glendale High School's classrooms were cramped and overflowing, its public areas, all in the north wing, were almost too vast. The auditorium was so large that no student concert or play could fill it, which gave productions a melancholy air of failure. The gymnasium was a high-ceilinged barn that always felt half empty, even when the boys' basketball team made a run for the state championship.

But the crowning idiocy of Glendale High School, as Glendale's original developer, Thornton Hartigan, had complained so publicly and loudly, was that the architect simply had not understood Maryland's climate, much less the quirkier weather peculiar to this valley. Glendale lay in north Baltimore County, physically closer to the Pennsylvania state line than it was to Baltimore, although most parents commuted southward to the city, or beyond. Because storms often cut a northeasterly path across the state, this northern part of the county could be under six inches of snow while the rest of the region was unscathed. And the winds were especially harsh here, whipping around the school's treeless lot as if still angry at those who had cleared so much of the valley's forests a century ago.

Yet the architect had sold the school board on four freestanding wings centered on a courtyard, a design more suitable to California or Florida. In inclement weather students had to choose between cutting coatless across the courtyard or taking the longer circuitous route, which meant being tardy. An in-house telephone system tried to make up for these vast distances, but this only overburdened the school's wiring, which was wholly inadequate to modern expectations. Students increasingly used BlackBerries, Treos, or other cell phones with e-mail capabilities, rather than rely on the school's sluggish Internet connections.

The call that interrupted Anita's monologue was an in-house one, a fact signaled by two short rings. Anita, looking vaguely annoyed at the phone ringing so early, picked up the receiver and said, "Main office." Then, "What? *What?* Don't you fun with me!"

Apparently the caller persuaded Anita that there was no fun involved, not as verb or noun, for it was then that she threw down the telephone and began to scream.

"We've been shot!" she shrieked, in violation of every protocol in which the staff had been trained. "There's a shooting — some damn kid has brought a gun to school — We've gotta evacuate, we've gotta get out —"

Barbara Paulson was out of her office so fast that she seemed a pink-suited blur, grabbing the receiver that Anita had thrown down. "This is your principal, Barbara Paulson," she said, which was how she began every announcement, answered every phone call. This verbal tic was much mocked behind her back by faculty, who speculated that Barbara presented herself this way at every occasion — the dry cleaners, the drive-through at McDonald's, the rare sexual encounter with her husband. Yet the tone was right for the situation, Alexa realized, stern and authoritative. If this was a prank, the student would never have the nerve to sustain it.

"Please repeat what you just told Ms. Whitehead." Barbara grabbed a pen and began jotting down notes on a "Panther Pride" pad that was handy. In reaching for the pen, she upset Anita's Diet Vanilla Coke, but she didn't seem to notice the soda that cascaded over Anita's desk, even as it splashed onto her skirt and jacket and

33

onto Alexa's mail, which she had put down on the edge of the desk when Anita started screaming. Alexa, not sure what else she could do, dropped to her knees and tried to gather the fallen papers.

"Yes — but —" Barbara had written *"SHOTS FIRED, NORTH WING"* — "I must know — hello? *Hello?*" The line had clearly gone dead. Barbara put down the phone and picked up the microphone for the school's public-address system.

"This is your principal, Barbara Paulson." The words echoed back to them from the hallway speakers. "I need everyone's undivided attention for a special announcement. Everyone — students, faculty, staff, and visitors — in the south, east, and west wings must leave the school immediately, under the emergency procedures we have practiced throughout the year. This is a Level II emergency. Repeat — this is a Level II emergency."

Her hands were shaking, yet her voice retained its usual metallic quality and her face was devoid of emotion, almost waxen. The Botox rumors that had dogged Barbara since spring break suddenly seemed plausible to Alexa. But perhaps Alexa's own face was blank and empty, too, unable to summon any expression appropriate to the moment, because what expression would be appropriate?

Barbara continued speaking into the microphone: "Those in the north wing, however, are asked to go into containment procedures, locking doors, drawing blinds, and staying away from windows until an all-clear is sounded."

Anita and the other secretaries happily followed the principal's instructions, grabbing their purses and all but running from the office. Alexa remained, because she thought Barbara might need her, but the principal barely seemed to register her presence. She called 911 and repeated the information she had gathered, while Alexa listened to her carefully worded answers. Yes, she had implemented the county's emergency plan — evacuation for those in the unaffected wings, lockdown for those classrooms near the reported shooting. No, she did not know if there were any injuries at this point.

"Glendale High School," Barbara repeated patiently. "Off Glendale Circle."

There was a pause while the dispatcher asked another question. Barbara braced the hand holding the phone, but both hands continued to shake.

"I wouldn't characterize it so much as a

school shooting," she said, "but as a shooting at the school."

Motioning Alexa to follow her, the principal turned out the lights in the office and closed the door, locking it behind them. The halls were already full of students and teachers, and Alexa plunged into the hallway, feeling as if she were trying to body-surf in those spindly, treacherous waves she remembered from the Outer Banks, a place she hadn't visited since she was four or five. The air had a crackly, electric charge, more like a winter day than a late-spring one, with some girls' hair dancing on end. The students were moving a bit too fast, talking among themselves in low voices that quickly rose in volume, despite the teachers' best efforts to enforce the no-talking rule. Others were ignoring the guidelines for a Level II emergency, holding their cell phones low by their hips, text-messaging with the ferocity of young Helen Kellers who had just discovered an accessible language. Alexa tapped one or two girls on the shoulder and shook her head in disapproval, but the girls just widened their eyes in fake innocence, as if they couldn't imagine why they were being singled out.

Out in the parking lot, Alexa realized

that the timing of the incident would make it nightmarishly impossible to account for everyone. While teachers had brought their roll books, they had yet to take morning attendance. Ten minutes before the first bell, the school was just full enough to be chaotic. There was no way to determine who had been inside or if the three wings under evacuation had truly emptied.

The staff tried to organize the chattering students, directing them to their homeroom teachers, insisting they turn off their cell phones, but it was like trying to gather feathers in a breeze. Some of the stoner-skater crowd — known as skeezers, for reasons Alexa had never grasped — drifted across the athletic field, heading to the fringe of woods where they gathered in all but the most intolerable weather. Alexa wanted to call after them that this was probably not the best time to get high. Then again, maybe it was. Certainly the police would have more pressing things to do than round up a few pot smokers.

Meanwhile students continued to arrive by car only to turn around promptly, sometimes taking other students with them, even as teachers yelled at them not to go. Parents, pulling up with dawdling freshmen and sophomores who had missed their buses, behaved no more responsibly, fleeing the moment they caught the scent of the emergency. Alexa imagined the stories that were starting in *their* heads, the tales of ordinary lateness — oversleeping, finishing homework — that would now take on epic dimensions. These parents were the lucky ones. They had the advantage of knowing *now* that their children were safe. Other parents would have to endure that horrible gap between partial and full knowledge. Once the police arrived, the driveways to the school would be blocked and parents would be directed to the nearby middle school to wait for their children. That, too, was part of the procedure of a Level II emergency. But it had all seemed so theoretical, so remote, during the training.

The faculty and those students who remained in the parking lot studied the school, as if the building itself might explain what was going on. It stared back, blank-faced, secretive.

Eve Muhly approached Alexa, standing a little too close, as usual, so Alexa could feel the odd heat the girl always generated, like a toddler who had just awakened from a long yet unsuccessful nap.

"Ms. Cunningham?"

"You can call me Alexa, Eve. You know that."

"Someone said it happened in the restroom?" Her voice rose on what should have been a declarative statement of fact. Eve often needed affirmation for the simplest assertions.

"*Who* said, Eve?" It was Alexa's automatic reply to anything that sounded like a rumor, even if she happened to know that the story was true. She never missed an opportunity to remind her students of the power of gossip, of mere words.

Eve looked around her feet, as if her informant were something she had temporarily misplaced or dropped. "Someone? I didn't see, exactly? But I definitely heard someone behind me as we were leaving, and she said she, like, heard it, she heard something."

"Those in the north wing were instructed to stay put." Alexa would never fall into the trap of calling it "containment." She eschewed jargon and euphemisms whenever possible, feeling it gave her more credibility with the students.

"Right. Like, if you were about to go into the bathroom and you heard shots, would you just stand there and wait for an *announcement* about what to do?"

Alexa looked at Eve closely. "Are you talking about yourself, Eve? Were you outside the bathroom when it happened? Did you call the office?"

"No, I'm just saying. Like, a hypo . . . hypo . . . hypothetical. *If* I heard shots, I wouldn't just stand around. I'd run."

"But you said 'she.' And you said she was going into the girls' room. So you know that much."

"Yeah. Well. I know a girl's voice from a boy's voice. And no one goes into the boys' bathroom, not even the skankiest girls. The boys' bathrooms are *nasty.*"

"Do you know anything else, Eve?" Alexa glanced at the girl's hands, but Eve was the daughter of old farmers. They may have tolerated her alliance with the skeezer crowd, but they were too thrifty to allow their daughter a cell phone. Eve had neither called nor been called in the frantic minutes since the school was evacuated.

"Someone said a name?" Eve squirmed like an insect impaled on a pin, equal parts misery and defiance. The poor girl constantly sought attention yet was mortified once she got it.

"A name?"

"Of the person who's, like, shot."

Alexa waited.

"They said —" Eve leaned even closer to Alexa and whispered — "Kat Hartigan."

"Kat? Are you sure?"

"It's what she said."

"Who, Eve?" But Alexa knew that even if Eve had any more concrete information, she wouldn't share it, not under the watchful eyes of her friends.

"Someone? I don't know. I didn't see her? I only, like, heard as I was walking out." Eve lifted up her hair and let it drop back on her neck, then disappeared into her group, blending in with them so thoroughly that she might have been a chameleon, taking on the protective coloration of a tree or a leaf.

And now that Alexa had the name — Kat Hartigan — it suddenly seemed to be everywhere, on everyone's lips. "Did you hear? It was Kat Hartigan." "Shut up!" "No, seriously. Kat." Kat. Kat. *Kat.*

The students and teachers shared the rumor with horror, shock, and just a little bit of smugness — the smugness born of knowing, the smugness born of being alive. All information was gossip, Alexa thought, even in the mouths of the best-intentioned people. As she told her students, gossip was not about content, and it was not necessarily false. Gossip was about self-importance, the thrill of knowing something and telling others. Those who passed along Kat Hartigan's name were not simply sharing a fact. They were establishing that they were inside the loop and therefore important. Later she would try to impress this fact upon her students, use this as a learning tool — assuming the school year hadn't just come to a premature end. It was hard to know what the school district would choose to do.

What was *she* doing, making lesson plans in her head, when a student might be wounded in the school, or even dead? It had to be a rumor, Alexa thought. Kat Hartigan didn't have an enemy in the world. She was the school's figurative and literal princess, crowned at the prom just two weeks ago. Many students envied her, but no one disliked her. She had the kind of gentle prettiness and self-deprecating manner that girls find tolerable and boys find preferable.

The police arrived, and now the school property was officially sealed off, with no one permitted to enter or leave. Media vans lined the street just beyond the school's driveway, and a few parents stood along the road's shoulder, craning their necks, gesturing at the students, some of whom ran back and forth, relaying Lord-knows-what information. Alexa felt bad for these parents and others, the ones gathering at the middle school. Of course, many of them would have spoken to their children by now, thanks to the omnipresent cell phones. Even those who did not have phones, girls such as Eve Muhly, could find a way to get word to their parents, assuming that they understood how worried their parents would be. It was all too possible for teenagers to forget that the news of a shooting would scare their parents. Teenagers took their immortality for granted.

And it was still possible, wasn't it, that everything would be okay? That Kat Hartigan would walk out of the school, tossing her hair and laughing in her apologetic way, embarrassed to have been the focus of so much attention, to have caused any interruption to the school day. Maybe it was a senior prank, a kind of emotional vandalism that Barbara Paulson hadn't thought to outlaw. The official news was not bad, not yet. Nothing had been established for the record. Alexa held to that hope even as the Shock Trauma helicopter came and went, even as an ambulance drove across the grass and back again, then left the school parking lot with its lights flashing. These were vehicles for survivors, for those who could be saved.

Then the coroner's car arrived, slow and deliberate. A man and woman ambled across the grass, and while their gait was not slow, there was no urgency to their movements. *Kat,* the voices began again. *Kat. It's Kat.* Eve Muhly caught Alexa's eye and made an "I told you so" face. Alexa summoned her with a stern "I'm not kidding this time" wave.

"Who did this?"

Eve shrugged. "I haven't heard anything about that."

"Eve."

"Everyone's saying Josie Patel must have been there, because she's so far up Kat's butt the only time she ever gets out is in the bathroom." She waited to see if Alexa would appreciate this bit of schoolhouse wit. "But I don't know for sure."

"Still, you must have heard something more." Alexa tried to pack a lot of weight behind those words, letting Eve know that she believed Eve was, if not an eyewitness, then someone who had seen or heard more than she was letting on. "Isn't there anything else you can tell me, Eve?"

Eve took on an air of injured innocence.

"Why, Ms. Cunningham, you're always saying we shouldn't talk about things unless we know them firsthand or have talked to someone who has firsthand information."

Alexa let her go again. An ambulance, a helicopter, a gurney. She thought of three families and the news that awaited them. The parents of the student in the ambulance were the luckiest — the injuries must not be too bad if the police had decided the student could make the trip along north county's congested roads. The helicopter was potentially bad, proof of life-threatening injuries, but at least those parents could hope for a good outcome. And everywhere else in Glendale, parents would be given the gift of learning that their dread was groundless, that their children were alive and well.

Only one set of parents wouldn't be let off the hook. Alexa had a mental image of these parents, alone in the middle-school cafeteria, seeing family after family reunited, watching the door nervously to see when their child would be returned to them.

But surely Barbara would get to the parents of the dead child as quickly as possible, would not prolong this agony of

45

wondering. Alexa could only hope that Barbara would manage to express herself warmly and openly, eschewing her usual bureaucrat-speak. *Not a school shooting but a shooting at a school.* What an utterly strange distinction to make in the midst of a crisis. She might as well have said, *Not a bank robbery but a robbery at the bank.* It was as if Barbara wanted to establish that Glendale High School could not be to blame for what had happened there, that it was as much a victim of circumstance as whatever students had been claimed by to-day's events.

Alexa glanced back at the building. It looked smug to her, as if it knew in what low esteem it was held and was happy for this moment of revenge against those who had reviled it.

3

When Baltimore County began training its police officers in the new response protocol for school shootings — "The latest *trend,* if you please," as Sergeant Harold Lenhardt liked to say — Lenhardt knew he could never follow it to the letter. Not that the policy wasn't sound, jokes about trends aside. Police departments across the country were all doing the same thing, under various names, abandoning the SWAT model that had proved so disastrous at Columbine. Some places called it homicide-in-progress. In Baltimore County they preferred to define it by the response, First-Four-In. This meant that the first four responding officers, no matter their rank, no matter their normal assignments, went in together, weapons drawn. The idea was to get to the shooter as quickly as possible, limiting the scope of casualties. Step over the dead, step over the wounded, the officers were told. Just stop the kid and contain the damage as soon as you can.

But what if you were the first guy? Lenhardt had wondered. What if you were there alone, outside a school, all by yourself? How could you wait for the others to show up? He didn't think he would. He was no cowboy, but if the point was to get in as quickly as possible, then what was so magical about the number four? If he got there first, he didn't think he'd wait for three others. One, maybe, as backup, but even that would be hard.

For now the question of how he would respond would remain moot. Lenhardt and his partner, Kevin Infante, had arrived at Glendale this morning forty minutes after the 911 call came in, summoned only once the first four officers had determined that there was, in fact, a homicide to investigate. The two wounded girls had been carted away, too, adding to Lenhardt's frustration. There were things to be done, opportunities to be seized, even in seemingly straightforward shootings such as this one, with a suspect already identified. And while even a seasoned homicide cop couldn't keep a scene pristine when paramedics were running around and victims had to be transported, Lenhardt and Infante might have been a little more vigilant.

48

"I just wish we had gotten here sooner," he told Infante, and not for the first time.

"It's a pendulum like anything else. It's only a matter of time before a cop gets killed doing it this way, and then they'll reinvent the wheel, go back to SWAT teams."

Lenhardt was studying an odd blood trail that seemed to lead to the door. That should make sense — the wounded girls could have bled on the way out, even with paramedics in attendance, and these drops would then be smeared by people running back and forth.

"The theory is they lack focus, these young shooters. Attention deficit disorder, you know? They get a gun, they come to school, they spray some bullets around, and then their attention wanders. I bet if you checked, you'd find the typical high-school shooter doesn't do well on the verbal section of the SAT."

"What?" Infante was staring so hard at a stain in the corner that nothing could pierce his concentration. As Infante's sergeant, Lenhardt had always admired the younger man's single-minded approach to the job. As his temporary partner, however, Lenhardt was finding Infante's one-track mind a bit of a drag. It killed a joke, having to repeat it.

"Never mind."

Of the two girls taken alive from this bathroom, only one of them, a girl with a bullet lodged in her right foot, would be of any immediate help to the detectives. The other survivor, believed to be the shooter, had lost a part of her face, as Lenhardt heard it, and although Shock Trauma might save her life, it was less clear what else could be salvaged — her jaw, her teeth, her brain. Much of the blood around them was undoubtedly hers. She had leaked a lot in the twenty minutes or so before she was transported.

The dead girl, who was still here with them, had died swiftly, from an almost freakishly precise gunshot wound to the chest, maybe straight to the heart, so there was very little of her blood. Was this marksmanship the result of luck or skill? It didn't jibe with Lenhardt's knowledge of Glendale — upper middle class, liberal. But then there were still pockets of farms in the area, rural families with old-fashioned values. A girl raised in such circumstances might be comfortable with a gun. If she knew how to use a gun, however, and had always planned to use it on herself, why had she fired into her cheekbone instead of her temple? And why shoot the other girl at all?

One thing he was willing to bet on: The dead girl, the one on the floor, wasn't the kind who knew anything about guns. She was a girly-girl, all in pink — pink sandals with cloth roses where the thong nestled between the big and second toes, pale pink pants, and a pale pink polo.

Lenhardt had the digital camera, one outfitted with software that made their photos impossible to alter. Infante was using the backup 35-millimeter because you wouldn't want to hang a murder investigation on something as temperamental as a computer. Clumsily — he still wasn't comfortable with the little Canon — he paged through the photos he had taken, looking at the blood, the scene, trying to find the story there. Something was off, but he couldn't say what exactly. He walked over to the windows, the better to see his photos in the diffused light they allowed in, then looked back at the floor. It was such a gray room — gray tile floors, gray stalls, gray walls, a long gray shelf above three white sinks. The only color in the room, aside from the blood and the dead girl, was an uncapped lipstick standing on the ledge, pink and moist. Lenhardt gestured toward it, and Infante bagged it.

"Aren't we meticulous," he said. "It's not exactly a fuckin' whodunit."

"No, it's not a whodunit. But it has the potential to be a gigantic pain in the ass."

"You can say that again. She was pretty, wasn't she?"

"Pretty in pink."

Neither one mentioned her body, although they might have if she had been a little older. She had a notable shape, with large, round breasts straining against the polo shirt, so much tighter and shorter than the polos Lenhardt remembered from the last time this preppy look was the rage. Not that the prep look ever went out of style in Baltimore. His daughter had wanted a shirt like this for Christmas, one with the little alligator, and he had almost fainted when he saw the seventy-dollar price tag. He was happy to spend seventy dollars on Jessica, but not for a polo shirt. "Dad," she had whined, "it's a limited edition." How in the hell could a shirt be a limited edition? Had this girl's parents balked at such an expense? No, a Glendale girl probably had a closetful of such shirts.

Her skin was pale, getting paler by the minute, but roses had probably bloomed in those cheeks, the round kind that grand-parents pinched. Assuming she had grand-parents. So many kids didn't nowadays, as people started families later and later. His kids, Jason and Jessica, had never really known Lenhardt's parents, although Marcia's were still alive and very doting.

"Remember Woodlawn?"

The question would have seemed a non sequitur to anyone else. "Woodlawn" was shorthand for a murder they had worked late last year, in which four members of a drug gang were killed by a competitor. It had been a particularly nasty scene — torture marks on all the bodies, the floor slick with blood — and their work on the case had been nothing less than inspired. It had taken them six months to identify a suspect and make an arrest, working with nothing more than a fingerprint on the cellophane from a cigarette pack. But when they made the case, it did wonders for the department's clearance rate. After all, four murders were one-eighth of the county's annual caseload.

"Yeah," he said.

"Now, that was a scene."

"Looked like a scrapple factory. An *abattoir*." Lenhardt savored the word, which had popped up on Jason's vocabulary test a few weeks back. He loved words and loved running the vocabulary lists with his son. *Abattoir, albatross, abdomen, aberrant.*

"Woodlawn was a *good* case," Infante said, and Lenhardt agreed. It had been easier to walk among those four men's disfigured corpses than it was to confront this one girl with a single bullet wound. Such men were supposed to die.

"I'm still bugged by this," Lenhardt said, pointing to the trail of blood that seemed to lead to the door. "The door was locked, right?"

Infante checked his notes. "Yeah, responders said the bathroom door was locked when they arrived. They spoke to the conscious girl — girl number three — through the door, and she convinced them that the shooter was down, but she refused to get up and open the door because of her injury. They had to find a custodian to unlock it."

"She was here, right? The injured girl?" Lenhardt followed the trail to a corner by the stalls.

"Think so."

"And she said she couldn't get up?"

"Right."

"So who locked the door?"

"Presumably the shooter, when she came in."

"But here, just here." He pointed to a faint mark, which had been smeared. "Doesn't that look like a footprint? Not a shoe but a foot?"

"It does look like someone's big toe. Maybe the girl who was shot hopped around a little at first."

"But it's leading *away* from the door. Wouldn't you hop toward it?"

"She might have been a little freaked out and disoriented."

Lenhardt revolved slowly, taking in the whole room. Except for the lack of urinals, it was no different from the boys' room. Three sinks. Three stalls. One of the doors, the middle one, had a hand-lettered sign taped to it, declaring it out of service. The door to the right was ajar, but the door to the left, the one against the wall, was shut tight. He pushed it, but it didn't give. Latched. What the fuck? It made sense that the out-of-service stall would be locked. But why this one? He bent down, saw loamy dirt on the floor.

He glanced at Infante, who was now measuring the room with a retractable yardstick. He had rank and seniority. He could make Infante do it. But it would be an argument, with Infante trying to get out of it by insisting there was no reason to do it at all, and Lenhardt had no heart for an argument just now. Lenhardt wished briefly that Nancy Porter, Infante's usual partner, were not on maternity leave. He had never put much stock in the idea that either gender brought anything special to detective work. If you were good at it, it was a personality type unto itself. But Nancy, with her keen eyes, might see something here that he was missing.

And Nancy, being a woman, would probably be less freaked out by the prospect of sliding under a locked stall door in a women's room.

Sighing, he removed his jacket and folded it, laying it with great care on the window ledge, next to the digital camera. His knees creaked as he lowered himself to the floor, and he worried about his back. He went in headfirst, gingerly, straightening up as soon as he could. Funny, it took him a second to realize that he could unlock the door then, freeing himself from this confined and alien space. He sat on the toilet seat — actually, he hovered over it, using his thigh muscles to avoid contact — and looked around. There was no graffiti, although the door and walls bore the sign of having graffiti scoured from their surfaces over the years. A relatively full roll

of toilet paper was in the dispenser. And —
he stood then, turning around — the toilet
was empty. So that was that — Nancy
Drew and the Mystery of the Locked Bathroom Stall. What did he think he might
find anyway? There were no casings, not
with the little six-shooter this girl had
used. Her bullets were all going to be
lodged in her victims, including herself.

Then he noticed the metal box on the
wall. Pulling a pen from his breast pocket,
he used it to lift the lid slightly, promptly
dropping it with a bang.

"Shit," he said. "Fuck me." Then,
"Hand me a Baggie, okay, Kevin?"

"What could you possibly have found in
there?"

"You don't want to know."

This is no job for a man, he thought as
he used tweezers to extract the tampon
from the bag inside the metal box and
sealed it in a Baggie. It was fresh, or reasonably so, which meant someone had
been in this locked stall — and left it,
without unlocking the door. Had the
shooter hidden here, waiting? If you're
waiting to shoot someone, do you have the
presence of mind to change your tampon?
And why would you leave without unlocking the door? He tested it several times,

slamming it shut to see if the lock engaged by itself. But, if anything, the door needed to be forced into position before the bolt could be engaged.

"Infante . . ."

"What?"

"Never mind. If anyone knows less about teenage girls than me, it's you."

"I know a lot about teenage girls." His tone was one of mock outrage.

"You're attracted to them. It's not the same thing."

4

The things we can do without thinking, Dale Hartigan decided, are nothing short of amazing. Breathing, for example. No, that was a bad example, because one didn't have to learn how to breathe, it wasn't a skill that one mastered and later did automatically. Breathing was instinctive, from that first whack on the backside, although doctors had stopped doing that, of course. Dale's generation may have started life with that stern little pat on the rump, but his daughter had arrived in a private birthing room, full of soft colors and kind lights. *That* was a good day.

So no, not breathing. Driving, on the other hand, started off as something that engaged every fiber of your being in the early going, then became unconscious over time. How often had Dale snapped to behind the wheel, the highway sliding effortlessly beneath his humming wheels, with no real memory of the last few miles? And he didn't think he was unique in this way, far from it. Every day people climbed into these contraptions that you weren't even supposed to operate while on ordinary cold medicine and never gave it a thought. It was a wonder there weren't *more* accidents. Yet here he was, more conscious than he had ever been behind the wheel, and everyone — the cops, Chloe — had kept saying he shouldn't drive, he mustn't drive, please don't drive.

Couldn't they understand that this errand was his only way of asserting his sanity? Every action — changing lanes, using his turn signal, braking, accelerating — proved he was functioning. Not that he was sure he wanted to be functioning, but what choice did he have? Dale was supposed to be the calm one, the capable one. And while his daughter's death entitled him to be otherwise, he wasn't sure he knew how to be anything else.

But if he didn't have both his hands on the steering wheel — "Two and ten o'clock, Kat, always at two and ten o'clock" — they would be engaged in some form of destruction, he was sure of that. One could literally tear hair, it turned out. And if one could grab one's hair with enough force to rip it, then it followed that one could rend one's garments, maybe even tear oneself from limb to limb, like those crazy Greek women, although weren't they motivated by bliss and joy? The Man-somethings. The Furies? No, that was another myth.

Until today Dale had never really believed that the human body could be shredded by human hands. In fact, he and Chloe had argued heatedly about it after seeing a production of *Suddenly, Last Summer* at the Mechanic several years ago, which she had found quite affecting and he had found profoundly stupid. (There was their marriage in a nutshell, Chloe responding passionately to things that Dale just didn't get.) Now such an act seemed as simple as tearing a piece of bread from a loaf. His hands, if allowed, could destroy a person, perhaps even take a building apart. Which, strangely, had been his first instinct. To punch the wall of Deerfield Middle, to go mano a mano with a school, and not even the right school at that.

Chloe, although long out of the habit of caring about Dale's needs, much less anticipating them, had somehow sensed what he intended to do, grabbing his wrists and holding him, then allowing him to hold her. Chloe looked wispy, but she was a former athlete who could easily withstand the force of Dale's embrace, as he squeezed and squeezed, taking in all the parts of Chloe that reminded him of Kat. Here was her hair, here were her eyes, except they weren't and couldn't be. He would never see his daughter again.

"I need to get to my father," he said later, at Public Safety Headquarters, where it was becoming all too apparent that he was of no use to the detectives. (Kat and Perri were no longer friends? He had missed that. Was Kat menstruating? *What the fuck?* Yet Chloe knew. She knew.) "If he hears it on the news, he'll be devastated."

"Dale . . ." Chloe said gently as he stood to go. Sure, she wanted to make up now, wanted to take back her hurtful words. *Too late, Chloe. This time I won't forgive you.*

"Maybe you should call," said the older detective.

"No, it has to be done face-to-face."

They had cajoled and argued, but they had to let him go, even if Dale was lying through his teeth. His father could watch television all day, hear the headline invoked over and over again — "One dead, two injured in high-school shooting" — and never stop to think it was his granddaughter. Thornton Hartigan had no imagination, absolutely none.

People make that claim all the time — "Oh, I have no imagination" — but it's almost never true. Who is so dim that he hasn't daydreamed, for just a moment, about winning a lottery, or enjoying the company of some remote object of desire? However, Dale Hartigan believed that his father's inability to fantasize was literal. He was like someone missing one of the less obvious senses, taste or smell. He had no vision, no original ideas — and, as a result, no compunction about stealing the ideas of others.

Take Glendale, created when Hartigan began buying acres of Baltimore County farmland in secret, later subdividing it and selling it at ten times what he had paid, building homes in exactly four models, then letting other developers come in and build bigger, grander places. That had just been a page out of Jim Rouse's playbook, who had done the same thing in Columbia back in the 1960s. Take the suburb's very name, *Glendale*. It was coined, disappointingly, for Dale and his twin brother, Glen. When fifteen-year-old Dale had objected, appalled by the wasted opportunity — a *town,* a name that maps would carry, an amazing opportunity wasted — his father assumed it was only because Glen's name had gone first.

"I couldn't call it Daleglen," he said, maddeningly obtuse as ever.

His old man was tough, his robust health almost frighteningly unnatural. At seventy-six, he could have passed for ten, fifteen years younger. All the widows in Charlestowne had made a move or two on him since he moved in five years ago, and Thornton had been a bit of an asshole about this late-in-life desirability, sampling the most appealing women, then discarding them all, preferring his own company. It was bad enough that men acted that way in their twenties, thirties, even their forties, but their seventies? Dale was embarrassed whenever he dined with his father at Charlestowne, all too aware of the frosty and sorrowful looks cast in their direction. His father, on the other hand, noticed nothing. Perhaps it wasn't imagination his father lacked so much as curiosity, or empathy. It never occurred to him to think about how things felt to other people. Except perhaps Glen, but then what man doesn't obsess over his failures?

The one time Dale had tried to caution his father on his ill-advised second act as the Casanova of Charlestowne, his father had simply turned the accusation back on Dale. "At least I'm a widower," he said. "It's not like I'm cheating on someone."

"Dad, I never cheated on Chloe."

"I wasn't talking about you."

But he was. People talked about Dale all the time after the divorce, which should be old news four years later. There was no persuading anyone that he had left Chloe without the intention of taking up with Susannah Goode, who had done some consulting work for his company when it was trying to develop some business properties in Washington Village in southwest Baltimore. Pigtown, as the old-timers insisted on calling it. In fact, that had been Susannah's charge, how to brand Washington Village so the name Pigtown would disappear. Washington Village hadn't really caught on, but Susannah had. They had worked together closely, and yes, sure, a latent attraction was there. It wasn't unnatural to notice that a woman was beautiful. But Dale hadn't slept with her until *after* Chloe threw him out. Maybe it was a little too soon after — two weeks to be precise — and maybe Susannah had nudged him into it, which ultimately destroyed his chances of putting his marriage back together again. The fact remained: He was separated before he ever touched her.

The irony was, the only person who believed him was Chloe.

"Because you didn't have the balls to do anything literal until I put you out," she had screamed at him eight months into the separation, when her lawyer made noises about adultery during one of their endless mediations on the financial settlement. "You were just going to go on having your stupid little crushes, getting moody for a few months, then rewarding yourself with some new toy when you sucked it up and moved on. So I tell you to get out, and what did you do? You fuck some girl!"

To Chloe's way of thinking, Dale's technical faithfulness up to the point she threw him out was just as wounding as a series of affairs would have been. Sharp-tongued and volatile, capable of going months without sex, she didn't see how his intermittent attraction to women had anything to do with her behavior, and she didn't see anything noble in his decision, time and again, not to stray. But logic had never been Chloe's strong point, which was how Kat had ended up with that hideous name on her birth certificate, Katarina.

"It's important to me," Chloe said when

Dale tried to back her off the name. "Why?" "Because of the 1984 Olympics." "But Katarina Witt was a skater. You skied." "You never understand anything."

Chloe and Dale had been married a year at the time, and her skiing ambitions had been thwarted almost a decade earlier. And it wasn't as if she had blown out a knee or suffered some other catastrophic injury on the eve of achieving greatness. *She just hadn't been good enough,* as she had admitted readily. When Dale met her, she was a hostess at a high-end steak house, talking a good game about graduate school and sports medicine but essentially searching for someone who had the means, or the potential means, to bail her out. Dale had been a city planner then, with no intention of ever working for his father, but Chloe had either seen through his own lack of resolve or known she could nag him into doing what she wanted as soon as they had a child. And what she wanted, it turned out, was life in Glendale. To be married, to be a mom.

This was fine with Dale, better than fine. If only Chloe had really channeled her energy into being a wife and a mother. But those things, once achieved, no longer interested her. She dressed Kat nicely enough, chauffeured her to the endless activities, went through the motions of motherhood with nary a complaint. But that was when Dale knew something was wrong, when he found himself thinking that way: *Chloe is going through the motions.* She moved with a slow, lazy grace and always seemed to need a beat or two to answer the simplest questions, as if she were under a spell, or suffering from some strange kind of stroke. Oh, she loved Kat completely, he never doubted that. She would have laid down her life for Kat without hesitation. It was in the day-to-day, the quotidian tasks of motherhood and parenthood, that Chloe failed to engage. Cooking, for example. She was simply god-awful, producing meals so bland and tasteless that it seemed a little passive-aggressive. A woman had to *try* to make food as bad as Chloe did. Even the ready-made stuff she picked up at the nicer markets somehow tasted blah by the time she got it home. And the house was never truly neat, much less clean. What did she do all day? Dale felt as if she were daring him to pick a fight with her, but he wouldn't. Kat did, though, especially after Dale moved out. She zeroed in on the very things that had so annoyed Dale and blamed her mother for the end of the marriage. Then Chloe would cry and say she wanted to be married, it was Dale who had moved out, going off to work one day and then calling from the office, as if Chloe were just another person to be fired by the Hartigan Group and its subsidiaries.

This was an out-and-out lie, but Dale never challenged it, because the truth was even harder to explain to one's teenage daughter. Chloe had packed his bags and left them on the porch, announcing she was tired of his "mooning." She told him to get out and call a lawyer. He did the former but not the latter, and it was less than a week before one of the biggest jackals in Maryland's domestic-law bar tried to subpoena his credit card bills. It was all a bluff, a test, but how was Dale to know that? He made the mistake of thinking Chloe was serious, that his marriage really was over. Distraught, threatened with the loss of access to his daughter, he had allowed Susannah to comfort him. After that, there was literally no going back. In front of the marriage counselor, caught up in the promised spirit of honesty and openness, he told Chloe everything that had transpired between him and Susannah — and she had told him their marriage was over, that this was the one transgression that could never be forgiven. "But it's my only transgression," he protested. "That's all you get," Chloe said.

When Dale looked back on the rest of his marriage, all he saw were petty grudges, the things that couples were supposed to work through. He longed, sometimes, for big problems, for the kind of reasons that made the end of a marriage comprehensible and acceptable. He wished that Chloe drank or had affairs. Or that they had become undone by the fertility problems that had plagued them after Kat's birth. (Kat had come so easily, and then they couldn't conceive at all. A mystery, especially given the fact that Chloe was not quite thirty when they started trying to make a sibling for Kat, who yearned for a little brother or sister.) He had loved her once, truly, and she had loved him. And then he didn't. Some — his brother, for example — had suggested that Dale would have been better off to have an affair, get it out of his system, then go home to Chloe and *keep his damn mouth shut.* As if everything happened in bed. But it wasn't just about sex. There was also the intense loneliness Dale felt sitting with Chloe, in their rare quiet moments. Outside of Kat he had nothing to say to her, and she had nothing to say to him. Maybe they never had.

When he saw her today, waiting for him at this middle school — he already knew, of course, had barked at the principal to stop her stuttering nonexplanations and just tell him, precisely, what had happened — it occurred to her that they were now two members of a tiny tribe, the only people who could ever understand each other.

But later, under the gentle questioning of the detectives, she had been cruel again, blurting out, "I wanted to send her to private school."

"Chloe —"

"I wanted to send her to private school, and you insisted on public school, and now she's dead."

"I can't believe you would bust my balls over that *now*."

"But it's true."

It wasn't. Chloe had squawked about private school after the marriage broke up, interested in finding another way to spend Dale's money. But Kat had been the one to end the discussion, saying she didn't want to be separated from her friends. Friends — that was good. According to preliminary information, the girl who had shot Kat was her oldest and dearest friend, Perri Kahn. Shot Kat, shot Josie Patel, then shot herself.

"Chloe, that's not fair."

She narrowed her eyes, ready to fight, as always, then realized there were witnesses. That was when she had taken his hand, pretended such concern for him, but it was too late. He left her to the detectives, finding a tiny crumb of comfort in having them on his side. Surely they understood now why Kat's parents had divorced, even if Kat never did.

The drive to Charlestowne was usually torturous, a battle through the worst spots on the Beltway, but the trip went swiftly today, and Dale arrived at his father's apartment a few minutes past three. A well-meaning resident, a woman with hair only a shade lighter than her lilac dress, held the door open for Dale so he didn't have to be buzzed through the foyer doors. He wanted to chide her — what good was a security system if the residents let anyone in the building? — but it was probably for the best, as his father would demand to know the purpose of Dale's mission if he called from the lobby, refusing to grant entry until Dale explained why he was here. ("It's Dale, Dad. I'm in the lobby, Dad." "Why?" "Because I have something to tell you." "What?" "I'd rather do it up-stairs." "I don't want to spend five minutes waiting to find out what you have to say. Just say it and I'll digest it, and then we'll talk about it." "Kat's dead, Dad!" "What?" "KAT IS DEAD." And the women wan-dering through the lobby would murmur to one another, "Poor boy, his cat is dead.") No, better to avoid the intercom altogether.

To his surprise, his father's door was ajar, the usually roaring television muted. And next to his father on the old plaid sofa, a relic from the family's earliest years, was Glen, his eyes red-rimmed. *Sad or stoned?* Dale wanted to ask his brother.

"Glennie just got here five minutes ago," his father said. "He told me everything."

"Everything?" Dale felt a curious mix of relief and resentment. How could Glen be in the position to know anything? He was just the uncle, not the father.

"Chloe called me," Glen said almost apologetically. That made sense. Chloe and Glen were still close, bound by their dislike of Dale. And Glen lived just twenty minutes from here, which was probably why their father had chosen Charlestowne in the first place. To be closer to Glen, to keep an eye on Glen.

"He says Kat was shot at school today, shot and killed. Is this true?"

It shocked Dale that his father could speak of it so directly, so unflinchingly.

"Yes, Dad."

He expected his father to ask how or why, not that Dale could answer those questions just yet, not that he ever expected to be able to answer such questions. What was a motive, after all, what could truly explain such an act? He wished he could say he had always found Perri suspect, or off in some vague way, but she had been a delightful little girl, funny and voluble. He hadn't seen her much since the girls entered high school, but that had been at his insistence. When he journeyed out to Glendale, he wanted his time with Kat to be exclusive, not spent with Perri and Josie.

"And the girl who did it — they think she's going to die?"

"She went to Shock Trauma. That's all I know."

"If they don't save her," his father asked, "then who will we have to blame?"

Dale assumed the question was rhetorical, an old man's inappropriate blurting.

But then he saw the legal pad on his father's lap, the one he usually used to take notes on his stocks as they marched by on CNBC's ticker. A list had been started, in his father's quavery spidery hand:

The girl

The girl's family

The school

The gun manufacturer

"Dad —"

"We have to stay on top of this," his father said. "You can't expect government to work for you. If I had waited for civil servants to do their jobs, Glendale would still be on wells and septic tanks."

"But thinking about a lawsuit —"

"I'm thinking about *everything*. All our options. And you should, too. That was my only grandchild."

"And *my* only daughter," Dale said, then realized his father was trying to help. His father was, in fact, offering him a gift of sorts — a project, a place to focus all his grief and rage. This was how he would survive what seemed impossible. Here his numbness would be an asset.

"You bet. Now, you get on that phone and you call my old friend Bert Pierce. He's the best criminal attorney in the area."

"Dad, we don't need an attorney."

"We don't need anyone else to hire Bert either. He's too good. You call Bert, and you tell him you want to put him on retainer, and the first call you want him to make is to the county executive, who might need to be reminded just how much money we've contributed to him and his allies over the years. Then Bert might want to talk to the chief of police, too, make sure they know we'll be looking over their shoulder every step of the way. Someone's going to be held accountable, Dale. We'll make sure of that."

Glen was still there physically, but his mind had drifted away. Dale felt he could almost see it leave — rising out of Glen's body, pausing at the muted television, then flying out the window, going wherever Glen's thoughts went these days. They were fraternal twins, and the likeness was not pronounced, but it was always a bit of a shock to see him, like a glance into some surreal mirror. *This is what I would look like if I smoked pot all day every day of my life for twenty years and dreamed of making it big, even while Dad's money was propping me up.* Dale sometimes suspected that Glen planned to move in with his father, as soon as he reached Charlestowne's minimum age of fifty. His father would love it. And Glen could sell pot to the glaucoma patients.

"Dale, are you *listening* to me? Are you paying attention?"

"Always, Dad. Always."

5

"*Saving Private Ryan,*" Colin said.

"The opening sequence is a nine or a ten," Peter agreed after careful consideration. "But if you come in after they've stormed the beach, not so much."

"*Fight Club.*"

"Eight."

"*Happy Gilmore.*"

"Seven. No *Caddyshack,* but solid. 'The price is *wrong,* bitch.' "

"*Mystic River.*"

"A two."

"But *Mystic River* is a great movie," Simone objected.

"It's not about good or bad," Peter explained, and not for the first time. Simone had always been determinedly obtuse about his and Colin's watchability scale. Or maybe it was just that she got bored when she wasn't the center of attention. "A watchable film is one that pulls you in, no matter what point you enter. You're flicking through the channels, and it may be the first minute or the last or any point in between, but you're hooked. It may not be a great film, the parts may be greater than the whole, but something about it makes it mesmerizing. You can't take your eyes away."

Simone furrowed her brow. "Like *Fitzcarraldo*."

"Oh, stop being so fucking pretentious, Simone," Colin said. "*Fitzcarraldo* is the opposite of watchable. It would have a score of, like, negative one. Which isn't a knock — *Schindler's List* and *Raging Bull* are low, too, on this scale. Great movies, but not watchable. You want to go with a classic that's watchable, then — *Citizen Kane*."

"*The Godfather*," Simone tried.

"Yeah," Peter mused, "but you always feel a little cheated if you miss the wedding scene. It's like a movie unto itself."

"*Scarface*!" Colin yelled, exchanging a high five with Peter, and they proceeded to chant in unison, " 'Say hel-lo to my leetle friend!' "

The three friends almost fell apart laughing over that. It was funnier still if you knew Peter was half Cuban. But then they were finding everything hilarious these days.

Peter Lasko, Colin Boyd, and Simone Simpkins — recent graduates of NYU's Tisch School, joined at the hip since sophomore year — were sharing what they kept billing as their last night together, starting with the two-for-one happy hour at their favorite downtown bar, a neighborhood joint where the workaday regulars grimly tolerated the high-spirited theater majors who kept discovering it year after year. This celebration was the last of many last nights over the past two weeks, a veritable Ramadan of leave-takings in which the three friends had toasted themselves and their futures over and over again, relived the triumphs of their college days, and pretended, ever so modestly, that they did not expect the world to continue to heap prizes at their feet. Simone was going to Yale — her parents were loaded, so she could afford it, but she still had to get in, and she had, which was no small thing. Colin had landed the part of Mark, the second lead, in a national touring company of *Rent*.

And Peter . . . well, Peter still couldn't quite believe what waited for him in a mere four weeks, the bit of last-minute luck that had transformed him from the under-achiever of the three into the undisputed shooting star.

"Did you know there's another Peter Lasko in SAG?" he asked now, hoping it sounded casual, even a little put-upon. "My agent says I have to change my name."

"Peter Pringle," Simone suggested.

"Peter Piper Picked a Pickled Pepper," Colin said, his diction theater-school perfect.

"Peter Paul," Simone said. "Tell everyone you invented the Mounds Bar."

"I was thinking" — Peter paused, not so much because he was shy about his real choice but because he wanted to make sure they understood he was no longer joking — "of Peter Lennox."

"Like the china?" Simone wrinkled her nose.

"It was my father's mother's maiden name. I'd use my mom's, but it would throw people off. I mean, you know, Sandoval. I wouldn't get calls for anything but gangbangers and gardeners. So . . . Peter Lennox?"

Colin and Simone nodded judiciously, although Colin had to add, "It will look great on the cover of *Vanity Fair*."

This was Colin's way of saying that he knew Peter entertained such fantasies. Well, Colin probably did, too.

The difference was that magazine covers weren't quite so theoretical in Peter's case, not anymore. He was going to play Guy Pearce's younger brother in a period piece, a film that was being described as *L.A. Confidential* meets *Memento*, and not just because Pearce had appeared in both of those movies. "Oh, the *other* Australian," Colin had said, and it was true that Pearce was not the star that Russell Crowe was. But Peter would take Pearce's career any day — and Colin would, too.

Ah, well, he could afford to be magnanimous. *Rent* may have seemed cutting edge a decade ago, but now it was about as daring as those shows you saw at places like Hershey Park. *Ladies and gentlemen, welcome the Lower East Side Singers!* Perky, perky, perky, Pulitzer Prize or no. A boy-band singer had played the same part that was now Colin's.

Simone squeezed Peter's knee under the table, her way of saying she was happy to sleep with him tonight, another *last*-last time. Simone's favorite film, or so she always said, was *Jules and Jim*; Colin and Peter had been accommodating her Truffaut-inspired fantasy for two years now, a setup that all three had found practical, as it left their emotions relatively free.

But since Peter had landed the role of the self-destructive Chick Webster in *Susquehanna Falls* — younger brother of Guy Pearce! totally Best Supporting Actor material! — Simone had seemed to be focusing exclusively on him, trying to get something more traditional going. Peter was having none of it, and not just because he didn't want Colin to feel shitty. This was not the time to have a girlfriend. So when Simone squeezed, Peter didn't squeeze back.

"Have you told your folks yet?" she asked, removing her hand.

"I'm going to surprise them, take the train home Sunday, crash there for a little while. The apartment is sublet as of next week anyway, and I can let my mom feed me." He patted his nonexistent belly. "Although I have to be careful. They hired me for my lean and hungry look."

"And for your resemblance to Pearce," Colin said. "That was what clinched it, right?"

"Yep," Peter said. "Luckiest accident of genetics ever, my Jewish dad and my Cuban mom."

Not to mention the growth spurt that had come so late that he had almost despaired of ever cresting six feet, only to zoom up six inches his first year at NYU, when girls like Simone were going with seniors or sneaking around with professors. Peter had come into NYU cute — cuddly cute, with a big personality to compensate for his lack of literal stature. But now he was six foot one and super lean, with his father's dark hair and pale skin, his mother's green eyes and sharp cheekbones. Yet he still had a short boy's personality, charming and eager to please. It was, Peter had discovered, a good combination.

Their glasses, the second beers in their first twofer happy-hour round, were almost empty, and they had to decide whether to stay for another round or go someplace else. Colin and Simone were restless, in need of novelty. But Peter was content with the familiar, and they were deferring to Peter more and more these days. He signaled the waitress for refills.

"Another school shooting," Simone said, glancing at the television over the bar, which was always tuned to CNN or the Yankees network.

"There was almost a shooting at my junior high," Colin said. "But the kid showed the gun to someone who ratted him out before he had a chance to do anything. Too bad — we could have used a little drama."

"Where's this one?" Peter asked.

Simone squinted, which was funny because she was wearing glasses. But they were plastic, just for show, picked up from one of the sidewalk vendors in SoHo.

"Glendale . . ."

"Glendale, Maryland?" Peter looked up. "That's where I'm from."

"I thought you grew up in Baltimore," Simone said.

"Glendale is just outside the city limits." At that exact moment, a chroma-key map popped up on the screen, showing Glendale in relationship to Baltimore. More exacting eyes might have noticed it was far from *just* outside, but neither Simone nor Colin was petty enough to call him on that discrepancy, not when Peter was watching a video of students standing around his former high school. The school was the only thing he recognized, of course. He had graduated four years ago, so the students were unknown to him, although he thought he saw his old drama teacher, Ted Gifford, hovering on the edges.

The text superimposed on the screen said ONE DEAD, TWO INJURED.

"That's not so bad," Colin said. "Relatively. Barely national news."

"I wonder why they don't give the

names," Peter said, more to himself than his friends. "Everyone I know has graduated, but a lot of my friends have brothers and sisters there."

"The names aren't going to mean anything to most people," Colin said. "Besides, they're probably minors, or their families might not have been notified yet. Don't be a drama king, dude. We leave that kind of narcissism to Simone."

"Hey." She mock-punched Colin with her tiny beringed fist.

"Right," Peter said. "Yeah."

And just as he was availing himself of that very reasonable assurance, the video jumped to a shot of Dale Hartigan, rushing from what looked like Deerfield Middle, his arm around a woman whose only visible feature was the part in her blond hair. That would be Mrs. Hartigan, whom Peter knew better, the Hartigans having already separated when Peter and Kat were dating. Peter had often wondered that summer how things might have gone otherwise if Mr. Hartigan were still in the house. Peter probably never would have gotten started with Kat if Mr. Hartigan had anything to say about it.

But it was hard for Mr. Hartigan to put his foot down about a fifteen-year-old girl dating a nineteen-year-old boy when he was shacking up with a woman sixteen years younger than himself. "You don't exactly have any moral authority on this subject, Dale," Peter had overheard Mrs. Hartigan say on the phone one night, when he was waiting for Kat to get ready. Yeah, Mr. Hartigan had been out to get rid of him from the start.

Of course, Kat's parents could be on the video just because they were prominent local residents. Mr. Hartigan's dad practically invented Glendale, as Peter understood it. Or Kat might be among the injured. *Don't be a drama king, Lasko,* which was how he always addressed himself in his head. He wondered if that would change over the years, as he grew into the skin of this new person called Peter Lennox. *Don't be a drama king, Lennox.* No, it didn't have the same ring.

He could call home, ask his folks, but that would take some of the steam out of his surprise visit Sunday. Besides, he had no regular minutes. All he had left were night and weekend minutes, and it wasn't either yet, not according to his wireless contract.

Peter glanced around the bar. There was a guy at a booth, working on a laptop, maybe grabbing a little of the wireless bleed from the Starbucks next door. Asking someone in a public place to use his Internet connection was an almost unthinkable gaucherie; you might as well ask to slip your hands down some guy's pants and cup his ass cheeks in order to warm yourself. For Peter — who had sung in this bar, and danced, and made himself ridiculous and obnoxious in probably ten thousand ways — going up to a stranger and asking if he could use his laptop was the most self-conscious thing he could imagine.

"It's a matter of life or death," Peter said as the man waffled. "Honestly."

And perhaps because the request was so outside the realm of accepted behavior, the guy slid his laptop toward Peter, saying only, "I've got Google open."

Peter's first Google search was unwieldy, returning dozens of versions of the same stories, with no more detail than what he had glimpsed on CNN. Then he finally thought to go to the home page of the local newspaper, the *Beacon-Light*. Yes, there it was — a story that claimed to have been updated within the past hour, along with the promises of streaming video from the paper's "television partner, WMDS, channel 7." Peter clicked on the link. The guy's computer was slow to load, and it blinked ominously at one point, as if it were going to lose the connection. But the story surfaced at last.

"Baltimore County police have released the names of the victims in today's shooting at Glendale High School but are withholding the identity of the girl who is expected to be charged, although she is 18 and will be treated as an adult.

"The victims are Katarina Hartigan, 18, who was killed by a single gunshot to the chest, and Josie Patel, also 18, who is being treated at Greater Baltimore Medical Center for a gunshot wound to her foot."

Peter quickly closed the page, as if it were something he would have been embarrassed to be caught reading, like really sleazy porn.

"You okay, man?" asked the stranger.

"Sure," he said automatically, wanting to retreat into the world of normal manners and customs. But when Colin repeated the same question moments later, he couldn't sustain the lie.

"No. I'm a long way from okay."

"Hey, that's from *Pulp Fiction*," Colin said. Then: "I'm sorry. Fuck."

"Did you actually know . . ." Simone's voice trailed off.

"Oh, yeah." He was tempted to add *in the biblical sense,* as if making a joke could help him regain his balance. The only thing was, it wasn't true, and he wouldn't say such a thing about Kat even if it were. There was a reason that Peter Lasko hadn't been cast to play the tough guy but the sensitive younger brother to the tough guy, the one who was going to die in the leading actor's arms, coughing up fake blood.

And if there were a part of his mind that whispered to him to remember this feeling, to use it later as he had been trained in his acting classes, it was only a faint voice at the back of his head, one he immediately silenced before getting blind-heaving-hurling-blackout drunk.

6

When Josie woke at 2:00 a.m., she had no confusion about where she was, not even for a second. *Hospital,* her brain supplied instantly, *GBMC.* Greater Baltimore Medical Center was the same hospital where she had been born, in the middle of a blizzard. At the school today, the paramedics had wanted to take her to Sinai, but Josie had wailed and screamed, determined to come here, and they had obeyed her, much to her surprise. GBMC was safe, familiar. GBMC was a place of happy endings.

Josie's birth was a famous story in the Patel family, one that Josie had asked her parents to tell over and over again when she was small. Then, about the time she turned thirteen, she decided it was all too embarrassing, that the problem with a story about one's birth is that it kept pointing back to the fact that one's parents actually had sex, which was simply too gross to contemplate. Besides, she had decided that it wasn't really about her after all. She may have been the title character, but it was her parents' adventure. Josie was little more than a series of contractions causing her mother to squeal, which made her father push harder on the accelerator, so the car skidded off the road. "You were so determined to be born," her father would say, "that you almost killed us all."

This was when her parents still lived in the city, in South Baltimore. GBMC was ten miles up Charles Street from the rowhouse the Patels were restoring in a then iffy neighborhood. There were closer hospitals, but her mother's ob/gyn preferred to deliver at the suburban hospital, which no one expected to be a problem. And even with the snow, her father was making good time until he came to that final curve.

It was then that the car — an ordinary Honda Civic, her father always pointed out, not an SUV or a minivan, for her parents were still young and giddy then, just beginning to be parents — had fishtailed and swerved off the road, hitting the gatehouse at Sheppard Pratt, the psychiatric hospital next to GBMC. This was when the road to Sheppard Pratt led *through* a stone gatehouse, which everyone just assumed was a charming relic. Josie's parents had never known that someone actually lived in this quaint structure, famous as it was, but on the night their car plunged off the side of Charles Street and into the side of the gatehouse, a caretaker had emerged, a parka thrown over his pajamas. He was angry at first, sputtering about what fools they were to take the curve so fast. But when he saw Josie's mother in her down jacket, which wouldn't zip over her belly, he stopped yelling and put her in his pickup truck, leaving Josie's father behind to wait for a ride in the tow truck.

(Her father always said here, "And for all that, your mother was another eleven hours in labor, so what was the rush? *She* could have walked to the hospital, and I could have gotten the ride in the pickup truck. I was the one who had hit my head on the steering wheel and cut my forehead. I was the one who had a cracked rib, although we didn't know it at the time." Of course, he could say these things, because everyone in the Patel family knew that Vikram Patel could have been dying in a ditch and he would have insisted that the gatehouse keeper take care of his wife first.)

Many years later the road to Sheppard

Pratt was redone, at great expense, so instead of going through the gatehouse, the road now swept to the side. It was an article of faith in the Patel family that Josie's birth had led, at least indirectly, to that bit of reconstruction. *My road,* Josie always thought when she passed it. Eight years later, then ten years later, her younger brothers had been born at GBMC, but far less dramatically.

Meanwhile Josie had been in GBMC several times since then — she was something of a regular in the ER because of her physical fearlessness — but this was her first overnight stay. Her parents had explained that the doctor wanted to keep her here for observation, but Josie hadn't felt observed so much as guarded. She had been given a sedative, but she vaguely remembered someone coming to the door and being turned away, on the grounds that she just couldn't speak right now. Part of her had wanted to call out, groggy as she was, and part of her had been glad to fall back into the dreamless sleep afforded by the pill.

Now here she was, at 2:00 a.m., wide awake. What were the rules? Was she allowed to ring for water? Turn on the television, or even the light, or was there someone on the other side of the curtain? Would they bring her a bedpan if she had to pee? Oh, God, she would rather hold it all night than pee in some basin, a nurse standing by. She had been allowed to limp to the bathroom throughout the afternoon, a nurse or parent supporting her. How bad was her foot anyway? It felt funny — throbbing and fiery, with a pins-and-needles sensation.

And then she realized her father was sitting in a chair in the corner, his chin resting on his chest, his bald spot staring at her. A few strands of hair, so much darker and glossier than her own, clung to his skin, but most of it had fallen back to the side from which it had been coaxed so painstakingly. Her father's comb-over was a source of great embarrassment to Josie, but her mother had forbidden her to tease him about it. "You can say all the hateful things you want about *my* appearance," her mother had said, "but don't you dare pick on your father. He works so hard."

He works so hard. Her mother was always saying that, as if it should have some special significance to Josie. *He works so hard.* Translation: You and your brothers need too much. *You can't imagine how hard it is to commute.* Translation: We

95

moved out here just for you. The strange thing was, Josie's mom worked hard, too, with virtually the same commute, but she sought no sympathy for herself. Josie was left with the sense that her mother was happy to make the sacrifices that children required, but her father had surrendered something infinitely more precious.

What, exactly? What else could her father have wanted from life? Here he was, asleep in front of her, murmuring, literally dreaming. Yet Josie could not imagine her father's dreams. For all her mother's complaints, he had a job he genuinely liked at Hopkins Applied Physics Lab, pretty much nirvana for a onetime math nerd. (He wrote code. At least that's what Josie thought her father did. She had always been a little vague on the details, even after going to the office with him on Take Your Daughters to Work Day, where the one thing that kept Josie's interest was the tray of doughnuts. She was only eleven.) He adored Josie's mother to a degree that was almost embarrassing, and he was just as affectionate with his children. If she had to guess, Josie would say her father was happy, although she didn't know why.

Josie's father had been a musician in college, playing guitar in a band. That was how her parents met, at a keg party in the middle of a field at Grinnell College. "His band was terrible, just terrible," her mother said. "Although they did a very good punk version of 'Pleasant Valley Sunday.' " Her father still had a guitar and played in the garage on the rare weekends when there was nothing else to do. He wasn't very good. Josie could recognize the chords he picked out only because some Glendale guys listened to a lot of vintage music — the Clash, the Rolling Stones, that sort of thing. Every now and then, her father would start plucking out the *der-der* opening of what Josie's mother called his signature song, and her mother would abandon whatever she was doing and go out into the garage and dance to the Monkees' idea of what was subversive, all those years ago — to Josie's utter embarrassment, although her brothers were still young enough to think it was funny. There was something so . . . well, teenage about her parents' devotion to each other. Her mother especially reminded her of the Glendale girls who went steady with the same boys all four years. Although, come to think of it, those girls always looked grim and exhausted, while Josie's mom beamed as if she still couldn't believe that

Susie Cobb from Janesville, Wisconsin, had landed worldly Vik Patel, the math whiz who played in a band, tossing his then full, dark hair back from his face, smiling his brilliant smile, so white in contrast to his walnut-colored skin.

"I couldn't believe someone so worldly was interested in me," her mother always said. Josie, who had learned the word "uxorious" when studying for the SATs, asked her English teacher if there was a corresponding word for a woman who worshipped her husband. Mrs. Billings had shrugged. "I guess it was assumed that wives were supposed to be that way about their husbands, that it was the natural order of things." *So sexist,* Perri had pointed out.

But being goony in love with your spouse clearly wasn't the natural order, not based on what Josie saw around her in Glendale. Perri's folks were nice enough, but hardly romantic. Mrs. Kahn did that humorous, put-upon thing, claiming that Dr. Kahn was terrible to her, but it was clearly all for show. As for Kat's parents — they had always been a little snappish with each other, even before the divorce. Kat may have been shocked when her parents broke up, but Josie and Perri had seen it coming from a long way off. Josie had always been keen to escape the Hartigan house, despite its wealth of toys and gadgets, making a beeline for the patch of trees and the old creek at the far end of the Hartigans' property. Yes, Kat had the coolest house but the worst parents. Josie had the worst house, and her parents were a close second to Perri's. Perri had the second-best house and the best parents, because they simply never got mad. Perri could do no wrong as far as her parents were concerned, although they did have very high standards in terms of effort. The only time that Perri had gotten in trouble for a report card was when she had gotten a 2 in effort.

But it was wrong, keeping score, now that Kat was dead. Dead for no reason. How could this have happened? Perri was crazy, an actual lunatic. Had she always been this way? Not when they were little, of course. No one's insane in the third grade, except for serial killers, the boys who blow up cats and set dogs on fire. It was only in the past year that Perri had gotten so weird, and everyone — Josie included — had chalked that up to her obvious jealousy of Kat.

Still, she was *Perri*. The smart one, the

funny one, the one with the best ideas. She was the one who had dropped them, although the school didn't spin it that way, couldn't see how much Kat and Josie missed Perri when she distanced herself from them last fall — suddenly, viciously, without any explanation. Just because they were two and she was one didn't make it any easier to bear. Especially given the fact that Kat was as strangely silent on the topic as Perri was.

The memory of how her two friends had looked, *after,* rushed over Josie, and she glanced around frantically. There was a plastic trash can near her bed, but she had to lean out at a perilous angle. She tried to throw up silently, but it was too hard maintaining that posture while vomiting, and the sound of retching woke her father.

"Oh, Josie." Her father tucked her hair behind her ears, fetched a towel from the bathroom, and wiped her face. He was still in his office clothes — the embarrassing short-sleeved shirt and polyester old-man pants — and his BO was a little funky. He must have sweated a lot today. Her father's sweat didn't smell like anyone else's — it wasn't worse, just different — and Josie had always feared that it had something to do with being Indian, that her own perspiration would have this same foreign undercurrent. So far it didn't, but you never knew.

"I was worried the codeine and the sedative would be hard on your stomach, but the doctor kept saying he didn't want the pain to get ahead of itself. How's the foot?"

"It feels kind of . . . fiery."

"Yeah. There may be some bone chips in there. They took the bullet out, but they still need an orthopedic surgeon to go over the X-rays."

"Am I going to be okay? I mean, totally normal, so I can — Dad, what about my scholarship? If I can't do acrobatics, if I end up with a limp . . . Dad, Dad —"

"You're the lucky one, Josie. We're the lucky ones. That's all that matters for now."

Her father's voice became thick and strange, as if he might begin to cry, an idea that made Josie even more frantic. "Dad . . . Dad . . . Dad."

"What, Josie?"

But she didn't know how to deny him his tears, so she said instead, "Can I have a Sprite or a ginger ale to settle my stomach?"

"You bet, Josefina." It was his private pet

name for her, one he hadn't used for years. "You bet."

He left her room, whistling one of the songs he liked to play on the guitar — "The Best I Ever Had" — as if he wanted her to be able to know where he was once he was out of view. A nurse must have reproved him, for Josie heard a soft but stern female voice, chiding in tone, and the whistling stopped abruptly. But Josie could still hear her father's shoes, slapping down the corridor in search of a vending machine. Oh, God, he was wearing his Tevas.

She thought she had nothing left to throw up, but the moment she tried to close her eyes, the room began to spin and the bile rose again, until nothing came out, her mouth opening and shutting almost convulsively. Wasn't there a movie where a woman had honked silently the way Josie was now? Or was she thinking about someone in real life, someone odd, someone her mother had told Josie to stop staring at, a long time ago, when Josie was little and didn't know better. Yes, that was it. Back when she was in middle school, there was a woman who looked like a goose, with a long, skinny neck and flying brown hair, and after each sentence she had opened her mouth wide and made a clicking sound deep in her throat. She had worked at the sandwich shop in the Strand, one of the first strip centers in the area. The woman looked straight at you while taking your order, and she seemed to speak more than was strictly necessary, as if to flaunt her disability, make you confront it. Her thin, long lips opened wide, and the strange snap echoed at the end of every sentence. "Do — you — want — cheese — with — that?" *Snap.* "What — do — you — think — of — the — weather — we're — having?" *Snap.* When they were in middle school and wanted to buy sandwiches after school, they used to take turns going in. (If they tried to enter the store together, they ended up laughing too hysterically, and they were not unkind, not really.) Whenever it was Perri's turn, she always convinced one of the others to do it for her. Kat would try to coax her: "It wasn't so bad, she's really very nice." "So why don't *you* go in every time?" Perri asked. "Because it's not fair," Kat countered. "We're supposed to take turns." Yet the next time it was Perri's turn, Kat or Josie would end up going for her.

The sandwich shop had disappeared, replaced by a Caribou Coffee, and the woman had disappeared, too. Things in Glendale were always disappearing, changing — the open spaces that were supposed to be left untouched, the original houses such as the Patels', which were now being torn down right and left. And now Kat was gone, and perhaps Perri, too. It had been horrible, waiting there with them, listening to the strange, labored sound of Perri's breathing, looking, then trying not to look, at Kat's waxy features beneath the fluorescent lights. There was no place to look safely, except the ceiling, which Josie had never noticed before. White, pockmarked, divided into squares by aluminum bands.

Finally the policemen had knocked, asking her to unlock the door, but Josie couldn't get up, she just couldn't. "Can you walk, honey? Can you crawl?" "Yes — no. I mean, I'm okay, but I can't get up, I just can't." "You don't have the gun, do you — what's your name? Who are we talking to?" "I'm Josie. I'm not the one who did this. It was Perri, and she's —" "Is she dead? Did she shoot herself?" "Yes. No. I mean, yes, she shot herself, but I don't think she's dead. She's . . . it's — Please find someone to unlock the door. I don't want to look at them anymore." But they had kept talking to her, disbelieving. "You don't have the gun, do you . . . Josie?

It's Josie, right? You're sure you're not holding the gun?"

"I never touched the gun." Finally a key turned in the lock, and she began to sob when she saw the police officers enter with their weapons drawn. Then everything had speeded up, with paramedics rushing in, taking away Perri, then Josie. *Yes, it was Perri,* she told them over and over. *Perri had done this. Shot Kat, shot Josie, then herself. Perri. It was Perri, only Perri.*

"What about Kat?" she had asked as they wheeled her out. "Aren't you going to get Kat?"

"Your friend has to stay here a little while longer," the attendant had said, soothing her as if she were stupid enough to think Kat was alive. "The important thing is to get you to the emergency room, have that foot looked at. You were smart to wrap it like you did and prop it up, but we need to attend to that."

"I don't want to go without Kat. She's my best friend. I want to be with her. You can't separate us. You can't, you can't."

She knew she was being hysterical and idiotic. But there was a part of her that clung to the idea that everything could be undone somehow, if they would just let her stay, give her five more minutes with the two girls who had defined her life for the last ten years, almost from the first day she had walked into Mrs. Groves's class at Meeker Creek Elementary School. One for all and all for one, the eternal triangle. She finally knew what she needed to make everything right again.

third grade

7

Josie Patel, assigned to the front row because she was the smallest student in Mrs. Groves's third-grade class, steeled herself not to look back as Seth Raskin and Chip Vasilarakis chose teams for kickball. If she swiveled her head the tiniest bit, it would be apparent that she cared, and nonchalance was the only thing Josie had going for her on that first day at Meeker Creek Elementary School.

As each pick went by and she remained unchosen, she reminded herself that she was a new girl, the only new girl in a room where everyone else seemed to be old friends. She was a short, skinny new girl with what she was just beginning to suspect was a disastrous haircut — boyishly short, an attempt to tame her cowlicky curls. Clearly she was going to be the last or next to last called. She tried to tell herself that it didn't matter, that she wouldn't always be new, judged solely by her size and her strangeness and her stupid hair. Still, it hurt. She felt odd-looking, with her dark skin and darker hair. Her old school, back in Baltimore, had been so small that differences hadn't mattered as much. Here she was the only dark-skinned girl. There was an African-American boy and three girls who were what Josie thought of as *real* Asians — Chinese and Japanese, with pretty, pretty hair, straight and shiny — but no one who looked like Josie.

"What are you?" a ghostly pale red-headed girl had asked her that morning before the bell rang.

"American," Josie said, although she knew what the girl was trying to determine.

"I mean your parents. Are they from Mexico or someplace like that?"

"They're American."

"Are you adopted? You look like Minetta, in Mrs. Flippo's class. She had to fly here on a plane from India when she was a little baby, and the plane ride was, like, a whole day. She flew through seven time zones."

"My grandparents' parents were from India," Josie admitted. "But my dad was born in Chicago."

"So you're *not* adopted."

"No."

"Oh." The redheaded girl's tone suggested this was a failing on Josie's part. She had a flat, thin face with watery blue eyes that looked even smaller behind her wire-rimmed glasses. "*I'm* adopted."

The redheaded girl abandoned her, going to whisper with a dark-haired girl from another class. That was okay. Josie didn't want to be friends with them anyway. The redheaded girl was funny-looking, and her friend had a sneaky look. She wouldn't settle for them. The redheaded girl was Seth Raskin's last pick, leaving Josie for Chip, who made a face and said, "*Her,* I guess."

Given the last slot for at-bats, Josie was worried she wouldn't get a turn before recess ended. What if she never got a turn? What if the game started over from the beginning, every day, and she was always at the end of the line, and the bell rang just as she approached the plate? At least being last gave her time to study Seth's fast, underhanded rolling style. The ball was the standard red rubber one, lighter than a soccer ball, but it gathered a stinging, intimidating force when kicked hard enough. Josie could tell which kids had played soccer by the way they approached the ball, where they placed their toes.

When her team was sent to the field, she was sent to far, far right, the loser's spot.

Few of the girls were any good. One on Seth's team was especially bad, her feeble kick sending the ball only a few feet from home plate. Tagged out at first, she made an elaborate curtsy, turning her incompetence into comedy. The other students seemed to like her, Josie noted, despite the fact that she made the last out, giving Josie's team another turn. Fourth in line now, she prayed, literally prayed, that she would get up to the plate before the end of the inning.

She did, with runners on first and second, one out. "I could take your turn," Chip offered. "I mean, if you don't feel like it."

"I feel like it," Josie said.

She let the first ball roll by, paying no attention to the groans behind her. It had too much spin. The second pitch came flat and direct, and she booted it into right field, straight at the redheaded girl, who didn't even try to catch it, just covered her face with her hands and squealed as the ball rolled away, the other outfielders chasing it. "Binnie!" her teammates yelled, in a way that made it clear they did not find *her* antics humorous. Josie scampered home. "Hey, she's *good,*" Seth said accusingly, as if Chip had tricked him by not choosing her until last.

"I played soccer in the city," she panted out. "My coach wanted me to be on a travel team, but my mom works and can't do all that driving."

It was a promising start. Yet being athletic was not enough to win Josie friends, not at first. All it gave her was some breathing room those first few weeks, as the girls studied her and she studied them back, trying to figure out where she might fit.

The boys would have been happy for her company, for Josie was not only agile but fearless, doing tricks on the monkey bars that few other third-graders dared. But Josie had already decided that she did not want to be one of those girls who have boys for friends. Her best friend back in Baltimore, Parson, had been a boy, and the grown-ups had been stupid about it, asking when they were going to get married. She wasn't going to make that mistake again. She preferred a best friend, but all the girls in Mrs. Groves's class already came in pairs. And while some of the girls began to court her — offering her stickers and pogs, which were very big then, inviting her to sit with them at lunch — the two she liked best didn't seem to notice her at all.

Perri Kahn — the thin girl from the kickball game, the one who had curtsied — and Kat Hartigan had a calm, quiet way about them, as if they were visiting the third grade from some far more desirable place. They were not the prettiest or most fashionable girls. They were not mean or bossy, although Perri's words were often sharp, shooting down the dumber kids with sharp one-liners. (Lifted from television, Josie would come to find out, but that was allowed. It was okay to copy a television program, as long as you thought of it first. Copying the copier was what was unforgivable.) Kat, who wore her blond hair in fat pigtails, was super nice to everyone and therefore forgiven for her consistent A's, about which she was borderline apologetic. "Hey," she said to everyone, even Josie, and it made Josie happy in a way that she could never have explained, getting her own personal "Hey" from Kat Hartigan.

Finally, the week after Halloween, a wonderful thing happened. Strep throat made its way through Meeker Creek Elementary, and Perri was out of school for an entire week. Well, it wasn't wonderful that Perri was sick. But her absence gave Josie a chance to slide into the empty seat opposite Kat during lunch, something that no one else had thought to do.

"Hey," Kat said, and Josie thought she detected a note of happy surprise in Kat's usual greeting, as if she had been nervous about being alone.

"Hey." Josie, who had fantasized about a day when Kat Hartigan might want to talk to her, realized she had not planned on anything to say next. "Do you always wear your hair in braids?"

Kat touched one of her fat plaits, so blond it was almost white. "My mom says I have to wear it this way if I want to keep it long. Otherwise it's too much trouble, and she says I'll have to get it all cut off."

"My mom made the barber give me this cut because my hair's so curly, but I'm going to grow it back out. It's already grown two inches since school started." Josie was sure of this, for she pulled a lock from her forehead every night and measured it with the purple ruler from her pencil case.

"I wish I had curly hair."

"It tangles even worse than straight hair. Even with cream rinse, it tangles."

Another silence fell, but it was more companionable, filled with chewing and discreet inspection of each other's lunches.

Kat had Lunchables, which were new at the time and the height of coolness. Josie had a turkey sandwich topped with a special kind of homemade relish. Her father and mother took their lunches to work, and they were firm believers that thrift should be balanced with small indulgences. So Josie's sandwich was fresh-roasted turkey on bakery bread from Graul's, her dessert a collection of iced petit fours. Without being asked, Josie pushed two toward Kat, who seemed delighted by this tribute, yet not particularly surprised.

"Where did you live? Before here?"

"Baltimore. In the city."

"That's where my dad grew up, but I've always lived in Glendale."

"Cool," Josie said, hoping it was the right thing to say. It must have been, because Kat then asked, "Do you want to come over to my house?"

"I have a sitter. My mom works. And I have gymnastics on Tuesdays, down at Gerstung." Gerstung was a serious gym, the kind whose students sometimes went on to the Olympics, and Josie's mom always said she should aim high.

"I have horseback riding lessons on Wednesdays. What about Thursday? If you asked, could you come over on Thursday?"

Josie and Kat, raised in an era where the simplest afterschool playdate required planning and permission, both understood the negotiation that had to be completed before Josie could visit Kat's home. Josie's mom would have to call Kat's mom, to make sure that Kat really could bring a friend home from school and that Kat's mom or some other adult would be there. Josie's mom would pick her up on her way home from work, while the sitter stayed with Josie's new baby brother, Matt. The two mothers worked this out by telephone that very evening.

Josie, who watched worriedly as this conversation took place, saw a strange look pass over her mom's face during the call.

"You didn't tell me," she said after hanging up, "that Kat was Katarina Hartigan."

"Yes I did, I absolutely did, I told you that her full name was Katarina but everyone calls her Kat." Josie was frantic at the idea that such a trivial matter could deny her this afterschool date.

"Don't get so upset, Josie. I just meant . . . she's a *Hartigan*. Her grandfather started Glendale. He built our house."

"Really?" Josie had a vision of Kat and her family in hard hats, pushing wheelbarrows, smoothing concrete between layers of bricks as if icing a multitiered cake. In Josie's mind the Hartigans were all blond and quite small, just like her — helpful, puttering elves from a fairy tale. She imagined Kat on a ladder, hammering up shutters.

Given that the Hartigans owned Glendale, at least in Josie's mind, she assumed their house would be the biggest and grandest, nicer than even the best houses her parents had inspected before moving here. But the house to which Mrs. Hartigan drove them on Thursday afternoon was old and strange, a lumpy stone structure that looked like a place you'd go on a field trip. The house was odd inside, too, with tiny rooms, low ceilings, rough plaster walls, and wooden floorboards that creaked underfoot. The kitchen, into which they entered from a side door — the Hartigans had no garage, just a circular driveway — was the only room of any size, and it felt crowded, for it was trying to fill the role of three rooms — kitchen, dining room, den.

Yet the things inside the Hartigan house were notable — a huge television set, a refrigerator with glass doors, a bright red stove.

"Aga," Mrs. Hartigan said when she saw Josie staring at it, and Josie nodded as if she understood. Mrs. Hartigan had white-blond hair like Kat's, only she wore it loose, almost to the middle of her back. She dressed in what Josie thought of as a Gypsy-ish way — a purple tie-dyed T-shirt and a gauzy, almost transparent skirt worn over velvet leggings. She gave the girls a snack — cranberry juice and Fruit Roll-Ups — and sent them to the family room to amuse themselves. Here, unlike the other homes in Glendale, the family room was not off the kitchen but in a separate room on the second floor. Kat had plenty of toys that were new to Josie, including a small chest of dress-up clothes.

The girls arrayed themselves in Mrs. Hartigan's cast-off dresses and shoes.

"What should we be?" Kat asked Josie.

"Be?"

"Perri usually makes up a story."

"Oh." Josie was not very good at making things up, but Kat seemed so sure she could that she felt obligated to try. "We could be . . . lion tamers."

"We're lion tamers?" Kat indicated her dress, a long peach-colored gown that she said her mother had worn in a wedding.

"Lady lion tamers. And models."

Josie thought Kat would laugh at this unlikely idea, but she seemed delighted.

"We're modeling clothes when a lion gets loose, and they call us to come get it."

"But we don't use whips. We . . . we talk to the lions and ask them what they want. And they say they want pizza."

"I love pizza," Kat said. "Do you go to Fortunato's?"

Josie shook her head. "No, my mom and dad make their own, from scratch. But we get Domino's sometimes."

"Fortunato's is in the city. My dad orders the pizzas half baked and brings them home and puts them in the oven to finish them, and it's like having delivery, only it's really hot. No one delivers out here. No one good. We have them every Friday night. Do you want to come over for dinner tomorrow night?"

Josie did but knew that this, too, would have to be negotiated. Her mother was reluctant at first, saying it wasn't polite to wear out one's welcome. But her father saw how much she wanted to return and agreed to come home early, if Mrs. Patel would run over and pick Josie up when the playdate was over. Yet when Mrs. Patel came to collect Josie Friday night, she didn't hurry Josie out to the car but stayed for the glass of wine that Mr. and Mrs. Hartigan offered, oohing and ahing over the Hartigans' house.

"It's great that you kept this old farm-house the way that it is," she told Mr. Hartigan. "It's a gem."

Mr. Hartigan, a dark-haired man with glasses, ducked his head and nodded. "It's the original Meeker homestead, goes back to the early eighteenth century, maybe the late seventeenth."

"It's a pain in the ass," Mrs. Hartigan said. "I can't believe I married into Hartigan Builders and I have to live in this relic."

"What's a relic?" Josie asked Kat.

"Something old," Kat said. "Old but nice."

"Something *old*," Mrs. Hartigan said. "Dale's family moved out here when the boys were in high school, and he's still sentimental about it, even though the family only lived here a few months before taking over one of the model homes."

Josie wasn't sure what "sentimental" was, but Mrs. Hartigan made it sound like a very bad thing indeed.

"It's a historic landmark," Mr. Hartigan said. "Where do you live, Mrs. —"

"Susie," Josie's mother supplied when she realized he was fumbling for her name. "We're in Glendale Meadows."

"That was my father's first development. I love those houses — they're so simple and efficient."

"And tacky," Mrs. Hartigan said. "Oh, I'm sorry . . . I didn't mean — It's just that Thornton's early stuff seems a little dated to me. All that redwood and rectangles. Very seventies."

"We keep telling ourselves *they'll* be historic landmarks by the time our children are grown," Mrs. Patel said, laughing. "But we were willing to live in a mobile home if that's what it took to get into this school district."

"Glendale Meadows is what Glendale was supposed to be," Mr. Hartigan said. "Affordable, energy-smart houses for middle-class families. The original vision for Glendale included apartments and even Section 8 housing. But my father's partners cared only for maximizing profits. They talked a good game, but once they got the public water and sewers, they abandoned the idea of mixed-income housing."

"Honey, your dad did the right thing. I mean, it was all very utopian and sweet, but people leave the city to get away from poor people. You don't want to live next door to people with cars up on blocks and old appliances in the backyard. The farmers out here are bad enough."

"Can we take our dessert to the family room?" Kat asked, and her parents nodded. The girls carried their bowls of ice cream to the television set, leaving the adults with their wine and boring conversation.

"This tastes funny," Josie said, forgetting that it wasn't good manners for a guest to comment on food.

"Oh, it's low-fat, sugar-free," Kat said. "My mom says I need to watch what I eat."

Perri's strep was so bad that she stayed out of school another week. Later Josie would come to learn that Perri never got sick the way other people did, the two- or three-day kind of way. Her colds bloomed into pneumonia, her sprained ankles ended up being borderline fractures. So Kat was Josie's for another week. They ate lunch together every day and were given permission to make another playdate, even though the Patels had not yet been able to *reciprocate,* as Josie's mom kept insisting they must.

Seth and Chip noticed that the two girls were spending time together and decided to taunt them. They would sing to the girls, during lunch and recess:

> Josie and her pussy — Kat,
> One is short and the other's fat.

Other students picked it up and sang along. It took all Josie's concentration not to break down in tears. It wasn't so bad, being called short. Certainly she had heard much worse — monkeyface, for example. Her real fear was that Kat would stop doing things with her, rather than risk hearing that song over and over. But Kat merely shook her head and laughed. "I'm *not* fat," she said. "Just big-boned, my mom says." She told Seth to stop. And the strange thing was — he did. Josie was beginning to realize that everyone craved Kat's approval. Was it because her grandfather had built all their houses? Because she got straight A's? But none of this was enough to explain the effect that Kat had on people.

Perri came back to school in mid-November. Pale, even thinner than before, she had dark shadows beneath her blue eyes that made her look angry and pretty at the same time. Perri was not pink-and-white beautiful like Kat, but there was something about her face, the eyes in particular, that made people want to look at her. Josie thought she resembled an old-fashioned girl, perhaps someone from Puritan times, which they were studying just then in preparation for Thanksgiving. The first day Perri was back, Josie waited nervously in the cafeteria to see if Kat would drop her now, if Perri would insist on a return to their closed-off twosome, but Perri accepted Kat's decision that Josie should be their friend.

"Three is an excellent number," Perri said. "All the best books are about groups of three. Nancy Drew has two friends. And my mom read me these books while I was sick, about three girls in Minnesota in the olden days, Betsy, Tacy, and Tib. Betsy wants to be a writer, and she's kind of the leader, so I guess I'm Betsy."

"Am I Tacy or Tib?" Kat asked eagerly.

"Tacy, because she has the prettiest hair." Perri paused. "And because Betsy and Tacy were friends *first*."

Perri wasn't being mean, only accurate, Josie thought. She and Kat had been friends first.

"So Josie is Tib."

"Yes. Although Tib had blond hair. They were always forming clubs, too. Do you want to start a club?"

"Sure," Kat said.

"Sure," Josie echoed.

The bell rang, signaling the end of lunch. They had to go to the playground now, although Perri was excused because of her recent illness. She was allowed to stay inside and read, with a teacher's supervision. Josie would have been miserable under such circumstances, but Perri was clearly delighted for a chance to skip recess.

"We'll decide on the club Thursday," Perri whispered. "At Kat's house."

Thursday afternoon was warm and bright, one of November's lingering surprises, and the three girls left the Hartigans' farmhouse with a basket of Fruit Roll-Ups and string cheese packed by Kat's mom. Under the rules they could not cross major streets without a grown-up. This meant they could not go north, toward Old Town Road, the major road that wove through much of Glendale. And the cul-de-sacs that lay to the east and south were of little interest, although one family did have a basketball hoop.

However, there was a wooded area behind the Hartigan farmhouse, and there were no rules forbidding them access to this, although Kat said they were supposed to watch for deer ticks in the summer. With the trees bare, they felt they had to walk as far as possible for privacy, all the way to the creek for which their school had been named. But no one had said they couldn't cross the creek, Perri pointed out, so they did, jumping from rock to rock. On one flat but mossy stone, Kat slipped a little, so her leg went into the water up to her shin. Kat laughed, but her fall seemed to make Perri nervous, and she took forever to cross. Only Josie crossed quickly and dryly, leaping with her usual fearless grace.

Once across the creek, they found a place where someone had held a campfire a long, long time ago. "Teenagers," Perri said. "They probably did drugs here." Kat and Josie nodded solemnly, having heard many stories about teenagers and the strange things they did. Felled trees formed a ring of benches, and Perri took a seat on one of these, indicating that Kat and Josie should do the same.

"It smells funny here," Josie said. "Like poo."

"The Snyders' farm is over there," Perri said. "Binnie Snyder smells like poo. Haven't you noticed?"

Binnie was the redheaded girl who had wanted Josie to be adopted, the last-chosen girl now that everyone knew what a good athlete Josie was. But Josie didn't remember that she smelled any way in particular.

"Her father is scary," Kat said. "He comes after people with a shotgun if they put even a foot on his property. So we have to be careful and not walk too far."

"That never happened," Perri said. "That's a made-up story."

"It did. He chased my father off."

"My dad says that's because your dad keeps trying to buy the Snyder farm and he doesn't want to sell."

It was the first time that Josie had seen any kind of disagreement between Perri and Kat, and she found it fascinating and frightening at the same time.

"Well," Kat said at last, "wanting to buy something isn't a reason for someone to chase you with a gun. All you have to do is say no."

They all could see the logic in that.

"I think," Perri said, "that our club should be named after the three of us, but it should be, like, a code. So we can talk about it but no one knows we're talking about it. We should take two letters from each of our names, so it sounds like an Indian tribe. So we'll be . . . the *Pe-ka-jos*."

Kat nodded, but Josie said, "Pe-ka-jos? That sounds like those little dogs, the ones with the smushed noses. What about Ka-jo-pe?" She thought she was being clever, not trying to put her own name first.

"Because that will look funny, written down. Besides, Pekajo was a real tribe that lived in Maryland a long, long time ago. We learned about them in social studies before you came."

Kat looked puzzled, as if trying to recall this lesson. Josie wasn't fooled, though. She may not have been at Glendale, but she had been in Maryland, and her old school was a good one, more advanced than Meeker Creek.

"Well, if we name ourselves for a real tribe, then it's not a *secret* code. It's just . . . dumb."

"Yours is dumb, too. It doesn't sound like a tribe at all."

They sat in silence, glaring at each other. Finally Kat spoke.

"What about Ka-pe-jos? It sounds like Navajo, sort of, if you pronounce the *j* like an *h*."

Perri and Josie nodded, pleased with the compromise.

"Now we take a vow." Perri began, "We, the founding tribal council of the Ka-pe-jos . . ."

Kat held her right arm straight in front of her, palm down, and Josie followed.

"Not like that," Perri said. "You look like Nazis." She put her right hand over her heart. "We, the founding tribal council —"

"But now it's just like the Pledge of Allegiance," Kat pointed out.

Perri adjusted her arm yet again, folding her hands as if she were praying. But she shook off that posture before the others could say anything. "We should join hands and stand in a circle."

Kat had to suppress a small giggle, earning a frown from Perri, but Josie had no problem feeling serious and grave.

"We, the founding tribal council of the Ka-pe-jo tribe, pledge to . . . um, be good friends and warriors, taking care of one another as best we can. We will do good deeds in the world when possible. All for one and one for all."

"Isn't that the Three Musketeers?" A new version of the film had just been released on video, one with all of Josie's favorite actors.

"So?"

Josie had no real objection. "Just saying."

130

"All for one and one for all. This is our vow."

"This is our vow," Kat and Josie repeated in unison.

Dry leaves rustled and cracked. The girls turned and saw two girls, redheaded Binnie Snyder and the dark-haired second-grader who often trailed her on the playground. The two clutched sheaves of autumn leaves to their chests. They looked embarrassed, which Josie thought odd. Kat, Perri, and Josie were the ones who had been caught holding hands, reciting vows. Binnie and Eve were just two girls in the woods, gathering leaves. But they turned and ran.

"They're doing the extra-credit project," Perri said, her tone outraged. "Binnie is such a suck-up. She's always competing to be first in class."

"Well, she's not," Kat said in her mild, reasonable way. "She wasn't even chosen for gifted-and-talented. She's only good in math." Binnie could multiply huge numbers in her head, in fact, but she made terrible faces while she did it.

"But they were spying on us. They'll tell our secrets. We have to make sure they don't."

"How do you do that?" Josie asked,

even as Kat nodded.

"You'll see," Perri said.

In school the next day, Perri passed a note to Kat, who sat between Seth and Chip. She smiled, refusing to show it to the now curious boys. Yet she left the folded bit of paper on her desk when she went up to the board to do her seven-times table. Chip swiped it, giving a short bark of a laugh, then slipped it to Seth as soon as Mrs. Groves stopped looking at them.

By the end of the week, everyone at Meeker Creek Elementary knew that Binnie Snyder and Eve Muhly had been pretending to be bears in the woods and had gone to the bathroom outside, wiping themselves with leaves. Some said they even had rashes on their bottoms, because they had foolishly used poison oak or sumac. Binnie insisted that it was Kat and Perri and the new girl who had been acting queer in the woods, holding hands and chanting, but it sounded weak, compared to what everyone now knew, or thought they knew, about Binnie and Eve.

"Was it wrong, what we did?" Josie asked Perri and Kat.

"They shouldn't have been spying," Perri said.

"I didn't do anything," Kat said.

Part Two

death, near and certain

Saturday

8

It was still early, not even 7:00 a.m., when Eve Muhly rose and hurried to the barn. Claude and Billy began scampering around the pen as soon as they heard her footsteps and, in their excitement, were almost impossible to harness. "Stupid goats," she scolded them, although her voice was as fond as her words were harsh. "If you want to go so badly, then stand still. Stand still." But she said the same thing every day, and they behaved the same way every day. There was just no reasoning with goats.

Their halters fixed, she led them down the paved driveway her father had put in a few years ago, when a new development had gone in behind their farm. It had amused her father, creating this shortcut, which only he could use, although teenagers sometimes tried to drive on the Muhlys' property late at night, tempted by the stock pond. They never tried more than once, however, as Eve's father was quite fearsome in such situations. "I have to be," he said. "We gave 'em a mile, and now they want to take every last inch."

Claude and Billy were small but fast, and Eve had to trot to keep up with them. She skirted along the rear property lines of the houses, glancing at the windows, still dark on a Saturday. While the owners had taken great pains to make their homes distinctive from one another in the front, the back views were strikingly similar — decks with French doors or soaring windows, with another set of small windows at the top, like two quirked eyebrows. When the development had first gone in and the hill was still bald, Eve had had the sensation of being stared at by a series of narrowed, un-blinking eyes. Now trees and gardens had started to compensate for this naked look, but she still felt as if the houses were watching her. That was okay. The houses, even the adults, could stare at Eve all they wanted. It was only her classmates that she wanted to avoid.

Eve would die, just die, if Val and Lila knew about the chores she was still ex-pected to do. Most of the 4-H kids walked their goats and lambs in the afternoon hours, just before supper. But Eve tried to keep those hours free for hanging out with

Val and Lila, and she could not imagine what they would think about a life that required goat walking, not to mention working in her mother's greenhouse and, once summer was truly here, taking turns at the produce stand. Val and Lila weren't snobs, but they simply wouldn't think that they could be friends with a redneck. So Eve hid that part of herself.

The goats walked and their pen mucked, Eve risked her father's wrath over the gas bill and stood in the shower for almost thirty minutes, slathering herself with strongly scented bath gel and shampoo, cheap but potent things she bought at CVS. Even so, she thought she caught a whiff of feed and manure beneath all those flower and berry scents. To her knowledge there were no high-school kids in the houses behind her family's farm, but what if someone she knew saw her walking the goats? She believed she would never live it down, and Eve had lived down a lot during her seventeen years, more than her share. That's how she had come to be friends with the skeezer girls in the first place, because she had held her head high and refused to be cowed when the divas started gossiping about her.

"Skeezer" was an ancient bit of slang in

this part of the county, older than Glendale itself, older than Eve's parents even. Its origins, while murky, dated back to a time when this valley was true country and Baltimore seemed as far away as the moon. The original skeezers had something to do with hot rods — the boys who drove them and the girls who liked them. Liked the boys *and* the cars, that is, because cars offered escape. Eve's mother often said she thought "skeezer" might be connected to an old comic strip called "Gasoline Alley," whose main character was named Skeezix. Then she would start to get all nostalgic about other comic strips she had liked — "Mr. Tweedy," the girls in "Apartment 3-G," "Mary Worth" — and Eve would end up tuning much of it out. Eve's mom was prone to memories.

Today's skeezers might have been called goths at another school, although they weren't quite that. Nor were they to be confused with "skeezy," a more recent coinage that suggested a combination of sleazy, skanky, and sketchy. They were mostly girls who hung with the skater punks, mellow and nonjudgmental.

Yet even the skeezers wouldn't be friends with an out-and-out redneck. The farm kids weren't exactly at the bottom of Glendale's social hierarchy, just separate, assumed to have different values and ambitions. When Eve's history class had read about the walled ghettos in Poland, she had thought that Glendale had managed to turn this idea inside out. The rich kids lived behind gates and curving brick walls, while the farm kids were left outside at day's end, forgotten. Sometimes even the teachers seemed to forget that the rednecks intended to go to college, that they couldn't just work on their family farms. That's how dumb the teachers were. Eve didn't know of a single full-time farmer left in the valley. Her father managed a fleet of school buses, and her mother boarded horses, while Binnie Snyder's father sold farm machinery and riding lawn mowers. The Coxes were Amway reps. Even the kids who actually liked farming knew they had to have something else going.

Again, this was not a subject that Eve could speak of to Val and Lila, her new friends. To keep their approval, Eve believed she had to give up things she had once loved — competing in the state fair, making jams and jellies with her mother, participating in 4-H. She was raising Claude and Billy for the livestock auction only because her father had laid down the law, insisting that Eve contribute to her own college fund, and he wouldn't let her take a job at any of the mall shops, although they paid much better than raising and selling goats. Plus, it wouldn't give you a pang, selling a sweater at the Gap, whereas Eve had never gotten used to handing over her animals at summer's end.

Eve's father was rigid, and she had decided early on that the only way to cope with such an unmoving, rock-hard man was to maneuver around him. A curfew of 10:00 p.m. was ridiculous for a seventeen-year-old girl, but that was Eve's curfew, and she wasn't going to change her father's ideas by arguing with him. So, since taking up with Val and Lila, she had learned to escape her room at night by climbing out on the porch and jumping to the ground. She figured this was between her and her conscience. And if she got caught . . . well, then, Eve's behind would be between her father's knee and hand. That was fair, that was okay. She knew the risk of disobeying her father, and she was willing take it. Besides, she hadn't come close to getting caught. Her father was already in his mid-fifties — Eve was a late baby, born thirteen years after her next-oldest sibling — and a little deaf. He slept, her mother said, the sleep of the dead. Her mother did not, but if she ever heard Eve's footsteps on the porch roof, she let it go.

Eve was naturally stealthy, had been from an early age. If there were a contest for keeping confidences, she would win that every time. She had started out by learning and then protecting her parents' secrets. These were small privacies, things that could be concealed in drawers or tins of flour, beneath the loose floorboard in the barn. A cache of money (her mother's), for example, or a bottle of whiskey (her father's). No one ever told Eve not to reveal the whereabouts of these things, because no one knew she had discovered them. Yet Eve understood instinctively that the fact of these stashes was as important to her parents as the items themselves. Her father wasn't a drunk — the level in his bottle stayed more or less constant for months, his breath seldom smelled. Nor was her mother saving up to run away or buy something outrageous. They just needed a part of themselves that wasn't wholly known. Eve understood.

Over the years she tested them a time or two — sliding a bill out of the lining of her mother's sewing basket, taking a nip of her father's whiskey. Her mother's eyes would look distant and troubled for a while, but the look would gradually fade. As for her father, he never missed a swallow as far as Eve could tell. Sometimes she wanted to tell them what she knew and assure them that their secrets were safe, that she loved them more for knowing they had things to hide, too. But she did not think her father would see it that way.

Now, however, she had a real secret, a huge one, one she must never tell. Eve had given her word readily, sure of her ability to keep any secret. Yet this one was so enormous she wasn't sure how she would hold it inside, or even if she should. The knowledge already felt oppressive, so omnipresent in her thoughts that she thought she might blurt it out at any moment, much like this one joke her father liked to tell, about the self-conscious boy with a wooden eye who asked a girl to dance, only to end up yelling at her, "Harelip! Harelip! Harelip!" She wanted to tell Claude and Billy, she wanted to say it out loud, just to hear the words, but she almost feared that the wind might carry it away, over the hills and into the world.

Ms. Cunningham was always telling her students that gossip was a weapon, that talking behind someone's back was a destructive act on a par with hitting someone from behind. Yet Eve was in the curious position of knowing even the meanest, evilest gossip could change a person's life for the better. Eve had been saved from her redneck-girl existence by a horrible story, one made all the more nasty because it was the word-for-word truth.

It had happened more than a year ago, the fall of her sophomore year, on a field trip to the Franklin Institute in Philadelphia. Eve had entered high school with the brief hope of starting over and forming a new identity for herself, but Glendale was not big enough to wipe out the knowledge of the dorky kid she had been for eight years, first at Meeker Creek, then in Hammond Springs. Eve was beginning to accept that she was a dork for life, a dork without even the consolation of being a brain, like Binnie, who was turning out to be some kind of supergenius. They didn't share a single class in high school. Binnie didn't even go on the same field trips, being a year older, so Eve sat alone on the bus to Philadelphia, odd girl out. She should have been used to it, but maybe you never get used to it.

The bus ride north had been the usual keyed-up affair, the popular kids swapping ring tones and text-messaging on their cells, despite sitting just a few feet away from each other. Text messages were meaner than whispers, impossible to over-hear or second-guess. Eve's ears burned as she listened to the near-silent conversa-tions behind her — *tap, tap, tap, tap,* burst of raucous laughter, *tap, tap, tap, tap,* more laughter. She assumed they were making fun of her, but what could she do about it?

Once at the museum, however, she had been approached by Beverly Wilson, whose sole claim to fame was being best friends with Thalia Cooper, the absolutely top girl in their class — the prettiest, the most pop-ular, a girl who disdained cheerleading be-cause she rode competitively and didn't have time to go to practices, although the JV coach had made a special point of pleading with her to reconsider.

"Thalia says you know something about horses," Beverly had said as they waited in line to walk through the supersize version of the human heart.

"Huh? Oh, yeah. Well, my mom boards some, for some city people who like to ride. My dad doesn't have much use for them, though."

"Thalia likes people who like horses."

Eve started to say, *I didn't say I liked them* — she thought horses disgusting, given that she spent much of her time cleaning up after them — but she stopped herself. Just the possibility of Thalia's positive attention was dizzying. If Thalia wanted a friend who liked horses, Eve could be that girl.

"Do you want to sit with us?" Beverly asked. "On the bus, on the way back?"

"Sure," she said, hoping she was hitting the right casual note.

Beverly left her then and rejoined the group of girls orbiting around Thalia, but that made sense to Eve. Things should not go too quickly. She had been invited to ride with them at the back of the bus, an almost-two-hour trip. It would be too much to expect that they would allow her to walk with them through the museum or unwrap her lumpy homemade sandwich next to their purchased burgers and salads. She ate alone, not minding, the promise of the return trip bright in her mind.

After a quick but dutiful inspection of the Liberty Bell and Benjamin Franklin's penny-speckled grave, they boarded the bus at six o'clock. Once they were on the highway, Beverly crooked a finger at Eve, summoning her to the seats two-thirds toward the rear of the bus. By custom, the final rows were reserved for the jocks, soccer and football players who hung over the seat backs, sweet-talking the girls, trying to get their attention. Eve was quiet, but she tried to make it an interesting kind of quiet, laughing at what seemed like the right moments, smiling and nodding otherwise. Sometimes Beverly would ask her sharply, "What's so funny?" Eve just shrugged and rolled her eyes heavenward, which made the other girls laugh, seemingly with her.

They were in the final thirty minutes of the trip, the sun down and the bus dark inside, when Beverly explained what she called the initiation. "We've all done it," she said, gesturing to Graham Booth, the least attractive of the jocks, a boy who liked to say he was descended from John Wilkes Booth, just to get attention. He particularly liked making this boast around the school's few African-American students, adding, "So my sympathies for the Confederacy aren't racist, just respect for family." It was clever, a vicious way of suggesting things that could never be said directly under Glendale High School's speech codes, and Graham seemed proud of himself for figuring that out. He was a large boy with messy hair and a grin that showed too much gum. But he was good at football, and that was enough, for a boy.

Eve bit her lip after Beverly detailed the initiation. "I've never done that."

"No one had. That's why we made it our initiation. Graham's big — big as a horse."

"Does it have to be Graham?" Kenny Raskin, the runty younger brother of Seth Raskin, was next to Graham, and Eve thought he would be preferable. Smaller, certainly. Besides, Kenny was as nice as Graham was mean.

"Yes. It's always Graham."

Eve walked to the final row, where Graham now sat alone, Kenny having slipped into the aisle to help block the view of the backseat. She wasn't afraid, not really, especially when she saw Graham wasn't as big as the horses, nowhere near. And it was over so fast, thank God. For some reason she thought it might be like squeezing a bit of milk from a cow or a goat. But it wasn't anything like that.

She took her seat among the girls, waiting to be congratulated, welcomed. The bus was suddenly so quiet, all the usual buzz gone. Perhaps people had fallen asleep.

Finally Beverly said, "That's a lot of calories, you know."

"Oh, but Eve doesn't have to worry about what she eats," Thalia said. "You can eat *anything,* can't you, Eve?"

Everyone laughed, and Eve joined them, thinking it was a funny line. It was only the next day, when she tried to sit with them in the cafeteria and Beverly said all the seats were taken, that she knew she had been tricked. She just didn't know why.

The strange thing was, the story didn't spread, not in the way that Thalia and Beverly had clearly intended. The sophomores knew, and then the rest of the students, but the story failed to jump the firewall to the faculty. Eve stalked through the halls for a week, fierce and proud, staring balefully at boys who attempted to taunt her. "It wasn't a big deal," she said, not understanding the double meaning of her words until she saw Graham blush brick red and punch the boys who dared to laugh. From then on she said the line deliberately to anyone who dared to approach her. "It wasn't a big deal at all."

After a week of this, Val Morrisey stopped by Eve's locker at day's end.

"Hey," she said. She was a big girl,

broad-shouldered, unremarkable-looking except for her eyes, a light, clear green.

"Hey," said Eve, steeling herself for some new form of taunt she hadn't imagined. Val had a legendary mouth, as quick and lethal as Perri Kahn's. Unlike Perri, she used it only for her own amusement, refusing to join the debate or drama clubs.

"Some of us were going to get some coolers at Caribou Coffee. You want to come?"

"I take the bus home," Eve said. "I live pretty far out."

"This guy I know, Tom, he has a car. He could drop you home, after." Val saw Eve hesitate. "He's my friend, and he'd take you home if I told him to, and if he tried anything — not that he would with me in the car — I'd knee him in the balls. Okay?"

"I'd have to call my mom. I mean, I don't have to ask for permission or anything. She'll just need to know that I'm coming home in someone's car."

"Here," Val said, proffering her cell.

It was that easy. Val liked Eve because she hadn't broken down in the face of the diva girls who had been intent on humiliating her. And whomever Val liked, Lila liked and the other skeezers accepted. Val and Lila even knew why Eve had attracted the divas' wrath. "You're cute," Val said, and Lila nodded a little reluctantly. "They hated that boys were looking at you." Eve finally had the new start she had wanted. The divas' only recourse was to go to Ms. Cunningham and tell the whole story, pretending it was because they were so very, very concerned about Eve.

Ms. Cunningham had summoned Eve's parents to school, which was what the divas had wanted all along. Again — why? That was the part that Eve still didn't get. Not even Val understood this strategy. Did they want her parents to come to school in hopes that their very queerness would destroy what she had with Val and Lila? Eve remembered a goat that had been born blind, the way the other goats had cowered in the pen, afraid of it, when it was the weakest and most helpless of all. Was she the blind goat of Glendale High School? No, she was just a girl who had been dumb enough to yearn openly for what she wasn't supposed to have. That was the lesson Beverly and Thalia had been intent on teaching her. Know your place, redneck.

In Ms. Cunningham's office, bracketed by her parents, Eve had a terrible moment.

She was still more good girl than skeezer then — she had not started smoking, much less using pot, although she would learn to do those things over time — and she could not imagine the punishment her father would fashion when he learned what she had done with Graham Booth. Her father always said the punishment should fit the crime, by which he meant it should have a certain Old Testament logic. Would he bind her mouth with duct tape? Make her swallow something even more disgusting? Did her parents even know about oral sex? It seemed unlikely. As Eve understood it, the activity had been pretty much abandoned until the former president made it popular again.

But Ms. Cunningham did not tell. She had meant to, Eve was sure of it, perhaps had thought Eve would volunteer the story, which showed how little Ms. Cunningham knew of Eve. In the end, however, she could not form the words, and Eve certainly didn't volunteer any information. Ms. Cunningham told Eve's parents that she was worried about Eve's thinness, to which her father had said, "You wouldn't be if you could see our food bill. The girl eats like there's no tomorrow."

Her mother put in, "It's just genes. I was

built the same way, as a girl."

Ms. Cunningham gave Eve's parents some pamphlets on eating disorders. Her father glanced at them, then stared at Eve. "Do you do this? Eat good food and throw it up? Because that's just wasteful."

"No, sir," she said. It was so easy, being sincere when telling the truth. It almost seemed like cheating. Then again, Eve was pretty sure she could be just as sincere when lying. Ms. Cunningham waited to see if Eve could be bluffed into saying anything, then finally sent the Muhlys on their way.

"That was a strange to-do over nothing," Eve's father grumbled. "Making a man come all the way up to the school just to ask why a girl is thin."

Eve supposed that Ms. Cunningham thought Eve owed her now, which is why she kept asking her questions yesterday. But Eve didn't see it that way. Besides, people didn't really want to know the truth. They thought they did, then got mad at the people who insisted on it. It was a lesson Eve had learned over and over in high school. Stick to the official version of things. Say what people wanted to hear. And no one, no one, wanted to hear what she knew now.

9

Harold Lenhardt had made sergeant twice in his life, first in city homicide, where he got his twenty and got out when the new commissioner proved to be a jackass, and now he was a sergeant in the county, going on five years. Funny, that "new" commissioner back in Baltimore was almost ten years and four commissioners ago. Time flies, whether or not you're having fun. His colleagues liked to tease him, ask if he was going to retire from Baltimore County when he got his *second* twenty, then head to Carroll, the next county over, and make sergeant yet again.

"It's not out of the realm of statistical possibility," he said this morning, as he and Infante reviewed their notes in preparation for a meeting with higher-ups who wanted to be briefed on the Hartigan shooting. "I'd only be eighty-three when I was done."

"Qualifying on the range might get

tricky," Infante said. "They say the hands are the first thing to go."

"Maybe *your* hands, Infante. Given how much extracurricular activity they see." Lenhardt made a pumping motion with his fist, one universally understood by men everywhere. Or *was* it? Did, say, Chinese peasants or aborigines in the outback do the same thing? It was the kind of topic you never saw tackled on the Discovery Channel, but why not? It could be interesting — the rituals of male bonding around the world.

"I thought when Nancy went on leave, you wouldn't be able to gang up on me," Infante mock-complained. "I'm still the butt of every joke."

"Not today," Lenhardt said. "Today the joke's on the guy who's not getting overtime. And that would be yours truly."

No overtime for sergeants, to paraphrase the title of a movie that Lenhardt's father had loved beyond reason. Gary Cooper? No, he had been Sergeant York. Andy Griffith? Yes, that was it.

Normally Lenhardt didn't mind not getting overtime. He saw it as proof of his professionalism and rank. When he worked an eighteen-hour day, everyone knew it wasn't because he was padding his time sheet. Besides, he was already drawing his city pension, so he didn't need the money as much as the younger guys. But on a brilliant Saturday morning in June, it was hard to leave his wife at the breakfast table and his children in their beds, hard to know that he had to miss Jessica's swim meet. Harder still to realize that Infante would make buckets of overtime on this case, whereas all he would get was grief. At home and here, if this meeting was any indication of what was to come. A veritable exacta of aggravation.

He looked over his notes, trying to find the holes that his colonel would be sure to highlight, if only to embarrass him in front of the chief. The first day had been hit-and-miss. After the interview with the dead girl's parents, he and Lenhardt had run the gun through state police and gotten an owner — Michael Delacorte, with a Glendale address. The parents of the girl at Shock Trauma had readily admitted that their daughter baby-sat for the Delacorte family, although that was before Lenhardt explained why it was of interest. Once informed of the gun, they had started backpedaling like hell. The parents, the Kahns, then insisted it was unthinkable their daughter would have stolen a gun, any gun. "She was opposed to violence," the mother kept saying, as if this assertion could somehow undo the inconvenient fact of one dead and two wounded, and a Shock Trauma doctor agreeing the Kahn girl's wound appeared to be self-inflicted if poorly aimed — more off the cheekbone than the temple. ER docs were notoriously bad at forensics, having been trained to save live people as opposed to autopsying dead ones, but even a first-year resident should be able to identify the entry wound. All in all, it was shaping up to be a pretty straightforward event. Girl shoots two, then self. So why the meeting?

And, more relevant to Lenhardt's way of thinking, why this nagging at the back of his own mind, a sense that things were far from right? He was not an instinct guy, more of a context one, so the problem had to be in his notes. What had he neglected to do yesterday, what were they going to bust his balls for?

The chief finally showed up, not that Lenhardt begrudged him being late to his own meeting. The chief was a good guy, solid and long-lived in a job where most achieved longevity through mediocrity. Lenhardt got along with his lieutenant, too, a city refugee like himself. The colonel

— the colonel was another story. Tall and lean with reddish hair, he was one of those guys who could score points only at someone's expense. He couldn't put himself up, so he settled for constantly putting everyone else down.

"I was on the phone late last night and early this morning," the chief began, and he looked haggard enough for it to be the literal truth. "It turns out the father of the dead girl, Dale Hartigan, is good buddies with our county executive, and he wants to be as involved as possible. Those were his lawyer's words — as involved as possible."

"Shit," Infante said, and he was only blurting out what everyone else was thinking.

"He wants to know where the gun came from," the chief continued. "He wants to know if there are federal charges that apply. The lawyer even asked if cases such as this could ever be death penalty — and then insisted his client would never support that, and it's his understanding Baltimore County won't go for it without familial consent. Hartigan is, in short, all over the map. But the one message that came through loud and clear is that he's going to ride our asses for the duration of this investigation."

"Nothing worse than a good citizen," Lenhardt said, and every man in the room nodded. You'd think it would be the other way around, but in Lenhardt's experience middle-class victims were just hell. People who paid their taxes, toed the line — they believed they should be exempt from crime, that it was a constitutional guarantee.

"I think the family's grief is perfectly understandable," the colonel said. "They've lost a child."

Lenhardt wished the gathering were large enough so he could catch Infante's eye, make a face, but he shouldn't risk it. Instead he said, "We've already traced the gun and established that Perri Kahn had access to it."

This was Lenhardt's way of saying, *We know how to do our job, dickhead.*

"I know," the chief said, "because as of this morning, *her* parents have hired Eddie Dixon. He called me at home to give me a raft of shit about you guys talking to the parents while their daughter was in surgery. So — good work. Any time Dixon is pissed, I figure that's a point for our side."

Dixon had a fearsome reputation as a defense attorney. A thin, light-skinned black man, he dressed in a style that Lenhardt called Park Avenue pimp — beautiful hand-tailored suits in not-quite-right colors. He was particularly partial to a shade of dove gray, for example, which he wore with a rose-colored shirt and matching handkerchief poking out of the breast pocket. His success in the city, where juries were prone to acquit, was understandable. It was harder to explain how Dixon had done so well in the county, where jurors tended to be law-and-order types. Lenhardt, who was three-for-one lifetime against the lawyer, chalked it up to Dixon's way with voir dire. He had an eye for the bleeding hearts wrapped in the most unlikely packages — stern-faced White Marsh men, starchy Ruxton women.

"That's an odd match," the lieutenant said. "You wouldn't expect a Glendale family to gravitate toward a city slick like Eddie."

"*He* might have gravitated toward them," the colonel said.

"More like orbited, circling Shock Trauma like the ambulance chaser he is. *Helicopter* chaser," Lenhardt amended, caught up in his own whimsical vision. "I think I saw him hanging from the chopper as it lifted yesterday. It was like the fall of Saigon."

"Were you there when the girls were taken out?" The colonel was not much for Lenhardt's brand of humor, which was Lenhardt's secondary complaint against the man. But then the colonel had never been a murder police, and that was Lenhardt's primary complaint. The colonel had come up through various property crimes — burglary, auto theft. Want to follow a serial number? He was your guy. Need tips on how to canvass pawnshops? No one better.

But when it came to the simple task of talking to another human being one-on-one, the colonel was in way over his head.

"No, both had been transported by the time we got there," Lenhardt said.

"First-four protocol," Infante put in. "And of the first four who went in, not a single one was homicide."

"So?" The colonel all but bristled at the implicit rebuke for the new policy, which he had helped implement.

"So," Lenhardt said, "some things didn't get done. No one thought to ride with the witness in the ambo, keep talking to her. They accepted what she said at the scene at face value and let her go unescorted."

"Why shouldn't they?" the colonel asked.

The question so appalled Lenhardt, went so directly to the heart of everything he believed, that he was left uncharacteristically speechless. In his head, however, he had an answer: *Because people lie, dickhead. Especially people at murder scenes.*

The lieutenant stepped in, all too familiar with the friction between his sergeant and colonel. "Did you get to her later, interview her at the hospital?"

"No, and that's another thing that bugs me. She was sedated when we finally got there, at her parents' insistence. Yet her injury is pretty superficial."

"She was shot by her friend, who killed someone else and then planted a bullet in her own jaw," the colonel said. "Even without an injury, she might have required a tranquilizer to sleep."

Lenhardt would concede this point. "Also, she's at GBMC."

"GBMC, not Sinai?" The chief frowned. "But Sinai has the trauma center for north county."

"Exactly. This teenage girl insisted on GBMC, and the EMTs followed her instructions because GBMC was slightly closer and can handle that kind of minor gunshot injury. So, on the one hand, she's so hysterical that she needs to be sedated, and yet she also has this moment of clarity in which she demands a certain hospital."

He let this information hang in the air, seizing the moment to begin passing around photocopies of his notes on the blood evidence in the restroom. Copies of the digital photos were attached, photos downloaded and printed with only seventeen malfunctions in the software and the laser printer. The chief may have been on the phone at all hours, but Lenhardt and Infante had been here until 1:00 a.m., at war with the computer.

"Here's some potential problems as I see it — there's some stuff that doesn't match the preliminary story, neat as it's shaping up. We've got a living witness who told the responders that this one girl did the shooting, and most of the evidence fits. But some doesn't, and those are the kinds of details that Eddie Dixon can make hay out of — like this trail of blood that seems to be leading *away* from the door. Or these two locked stalls."

He didn't feel he had to mention the *thing,* as Infante insisted on calling the tampon. But it was another piece of the puzzle, or would be if it turned out that it didn't match one of the three girls. The principal insisted that the restrooms were cleaned at day's end, so it had to be from that morning, and the school's doors had been open for only twenty minutes. Once these facts came up in discovery, Dixon was free to spin any fairy tale he wanted, defense attorneys not being bound by the facts, much less the burden of consistency. Their entire case was going to rest on the girl in GBMC, and Lenhardt was already troubled by her behavior so far. Why had she refused to open the door when rescuers arrived? Why hadn't she crawled or hopped, if only to get away from the considerable carnage around her? He knew rookie cops who had thrown up on their shoes at lesser sights.

And why did she care which hospital treated her? Oh, how he wished he had been one of those first four. He would have knelt next to her, held her hand, ridden with her in the ambo, gotten her life story, been her best friend, her favorite uncle. Twenty-four hours later that opportunity was gone.

"You've linked the girl in Shock Trauma to the gun, at least indirectly," the chief said. "What about the witness? Have you got anything concrete?"

"She's a person of interest," Lenhardt said. "And once we talk to her at length, she may be a lot more interesting. Even accounting for fear and shock, her actions don't track. Maybe today she'll be clearer. That's what I'm hoping for."

He thought of his daughter in the same situation. Of course, she was only eleven, but Jessica could be very cool in an emergency. She had a breezy confidence that astonished him at times, a certainty about herself that had only started to wobble in the past year, her first in middle school. Jessica was prepared for disaster, too, but that, sadly, was a part of life for cop kids.

Don't ever tell anyone that Daddy is a cop, or that Daddy has a gun.

This was the brave new world of post-9/11, when no law-enforcement official was ever truly off duty. Earlier this year they had shown the officers a video from a robbery in a parking lot, where some thug confronted a man and his daughter, demanded money. Even as the guy reached for his gun, the little girl piped up, "You can't do that. My daddy's a policeman." And bam, bam, bam, the guy was dead, killed in front of his child. They were told to instruct their families that Daddy's job — or Mommy's — was a kind of secret among strangers, that it was up to Daddy (or Mommy) to let people know.

It still broke Lenhardt's heart to think of the night he found Jessica crying in her bed because she thought this meant that her dad couldn't come to Career Day anymore. She took things so hard, Jessica did. *Our daughter has no small emotions,* as Marcia liked to say, but she could laugh when she said it, whereas Lenhardt brooded on the fact.

Still, he believed that if Jessica were in a locked room with one dead girl and another who appeared to be well on her way to dead, she wouldn't have lingered. She would have gotten to that door by any means possible, unlocked it, and gone down the hallway on her belly if she had to. His daughter was scrappy, more of a fighter than her older brother, truth be told. Jason was a dreamer, safe in a gauzy world of his own making. But even Jason would have the instinct to save himself.

So why had the other girl stayed? Did she think the shooter might have the wherewithal to come after her? It was a foolish notion, but if you had grown up on a steady diet of horror movies in which the killer kept getting up again and again, you might think it possible. Had she been hiding in the stall and emerged only after it was all over?

"Like I said, ninety percent of what I'm seeing and hearing matches up with the shooter being the girl in Shock Trauma," Lenhardt said. "But I don't think anyone in this room is going to be happy with a ninety percent certainty if the case falls apart in court. The dead girl's father is already busting our balls. Imagine what he'll be like if we fuck this up."

"I thought it was a given in homicide that the obvious solution is the obvious solution." The colonel smirked at what he thought was a brilliant ploy, throwing Lenhardt's oft-repeated words back at him.

"I never disdain the obvious," Lenhardt said. "But I don't let myself get seduced by it either."

10

"Is it too late for tulips?" Susannah Goode asked the funeral director.

"Probably," said Stan Jasper. "And they're not a flower we work with, normally."

"Oh. I hadn't thought about that. Still, if they were in season . . . She loved tulips."

"Whatever you choose, I'd recommend a palette of white. White, or pale yellow, or pale pink. Very appropriate to one so young."

"Yellow," Dale Hartigan said. "Roses." Susannah squeezed his hand. More correctly, she squeezed his fist, because Dale's hands had been pretty much balled into fists for the last twenty-four hours, except when occupied by tasks that insisted on uncurled fingers. Driving. Eating, except he hadn't been able to eat, no matter how others urged him. Drinking, which he had done, well into the night, after the last phone call to his father, who wanted to know what the chief had said. He should be hungover today, yet he had never gotten drunk, much less achieved the total numbness he was going for. It was as if he had cried the liquor out before it could reach his blood.

"We work with a florist whose roses are exquisite."

"Yellow roses are often quite bright," Susannah pointed out. "Not pastel."

"Oh, no, the ones we use are very, very light in hue."

Dale had a weary moment of insight: He was being bilked. Well, not bilked, exactly, but the unctuous funeral director had sized him up nicely: Dale Hartigan, a well-fixed man who would spare no expense in burying his daughter, a businessman who would have no stomach for this negotiation. One man's tragedy was another man's workaday life, pure and simple. Stan might have been Dale, pricing out the electrical work on his latest project or girding for battle with the historic review board. Kat's death was just a job to so many people — the police, the assistant state's attorney, the medical examiner.

Then again, it could be argued that someone such as Stan, who worked in an industry that few found desirable, was entitled to charge a premium. Dale had thought the funeral business might have changed, that it would be more like that television show, with lots of loquacious, quirky types whose own dramas could distract the bereaved from their problems. But it was still pretty much *The Loved One* — essential yet vaguely suspect, like aluminum siding.

The interesting aspect about the funeral business, from a businessman's standpoint, was that it didn't have to chase its customers when they headed out to the suburbs. Other merchants needed to go where the customers were, but Baltimore's mortuaries had stayed in place for generations, confident that their customers would come to them when the time was right. *Who ya gonna call?* Oh, shit, Dale was totally losing it, quoting *Ghostbusters* in his head, sitting like a bump in a funeral home while his girlfriend planned his daughter's funeral. "Yellow roses" had been his only real input so far. Yellow roses and his credit card. But then, he needed all his energy to keep from breaking down every five minutes. Once, when he was seventeen, Dale had been rear-ended in a pretty bad pileup on I-83. A runaway semi had come tearing over a hill and confronted an unexpected backup. It had careered from one side to another, tearing open a Corolla, throwing a big boat of a Chevy into Dale's father's Pontiac. But he was young, his reflexes good, and he had braked before hitting the pickup in front of him. When he got out, he was astonished to see the damage to the cars, his and all those around him, more astonished that he hadn't been injured. Yet, within a few hours, he was vaguely sore and achy.

That was how he felt now, times a thousand. He felt as if he had been broken into pieces and glued back together, like a little pitcher or vase. He looked the same, but if you poured anything into him, it would all leak out. He couldn't hold a thought, much less a conversation.

"And the casket?" Stan Jasper prompted. Dale pointed blindly toward a photo in the glossy brochure before him, and Susannah nodded, signifying that his random choice was a suitable one.

Dale had helped to plan one funeral before, his mother's eight years ago, but he found he had no memory of it. Even if he did, he couldn't see how it would help get him through this. The cliché held: Burying a parent was part of the natural order. Burying a child was not. His only child.

Now he got it, the old saying about the monarchy, an heir and a spare. The parents of only children had forgone the spare, which mattered not as an issue of primogeniture but as one of emotional safe harbor. If you had only one, you could lose everything.

Chloe had wanted a second child, but Dale could never see the point and had been secretly pleased when she couldn't conceive again. Kat was so perfect that he worried he would favor her over any sibling who followed, even a son. Besides, Chloe's interest in conceiving had been as flighty and temporary as all her plans — going back to school, becoming a certified yoga instructor, starting her own aromatherapy business. In the last instance, she had actually commissioned a sign, a hand-painted piece of wood proclaiming JUST GOOD SCENTS. The sign had cost four hundred dollars and was still, as far as Dale knew, tucked somewhere in the overstuffed garage, probably between Chloe's kiln and Chloe's skis.

"We aren't as familiar with the, uh, liturgy as we should be," Susannah was telling Stan Jasper. "And we don't have a pastor, not really. But we would like the service to be, well, original. That is, it should be specific to Kat. Would it be appropriate, say, to use one of her favorite poems?"

"That would be utterly appropriate," Stan said in his professionally assuring tones.

" 'Dover Beach,' " Dale said.

"Sweetie?" Susannah squeezed his fist again.

"She was rehearsing a poem called 'Dover Beach,' or a piece of it, for the graduation ceremony. 'We are alone as if . . .' something, something. I remember something about ignorant armies. She picked it out herself."

"A poem would be nice," Stan said carefully. "Although that one sounds a little — well, we don't have to work out all the details right now."

"Still, we'd like to make as much headway as possible on the arrangements," Susannah said. "And Mrs. Hartigan may have some thoughts."

"Will she be calling me?"

"Perhaps," Susannah said in the tight, careful voice she used whenever the subject of Chloe Hartigan came up in any context. "Dale went out to see her this morning, but she didn't feel up to coming today."

That was one way to explain it, Dale thought. Upon hearing that he wanted an Episcopalian priest to officiate, Chloe had pitched a fit and then pitched a book at Dale's head. A thin book, to be sure, *The Prayer of Jabez*, but it had smarted a little. She had thrown a book at his head and called him a hypocrite and a stupid cunt, and he was still puzzling over both charges. The latter was a word Chloe had never used, even in her most Tourette-like rages. Had she been so upset that she had garbled her insult, saying "You stupid cunt" as opposed to "You *and* your stupid cunt"? He wondered if other families would tell Stan Jasper all of this, pour their hearts out. Or perhaps death, the ultimate bodily function, made people overly decorous and circumspect. Right now, for example, he knew he felt some odd need for the undertaker's approval.

Yet here was a guy who was going to touch Dale's dead daughter, who was going to oversee her final choice of dress, arrange her hair, supervise her makeup, pump her full of formaldehyde, or whatever it was these guys did. *He's going to see my daughter naked,* Dale thought, and no man ever had. At least he was pretty sure that Kat was still a virgin, de-

175

spite dating that college boy, Peter Lasko, a few summers back. Dale had disliked that guy from the moment he met him. There had been something predatory about him, swooping in to pluck Kat, then newly hatched from her baby fat. A nineteen-year-old college boy going after a girl who had just finished her first year of high school. He was slick, an opportunist. He had wanted to be an actor, for God's sake, although Dale was pretty sure his greatest role was the nice-boy act he put on for Chloe, who ate it up sideways with a spoon. She had no judgment about people.

Then again, she always swore she liked Susannah.

"She's so accomplished," was what Chloe said. "She's a great role model for Kat." Dale kept waiting for the other shoe to drop, the insult that he was sure Chloe was holding back for the perfect moment. But she remained sweet as pie to Susannah. It was her way of underscoring the fact that Dale was her only enemy. Dale was the person she blamed for everything that had gone wrong in her life, even things that happened long before he showed up. Why? Their marriage counselor had spoken of the concept of shame, of the way that certain experiences left holes in people.

Chloe had never gotten over her haphazard family, or the fact that her dreams were squashed so young. (Yet Dale's father was as big a piece of work as anyone, and Chloe always mocked him for bringing that up.) Her ob/gyn had cited postpartum depression, but did postpartum last for fourteen years?

After the tumultuous years with Chloe, it had been hard at first to trust Susannah's sweet, steady competence. "She has the best disposition," Dale told his father when they started dating. "I hate to tell you this," his father said, clearly not hating it, "but you said the same thing about the other one once upon a time." Now, four years in, Dale had been proven right about Susannah. Always calm, always capable, never letting her emotions get the better of her. These were the things he loved about her.

Until right now, when he kind of hated her for these very qualities. How could she be so collected, so efficient? Maybe Susannah had never really cared for Kat. Maybe she was secretly glad Kat was dead. Now *she* would want a baby, and Dale had been very clear on that score — no more children. He was done.

"We expect a lot of people," she was

telling Stan Jasper in her lovely low voice, a voice that Dale had never heard raised except in joy or excitement. "Kat was a very popular girl, and . . . the nature of what happened makes this something of a public event. Yet we still want the service to be intimate, to reflect her."

"I'd recommend a private service," Jasper said, "followed by a more, ah, inclusive burial service. Or even a memorial service at the school, which would allow her little friends to grieve, without putting too much of a burden on you."

Oh, he was such a shit. Susannah had loved Kat, too. There had been tensions, of course. It wasn't easy for Kat to have a de facto stepmother who was only fourteen years older, even if Susannah was far more mature than Chloe would ever be. But Susannah's cool competence, so comforting in other aspects of their life together, was also present in her relationship with Kat, and that had worried Dale a little. She admired Kat, complimented her, had even been instrumental in helping Kat get into Stanford, but she was unusually insistent, in Dale's opinion, about not wanting to replace Chloe in Kat's heart. One could argue that Susannah was being sensitive and responsible in not pressing for too intimate a connection to Kat. Yet Susannah's reserve had always bothered Dale.

Then he remembered Susannah yesterday afternoon, crying wholeheartedly upon hearing the news, holding him as tightly as anyone had ever held him — outside Chloe, who used to grab on to Dale so hard when she was angry or sad that it had frightened him a little. Susannah felt this as deeply as she could — but she could never feel what he did. The irony of Kat's death, if such a thing could ever be termed ironic in any aspect, was that the only person on earth who understood what Dale was going through was a person who was determined to hate him. That was Chloe's religion, the Gospel According to Hating Dale. What did it matter if an Episcopal priest or Chloe's Buddhist-monk friend officiated at the service? The only person who could please Chloe was someone who got up and reminded the mourners that everything was Dale Hartigan's fault, forever and ever, amen.

"You haven't been in an Episcopal church since we got married," Chloe complained. "And that was only for your parents." So hypocrite, okay. But why a cunt? Wait — now he got it. She had been going for his soft spot, mocking his masculinity. A real man would be able to take care of his daughter, Chloe was saying. Never mind that she was the custodial parent, that if anyone could have seen this storm gathering on the horizon, it should have been Chloe, who was part of Kat's life on a daily basis. She knew about this strange feud with Perri, as it turned out, but had written it off as a rite of passage. "All girls fight," she had said. No, this, too, had to be Dale's fault somehow.

She hadn't thrown *The Prayer of Jabez* at him because of the Episcopalian minister. That was a lie, the only thing he could think of to explain the red mark on his forehead to Susannah. Chloe had tossed the book at him because Dale had agreed that Kat's death was all his fault — but not for reasons that Chloe wanted to hear.

"If I hadn't let you pack my bags and put me out that first time," he had told her. "If I hadn't made the mistake of telling the truth, in hopes of making a truly fresh start with you. If I hadn't accepted your edict that our marriage was over, if I had parked myself on our front porch and refused to move until you heard me out —"

"You stupid cunt," she had said. "You think everything is about you."

180

And the book had landed before Dale could finish his thought, which was simply, *If I hadn't left, I would have been here to protect her.*

II

Josie was alone with her mother when the two strange men appeared in her hospital room. She could not have told you who they were, but she quickly understood who they were *not*. Not doctors, because they wore suits and ties and hovered in the doorway waiting to be invited in, while the hospital staff always sailed right in. Not from school. Not friends' fathers, because she didn't recognize them, and one looked a little too young to be anyone's dad. Not her parents' friends, because — But she had no words for this knowledge, just an awareness that these were not men from her parents' jobs. Something about their suits, their ties, even their hair, told her they were not part of her family's world.

"Mrs. Patel?" the older one asked. Josie, who had endured a lifetime of such puzzled looks, knew he was trying to connect the blond woman in the chair to the dark girl in the bed. He also didn't say their name quite right. It was more "Pattle" than "*Pa*-tel" in this stranger's mouth. If her father were here, there would be no confusion. But Josie's father was in the parking lot, arguing with his insurance company on his cell phone. Josie was to be discharged today, but with television trucks cruising the cul-de-sac in front of their house, her parents felt it would be easier to safeguard her privacy at the hospital. Her father had assured Josie it was just a matter of getting the right person on the phone, but there were apparently many, many wrong people en route to that right one, bored men and women in windowless cubicles in distant states who did not understand the magnitude of what had happened at Glendale, or Josie's singular role in it.

"Mrs. Patel?" The older man had to repeat himself, for Josie's mother was just looking at him over her magazine, fatigue making her punchy. She had gone home last night to take care of Matt and Tim, but she told Josie she hadn't slept.

"Yes?"

"I'm Sergeant Harold Lenhardt from Baltimore County Police, and this is my partner, Detective Kevin Infante. We'd like to ask your daughter, Josephine, some questions if she's up to it."

"Josie," said Josie, shocked to hear the old-fashioned name that her family had never used. Then she wished she had not responded so quickly and forcefully. She should have pretended to be tired, or spacey from the painkillers. Then these men would have to go away. Why did she have to talk to police? Wasn't it obvious what had happened?

"I suppose —" her mother began.

"It's important," the older man said, the one who had identified himself as a sergeant. "It's best to talk to witnesses when their memories are freshest. Every day that goes by, things will be harder to recall. Especially in a trauma like this, where a healthy brain will be working to suppress memories."

"Josie's brain is very healthy," her mother said, clearly not hearing all the words.

"Of course she is. It's just, from our point of view, it's never too early to start preparing for a trial."

"There's going to be a trial?" Josie asked.

"Maybe," Lenhardt said. "If . . . well, for now, we have to assume that someone will be charged. That could change."

Because Perri might die, Josie realized.

The very concept still stunned her, despite seeing Perri's face. Perri dead was even more shocking than Kat dead.

"Even if there's not a criminal trial," put in the younger cop, Infante, "there could be civil ones. Lawsuits against the gun manufacturer, for example. Or the school."

"Oh, Jesus," Josie's mom said. "We would never be a party to such things."

"You're not the only family affected," Sergeant Lenhardt reminded her, almost apologetically. "But I wouldn't worry so much about civil trials right now. We just need to have a clear picture of what happened, so the state's attorney can decide what sort of charges are merited. There are a lot of distinctions, even within a homicide case."

"Homicide?" Josie asked.

"A girl is dead. You knew that, didn't you? The Hartigan girl died immediately."

Josie nodded. Of course she knew. She just hadn't thought of it as a *homicide*. It was such a television word, freighted and somber. It was hard to see how it had shouldered its way into her life.

"But I don't know what I can tell you. Perri came into the bathroom and started shooting. It was . . . crazy."

"Just walked in and opened fire? Didn't

185

say anything or do anything else?" Sergeant Lenhardt pulled a microcassette recorder from his blazer pocket. "Mind if I tape this? My own memory's not the greatest, and Infante's notes" — he gestured to the younger man, who had produced a narrow steno pad and pen — "are darn near illegible."

"No problem," Josie said. Her voice sounded faint and thin in her ears.

"So you're in the bathroom with Katarina Hartigan."

"Kat. No one called her Katarina."

"Okay. You and Kat are in the bathroom. Is anyone else there? Does anyone come and go before Perri Kahn comes in?"

"No." The other detective seemed to find that interesting, underscoring whatever he had written on his pad.

"And why are you there?"

"Well, you know, the usual reasons."

"Of course. That was silly of me. Why does anyone go to the bathroom just before school starts? In my day kids smoked, but I guess that's not so common anymore."

"Some girls smoke," Josie said. "But not in the bathrooms. You get suspended for that. The whole school is smoke-free, by state law, so the kids who want to smoke

186

go to the woods, just beyond the athletic field. That's not school property."

"Yeah. You don't look like a smoker anyway."

"I'm a gymnast. I have an athletic scholarship to College Park. At least . . . I did." Josie indicated her foot. She had been proud of that scholarship. Maryland was the first school in the country to offer cheerleading as a Title IX program, and it was hard to get into College Park. Only five students from her class had made it.

"A gymnast. That's very admirable. So you and Kat are . . . well, where, exactly, when this other girl comes in?"

"Standing by the sinks."

"Washing hands? Putting on makeup?"

"Kat had a lipstick."

The other police officer wrote something, then waited for her to continue.

"And Perri came in —"

"You knew her, right?"

Josie hesitated, and her mother, ever helpful, rushed in, "The girls have been close friends since they were eight, all three of them, although their interests took them in different directions in the past year. Josie and Kat were doing cheerleading, and Kat was knocking herself out with all sorts of extracurriculars, to make sure she got into Stanford. Perri had concentrated on drama."

You can say that again, Mom.

"Oh. Oh. So did the three of you normally meet in this bathroom before school? I mean, would someone know you would be there?"

"No. We didn't even have homeroom or classes in the north wing, Kat and I. But Perri's homeroom teacher was the drama teacher, so she was in that wing."

"So why were *you* there?"

"Because Kat said she needed to do something in that part of the school."

"What?"

"She didn't say."

"So you just followed your friend on some errand, although you didn't know what it was?"

"They were extremely close," Josie's mom said. "Kat drove Josie to school almost every morning."

"If you don't mind, ma'am, it's better if we just let your daughter tell the story." Josie's mother blushed, embarrassed at being corrected in any way, although the sergeant's manner was gentle.

"So you and Kat are in the north wing, getting ready to do something — you don't know what — and it's a place where you don't normally go, at least before school, and this other girl that you know, who used to be your good friend, although you don't see her so much anymore, just comes in and starts shooting when she sees you, although she has no reason to suspect that you'll be there."

It did sound odd, the way he said it. "I guess that's what happened."

"It's not a test, Josie. The only right answers are the ones you know."

Josie's head was beginning to ache, her foot to throb.

"She shot Kat," she said. "Then she shot me in the foot when I tried to grab the gun from her. And then she shot herself. Those *are* the right answers."

"Did she say anything? Perri Kahn, I mean."

"Not really."

"Not really?"

"I mean no, no, she didn't say anything."

The sergeant did not say anything for a while, and yet the detective wrote and wrote and wrote, filling his pad. What could he be writing if nothing was being said?

"So you're at the sink, and Perri comes in," the sergeant began, as if there had been no long silence. "Is the gun in her hand, or does she have to get it out of something?"

"It was in her knapsack, but in the outside pocket. I think."

"So" — the detective pantomimed holding a knapsack in his left hand, pulling a gun out with his right — "she just comes in, whips out the gun, and starts shooting. No preamble, no warning."

"Yes."

"Doesn't do anything else?"

"No."

"Doesn't lock the door?"

Shit. "Well, yeah, she must have locked the door."

"Really?" The sergeant returned to his mime with the knapsack and the gun. "How does she do that if she comes through the door and immediately gets her gun out?"

"I didn't see her lock the door, but she must have, because it was locked when the police came."

"You didn't know the door was locked until the police got there and asked you to open it?" Her words, recast as his, sounded odd. Suspect, even.

"No, not for sure."

"You didn't go to the door at any time?"

"No."

The sergeant made a great show of being puzzled. If he had been in one of the school's productions, Josie thought, the drama teacher, Old Giff, would have told him to dial it down a notch. That had been his most frequent note to Perri. *Dial it down a notch, make it real.*

"The thing is, there's this trail of blood. Just a little, from one corner to the door. Dot, dot, dot, like a trail. As if it were leaking from something, but not a lot."

"I was still bleeding a little when the paramedics took me out," Josie said.

"On a gurney?"

"What?"

"They took you out on a stretcher with wheels, the kind that goes up and down?"

"Yes." She remembered the way it had risen and collapsed beneath her along the way, bringing her up to the paramedics in the bathroom, then down again at the door to the ambulance, up again at the hospital. Up and down, up and down. It had reminded her of her old trampoline after a fashion, although there had been no joy in these movements.

The young detective turned a page, filled it with a big, looping scrawl, turned another page.

"Probably not important," the sergeant

said. "Now, who got shot first?"

"Kat."

"Perri just walked in — locked the door, although you didn't see her lock the door or notice her turning back — pulled the gun out of her knapsack, and bam, shot Kat Hartigan right in the heart."

"Yeah. I mean, I grabbed for the gun, but I couldn't reach her."

"How far away was she?"

"Not far."

"Three feet? Six feet? Nine feet?"

"I'm not good with distances."

"If we were to go back there, could you —"

"I don't want to go back there," Josie said, feeling dangerously out of control. "Ever."

"I get that. I get that. And then what? After Kat was shot?"

"Perri shot me in the foot. I made another grab for it, but she's taller, and she just aimed the gun down and fired. Then she stepped back and shot herself." It was no effort to cry here, none at all. The only effort was making sure she didn't choke on the sobs that started. "I didn't know what to do. My foot hurt, and it was bleeding, and they say you should elevate injuries, so I just sat down where I was, and I put my leg up, and I waited." She remembered how endless it had seemed, the long minutes before the paramedics arrived, the principal's voice on the PA system, the distant sounds of the school emptying. "I waited an awfully long time."

"But when the police came, you wouldn't unlock the door."

"I couldn't. I was scared. I thought if I moved, I might lose too much blood."

"So it was less scary sitting there with your dead friend and your old friend . . . well, she must have looked pretty bad."

"Yes. No. I don't know. It was all awful. Everything was awful."

"Detective," her mother began.

"Sergeant," the older man corrected. "Sergeant Lenhardt."

"This interview seems a little rough to me. I'm not sure what you want Josie to say, but you don't need to make her feel as if she did anything wrong. *She's* the victim."

"Oh, right. Right. I'm sorry, I don't mean to be harsh. Far from it. The thing is, while this whole shooting is obvious from my department's point of view, it might not seem quite so obvious in court. So let me just make sure that I'm absolutely clear on this: Perri comes in, says

nothing, takes out her gun, shoots Kat —
how many times?"

"Once."

"Right, once. Then she shoots you in the
foot while you try to grab the gun, steps
back, and . . . well, we haven't talked to her
doctor, but it's my understanding it goes
up through her jaw. How tall are you,
Josie?"

It was a question she hated under any
circumstance.

"Five-one."

"And how tall was Perri? Approxi-
mately?"

Her mother answered: "At least five-
eight, maybe five-nine. She stooped hor-
ribly when she was younger, but she was
more comfortable with her height once
they started high school."

"Uh-huh, uh-huh. Josie, did any of the
responding officers test you for gun residue?"

"Why would they do that?" Josie's
mother asked.

"Oh, it's just routine. But no one
touched the gun except Perri. Right, Josie?
She was the only one who held it."

"I might have touched it when I tried to
grab it from her. Everything happened so
fast."

"But if we wanted to test you, right now, you'd say yes, right? Because you didn't fire the gun, and a test could prove that even twenty-four hours later. Besides, we'll need your fingerprints, just in case. I could go out to our car —"

"I don't feel good," Josie said, putting her hand beneath the sheet and hugging her stomach, which was beginning to jump around alarmingly. "I'm nauseous and hungry at the same time."

"Josie, are you . . . um, menstruating? Or was Kat? Is that why you were in the bathroom?"

"What?"

Josie's father entered the room, brandishing his cell phone as if it were the Olympic torch. "I all but had to call the CEO at home in Louisville, but they okayed another night's stay as long as a hospital psychiatrist signs off on it, which I've been assured is no problem. When I told him how many television cameras were outside our house — Who are these gentlemen?"

"Police," her mother said.

"Why are you talking to Josie? I mean, why now? Couldn't this have waited?"

"She's the only witness, sir." Was it Josie's imagination, or did the sergeant stare at her just then?

"Daddy, I'm tired and it's hard to remember everything, and they're asking me questions about my period and stuff."

"What?"

"It's not quite —" Sergeant Lenhardt stood, as if he knew it was time to leave. Was he scared of her dad? No one had ever been scared of Josie's dad. It was kind of cool.

"My daughter has been through enough this weekend," her father said. "She saw her best friend killed and was shot trying to take the gun away from a girl who was also her friend. Girls who were like sisters to her. This is unconscionable."

"No one's implied that your daughter's lying or that she wasn't brave," the sergeant said. "We're in the difficult position of having to collect information in the expectation of facing a very skilled criminal defense. As I said, your daughter's the only eyewitness. I mean, who can talk. Who knows what the Kahn girl will say if she recovers?"

Now everyone in the room was silent, everyone and everything, except the younger detective's pen, hurrying across his pad.

"Does my daughter have to talk to you?"

"Excuse me?"

"Is she required to talk to you? Do citizens have to talk to the police when they're not charged with anything? Because I am a citizen, Officer, a second-generation American, for your information, so don't think I can be bullied."

"Well, it could be argued, Mr. Patel" — he still didn't have their name quite right, Josie noticed — "that a witness to a murder who doesn't cooperate is obstructing justice, which is a felony in its own right."

"In that case — since you're throwing charges around — I think I'd like my daughter to have a lawyer before she talks to you again."

"That's your legal right, Mr. Patel, but it's not really necessary. Just gunks up the works, makes your neighbors think things are different than they are. No one's accusing your daughter of anything. We're simply trying to make sure we're clear on the details of what happened."

"I'm very clear. My daughter's been through the most traumatic experience of her life. She's seen her best friend killed and suffered a painful injury. If you'd like to talk to her further, I'll bring her to your offices next week. With a lawyer."

The sergeant and the detective shuffled out, heads down. Josie almost felt sorry for them — until she caught the look on the older man's face. He wasn't the least bit ashamed or cowed by her father's lecture. He was just pretending.

"Daddy?" she said as soon as the detectives left. "Could I have a snowball? Raspberry? Or fireball, with marsh-a-mallow?"

"Marsh-a-mallow" was an old family joke, Josie's childhood mangling of the word.

"The hospital might have smoothies or frozen yogurt, but I don't think —" her mother began.

"Of course you can have a snowball," her father said. "I'll ask where the nearest stand is, so it won't be all juice."

Josie settled back on her pillows, exhausted. Exhausted, and just a little exhilarated, too.

12

"Do you want anything from downstairs? Zip's going to the food court."

"Did I see a Mama Ilardo's down there? I love the sausage and pepperoni thick crust."

Eloise Kahn paused, and Dannon Estes wondered if she was going to suggest a healthier alternative, as she often did when Dannon dined with the Kahns. He couldn't blame her. Eloise, as she insisted on being called by Perri's friends, knew that Dannon was troubled by his weight and acne, not to mention his height. *There's nothing you can do about your height,* Eloise would tell him in her gentle way, *but the first two conditions actually respond to diet and behavior changes, even medication.* If he wanted to be thin, if he wanted clear skin, he could have them. He just had to make different *choices.* It was one of Mrs. Kahn's favorite words — choices.

But perhaps Eloise Kahn was less wedded to this view of self-control. For all her good choices, she was now hunkered down in the corridors of Shock Trauma, one of the most despised people in the Baltimore metro area this weekend. The other being her husband, of course. And Perri, too, although Dannon had a hunch that Perri didn't make a very satisfactory villain, being comatose. So her parents had to shoulder all the blame for now.

"Sure," she said. "Sausage and pepperoni, thick crust. What do you want to drink with that?"

"Mountain Dew."

"One slice?"

He held up two fingers, embarrassed by his greed, but he had been here since 10:00 a.m., when his mother had finally agreed to drive him down rather than continue to listen to his insistent wheedling.

Eloise nodded. "You got it. I'll go tell Zip before he gets on the elevator." She walked down the hall, her feet dragging along the linoleum, in marked contrast to her usual gait, which was bouncy, more girlish than Perri's. At the end of the corridor, she turned and called back to him.

"Are you sure that's all you want?"

"Yeah," he said, although it was far from

all he wanted. But what Dannon really craved was not available at the food court, or anywhere else. He wanted to be liked. He wanted to be taller. First and foremost, he wanted to be someone else — not merely a taller, cooler, clear-skinned Dannon Estes but someone altogether different. An outlaw type, the kind of silent guy who glided through life letting others project their dreams and desires on him, like Keith Carradine in that old movie. Not *Nashville*, but the other one where all the women were crazy in love with him. Except that Dannon would want other Keith Carradines to love him. That was his exact type. Tall, lanky, hetero, but maybe not wedded to it.

For now his only claim to outlaw status was that he was willing to be here, keeping a vigil with Baltimore's newest pariahs, part of a tiny minority who wanted to see Perri live. Oh, other people probably wanted Perri to survive, too, but only to see her punished. Dannon and the Kahns clung to the idea that Perri could somehow explain it all if she would only regain consciousness. It had to be a mistake, some freakish accident. This was not Perri.

The Kahns, for once needing Dannon almost as much as he needed them, had lied and told hospital personnel that he was Perri's brother and eighteen, neither of which was true. Both lies would be exposed once Dwight made it home from Japan, where he had just started a new job in some bank. Dannon felt noble, and then he felt stupid: What did Dannon Estes, wardrobe master for the drama club, really have to lose by being here? Until Perri came along, he hadn't had a real friend in all of Glendale. He was the fringe of the fringe of the fringe, a movie-besotted geek whose only friends were AMC and TCM and the Sundance Channel.

Then, last fall, Perri Kahn had taken him under her wing suddenly, excitingly, need ing a coconspirator in her scheme to get the drama department to mount Stephen Sondheim's *Anyone Can Whistle*. They hadn't won in the end, but they should have, and Dannon was flattered to discover that Perri still desired his company when she no longer needed him as a political ally. A year older than Dannon, one of the acknowledged stars of Glendale's drama department, she had barely spoken to him during previous productions — *Carousel*, *The Lark*. Perri had been a big wheel in the drama department since scoring the title role in *Mame* in the summer production, back when she was all of sixteen. Dannon had loved helping to create the illusion of glamour the role required. Watching from the wings as Perri descended the mock staircase in a gold dress that Dannon had found in a consignment shop, he had been as smitten as Mame's nephew in the play. Life really was a banquet, and most poor sons of bitches were starving.

Perri wasn't supposed to say "sons of bitches," of course. She was expressly forbidden, told to say sons of guns instead. So on opening night she substituted "bastards." That word, she blithely told a furious Barbara Paulson after the performance, had not been prohibited. Eloise and Zip had defended her, as they usually did. Eloise and Zip were big on integrity and principle.

Of course, Dannon, watching from the wings, didn't know that then. He hadn't gotten to know the Kahns until this fall, when it turned out that hanging out with Perri also meant spending time with her folks, a kind of accelerated intimacy that almost left him breathless. Eloise and Zip Kahn had treated Dannon as if he had been part of Perri's life since grade school, automatically including him in all sorts of outings and celebrations. Overwhelmed by

203

their kindness at first, he had begun to understand there was an element of relief in it for them, too: Dannon was filling Kat and Josie's spot in the Kahn family. Tight as the Kahns were, they liked to have outsiders around to validate their closeness, their specialness.

The senior-year rupture in Perri's friendship with Kat and Josie had been the gossip of the school, as much discussed as the breakups of the all-but-married couples, the ones who started going together in middle school. But no one knew anything. Even broken, the three were a closed unit. Dannon could tell Perri was angry and unhappy. But the origin of the grudge remained a mystery to him, despite his famed eavesdropping skills. (Oh, there were some advantages to never being noticed.) There was no backbiting, none of the diplomatic back-and-forth that some other girls employed when quarreling, with some poor intermediary sent between two camps. Instead Kat and Josie walked through the halls as if nothing had happened, and Perri stalked around in her increasingly odd garb — lots of black, a man's cashmere coat that Dannon had helped her find at Nearly New, and a battered homburg. Eloise just laughed and said Perri looked like a goth Annie Hall.

He wondered who was outside Josie's hospital room, who would stand beside Kat's grave when she was buried. Probably everybody in the school. He wasn't sure he could stomach the hypocrisy. Not that he disliked Kat. She was so unobjectionable that she was objectionable, as Perri had said in an unguarded moment just a few weeks ago. She was part of a larger problem, the very blandness of Glendale High, a culture that valued inoffensiveness above everything else. *How are you? You look great! Shut up, there is no way I'm going to be elected prom queen.* Yet she had said these things with genuine warmth. No one had ever caught Kat Hartigan being two-faced. She may not have known Dannon's name, but she had always been nice to him.

No, back in middle school, Perri was the one who had been in charge of making Dannon's life miserable. She had been vicious and tart-tongued, as bad as the mainstream popular kids she later disparaged. Her genius for dissection was fearsome, her instinct for weakness frightening. And back then her alliance with Kat and Josie, whom everyone liked, made her fearless. Safe within that ironclad friendship, she had mocked everyone who was the least bit off — Binnie-the-Albino Snyder, Fiona "Stiffie" Steiff, Bryan "Aimless" Ames, Eve Muhly. And Dannon.

"Dannon has bigger breasts than any girl in the seventh grade," Perri once said in that calculated undertone that sounded like a whisper but was pitched to be overheard, and he was "Boob Boy" for the rest of middle school. Reunited with Perri and her crowd in high school, he had waited nervously for the abuse to start again, but Perri seemed to have settled down. Or maybe she had just learned to channel her dark energy into villainous roles. She had been a most memorable Mrs. Mullins in *Carousel*.

When Perri found out Dannon knew even more about theater and old movies than she did, their friendship really took off. She drew him into her family, invited him to attend *Bounce* at the Kennedy Center. (Dannon tried not to think about for whom that ticket had been purchased, months earlier. Kat? Josie? Some boy she had dated? But Perri never seemed to get that tangled up with her boyfriends.) The Kahns' beaming attention was so seductive, relative to his own mom's strong but spotty love. They sought his opinions and encouraged vigorous debate, as long as it was backed up with thoughtful reasons. They pushed him to take his ambitions seriously, whereas Dannon was pretty much used to being told by his stepfather that all his dreams were out of reach. Once Mrs. Kahn learned of his interest in fashion design, she began giving him college catalogs for places like RISD and Pratt Institute. A chance remark about film school brought a similar torrent of catalogs and books.

At times Dannon would find himself feeling overwhelmed by the Kahns' cheerfully high expectations for him. And then he would wonder what it was like to be Perri, but he had never dared to ask, because the last thing he wanted to know was that the Kahns had any shortcomings. Because if Perri's parents were wrong, then there were no good parents, and who needed to know that?

He had known about the gun. Should he tell her parents? Was it his fault? He had known about the gun, but Perri had said it was a caper. Well, she hadn't used that word, but she had implied it. All Perri had said was "I stole a gun." "Why?" " 'Seemed like a smile,' " she said, quoting one of their favorite actors in one of their favorite movies, Kevin Bacon in *Diner*. Six Degrees of Kevin Bacon. Perri and Dannon had loved that game, because their mastery of old movies made them unstoppable. Their Holy Grail was to link Kevin Bacon to Fatty Arbuckle, and just because they hadn't done it yet didn't mean they never would. Unless, of course — but he had to be hopeful. Perri alive was better than Perri dead, right? Even if she faced a lifetime in jail, her parents would want her alive. All the Kahns ever wanted was for their daughter to be the best at what she did.

Dannon had tried so hard to come up with a way to save Perri without ratting her out, which would have lost him her friendship. *I tried, I tried,* he thought frantically now, not sure if he sought to convince God or himself. *But she didn't tell me she was going to kill Kat.* She didn't say anything like that. "A little theater," she had promised, nothing more. "Think *Much Ado About Nothing.*" There was no shooting in that play that Dannon knew of, although, granted, he wasn't the Shakespeare fiend that Perri was. Still, if the Kahns knew that he had been Perri's confidant *before* the fact . . .

"Here's your food, Dannon," Mrs. Kahn said, handing him a cardboard plate that was barely up to holding the two huge slabs of pizza. "What's making you look so thoughtful?"

"Oh, thinking of that Kevin Bacon game," he lied. "Still trying to make my way to Fatty Arbuckle."

What would the Kahns have done if Perri had told them she had a gun, if she had told them she planned to make a rumpus? (That was another one of Perri's sayings, when she planned mischief: "Let's make a rumpus.") Of course, Dannon knew they would have talked her out of it, sent her to a psychiatrist, gotten Perri whatever help she needed for whatever kind of breakdown she was having.

But a part of him, the evil part of him that Perri had so encouraged, couldn't help imagining the Kahns reacting with their typical enthusiasm: *You want to shock everyone in Glendale, dear? You want to kill your friend? Then you must be the best killer of your generation.* They would have heaped books and documentaries on Perri, maybe hired a pistol expert to train her in shooting.

Dannon blinked back tears. He knew that voice in his head. It was Perri's, sarcastic as ever. *Get out of my head, Perri. Get back into yours, fix yourself, wake up, explain what happened. Please, Perri, please. Make this make sense. Tell us it's not what it looks like.*

And he saw her again, Mame on the staircase, trumpet in hand, her angular thinness rendered glamorous in the gold sequins he had found for her. Life *was* a banquet, and Dannon was the poorest son of a bitch of all, still starving despite the two huge slices of pizza he had crammed into his mouth, barely noticing their taste. What would Perri do? Would she want him to tell, or would she want him to be quiet for now? The answer only mattered if you thought she was going to be all right, and that was pretty much Dannon's religion right now. Clap for Tinker Bell, boys and girls. Clap if you believe in fairies.

If Perri were here, she'd probably got a laugh out of that, Dannon Estes of all people, asking an imaginary audience to believe in fairies. Yet if anything ever got through to Perri, it was definitely applause.

sixth grade

13

The summer before the girls were to enter sixth grade, a new middle school was completed and the students in the Glendale subdivisions had to be split between the old and the new. Perri and Josie remained in the district for the original school, Hammond Springs, but Kat wound up on the other side of an invisible line and was assigned to Deerfield.

No one liked this idea, of course. Kat was terrified at the idea of being alone — separated not only from Perri and Josie but from virtually every classmate she had known since kindergarten, with the exception of Binnie Snyder. Perri had become so enamored of the idea of the three of them that she viewed the new school as a specific plot to break them up. Josie didn't care so much if they were two or three, but if there were going to be just two, she would prefer it to be Kat and her. While she and Perri sometimes spent time alone

— and even had fun that way, for Josie rather liked Perri's cruel wit, as long as it was directed at others — she was nervous she wouldn't be able to meet Perri's standards, day to day. Kat was their anchor, the one who kept them steady.

"We're a triangle," Perri said. "And a triangle that loses one of its points is nothing but a line."

"Wouldn't we be two lines?" Geometry was not Josie's best subject.

"No, just two points, a single line. It takes three points to make a shape." Perri, like Kat, was in gifted-and-talented math.

"It won't be so bad for you," Kat said. "You'll have each other, while I'll be alone. What am I supposed to do, ride the bus with Binnie?"

"The new school is prettier, though," Josie said, thinking that might be a consolation.

"You're not going," Perri assured Kat, but even her agile mind failed to concoct a plan. It was the beginning of summer, but the season's normal joys were small consolation to them as they contemplated summer's end.

Yet the girls had an unexpected ally in Kat's father, who believed that Deerfield, despite its newness, was not as desirable as

Hammond Springs. "Teachers are what make schools good," he said. "Not buildings." (Perhaps this was a lesson that he had learned from the high school, whose physical problems were manifest now that it was three years old.) Meetings were held, phone calls were made, and somehow, midway through August, the invisible line jumped over the Hartigans' house and it came back into the Hammond district, along with the Snyder and Muhly farms.

So it was with giddy relief that the girls met at the Ka-pe-jos' old campsite, the ceremonial grounds, although the tribal name had fallen into disuse over the last year. No one had said they should stop speaking of the Ka-pe-jos or relinquish their vows. A day just came when it seemed natural to stop doing those things. Josie assumed that a new game or ritual might replace the old, and she had waited hopefully to see where Perri's imagination might lead them. But so far the abandoned campfire was a place to meet and talk, nothing more.

It was the last Sunday in August, and they had not seen each other for almost a month. Kat's family had gone to Rehoboth, while Perri's folks had taken her to New York City, where, as she kept telling them, she saw five plays in seven days. Josie hadn't gone anywhere, except to a dreary day camp. Her parents had spoken of a long weekend in West Virginia, but something had fallen through, Josie wasn't quite sure what, and her parents had bought her a trampoline instead, much to the neighbors' disgust. "They're not safe, you know," Mrs. Patterson told Josie's mother. "About the only more dangerous thing you can have on your property is a pool." Josie's mother just shrugged and said Mrs. Patterson's children didn't have to play on it.

In mid-August, Josie's grandparents had arrived from Chicago, and that was fun, although their foreignness had embarrassed Josie when they went to places like the mall or Moxley's ice cream. She didn't know what was worse, her grandmother's sari or her *bindi*. Still, it was nice to have such a rapt audience for her trampoline tricks, although Grammy Patel seemed a little shocked by some of the things Josie did. "Is it safe? Is it *nice?*" she had asked Josie's mom, who had assured her that Josie was trained to do these amazing things and no one cared if an eleven-year-old girl's limbs were exposed. Josie had flown into the summer sky, tucking and turning and twisting, and her grandparents had clapped their cautious, bewildered approval.

But now, with school beginning, Kat and Perri were finally back. In acknowledgment of the reunion's importance, Josie's mother had provided cupcakes — extremely fancy ones, from Bonaparte's in the city — and helped Josie pack them in a wicker basket lined with a napkin. There were six cupcakes in all: two with pink frosting, two with white, two with orange. The white-frosted ones had devil's food bases, while the others were plain vanilla cake.

"Everyone should choose one first," Josie said. "And then we'll go in reverse order to choose the second, so it's fair."

"It's not fair to the one in the middle," Perri objected. "The one in the middle always goes second, while the other two both get to go first at least once."

"But my way, if there's one kind you really want, you'll get it. And the middle person has a choice between the last two, while the one who goes last has to take what's left."

"But what if the last two are the same kind? That's not a real choice."

"*I'll* go second," Kat said, ending the disagreement, as she so often did.

Perri nodded, picking a devil's food with white icing. Josie wanted to point out that Kat's going second did not mean Perri necessarily got to go first, but she had provided the cupcakes, so she should act as the hostess. Her mother was big on those kinds of manners.

Kat took an orange one. Josie picked a devil's food, then a pink, leaving a pink and an orange. Kat began to reach for the pink one, but after a quick glance at Perri, whose gaze was fixed on the pink with an almost unsettling ferocity, Kat chose the remaining orange instead.

"I didn't know you liked orange that much," Josie said. "Not enough to pick it twice."

Kat shrugged, glancing sideways at Perri, as if seeking her permission for something. Perri was already licking the pink frosting from the top of her cake, so there was no going back, or trading.

"Your mother should have gotten two kinds, not three," Perri said. "Then we all would have had the same."

At least my mother buys cupcakes, Josie wanted to say. Perri's mother was big on healthy foods — fruit, yogurt, granola bars, and not even the good ones but dry, dusty things that stuck in the throat.

But Josie did not want to risk ruining this moment of reunion and celebration. She lifted her cupcake as if it were a goblet, the kind of gesture that Perri usually thought to make. "A toast! A toast to . . . Kat not having to go to Deerfield!"

"To Kat!" Perri echoed. "To middle school! To Seth Raskin!"

They giggled at that. Seth Raskin was now the best-looking boy in their grade. Perhaps he had always been, but that information had begun to interest them only in the past year. They were all too aware that girls in middle school, the advanced ones, went with boys. And while they swore to each other that this was not something they wanted to do, if one were to have a boyfriend, Seth Raskin would be the one to have.

"To me!" Kat said, raising her orange-topped cupcake, her laugh spilling out.

"No, like this," Perri said, changing the game, taking charge. She took her second cupcake, the devil's food one, and smashed it into her face, so her nose was covered with white icing. Josie did the same thing with *her* white-frosted cupcake. Kat, however, hesitated.

"Drink, knave!" Perri commanded. "Drink deep from your cup . . . cake."

This made Josie laugh so hard that she had to roll on the ground, pine needles gathering in her hair and sticking to the frosting on her face.

"You look like a cat," Perri howled, and Josie laughed harder, arranging the pine needles so they did, indeed, resemble whiskers.

"*I'm* Kat," Kat said, and she scooped up some pine needles, but she couldn't make whiskers because she still hadn't smashed her cupcake in her face. Josie's mother was always saying that Kat was dignified. Josie wasn't sure exactly what this meant, but she thought it had something to do with how Kat was less prone to silliness than Josie and Perri were. Kat was, however, a wonderful audience for their antics, egging them on. Perri tried to say funnier things, while Josie did cartwheels and climbed trees, all for the honor of hearing Kat's giggle.

"Drink, my lord," Perri said, her hand closing over Kat's and pushing the cupcake up toward her face. "Drink the mead of Hammond Springs Middle School, or you'll have to go to Deerfield."

Kat hesitated, and Perri did it for her, not only pushing the cake into her face but giving it a little twist. Kat's eyes opened wide, and she looked for a moment as if she might cry. Instead she laughed, using her fingers to wipe the frosting from her face. Yet it was a softer, more controlled version of her usual laugh, and the girls, in a swift shift of mood not uncommon to them, were suddenly quiet and reflective.

"We get our own lockers in middle school," Kat said. "With combinations. I'm worried I'm going to forget mine."

"We could share our combinations," Perri said. "And then if one of us forgets, we'll be okay."

"We might not be in all the same classes," Kat said. "Or even have the same lunch hour."

"Oh?" Perri said. "Can't your dad fix that, too?"

If there was a hint of challenge in Perri's voice, Kat chose not to hear it. "No," she said. "I don't think my dad would worry about that, as long as I'm in Hammond Springs. Deerfield may be new, but Hammond Springs has the *proven* teachers, my dad says. He says Deerfield was built for newcomers."

"If Deerfield had been the good school, would your dad have worked it out so Josie and I went there?"

"Sure," Kat said.

"How?"

"I don't know. But he would have."

I was a newcomer, Josie thought. What was wrong with being a newcomer? But that was three years ago. Mr. Hartigan must mean the people in the newer developments, the ones that had created the need for Deerfield. Mr. Hartigan hated these places, so much larger and grander than the houses the Hartigan Group had built. Kat's grandfather had sold the business this year, and Mr. Hartigan had started his own company, renovating old buildings in the city. He was tired of showing people how to live, he told the other adults. He was going to settle for helping them work and shop.

The phone rang late that night, after Josie was in bed but still awake. Her parents didn't like phone calls after nine, because her father had to get up for work at five-thirty in order to leave the house by six-thirty. His job was on the other side of Baltimore, and he preferred heading out an hour earlier than necessary, when the roads were still relatively empty. He always said he'd rather have a quiet hour at his desk than leave later and battle traffic.

"Josie, sweetie?"

"Hmmm." She was reading an American

Girl book, although she knew she was getting too old for them.

"Which cupcakes did Kat eat today?"

Her mother's carefully neutral tone told Josie that someone was in trouble. Had they gotten frosting on Kat's shirt? Mrs. Hartigan was fussy about Kat's clothes. No, Perri had been precise in her aim, smashing the cupcake into Kat's face. Maybe Kat wasn't supposed to eat cupcakes at all. This past year her mother had stopped giving her Lunchables, sending Kat to school with turkey sandwiches and carrot sticks. But Kat remained as round-faced as ever. Perhaps it was because Josie always shared her lunch with her.

"She really didn't *eat* any," Josie said.

"Really? Not even a bite?"

"Well, she might have had a little orange frosting. Why?"

"That was Mrs. Hartigan on the phone. Kat's allergic to orange flavoring, of all things, and she has a horrible rash on her face and hands. She may have to miss the first day of school."

Josie felt a flip-flop of panic in her stomach. Her parents were easygoing, but that simply made her more nervous about doing anything wrong. It wasn't her idea to push the cupcake into Kat's face. She shouldn't be blamed.

"I didn't know Kat had allergies."

"She had a workup at the beginning of the summer, apparently. Although I have to say . . . I've never heard of an allergy to flavoring. I wonder sometimes if Mrs. Hartigan is a little —" Her mother broke off, as if she had noticed Josie's sharpening interest. It was always fascinating when adults talked about other adults. They said the meanest things in the nicest ways and then acted so surprised if anyone suggested they didn't like another adult, as if part of being grown-up was liking everyone, or pretending to.

"The important thing is, Kat's going to be fine. It's just a rash. Probably psychosomatic, for all we know. Kat's a little delicate, isn't she?"

Josie thought about this. Although Kat wasn't athletic, she was strong and solid, even brave in her own way. She had let Perri push the cake in her face, knowing she was allergic to the flavoring. When she fell or slipped, she always got back up and kept going, laughing at her own clumsiness. Perri was the one who used her injuries and illnesses to make excuses, who hesitated when she had to do something physical.

Then again, Josie had the feeling that her mother was trying to say something nice about Josie, in a roundabout way — that Josie *wasn't* delicate, that she didn't have allergies, and if she did, she wouldn't be so silly as to eat something that she knew would make her sick.

"I guess so."

"Sometimes I think the mothers who don't work — outside the home — tend to be a little more hysterical about the small things."

"Mrs. Hartigan is *nice*. She lets us play with her makeup and fixes us special treats when we're over there."

Her mother reached toward Josie as if to smooth hair away from her face, then let her hand hover in space as if awaiting permission. Josie had gotten touchy about her parents' touchy-feely ways. Finally her mother went ahead and did it anyway, and Josie didn't protest.

"Do you wish I didn't work?"

Josie thought about this. The truth — yes! — would make her mother feel bad. But she didn't want to tell an out-and-out lie either.

"No, but I don't like having a babysitter. I'm going to middle school now. I can look after myself, if not Matt and

Timmy. Do we still have to have Marta?"

"Yes, according to the state of Maryland. Want to know something funny? When I was your age — well, just a little older — I was baby-sitting. Taking care of little babies, changing diapers. Diapers with *pins,* not the sticky tapes. Looking back, I'm just so glad nothing happened to the children in my care. I was completely over my head."

"If you didn't work, I could have gone out for travel soccer."

"Really? You never said anything at the time. I thought you decided you'd rather concentrate on your gymnastics. You can't do everything. If you took up a team sport, you wouldn't have any time for Kat and Perri."

"Yeah, I know."

"We both have to work, your dad and I, if we want to live in a place like Glendale."

"Yeah," Josie said again.

"Not to mention having money for extras — like gymnastic lessons and trampolines and day camp."

"Yeah."

"Try saying 'yes' sometimes, Josie. It's not that much effort to put the *s* on the end of it." But she hugged her, and Josie had a moment of wishing she could be a little kid again, someone who got tucked in every night, really tucked in, with a story and a song, the way her brothers still did. Middle school was so very, very grown-up.

"Did you truly have an allergic reaction?" It was two days later, and Perri was studying Kat's skin, as smooth and pink as ever.

"My mom took me to the emergency room, and they stuck me with a pen."

"Like a marker?" Josie was puzzled.

"No, a special pen that sends something to your heart so your throat won't close up and keep you from breathing. She thought I was going to die."

Kat's manner was calm as ever, her voice low; they had to lean in to hear her over the din of the lunchroom. The middle-school cafeteria was thrillingly chaotic, much noisier than elementary school.

"Did *you* think you were going to die?" Perri's question struck Josie as odd. If your mother thought you were going to die, then of course you thought so, too. But Kat shook her head. Her hair, now worn loose from a center part, had grown quite long, and Josie noticed that a few of the older boys glanced at Kat's shining banner of hair as it moved back and forth.

"I wasn't scared at all. In fact, it was kind of interesting. I felt like Violet Beauregarde in *Charlie and the Chocolate Factory.* Remember when she ate the gum and she turned into a giant blueberry?"

" 'Take her to the dejuicing room!' " Josie shouted in a fairly good imitation of the movie Willy Wonka, and the others laughed, which made her happy. She so seldom said something funny on her own.

"Exactly," Kat said. "I just assumed they would take me to the dejuicing room and I would be fine. And that's what the pen did. It dejuiced me. Everything stopped swelling, and I was okay."

"But how could you be so sure that you weren't going to die?" Perri did not want to let that part of the discussion drop.

"That's not how death happens. From a cupcake, I mean."

"A person can drown on a teaspoon of water," Perri said with great authority. "So I suppose a cupcake can kill."

"Well, it didn't kill *me*."

"How would you like to die?"

"Perri — that's gross." Kat had finished her lunch — a cup of yogurt, an apple, and a chopped green salad packed in Tupperware, with an individual packet of salad dressing. Josie slid two of her oatmeal

228

cookies over to Kat, who smiled gratefully.

"No orange flavoring," Josie said. "Everyone wants to die in their sleep."

"Yes, but what if that wasn't a choice? What if you had to choose from choking . . ." Perri paused for a moment. Her brain sometimes reminded Josie of a computer, taking a few seconds to switch from task to task, then humming along, faster and faster. "Choking or suffocation. Then burning up, plane crash or . . ."

"Being shot," Josie supplied.

"No," Perri said. "That's instant, so it becomes the easy choice. We need a list of things that are painful and scary."

"You die instantly in a plane crash."

"No you don't," Perri said. "That's why people get money when they sue the airlines. For suffering."

"How do you sue if you're dead?" Kat asked.

"Not the dead people. Their families. Okay — so being smothered. A fire. Plane crash. We need one more."

"Need?" Kat asked.

"Our statistics project. Oh, that's right, you weren't there on the first day when Mr. Treff explained it. We have to conduct a survey, then chart our results, along with demo . . . demo . . . demographics on our survey sample. It's a poll, like the ones they do during elections, but we can ask anything we want. Mr. Treff said."

"Drowning," Josie said.

"What?"

"Death by drowning. That should be the last one."

"That's awfully like suffocation," Perri objected.

"Well, burning up and dying in a plane crash are alike, too."

"That's okay," Kat said. "For things to be alike. After all, the idea is to find out what people *pick*. Maybe it would be interesting to see if certain people pick drowning while other people pick suffocation."

They bent their heads together, pleased with themselves. Although no one made the point out loud, Josie knew they were all thinking the same thing: This was a way to get noticed, to make their mark in the new school. Other students would ask boring questions about television shows and desserts. Only they would investigate death.

And so the very next afternoon, a full week before the assignment was due, they set out, notebooks in hand, and began to canvass the neighborhood. The kids they met — school peers, high-school students, younger kids — were happy to answer their questions. ("That is *sick*," said an older boy who was hanging out with Perri's brother, Dwight, a high-school senior. But he clearly meant it in a good way.) Mothers and baby-sitters, however, frowned and told them not to ask such questions.

"It's our homework," Perri replied. "It's for school. We have to do it."

By Saturday they had polled forty people, but Perri was not pleased with the results. For one thing, far too many people were picking drowning, with plane crashes a distant second. Perri, however, claimed she was more disturbed by what she called demographics.

"We're doing okay on age, but we don't have enough over-eighteen men."

"We have our fathers," Josie said. Her own father had loved the assignment, if only because he liked to see Josie get excited about anything mathematical.

"That's all we have. And they all picked drowning."

"Do you want to go out in the neighborhood and see if there are fathers around?"

"We could, but it's so inefficient. We need to go to a mall or someplace where there are a lot of men."

"My mom would take us to the mall," Kat said.

"Men at malls would all pick drowning," Perri said. "Just like our fathers. We need to find a wider sample."

"We're not supposed to worry about the results," Josie said. She suspected that Perri disliked the "drowning" responses because the choice had been Josie's contribution to the poll. "That's why we vary the order of the possible answers, to control for people picking the first or last thing automatically."

"Still," Perri said, "it's a very narrow sample, just people we know."

"How are we supposed to talk to people we don't know?" Kat asked.

"That's my idea. Let's get our bikes and meet at Kat's house on Saturday."

Glendale had bike paths that connected its various developments, and now that they were in middle school, the girls had been given wide latitude to travel these routes. Still, Old Town Road was forbidden territory, so Josie was shocked when Perri led them to the edge of that busy two-lane strip, almost a highway in its own right.

"We're not supposed to go on Old Town Road."

"We won't," Perri said, turning right on the shoulder. Josie and Kat had no choice but to follow. Perri was right, they weren't exactly on the road, although Josie suspected their parents would not be impressed by this technical compliance with the rule. They rode about a mile, passing a feed store and a tractor dealership, until Perri came to a stop at last in a gravel parking lot outside a windowless concrete building labeled, simply, Dubby's.

"We can't go in a *bar*," Kat said.

"Sure we can. My dad brings me here for mozzarella sticks and cheeseburgers. We can't sit at the bar, but we can go into the restaurant part."

The air inside was smoky, the smokiest air Josie had ever smelled, and there were other smells beneath it, mysterious and unknown. The girls blinked rapidly, their eyes adjusting to the gloom. Suddenly a woman flew at them out of the darkness, like one of those shrieking bird persons they had studied in their mythology unit in fifth grade.

"Little girls can't come in here by themselves. What are you thinking?"

Josie and Kat shrank back, happy for an excuse to flee. But Perri didn't seem the least bit intimidated. "We're here on a school project. We would like to quiz your customers for an exercise in polling."

A man at the bar — an enormous man, with a belly that came so far down his legs that it appeared to rest on his knees — turned to inspect them with interest.

"My customers don't come here to talk politics."

"This isn't about politics," Perri said. "It's a survey on how one would like to die."

The man frowned, then started to laugh, and Josie wasn't sure which reaction scared her more. He was a white man, but with skin so tanned that he was darker than Josie's father. He had dark hair sprouting from his ears, broken yellow teeth, and truly terrifying eyebrows, scraggly and wild.

"Next commercial," he said, waving a huge, puffy hand toward a television tuned to a baseball game. "But that's it. Then you're out of here."

They agreed, interviewing all seven patrons as soon as the beer commercials began. The men did not appear happy about answering the questions, but when they glanced at the man who had given the girls permission, they reluctantly went through with it. One especially mean-looking man studied them for a long time before he answered their questions.

"Do you know my daughter?" he asked. "Eve Muhly?"

"She's a year behind us," Perri said. "We knew her back in elementary school." She made this sound as if it were a long, long time ago.

"Is she a good girl?"

The only thing to say to such a question from an adult was yes. Even if another kid was hateful to you, it was wrong to tell an adult. And back then Eve was pretty well behaved in the way that parents cared about, if smellier than ever. No one remembered the story that Perri made up about her back in third grade, but Eve was still famous for smelling, and picking her nose. For being, in general, a mess.

"She's okay," Perri said.

"What does that mean? Is she good or is she not?" The man's voice rose, and Josie thought, *I'd be so scared if he were my father.*

"She's good," Perri said hastily. "Very good."

"What's your name?"

"Perri."

"Isn't that a boy's name?"

"No, there's a writer my mom likes. I was named for her."

"Are you friends with my girl?"

"N-n-not really."

"Why not?"

Perri was speechless, something Josie had never seen, and Kat stepped in. "We're not *not* friends with her. She's in a different class from us. But she plays with Binnie Snyder sometimes."

"The Snyders are our neighbors, so I know them. What's *your* name?"

"Kat Hartigan."

"As in Thornton?" Kat nodded shyly. People were usually impressed when they learned that fact, but she almost never volunteered it. She was clearly surprised when the man added, "That old crook. He bought all that land on the sly to keep the prices low."

"What do you care?" the owner asked Mr. Muhly. "You didn't sell, and now your land is worth three times what it was. Anytime you want to give up your acreage, you'll have a buyer."

"And then what would I do with myself? Sit around here like the rest of you? That farm has been in my family for almost two hundred years."

"I'm just saying you've got no beef with him."

"Well, if he hadn't started building houses out here, someone else would have, sure enough," Mr. Muhly said. "But I don't have to like it."

The commercial break ended, and the girls started to go, for that was the agreement. But the owner insisted on giving them free Cokes and french fries. He even seated them at the bar, although Perri said later she was pretty sure that was against the law. He seemed to find them amusing, Perri in particular. As the girls prepared to leave, strapping on their bike helmets, he suddenly grabbed Kat's right arm by the wrist.

"Hit it," he said, indicating his left thigh.

Kat looked to Josie and Perri, but Josie didn't know what to tell her, and Perri again was at a loss for words. They were supposed to be on guard against strange people, of course, especially those who made unwelcome touches. But this man had let them take over his bar and fed them. Besides, what could he do to Kat with Josie, Perri, and a roomful of men watching?

"Hit it," he repeated. "Hard as you can."

Kat complied, but her punch was clearly too soft to please him. So he struck himself, producing a strange, hollow noise on contact.

"Fake," he said. "Fake! I lost it in an accident when I wasn't much older than you, working on my father's place. A tractor flipped over on me."

"Eleven-year-olds don't drive tractors," Perri said.

"My daughter, Eve, drives a tractor and a truck, and she's only ten," Mr. Muhly put in. "And she doesn't wear a helmet while doing it."

For the rest of the weekend, Josie lived in apprehension, sure that her parents would find out about the visit to Dubby's. Then, just as she was beginning to believe they had escaped detection, the three were summoned to the principal's office on Monday, with Mr. Treff in attendance. Josie assumed they were going to be suspended for going to a bar, and Perri cautioned them to volunteer nothing until they knew what was up.

It turned out that one of the mothers had complained about their "morbid" assignment.

"I know it seems unfair, after all the work you've done," the principal said. "But we really need you to pick another topic. Mr. Treff will give you an extension, to make up for the week you've lost. But we just can't condone such a, uh, ghoulish exercise."

Josie and Kat hung their heads, ashamed of being ghoulish. But Perri, although her face was quite pink with embarrassment, challenged the principal.

"It's a perfectly good survey," she said. "I'm not going to redo it."

"Then you'll receive a zero, and it will pull your grade down for the semester."

"My parents will understand. They'd rather that I get a zero than agree to something that I thought was unfair. There's a principle involved here."

"And what would that principle be, Perri? The right to ask people gruesome, disturbing questions?"

The principal clearly thought this point would end the discussion, but Perri shook her head. "That's part of it. Freedom of speech and all. But the principle is that we were given an assignment and we did it according to the rules outlined, and now you're changing the rules, saying we have to do it over, to get credit we've already earned. That's not fair."

"There are limits, Perri. There are always limits."

"Then Mr. Treff should have made it clear when he gave us the assignment."

"If Mr. Treff failed to tell you that it was wrong to kill people in the name of an assignment, would you assume you could do that?"

"No, but murder is illegal. We didn't do anything against the law."

"Perri, you're a bright girl, but sometimes you have to accept the rules without arguing. Redo the assignment or get a zero. Those are the choices."

Kat and Josie redid the poll, asking people in the neighborhood to pick their favorite desserts. They had no intention of going back to Dubby's, however, so the sample was a little smaller although the answers ultimately more diverse, people having more emphatic ideas about dessert than death, as it turned out. Perri handed in the charts and graphs based on the death survey, refusing Mr. Treff's attempts to give her extra-credit projects that might have made up the damage done by the zero he was forced to give her. Perri got a C in math that semester. On the Friday after grades came out, her parents took Perri, Kat, and Josie to Perri's favorite restaurant, Peerce's Plantation. She liked it because it seemed so grown-up and grand, with its striped awnings and views of the reservoir.

"Is this because you got all A's except for

math?" Josie asked Perri. But it was Dr. Kahn who answered her question.

"This is *because* she got a C in math — because she stood up for what was right."

"Were Kat and I wrong to redo it, then?" Josie had gotten a B in math, barely. She hated to think what would happen if she had taken the zero. Kat had gotten her usual A. Only Binnie Snyder did better in math than Kat, and Kat was the best in all the other subjects.

"Not wrong," Dr. Kahn said. "Practical, under the circumstances. The principal was a bully, and it's hard to stand up to a bully. And you couldn't know, sitting in his office that day, how your parents might react if you argued with him."

Josie did know, however. Her parents would have told her that sometimes you have to do things you don't think are fair, because that's the way the world works. And Kat's father would have said that she had to get A's now so she would keep getting A's later. Getting good grades was like anything else, Mr. Hartigan always said. You practiced until it became second nature.

"I didn't mind doing it over," Kat said.

"Oh, Kat," Dr. Kahn said, tugging a lock of her hair. "You never mind anything."

"I didn't like hitting that guy's leg. That was gross."

"What?"

Josie felt Perri's leg brush past hers beneath the table, landing a quick and careful kick on Kat's shin. So Perri's parents didn't know about the trip to Dubby's. Would they have supported that principle? Would they admire Perri for figuring out a way to get around *their* rules?

"Nothing," Kat said. "Just something that happened in gym."

"What were the final results anyway?" Mrs. Kahn asked. "I know I picked a plane crash, but what did others say?"

"Forty-two percent picked drowning. Twenty-eight percent chose plane crash. Then there was twenty-five percent for suffocation and only five percent for fire."

"Which is funny," said Dwight Kahn, whose eyes Josie could barely meet, given that he was a high-schooler, six whole years older than they were. "Because most fire victims die from smoke inhalation, not burning."

"We knew that. We specified being *set* on fire," Perri told her brother. "And everyone who picked that was male, between the ages of ten and eighteen."

They were eleven. They were in sixth

grade, a much more innocent version of sixth grade. September 11 was literally un-imaginable, except for those who were planning it. When 9/11 came in the fall of sophomore year, it turned out that one of those killed in the World Trade Towers was Dwight's friend, the older boy who had thought their survey was so funny. He was a trainee at an investment firm, high in the second tower.

"I remember him," Josie told Perri. "From the survey. He wanted to die in a plane crash. Remember, Dwight's friend?"

(Actually, they knew by then that Dwight's friend had been his supplier, that Dwight had run a thriving dope-dealing ring in Glendale all through high school, but it was not a topic that the candid Kahn family liked to discuss, now that Dwight had straightened out.)

Perri looked disgruntled at the mention of Dwight's friend, perhaps because Josie was getting too close to the forbidden sub-ject of Dwight's pothead phase, or just be-cause Josie was claiming a first-person connection that Perri considered her pri-vate property. It was a time of much weeping in Glendale High School, with girls erupting like geysers, and there was almost a competition of sorts, as unseemly as that might sound, to form connections to these events, at once so close and far. To speak of funerals attended and friends of friends of friends who had perished, to repeat stories of close calls — the local family that had almost flown out of Dulles that day, the cousins who lived mere miles from where the one jet crash-landed in Pennsylvania.

"Well," Perri said. "He got his wish."

Part Three

falling in love with jesus

Sunday

14

Lenhardt lay in bed, listening to his family get ready for church. Week in, week out, it was one of his best moments — alone yet not alone, the sounds of his wife and children drifting up to him from the downstairs rooms. The chatter was sharp at times; getting two children to church was seldom a smooth process and even required taking the Lord's name in vain a time or two.

But, overall, it was a comforting, lulling murmur. On winter Sundays, Lenhardt exulted in the warmth that Marcia left behind, rolling into her spot, picking up her scent, very clean and soapy. On a warm June morning such as this one, he kicked off the lightweight blanket and stuck a leg outside the sheet, a thermal balancing act he had learned from his first wife. That had been a young marriage, a starter marriage, the kind of mistake that only two twenty-two-year-olds can make. The divorce had been more like a breakup, with record albums to be divided — and not much more. Except, sadly, an infant daughter. Lenhardt had paid his support dutifully for eighteen years, but his wife moved to Oregon and remarried before the girl, Tally, was two. She thought of her stepfather as her daddy, and maybe he was. To this day Lenhardt sent checks on Christmases and birthdays, but nothing ever came back, not so much as a post-card.

The hallway floorboards creaked, a sound signaling a child's excessive, overdone caution, and Lenhardt cracked an eye as the bedroom door whined open. Jessica's pillow was just about to land on his head when he snaked his arm to the left, grabbed Marcia's abandoned pillow, and thwacked his daughter softly on the back.

"Got you first!" Jessica crowed, doing an up-and-down victory dance.

"But you can't get me now," he said, taking her wrists in his and pulling her onto the bed. He began tickling her, and although Jessica managed to free a hand, she was helpless to defend herself. She writhed and giggled, quite out of breath.

"Jessica —" Marcia's tone was even, but Lenhardt recognized she was near her breaking point. "You just brushed your hair. Now it has to be brushed all over again."

"No." The girl took refuge behind her father. "I'll do it myself."

"Okay, but quickly. We need to leave in five minutes. Besides, you're supposed to let your father sleep on Sundays. It's his only day to sleep in."

"I've been thinking about that," Jessica said, tucking her legs beneath her and making no move to reach for the hairbrush that Marcia was now extending toward her. "Why can't Daddy sleep in on Saturdays the way the rest of us do when there's no swim meet?"

"Daddy worked yesterday," her father pointed out. "In fact, Daddy's going to work *today*."

"I mean, when you don't have to work. Why don't you go to church with us?"

"Well, I have chores, and things to fix."

"Why can't you do your chores later?" she persisted.

"Jessica, get out of that bed and brush your hair, or I'll use this on your bottom instead."

The girl rolled her eyes, knowing that neither parent would ever raise a hand to her. But she did as her mother said, although she managed to do it in a way that indicated it was a mere courtesy to two inferior beings. Lenhardt slid out of the bed after her and headed into the shower, marveling again at his daughter's bullshit detector. Jason was two years older, but he had never questioned Lenhardt's absence from church. Jessica had an instinct for stories that didn't quite hang together. Maybe it was a genetic thing.

Lenhardt had given his wife's Methodist church a try, but he had never felt comfortable in the generous, light-filled space that Marcia called a church. Old habits died hard. He said "trespasses" instead of "debts" during the Lord's Prayer, started to cross himself, and while his knees didn't miss the literal ups and downs of the Catholic mass, his heart did, a little. "Church" should be one of those tall, gloomy piles that made you feel guilty as soon as you were over the threshold. No, he was just too old a dog to learn new tricks. So Marcia allowed him to abstain, as long as he promised to show up for the big things and didn't expose the kids to his own doubts about the whole enterprise.

Well, he was working today, that wasn't a lie. Less than fifteen minutes after his family headed out to church, he was en route to the Glendale address that the gun registration had kicked back for Michael Delacorte. Somewhat to his surprise, Glendale wasn't that far from his own house, a quick detour off I-83. He had always thought of that rich suburb as a world away. But then, there were no true neighborhoods out here in north county, not like in the city, just one development running into another, sort of like what happened when Jessica tried to make cookies. Lenhardt had grown up in Remington, a lower-middle-class enclave best known for its rat problem. Word had it that Remington was getting semidesirable these days. And why not? It was good housing stock, brick and stone, ten minutes to downtown. People were tired of driving so much, in Lenhardt's opinion. He wouldn't have moved out here if he hadn't landed the job in the county. There was a guy down at the University of Maryland who released a study, year after year, showing that commuting was the single biggest waste of Americans' time.

"What about books on tape?" Infante had asked whenever Lenhardt cited this study, trying to play devil's advocate. "You could learn, like, lots of stuff."

"Such as?"

"Civil War battles. Or art history, like

they have in that one book everyone's reading now. Or you could read the classics you didn't read in school."

"I read *The Great Gatsby* when Marcia was doing it for book club," Lenhardt said. "Green light, big thrill."

Once in Glendale it took him a few wrong turns to find the place he wanted, Windsor Park. Like most of the developments out here, it was set on a series of loops, with loops coming off the loops, so it was easy to get lost. The planners probably thought this layout discouraged burglars and thieves, and they would have been right, if communities such as this were targeted by the usual schmo amateurs, the addicts and teenagers interested in a quick buck or a joyride. But a pro wouldn't be deterred by Windsor Park's layout. A real thief would study it, driving the streets in the bland white van of a contractor, figuring out when people came and went, who had dogs, what drew attention. Such a guy might even take a job as a workman, given the endless renovations and remodelings, which would afford him the chance to find out who had alarms — and who set them. You'd be surprised how many people didn't use their expensive alarm systems because they didn't want to turn the bypass code over to the maid, or some nonsense like that. The smarter thieves cut phone wires, waited to see if anything happened — some homes had cellular backup, but not many — and then went in with a pillowcase.

Lenhardt had a dog, a sweet mutt who barked her head off if someone outside the family so much as touched the front door.

The Delacorte residence, however, had walled itself off behind a fence, with an electronic gate across the driveway. Lenhardt pressed the button on the intercom system, checking his watch. Ten was a little early for a Sunday visit, but that's why he had chosen this time. More likely to find people at home, assuming they skipped church as he did.

The voice that came back to him was alert, harried even. "Maurice? What are you doing at the front gate? You know you're supposed to come to the side."

"Mr. Delacorte? I'm Sergeant Harold Lenhardt from the Baltimore County Police Department, and I need to speak to you."

"Now? What about?"

A fair question. The man had no way of knowing that his gun had been used in the

Glendale shooting, may not even know it had been stolen, given that there was no report on it. The only information released to the media so far was that the shooter had used a licensed handgun.

"It's not something I can talk about over an intercom."

"I'll open the gates."

The gates rolled open, and Lenhardt found himself thinking of Graceland, a trip to Memphis when he and Marcia were about six months into their relationship, that time when it's still all roses and valentines — no voices raised, no disappointments. You couldn't go fifteen years without a few shouts and recriminations, of course, especially when raising kids. There was no doubt in Lenhardt's mind that the long haul was better, overall, than the superficial pleasures of those early months, when nothing was at stake. Still, there was something to be said for beginnings, especially when they were behind you.

The house in front of him was an expensive, showy affair, even by local standards. Everywhere Lenhardt looked, he saw expense — the triple-hung windows, the heavy door, the beige brick, the landscaping.

The owner, so quick on the intercom,

was slow to answer the door.

"Will this take much time?" he asked, panting as if he had come from a long distance. The man presented puffy — round-cheeked, with deep creases beneath his eyes, a stocky figure not unlike Lenhardt's, but softer, doughier. "I have to go to my office, and I want to be there by noon."

"On a Sunday you can get to downtown Baltimore in thirty minutes."

"I don't work in Baltimore."

"D.C.?"

"Harrisburg." There was an impatient edge to the man's voice, as if Lenhardt should have known where he worked. The name Delacorte did sound slightly familiar, but it didn't bring up any ready associations.

"This will take just a few minutes, I'm sure." People started out high-handed with detectives all the time, but the law-abiding types usually settled down pretty fast.

Delacorte led him into the living room, which looked unused, as most living rooms did these days. But this one was antiseptic in a way that Lenhardt couldn't pinpoint, like a room in a model home.

"I have to ask you a few questions about your gun."

"I don't have a gun."

Lenhardt took out his notes, although he was sure he had it right. There couldn't be another Michael Delacorte in Glendale.

"State police records show that Michael Delacorte has a .22 registered to this address, has had for the past year."

The guy's eyebrows shot up. "That's my wife. Michael."

"Your wife? My mistake. You see a name like Michael, you don't even think to glance at the gender."

"She's used to it. In fact, she rather likes it."

"So . . ."

"So?"

"Is she here? Mrs. Delacorte."

"She moved out a month ago." That explained the bare look of the house. The wife had gone through, taking all those little personal things that women strew about, photographs and candlesticks and vases.

"And did she take her gun with her? Or say anything about it being missing in the past few weeks?"

"Until five seconds ago, I didn't even know my wife had a gun. I'm still trying to process that information. It's an interesting footnote to everything that's been going on around here." He laughed in a self-deprecating way, as if Lenhardt should be intimate with his troubles. Yet Lenhardt still didn't have a clue who the guy was, had yet to learn his first name, in fact. "Why do *you* care?"

"A .22 registered to Michael Delacorte was recovered Friday from Glendale High School."

"From Glendale — oh, my fucking God, that's *all* I need."

Could this guy be more self-involved? But then it hit Lenhardt — Delacorte. Stewart Delacorte. Another business guy under indictment, or about to be, something to do with stock manipulation in a furniture company that had been in his family for generations, gone public, then gone pretty much to hell.

"We're trying to figure out how the gun came to be in the girl's possession."

Delacorte was in responsible-citizen mode now, keen to help. "We had a babysitter, a regular, came every Thursday. I think she was a Glendale girl."

"You know her name?"

"I might, if I heard it."

Lenhardt carefully read off three names, although he didn't need to refer to his notes to do that. He just wanted to make sure that he didn't lead this guy in any way, that each name was repeated in the same careful, uninflected tone.

"Katarina Hartigan. Josie Patel. Perri Kahn."

"Dale's daughter? But she was the one who was killed, right? Poor guy. When I read that in the paper, it reminded me there's always someone whose troubles are worse than your own."

"So Kat was your baby-sitter?"

"Oh, no. I just know Dale from, you know, around. He's a good guy. So I recognize Kat, but those other names — it could be either one. I'm sure it was one of those *y* names. Josie. Perri. Terry."

"But you saw the baby-sitter, would know her if you saw her again, right?" Perri's parents had already confirmed that their daughter baby-sat for this family, but Lenhardt was keen to determine that the other girls couldn't have procured the gun. The Kahns' lawyer would sure as hell find out if they had access, if Kat or Josie had so much as rung the doorbell in the past three years.

Delacorte looked a little sheepish. "I suppose so. I — I worked a lot. That's the reason Michael left. Part of the reason. The baby-sitter was . . . thin. Kind of bony."

That description could apply to Perri Kahn or Josie Patel.

"Tall? Short?"

Delacorte shrugged.

"Um, ethnic?"

"Ethnic?"

"Like, Asian or Indian. Not American Indian but the other kind."

"Oh, no. I don't recall ever seeing anyone like that in the house."

"And there was only the one babysitter?"

"On Thursdays. She came in on the nanny's day off, because, you know, God forbid Michael would have to spend an entire day alone with Malcolm."

"Why did your wife have a gun?"

Delacorte gave Lenhardt what he obviously thought of as a man-to-man smile. "I don't know, but believe me, I'm thinking about it."

"How do I get in touch with her?"

"Beats me. She won't tell me where she's living and hasn't let me see my son since she moved out. Is that even legal?"

"Not exactly. But you need a family lawyer —"

He held up a hand. "I know. The question was largely rhetorical."

"You got a number for your wife?"

"A cell. She won't answer when I call,

though. She always makes me talk to voice mail."

"I thought *I* could call it."

"Oh. Oh, of course." Delacorte began to wander the room, pulling open drawers in various end tables and chests, looking for paper and pencil. Lenhardt felt a stab of pity, watching a man roam his own home, incapable of finding so much as scrap of paper.

He handed him his own pad and pen, asking, "Who's Maurice?"

"My driver. It's about an hour to Harrisburg. I can't afford that much downtime, so he drives, I work. I moved here because I thought I could commute by helicopter, but the neighbors went berserk on my ass. That's how I got to know Dale. He tried to broker a compromise, but there was no dealing with these nuts. I could have fought them in court, but it wasn't worth it, not with everything else going on."

"Why are you going in on a Sunday, though?"

"The usual things," he said. "Papers to go through. Some things to box up and put into storage."

His tone had the vague, innocent air of a lying kid, and he was no longer making eye contact.

"It's illegal, you know. Getting rid of stuff once an investigation is under way."

"Thanks for the free legal advice, Sergeant. Helps defray the cost of the official advice that costs me six hundred dollars an hour. Got any other pearls of wisdom for me?"

Lenhardt knew he was being put down, but he pretended to take the guy's words at face value. "Okay, one more tip: Everything you steal, your wife is entitled to half of, under Maryland law. So if she knows where you hid all your assets before you gutted your company, you'll have to cut her in."

He left in a good mood, even though he hadn't established anything other than the probability that Perri Kahn was the only girl who could have taken the gun from this house. It would be interesting to pin down the when, which would suggest just how long she had been planning her morning of havoc. And Delacorte hadn't been able to place Josie in his home, a complication that Lenhardt had been happy to sidestep, even if he did think the girl was lying her head off.

What if she stalled on purpose? The thought hit him with a happy shock as soon as he was back on the highway, another possible resolution to the inconsistencies that were nagging at him. What if she hoped that refusing to open the door, pretending to be incapacitated, would be more likely to lead to the other girl's death?

He filed it away and continued to the office, where he and Infante were going to write up the paperwork necessary to get permission for a medical examiner to eyeball the girl's wound. According to the X-rays, the trajectory had been remarkably straight, as if someone had held the gun directly over the girl's foot and fired. As if she had stood still, polite and proper, the best-behaved kid lining up for a flu shot.

15

Alexa had her Sunday routine down pat —
the gym, then the farmers' market under the
expressway, shopping for whatever new
recipe she had picked out for that night's
supper, usually something from *Gourmet*, or
Food & Wine, or Nigella's column in the
New York Times, but not Martha, never
Martha, even before her legal problems.
Martha Stewart was cold, while Nigella
Lawson had an earthy sensuality that Alexa
believed was not unlike her own nature.
Warm, giving. And although Alexa sometimes invited Washington friends to her
Sunday-night suppers, entertaining was not
the point of her ritual. In fact, she prepared
meals just as elaborate when alone — single
portions of pot-au-feu, soufflés, paella. She
refused to be one of those women who were
stingy with themselves, postponing pleasure
until the proper husband or boyfriend
showed up.

That was one reason it had been so important to buy her own house, rather than settling into some sterile rental. The house needed quite a bit of work, but Alexa was patiently renovating one room at a time, which meant living in a perpetual cloud of dust. Only the kitchen had been done before she moved in, because the kitchen is the heart of any home. She had a hunch that granite was over, and she couldn't afford it anyway, so she had gone with an almost retro look, all white wood and milk glass. In the eighteen months since then, she had completed the downstairs half bath and the dining room — refinishing the floor, installing her own moldings, even finding an old chandelier at a flea market and rewiring it herself. It was a beautiful, sensuous room with cranberry red walls and a mahogany dining room set that Alexa had unearthed at an antique store not far from Glendale.

The antique stores and flea markets in north county had been her primary solace after being assigned to Glendale by the nonprofit that was underwriting her pilot program. A certified teacher and guidance counselor — Alexa preferred to think of herself as an ethnographer — she had designed a curriculum intended to tap into current concerns over girls' self-esteem.

Unlike others in the field, who concentrated on psychology and sociology, Alexa had designed her program around language, the girls' weapon of choice. She had assumed she would find a berth in Montgomery County, which would make it possible to keep her apartment in D.C.'s Adams-Morgan, close to her friends from graduate school. When she found out she was being sent to the distant reaches of north Baltimore County, she had insisted on living in the city, a curious choice in the mind of her new colleagues, who couldn't see why anyone would choose the city over the suburban apartments and condos, especially with so many move-in specials available. "I suppose you get a lot more house for your money in Baltimore," Barbara Paulson, the principal, had said, in a tone that suggested she didn't understand at all. "And the reverse commute isn't so bad."

The truth was, Alexa had gotten very little house for her money, a tiny bungalow, Craftsman era but definitely not a Craftsman, on an unusually large lot in Beverly Hills, a neighborhood ripe for a yuppie influx that would send prices soaring. If she just sat on her investment for a year or two, doing nothing, the house's value would probably triple from the land alone. But Alexa could not live that way. She needed a *home,* for emotional reasons so psychologically naked that they made Alexa, with her double degrees in rhetoric and psychology, a little sheepish.

She had done well by the house, but she was ill suited to harnessing its greatest asset, the wild and overgrown lawn. A neighborhood man had helped her with the basics — clearing out the weeds, cutting back on the overly rambunctious border plants — but the yard would have to wait for someone with a greener thumb to realize its true potential. Alexa's primary grudge against gardening was that it was never done. A room might take three months to renovate, especially if one were doing it in piecemeal fashion, but once finished, it was finished for years. A kitchen might take three hours to clean after a particularly ambitious day of cooking, but it would still be tidy the next morning. One could work in a garden every day, from first to last light, and a half-dozen tasks would remain, while another dozen would spring up overnight. Gardens were just so ceaselessly needy.

Teenage girls were, too, of course, but Alexa did not find them as exasperating —

quite the opposite. When she stood in front of a group of girls, she felt an almost spiritual thrill. Not holy per se, but as if she were the holder of simple but essential truths that could free them. They needed only to understand the power of words and stop using them to harm and harass. That was Alexa's gospel, and she had been making progress at Glendale, in the same way she was making progress on her house — one room at a time, one project at a time, and, right now, on her hands and knees in the living room, one strip of Pergo at a time. It was much harder than the guy at Home Depot had suggested, however, and Alexa was trying not to cry at the seeming impossibility of fitting the floor into her slightly off-kilter living room.

Secretly, selfishly, she wondered how her pilot program would be affected by Perri Kahn's — But Alexa did not know how to describe the actions of her star pupil. "Act"? Far too weak. "Crime"? Not if she were mentally ill, which she must be. But how could Alexa have missed the warning signs of such a profound psychosis? She had approved of Perri's break with Kat, seeing it as an important stage in the girl's development. True, Perri had been gloomy this year, emotional and secretive, and her papers had been increasingly fixated on violence, but in a cool, analytical way. She had written a particularly smart piece on the role of minorities as sacrificial totems in horror films, showing how even those movies that seemed to subvert this trope ended up serving it. For proof she had offered some B-movie about a snake, in which Jennifer Lopez and Ice Cube emerge heroic, yet all their efforts center on helping the injured blond hero, just as Sigourney Weaver had battled aliens to save a similarly comatose white male. Perri had been an absolute delight to teach, but Alexa knew that this was not information anyone wanted just now.

If Perri Kahn had shot, say, Thalia Cooper, then Alexa might have understood. Thalia was the stereotype, the mean girl who hid her cruelty beneath her bland, blond good looks, sending the pinch-faced Beverly Wilson to do her handiwork. If a boy was heard to remark approvingly on any facet of a girl that Thalia did not deem respectable, then Thalia tried to destroy that girl. That had been the whole motive behind her attempt to humiliate Eve Muhly. Eve had been getting too much attention for her ridiculously lovely body, a scale model of voluptuousness, not that

Eve had a clue what to do with it. Of course, now that Eve hung with the skeezer girls, she dressed in such baggy clothes that one could say Thalia had won, after a fashion. No, if someone had shot Thalia, it would have made perfect sense.

But Kat Hartigan was almost as nice as everyone said she was. As a new arrival to Glendale, Alexa wasn't quite so inclined to be gaga over Kat. And as a guidance counselor with unrestricted access to student records, she knew that Kat's admission to Stanford had rested heavily on the status of her father's girlfriend, an alum who'd gone to bat for her big-time, recruiting other area alums to write her letters of reference. Her grades were impressive, straight A's across the board, but her SATs were average by Glendale standards. Kat simply could not crack 1400 despite the money her father lavished on coaches and tutoring programs, making Stanford a reach for her. Strangely, reading comprehension was her downfall. She soared through the vocabulary on verbal only to hit a mental block when asked to interpret words in context. But Kat — well, Kat's father — was nothing if not sly about the process. By the time the girl applied for early admission, she had found multiple ways to sweeten her application and compensate for her board scores.

For all this — the money, the connections, the doting father, the grandfather who had helped to build the town where all her friends lived — Kat was genuinely sweet-tempered. A little dull, perhaps, because of the very earnestness that made her so nice, a perfectionist who panicked at the smallest error. Sometimes she was almost *too* solicitous of others' feelings, as if her parents' divorce had left her with a profound fear of even mildly disagreeable discussions. She was a nodder par excellence, someone who gave her wholehearted approval to the tiniest projects and pronouncements, to the point where she risked being patronizing. Yet Kat was nothing if not achingly sincere. While Thalia and Beverly stalked the halls of Glendale, looking for new victims to terrorize, Kat had reigned from a base of niceness.

At a standoff with the Pergo, Alexa decided to take a break, pour herself some iced tea — homemade, with mint leaves, which still grew wild in a corner of her barely cultivated yard — and carried the glass to her back steps, along with her cordless phone.

She eyed the phone, trying to think of someone to call. She had checked in with her mother Friday night, of course, and the conversation had been almost as gratifying as it should be, her mother properly awed and frightened by her daughter's brush with danger. Alexa had hung up with a rare feeling of satisfaction. Stories that one looked forward to telling so often fell flat. Yet this one became better with each telling, even as she called her best friend from graduate school, then took a call from an old high-school classmate who had heard the news all the way in San Diego.

But she had not called her older brother, assuming he would call her. Given their age difference, he had always been protective of her, especially after their father "decamped." That was her mother's preferred term, for it was at once literal and cruel, a reference to the fact that Mitchell Cunningham's last act had been to pack the family's camping gear in the trunk of his station wagon. He had been trying to find a place to fit the grill when his wife and daughter returned from church. Oona Cunningham told this story on herself to this day, as if being blunt about her own fate could keep anyone else from hurting

273

her. But she had been better when Evan was home, before he went away to college. The ensuing eight years that Alexa spent with her mother felt forlorn and temporary — too much takeout, too many meals eaten in front of the television. It was as if a woman and a girl, living alone in a house where a father and a son used to be, did not count for anything.

She dialed her brother's cell, knowing better than to expect him to stay home on such a beautiful day. While Alexa sought relief in domesticity, Evan needed endless distractions. But then, his New York apartment was small and depressing. No one would elect to spend time there. Alexa had offered to give it a perk-up — make curtains, show him how a few pieces from Target and Pier 1 could tie it all together — but Evan hadn't been interested.

"Alexa!" He was breathless. He was always breathless, always in a rush.

"Hey, Evan. Is this a bad time?"

"Heading uptown to a softball game. What's up?"

"Oh, I've been running around a lot and just wanted to make sure you hadn't tried to call me this weekend."

"No. Should I? Was there something with Mom?"

"Nothing important. But I thought you might get a little unnerved, my school being all over the news."

"Your school? Christ, was that your school? Oh, my God, Alexa, I didn't put it together. I mean, yes, Maryland, but when it wasn't Bethesda–Chevy Chase and when it wasn't Baltimore . . . I always think of you as being in *Baltimore*."

"I am in Baltimore," she said lightly, letting him off the hook. "It's the school that's in the suburbs."

"Did you see anything? Were you there?"

"I was in the office when the call came in, saying there were shots. And I'm going to coordinate the grief-counseling effort."

Evan started to laugh, then caught himself. "I'm sorry, Alexa, it's just that — I don't know, I've never understood the need to qualify counseling with the information that it's about grief, you know? It's not like there's a lot of *joy* counseling."

She could have reprimanded him for his insensitivity or pointed out that there were, in fact, other types of counseling. Job counseling for one, as Evan should know, having changed careers three times so far. He currently worked as a graphic designer in downtown Manhattan, a job he had managed to hold for a personal best of four years, even after his firm cut back positions in the wake of 9/11. The day the towers fell, Alexa and her mother had tried frantically to call him, encountering overloaded cellular systems and no answer on his landline. Turned out he had slept through it all. Stranger still, he had not really known anyone among the dead, not intimately. "I haven't lived in the city that long," he said, unconcerned about his lack of connection, but that detail had bothered Alexa. She worried that Evan was more like their father than he knew, simply skipping the wife-and-family part and going straight to a selfish, solitary existence.

"I'll let you go," she said, keen to say it first. "I'm laying a new floor."

"Is that *all* you're laying these days? What's wrong with Baltimore men?"

"Evan!"

"I'm serious. I've been to Baltimore. You raise the city's aesthetic standards by several percentage points."

"Bye!"

She dawdled on her back steps, less than eager to go in and confront her crossways pieces of Pergo. When she did return, she found that something — the tea, her brother's heartening belief that her solitary state said more about her surroundings than it did about her — had soothed her, and the task fell into place. By day's end her living room had a maple-hued floor. And only the most eagle-eyed spoilsport could identify it as anything other than the wood it pretended to be, much less find the spot where she had to cheat it, just a bit.

Fuck Evan, she thought as she began to prepare that night's dinner, a Thai recipe modified from the *New York Times*' Minimalist column. Grief counseling mattered. She was going to help the students of Glendale get through this tragedy, making up for the way the school had botched a more ordinary situation a year ago, when three star athletes had been killed in a car crash. Then, still shy about asserting herself, Alexa had hung back and watched as Barbara Paulson did everything wrong, encouraging an atmosphere of hysteria and gossip that only summer's arrival had stemmed. This time they would get it right, allow students to express their feelings without encouraging their paranoia.

And, when the opportunity arose, she would find a quiet moment to talk to Eve Muhly, see if the girl really did know more than she was telling. It was hard to see how she could — a middling junior such as Eve would have had little contact with outstanding seniors such as Kat and Perri, or even Josie. But there was no doubt in Alexa's mind that Eve had wanted to confide in her and could feel that way again, given the opportunity.

16

Out-of-towners have been known to compare the train's-eye view of Baltimore to Dresden, circa 1946, but Peter had always loved Amtrak's approach into the city. For Peter the butt-ugly scenery was charming — the old Goetze's caramel factory flashing past, then the backyard views of dilapidated rowhouses, the occasional church spire. He began to gather his things when he saw Johns Hopkins Hospital high on its hill, prim as Margaret Dumont in a Marx Brothers movie.

He had been astonished, upon entering NYU four years ago, to find out that Baltimore had a kind of retro cachet. Who needed to know that he was really from the suburbs, and a distant one at that? True, New Yorkers could be a bit patronizing, even when professing admiration for a place; when they cooed about Baltimore's charms, they sounded as if they wanted to bend over and pat the city on its collective

head. But Baltimore had a dispropor-
tionate amount of work for actors, with a
movie or television show almost always in
production there, and solid Equity the-
aters. The guy who had won the Tony this
year had done *Peter Pan* at Center Stage
less than a year ago. You couldn't build a
career here, not yet, but maybe that would
change. His mother would like that. But,
for now, he had to go to Toronto, where
the dollar was strong and the scenery ver-
satile.

He was actually a little nervous about
telling his parents about the job — and
about the money he needed, short term,
before the paychecks started. That was
part of the reason he had decided to do it
in a grand way, show up for Sunday dinner
with . . . well, with just himself, as it
turned out. Penn Station no longer had a
florist, go figure, and there was nothing in
the newsstand that would make a suitable
gift for his mom. *Hey, Mom, here's a
Goldenberg Peanut Chew.* No, not even
his self-indulgent mother would be impressed by such a lame gesture.

A cab to Glendale was at least forty dollars, which wouldn't seem like a lot of
ducats in a few weeks, but try explaining
your prospects to an ATM. Peter decided

to take Light Rail to the end of the line, where he could summon a cab for the rest of the journey. Best of both worlds — he could arrive in style and still have some money in his pocket.

The ghost-white train, near empty as usual, wended its way north. Things were so green here, so lush, and the wooded hills buzzed with the roar of seventeen-year cicadas, a phenomenon that hadn't reached as far north as New York. Peter was never conscious of missing the countryside while in New York, but he was always glad to see it when he returned home. Other kids at NYU seemed to get a kick out of knocking the places they were from, disavowing them, as if that were part of the New York ritual. To be truly cool, you had to reject your hometown. Unless, of course, your hometown was New York, in which case you just spent the first semester sneering at people who had never ridden the subway or eaten soup dumplings in Chinatown.

Short, eager, and a quick study, Peter had seen immediately that he shouldn't talk about his high-school glory days, that reminiscing about your past accomplishments merely indicated that you didn't think you had any future ones. *Everyone* at

Tisch had been a star back home. Some already had done professional gigs, usually commercial work. Simone had a line in *Good Will Hunting*, when she wasn't even in high school yet. No one needed to hear about Peter's Tony in *West Side Story*, his Billy Bigelow in *Carousel*, or his Biff in the community-playhouse production of *Salesman*. They were all former Billys, they were all former Biffs — and Romeos and Don Quixotes and Lieutenant Cables.

But they were not, Peter realized, all good-looking. And he was, not that he would ever be the kind of asshole who said such a thing out loud. Instead he pretended not to know, ducking his head sheepishly when girls talked about his long eyelashes and tight curls, the lone dimple in his left cheek. He pretended not to know, and they pretended not to know that he was pretending not to know. But when he finally got his height, it was almost disingenuous to claim he didn't recognize the effect he had just walking into a room. It was a weird responsibility of sorts, being good-looking.

That was another thing he could never say without being judged a Grade-A asshole. But it happened to be true. Sometimes, when he was with a girl, just at that moment when things were beginning to cross over to the point where something significant was going to happen — not necessarily intercourse, but definitely some sort of satisfaction — he would catch this look on the girl's face, something wistful and confused. It made him feel bad, as if he had led her astray somehow. Yet it wasn't his fault that girls projected things on him because he was handsome, because they had seen him onstage and they thought they were making out with Curly or Tony or the Rainmaker, and he was really just Peter Lasko, and he wasn't going to sing some ballad to them when it was all said and done, wasn't even going to spend the night if he could help it.

Kat wasn't like that, he reminded himself. *Yeah, but you never got with Kat,* the no-bullshit part of his brain chimed in. *Never got below the waist at all.*

Well, Christ, she was only fifteen. For all he knew, even the lightweight stuff they had done that summer was illegal. Her father had certainly tried to suggest as much in that scary little heart-to-heart that Mr. Hartigan had claimed was all about his interest in Peter's future. He had faked being buddy-buddy, but Peter had never doubted that the guy would have come at him if he hadn't gotten his way.

The Light Rail slid into the Hunt Valley station. It was only seven, the sun still bright and high above the ridged countryside to the west. His family sat down to supper early on Sundays, and his mother had never gotten out of the habit of putting on a huge spread, even after Peter left home. It was great when he was in a production, especially something where he was moving a lot, and he could come home from a Sunday matinee, fall facefirst into his mom's food. Some Glendale kids had been weird about his mom's being Cuban — and the fact that she was a green-eyed blonde, one of the hot moms, really messed with their minds. But once they came over and had arroz con pollo, or frijoles negros, not to mention plantains, they wanted to join the family. His dad had met her in Miami, while visiting Peter's great-grandparents, and she didn't have an accent or anything. But that Sandoval name had its advantages, especially when he was applying to colleges. He always assumed that lucky little biographical detail had pretty much cinched NYU for him.

It turned out there was no taxi stand at the end of the line, and it took almost forty-five minutes for Hunt Valley Cab company to dispatch anyone, so it was after eight when Peter pulled up in front of the house. His plan was to come through the front door, super casual, and yell "I'm home!" like he was coming back from lifeguard duty or rehearsal. His mom would practically burst from happiness, he figured, despite seeing him at graduation a month ago. And his dad would be on the verge of tears, too, although he would try to hide it. They were cool, his parents. Well, not exactly cool — his father actually wore a pocket protector to work — but warm and loving in a way that Peter no longer took for granted, not after knowing Simone and some even freakier girls at NYU, girls who had grown up in empty mansions and thought the Gossip Girls books were documentaries.

The front door was locked, which was unusual. Maybe people in Glendale were spooked after the shooting, although it wasn't as if some maniac was at large. No problem. It would be more in keeping for him to go through the garage and into the kitchen, where his mother was probably still puttering with the dishes and his father was trying to read the Sunday paper and watch television at the same time. Peter punched in the garage-door code, grabbed the key that his mother still hid beneath a Frisbee on the utility shelves, and let himself in.

But while both cars were in the garage, no one was inside the house. And something about the stillness — not to mention the air, which was warm and stuffy, the thermostat set unusually high for a June night — told him no one had been here for at least a day or two. There were no newspapers piled on the kitchen counter, no glasses in the sink. (His dad was a bit of a chauvinist, just put his dishes in the sink and figured Peter's mom would get them into the dishwasher. She did, muttering to herself but not really minding.)

Peter wandered through the house, looking for clues to his parents' whereabouts. There was no notation on the calendar, and only a few days' worth of mail had been dropped through the slot. Mail slots had been a huge controversy in Glendale back when Peter was a kid. All the developments had started out with community mailboxes. But no one really wanted to commune by the mailboxes, it turned out. The Glendale Association had finally surrendered, and door companies had done a thriving business in the older sections.

Glancing through his parents' bedroom

window, Peter saw the neighbor to the north, Mr. Milford, come out into his backyard and start his sprinklers. Peter ran downstairs and into the backyard, calling to him over the fence.

"Why, Peter Lasko!" Mr. Milford said. "I understand you're a college graduate now. What brings you home?"

"I wanted to surprise my parents. But they seem to have surprised me. Did they run away from home? Join the circus?"

"Your dad won a golf trip to Hilton Head in the United Way raffle down at his work. Isn't that something? Me, I couldn't win a goldfish at one of those carnivals where everyone wins the goldfish. Four days and three nights. I think they come back Tuesday. You need anything?"

Money, Peter thought. *A good meal.* But he still had twenty dollars in his pocket, and there was always plenty of stuff in his mother's freezer. He'd last until Tuesday.

But the freezer, while packed with leftovers, didn't intrigue him. It was one thing to have your mom bring all the goodies to the table, hot and ready, another to defrost them in the microwave and eat them alone, in front of the television. And his father's liquor cabinet wasn't anywhere near as intriguing as it used to be when Peter was underage. Besides, he wasn't eager to drink again, not after Friday night's excesses. Saturday had been a bit of a lost day, and alcohol was hell on the complexion. Peter hated having to think that way, but his appearance was his business, no different than his father having to know the tax codes for inventory, or whatever it was that he did know.

He slipped his mother's key ring from the pegboard next to the refrigerator and helped himself to her Jetta. Even now he wouldn't dare touch his dad's car, although it was nothing special, just a Buick. But dad's car had always been off-limits. When Peter got rich, he was going to buy his dad a car, something so extreme it would make him laugh that he had ever prized the Buick so much. Peter drove aimlessly, thinking he might get a sub at Dicenzo's, then remembering they weren't open on Sundays. He went to the Dairy Queen instead, the one on Old York Road. Now, here was something you couldn't find in New York. He settled at one of the picnic tables with two chili dogs and a Snickers Blizzard, although he'd pay for it all with double workouts tomorrow. In the meantime . . . heaven. Thomas Wolfe didn't know what the hell he was talking about. Everything was just as Peter remembered it.

Except, of course, Kat, who was dead. He hadn't thought of her consciously for some time, but he realized now he had been looking forward to her hearing about *Susquehanna Falls*, maybe feeling a little wistful toward him. *Suffer*, as Conrad Birdie snarled to his adoring, panting fans in *Bye Bye Birdie*, twitching his hips all over Sweet Apple, Ohio. Peter had played that part, too, back in middle school. His first big role, when he was a total runt, and no one knew that he could sing and dance and act, least of all Peter himself.

Of course he had seen Kat, in passing, over the last three years. She was always polite, always sweet. Given the way they behaved, people who didn't know the story might have assumed she dumped him, instead of the other way around. That was Kat, the ultimate good sport. Besides, what was the big deal? They had gone together less than two months, just a summer fling. He was going to be a sophomore in college. She was going to be a sophomore in high school. It wasn't fair to her, he had said more than once, and she had nodded, as if she believed that Peter was the kind of guy who worried about what was fair for others. But that was how summer romances were supposed to go. It was one thing to run around with a fifteen-year-old girl the summer you were nineteen, to regress to dry-humping in the backseats of cars, fighting for every inch of skin. Freshman year at NYU had been one long drought, his classmates going with older boys. But it wouldn't always be that way, Peter knew. And, sure enough, he had met a girl his first week of sophomore year, a girl who came to his room just to fuck, like it was a study break or something. And then Simone, with her *Jules and Jim* fantasy. Who needed a fifteen-year-old virgin, no matter how beautiful, no matter how sweet?

The problem was, he had fallen in love with Kat, just a little. And Kat, for her part, seemed to be the first girl, the only girl, who had loved Peter, as opposed to some stage version of him. She didn't want Tony or Biff or Conrad. She liked Peter, the lifeguard at the Glendale pool. There were moments, wrestling with her in the backseat of his mother's car or in her family's empty house, that he had been torn between wanting to force her to do something, anything, that might give him some release and wondering if they should get engaged. Which was crazy but might have at least persuaded her to sleep with him. That's how insane she had made him.

Instead he broke up with her, and Kat had accepted it with an almost disturbing ease, turning to the stars of the high-school crowd for her dates. Peter couldn't help wondering, in the end, if *she* had used him, if she had figured out that getting Peter Lasko on the string for a summer would give her a big social boost at Glendale. Because while Peter in high school had been a kind of B-plus guy — drama guys seldom being the A guys — he was an A-plus once he graduated, while Kat was a wallflower before she took up with him. Kat, who'd never even had a boyfriend before Peter, suddenly started dating athletes and rich boys. It was hard, in retrospect, not to wonder if it was all a plan, if he had been the one in love and she had been the cool, calculating one. Like her old man, although Kat would bristle if anyone suggested that her father was less than perfect.

And now she was dead, and Peter would never have the chance to make things right with her. He had been counting on that opportunity, he realized, banking on it. In the back of his head, he had always hoped to have a chance to make amends with Kat Hartigan.

On the way home from the Dairy Queen, Peter detoured by the school, but there was nothing to see out front, not even yellow crime-scene tape. They wouldn't seal off the whole school, obviously. The tape was probably in back, where it had happened. He had managed to learn that much in the last forty-eight hours. Kat, shot to death in the girls' room, Josie Patel wounded, Perri Kahn the suspect, although she was said to be pretty fucked up. In the Associated Press article that Peter had read in one of the New York tabloids, these names were rendered meaningless — for they were meaningless to whoever had written the account. But each one carried a world of significance for him. Perri, the drama queen. Josie, the little hanger-on. Kat — but he couldn't sum up Kat in a word or two. Homecoming queen, A student, granddaughter of Glendale's founder — you could pile up as many words as you liked, but they didn't get to the heart of Kat.

He still wasn't ready to go back to his parents' empty, quiet house. He decided to cruise past the community center, still ablaze with lights from some sort of show or recital inside. Peter parked his car and got out, leaning against it, enjoying the air. New York was great, but you couldn't walk a block without smelling something foul, especially this time of the year, when garbage seemed to bake in the alleys. Here muted notes drifted on the summer breeze, but he couldn't identify the tune. Was it the summer show? No, way too early. Those were always staged in July and August.

The community-theater program in Glendale was quite good, better than those NYU snobs would ever know, the final show as tight and professional as anything Peter had seen in college. Peter had done *Godspell* here, the summer he was eighteen, when he was college bound. He had worked as a lifeguard all day, then sung and danced every night, so he was tanned and cut, yet very thin, which suited the role of God's only son. He had fans, honest-to-God groupies who had hung around this parking lot waiting for him to come out. Perri and Josie had been among them, even some of the redneck crowd. But not Kat, never Kat. He knew because he had asked her, after they started dating.

"I'm not the kind of girl who goes around falling in love with Jesus," she had said. Kat could be droll that way. No one seemed to notice, because she was pretty and Perri was so famously mouthy, but Kat got some good lines off, in private. *I'm not the kind of girl who goes around falling in love with Jesus.*

Almost without thinking, Peter broke into the old soft shoe, the one from "All for the Best," right there in the parking lot. This was the Act 1 number with Judas, the one that always killed. *Yes, it's all for the best.* He still remembered all the moves, even the time step that the choreographer, a high-strung type, had almost despaired of Peter's mastering.

Judas got all the best lines in that duet. But Jesus got the girls. Oh, yes, Kat Hartigan notwithstanding, Jesus got *all* the girls.

ninth grade

17

Thirty years ago, back when Thornton Hartigan was still wondering if he would ever find developers and investors for the acreage he had acquired so stealthily, a New York couple bought a large, run-down farm in the nearby Monkton area. Harvey Bliss and Sylvia Archer-Bliss were the kind of people described by their new neighbors as artsy, which is to say they wore a lot of black and kept their sunglasses on while shopping at the Giant. They also had an asexual quality, the comfortable air of a couple more like friends than husband and wife. But they were split on what to do with their new property. Harvey dreamed of a restaurant, while Sylvia wanted a dance studio.

"A real one," she said, "for serious students, not potbellied little girls tiptoeing around in leotards." Sylvia had been a dancer, her career stunted by her uncompromisingly plain face. She hinted to her students that the song in *A Chorus Line*, the one about the dancer who transformed herself through plastic surgery, had been inspired by her own career. The claim was dubious, but Sylvia's talent was genuine, and the dinner theater that she and Harvey eventually opened was so good on all counts that it was possible to forget, as a *Beacon-Light* critic wrote, that one was at a dinner theater.

The dinner theater led to a school, which eventually inspired a summer day camp in partnership with the Glendale Arts Festival, and Sylvia found herself enduring the amateurish children she had hoped to avoid. The parents were the real problem, as many were uncomfortable with the program's rigid meritocracy. *Shouldn't the summer program be more inclusive?* wheedled the parents of the hammier students, those whose only talent was a profound lack of embarrassment at their ineptness. *Isn't participation more important than professionalism when young children are involved?* Sylvia, who had learned to tone down her New York candor after years in the Maryland countryside, pretended to accede to their wishes by creating two casts for each show. The parents were appeased, more or less, although one bossy mother insisted on having the last word. "Don't call the different casts 'A' and 'B' or 'One' and 'Two,' as the children will infer that one is better than the other."

And so the summer they turned fourteen, it happened that Perri was in the "Creamy" cast of *Peter Pan*, while Kat and Josie were in "Crunchy." You could argue all day about the relative merits of creamy versus crunchy peanut butter — and the cast members did, with almost everyone swearing allegiance to crunchy — but the bottom line was that everyone knew that Perri was the standout, which meant Creamy had to be the superior cast. Kat and Josie had attended the camp only because Perri begged them to, intent as ever on the trio's staying intact. Yet Perri voiced no objections when they were placed in different casts.

Josie's parents were all for Sylvia's day camp — it solved the summertime dilemma of making sure that Josie, now allowed to spend her days alone, did not fritter her time away. The fees were steep, but affordable since Josie had dropped out of the Gerstung gymnastics program. It was Mrs. Hartigan who balked, pointing out that Kat was shy and self-conscious, with no aptitude for performing.

"She says I just want to do this because Perri is doing it," Kat confided at the campfire one weekend afternoon.

"So?" Perri asked. "What's wrong with that?"

Josie knew but didn't say anything. Her own parents had said similar things, if less directly. *Of course you can go to drama camp — if that's what* you *really want.* "But you're allowed to have your own ideas," her mother added, as if Josie didn't know that. "You don't always have to do what Perri says." The thing was, Perri had the best ideas, and she had so many of them.

So the girls went to drama camp, where the ratio of girls to boys in their age group was roughly six to one. Despite these lopsided numbers, the counselors stuck to their plan to stage *Peter Pan*, which had only three female parts. (And one of them, Tiger Lily, lost her big number because it was judged irredeemably racist and insensitive, with its peace pipes and pidgin English and chorus of "ugh"s.) But Sylvia decreed that if boys could play girls in Shakespearean times, then girls could play boys' parts today. Not just Peter Pan but Captain Hook and Mr. Darling, Wendy's brothers, even Smee. Nonetheless, most of the girls wanted to be Wendy, except for Perri, who sought and was given the "Creamy" Hook.

Josie was a nonspeaking lost boy, until Sylvia realized how agile she was and asked her to take the part of Michael, Wendy's brother. "You don't have a dancer's personality," Sylvia said, "or even a dancer's arches. But you move very well. And that's important for flying."

Flying! Actual stage flying! It turned out that Sylvia had called on old contacts to obtain the patented wire system, Flying by Foy, used by theatrical companies whose actors needed to take flight. Even Perri was jealous, for Hook did not fly at all, and Josie was exceptionally good at flying, even better than the girls chosen to play Peter in either cast, so good that Sylvia urged the Patels to let Josie audition for a Baltimore production of *A Midsummer Night's Dream*, which needed flying fairies. Josie could tell this bothered Perri a little, and she felt bad because theater wasn't important to her, except for the flying. It was a relief to soar through the air again, given how her instructors at Gerstung had not encouraged Josie to pursue gymnastics competitively. She had the technical skills, they told her parents, but not the mental ones. She choked at meets, flubbing moves that she executed flawlessly in practice.

As for Kat, she asked to be Nana, the sheepdog nanny. She liked dogs. Moreover, she liked being hidden inside the huge, shaggy costume. "Eight hundred dollars for theater camp," Mrs. Hartigan said, "and we don't even get to see your face."

They performed the play four times, with Creamy taking the night shows and Crunchy the matinees, the stars in one cast appearing as chorus in the other. The Sunday matinee was especially lethargic, and the girl playing Mrs. Darling disappeared mere minutes before curtain. (On a bathroom break, it was discovered after the fact.) The result was a show that opened on an empty stage and remained empty, the pianist in the pit playing the strains of "Tender Shepherd" over and over again. "*Do* something," Sylvia muttered to no one in particular. Kat, waiting in the wings for her entrance, took this admonition literally, removing her dog's head and beginning to sing the lullaby in a pure, true voice that no one had ever suspected of her. The voice soared out like birdsong, serene and effortless. Then Mrs. Darling showed up, and the play went on, although it never quite recovered from its limp, improvised beginning. Perhaps it was because people in the audience kept waiting for that beautiful voice to return.

"Did you know that Kat could sing like that?" Sylvia demanded of the Hartigans afterward. Mrs. Hartigan shrugged, still miffed about her daughter's costume, but Mr. Hartigan said he believed Kat could achieve any goal she set for herself. Three months later he moved out, proving that Kat could not, in fact, achieve any goal she chose, for she certainly would have rescued her parents' marriage. But that would happen in the fall, after Labor Day. The rest of the summer was spent in blind devotion to Jesus.

Not Jesus per se, of course, but Jesus as embodied by Peter Lasko, in Sylvia's centerpiece production, the one performed throughout August in the Glendale community center. The girls, accompanied by Mrs. Kahn, first went to the show because of their newfound devotion to theater. Before the lights went down, Perri was a little superior, telling Josie and Kat that *Godspell* was second-rate, with a treacly, unmemorable score, not at all in the class of Stephen Sondheim, someone of whom she now spoke incessantly, almost as if they were dating. She also told Kat and Josie that some Jewish parents in Glendale — "Not yours," Mrs. Kahn interjected — had tried to talk Sylvia out of mounting it, saying it was a flat-out attempt to proselytize. So the play already had a certain forbidden aura before the first notes sounded on the shofar and the cast began moving through the audience in preppy clothes that Sylvia had chosen in an attempt to rethink *Godspell*'s hippie legacy. Throwing fake money in the air — the stock market was still riding high — they began to exhort the audience to prepare for the way of the Lord.

And then Peter Lasko bounded onto the stage, dressed in khakis and a button-down shirt, instead of the traditional suspenders and Superman T-shirt that Josie knew from the CD's cover. "Interesting concept," whispered Perri's mother. "I guess at the dawn of the new millennium, Jesus is a CEO."

Josie had no idea what Mrs. Kahn was talking about, nor did she care. She thought Jesus was the best-looking boy she had ever seen. Could such a person really have emerged from Glendale High School just a few weeks ago? Would there be other boys like that at the high school? The show unfolded before her dazzled eyes, and even a more objective critic than Josie would have to admit that Peter Lasko was an extraordinary performer, almost too extraordinary, for his professional sheen revealed the limitations of the rest of the cast. He was like Perri in *Peter Pan*, with a sweet tenor that was better than anyone in Josie's current collection of CDs, even Nick Lachey of 98 Degrees or the boy who sang about the angel. (It was okay to like Nick Lachey back then, especially if you were fourteen.) Josie's nonexistent theatrical ambitions caught fire as she watched, inspired not just by Peter's obvious talent but by the realization that the stage was a place where a boy really might take one's hand and sing, *You are the light of the world*. And where a girl could lasso that boy with her mink stole — "Traditionally it was a feather boa," Perri's mother whispered — and bring down the house with the line "Come here, Jesus, I've got something to show you."

Upon learning that Peter Lasko was a lifeguard at the Glendale pool, the girls began spending long afternoons there, splashing hilariously in the five-foot section, which happened to place them at *his* feet. At the campfire, in their bedrooms, the girls rehearsed the sexy number, the one with the mink stole, swooping around and shimmying their shoulders. At least Perri and Josie did those things. Kat insisted she wasn't interested in boys. She said it was silly, to talk about love at fourteen, when most grown-ups couldn't figure it out. She said she never planned to marry, or not until she was really old, thirty or thirty-five. Her parents were still together then, but fighting more and more. Up in Kat's room, under the sloping eaves, Josie had heard Mrs. Hartigan screaming at Mr. Hartigan and Mr. Hartigan responding in a lower, pleading voice. Kat stared at the ceiling as if she couldn't hear anything.

"I don't want to get married either," Perri said. "But maybe we should have boyfriends, once we go to high school. Lots of girls in middle school had them."

"My father wouldn't let me go out with boys yet," Josie said quickly, as if this explained everything.

"There are ways to have a boyfriend without a parent knowing," Perri said. "You didn't have a boyfriend because no one liked you that way."

"Shamit did," Kat said. "He gave her a card on Valentine's Day, and that little tiny box of Godivas."

"Shamit doesn't count," Perri decreed, and while Josie agreed, she was annoyed at Perri's firmness on this topic. Why didn't Shamit count? Because he competed in things like science fair and spelling bee? Because he was Indian? Because his parents were *Indian*-Indian, Sikhs with accents and odd ideas? It was one thing for Josie to assume that Shamit had chosen her for her last name, another for Perri to say it out loud.

"Why did you fall in love with Daddy?" she had asked her mother.

"Because he was drop-dead gorgeous," her mother had said promptly. "And *exotic*. I never saw anyone like your dad until I went to Grinnell. Actually, that's not quite true. When I was young, there was a magazine called *16*, and it used to run features about a young actor named Sajid something. I could never figure out what he was famous for, other than appearing on an episode of *The Big Valley*. But he was so handsome. Maybe that's why I fell for your father, all those years later, because of my unrequited crush on the mysterious Sajid."

She then produced a photograph from college, and Josie could almost see that her father had been attractive once, if not her idea of drop-dead gorgeous.

"He played rugby," her mother said dreamily. "Senior year, we found an apartment off campus and furnished it with items people put out for bulk trash — tables and chairs that looked perfectly good with just a coat of paint. I made deep-dish pizza from scratch, and we had our first dinner parties, if you want to call them that. Our curtains were made from Indian tablecloths, and we served Bulgarian wine that cost two dollars a bottle."

It was so much more than Josie wanted to know, yet also less. She wanted to be assured that her romantic horizons were as open as anyone's, but her mother's anecdote seemed to suggest that the only 100 percent American boys who might like her would be in pursuit of some exotic fantasy figure they had seen in a magazine. And the Indian boys, the Shamits of the world, would like her either in spite of the fact that she had an Anglo mother or because of it. She couldn't win.

"I'm going to go out for cheerleading," she announced after Perri brought up the subject of boyfriends. "Freshmen can try out for junior varsity at midyear."

"Cheerleader? We're not cheerleaders," Perri said.

"I could make it," Josie said, aware that her use of the first-person singular was cruelly accurate. She could make it, while Perri, with her gawky height and complete ineptness at all sports, would be hopeless. "I'm good at that kind of gymnastics — cartwheels and round-offs. And I'm light, so I could do the things they need the smaller girls for."

"You'd be great," Kat agreed. "Do you think our parents would let us make a little fire here, grill hot dogs and roast marshmallows?"

"We can ask," Perri said, "but they'd probably insist on supervising."

It did not have to be said that no activity, no matter how desirable, was worth bringing outsiders to their circle. Even if they did not consider themselves the Ka-pe-jos anymore, even if they visited the circle only once a month or so, the place was still sacred.

When Kat's father moved out, she refused to talk about it, even to Perri and Josie, and she stopped eating. By the end of their first semester as freshmen, she was almost too thin — and too beautiful, if such a thing were possible. Kat's fat had been like Nana's suit, hiding something gorgeous and true, and Josie was almost worried for her friend as she observed the commotion she created in the high school. Kat, however, seemed oblivious, wearing her old clothes, ill-fitting and baggy as they were, and ignoring the boys who buzzed around her. And it turned out that cool kids didn't have boyfriends and girlfriends anyway. Everything was about hooking up, hitting this or that, friends with benefits. Given that choice, Kat preferred safe, platonic relationships with boys they had always known, such as Seth and Chip.

Her only concession to her new body was an increasing physical ease. She began running and going to the gym. She asked Josie to show her how to do some of the simpler gymnastic tricks, and although they never said it was a secret from Perri, it somehow became one. Yet when they both made the JV squad freshman year, Perri congratulated them wholeheartedly, and no one seemed more impressed when Josie scrambled to the top of the pyramid, her tiny stature finally an asset. Similarly, when Perri landed the role of Joan of Arc in *The Lark*, a remarkable honor for a freshman, Josie and Kat attended every performance and sent her roses at the final curtain call. And in the school talent show, they appeared together, doing their own riff on the updated version of "Lady Marmalade," although they were not allowed to dress quite so provocatively.

They had trumped the system, built a friendship that transcended the confines of the school's cliques. Yes, they were cheerleaders, but they didn't take it seriously, and Perri may have been a drama geek, but she wasn't a geeky one. They ate lunch together and continued to see each other on weekends. It began to seem their friendship could survive anything.

Then Peter Lasko, home from first year of college and back in his lifeguard chair, had fallen in love with Kat. Perri had always said she wasn't jealous in the slightest, and she did have a sort-of boyfriend of her own that summer, the boy who was playing Beau to her Mame in the summer production. And when Peter dropped Kat, brutally and swiftly, their friendship continued as if it had never been interrupted, as if Kat hadn't spent most of the summer with Peter. There were no recriminations, no envy. If anything, Perri seemed to forget that she and Josie were the ones who had once hung around the community theater's rear entrance waiting for Peter to emerge. She told Kat he wasn't anyone special, that Kat

311

was better off without him. These were the right things to say, of course, and Perri said them with uncharacteristic tenderness.

But if Josie were pressed to find the precise moment when things began to fall apart, she would go back to that summer when Perri was Mame, when Kat was newly thin, when Josie was learning to fly to the top of the pyramid — and Peter Lasko had taken Kat from them, however briefly. Although they never acknowledged it out loud, it proved that something, someone, could come between them. Separated once, they were all the more vulnerable to being separated again.

Part Four

last year's funeral

Monday

18

"What do *you* want?" Chloe said by way of greeting when Dale made the long trip up from the city Monday morning, marveling all the while at the heavy traffic in the other direction. The commute hadn't been part of his life for four years, and memory was imperfect, always. Still, the congestion had to be exponentially worse than it had been even a year ago. Why did people live like this? Oh, because his father had enabled them to — his father and the builders and the state officials, who delivered the wide, smooth roads, which persuaded people that the trip to the city would be a snap. After all, it seemed an easy enough drive on a Sunday afternoon, when optimistic families made the journey to tour the open houses. On a Sunday you could make it downtown in thirty minutes. But come the first weekday after all the paperwork was signed, it would take almost an hour.

"The funeral director thought it would

be nice to have a photograph of Kat at the service. He'll have it enlarged, but it requires something more formal than I have." Dale had many snapshots of Kat, in his condo and the office, but they were not only too casual but also too old, the most recent taken during her sophomore year. How had he gone two years without acquiring a new photograph of his daughter?

"Do you want the painting?"

"God, no." After all these years, he still couldn't tell whether Chloe was ironic or obtuse. "She was ten when that was painted."

"Eleven," Chloe contradicted, then waited, presumably for him to acknowledge that she was correct. Chloe loved to catch Dale in errors, no matter how small, and insisted on verbal affirmation that she was right and he was wrong. Today, however, he stayed silent. "Okay, wait here, while I go look for something."

Wait here? *Wait here?* It was as if he were a repairman or some shifty delivery-person, denied permission to venture farther than the foyer. This was his house, no matter what the deed said, no matter what the lawyers had decided when they were carving up Dale and Chloe's property so gleefully. The old stone house, the last original structure within the boundaries of Glendale, had been his father's wedding gift to the couple, and Chloe had complained about it endlessly. But came the day when this house was all she wanted — the house and the eight acres behind it, which were virtually worthless as long as the Snyders and the Muhlys refused to sell their land. She had claimed that she wanted the house for Kat's sake, but Dale never doubted that Chloe's real purpose was to deny him something he loved.

Defiantly, he left the foyer and wandered the first floor. Given its age, the old farmhouse was a quirky place, in some ways the polar opposite of the homes that Glendale's architects had designed and refined over the years. Its rooms were small, the ceilings low, the pine floors almost wavy with age. It was, in short, lousy with charm — beamed ceilings, plaster walls that made it a bitch to hang anything, a huge kitchen with a stone fireplace. While other families gathered in the "great rooms" that were endemic to all the Glendale homes, no matter the price range, the Hartigans themselves had spent most of their time in this kitchen/dining room, not unlike the families who had lived here since it was first built in the late 1700s.

And it had been redone, Dale realized with a start. Redone at great expense. New cupboards of wide-planked pine paneling, with the same finish on the dishwasher and the refrigerator, a design trend he loathed. Why should appliances be forced to disappear from the kitchen in this trompe l'oeil scheme? Chloe also had installed a new freestanding sink, although "new" was a bit of a misnomer, for the piece was an antique, cleverly reworked. In fact, Dale had seen this very island at Gaines McHale, a high-end antique dealer that also trafficked in custom-mades. "Trafficked" was the right word, for it was a pricey place, more ruinous than a cocaine addiction for Baltimore's décor freaks. At Gaines McHale such a piece would cost at least twenty-five hundred dollars. Perhaps this was the reason Chloe had ordered Dale to stay in the foyer. She didn't want him to know how much money she was spending, even as she was bitching about how hard it was to make ends meet.

The portrait of Kat, in all its tacky glory, still dominated one wall over the dining room table. The painting had been his Christmas gift, the year Kat turned ten. (Chloe was wrong about that. Kat was definitely ten, not eleven.) Behind his back,

Chloe had hired a society painter, someone best known for painting dogs. But the painter was technically quite skilled, and her work usually appreciated in value. Unfortunately, she had let Chloe call the shots on Kat's portrait, and the result might as well have been painted on black velvet and offered at one of those starving-artist sales at the flea market.

In the painter's version, a falsely thin Kat was imprisoned in a white ruffled dress, quite unlike anything she had ever worn in real life, posed amid the ruins of some ancient civilization. But while the landscape was ominous and foreboding, the sky above it was cloudless blue, marred only by the yellow of a kite flown by Kat. If the painting had been the work of some addled religious zealot or prison inmate without any training, it would have been a masterpiece of outsider art, suitable for the Visionary Arts Museum. As it was, it was simply an embarrassment, a reminder that Chloe's membership in the bourgeoisie was an eternal high-wire act.

Chloe picked up on Dale's horror the moment he unwrapped it. He tried, he really tried, to pretend to the emotions that would make Chloe happy, but she had always been quick to see through him.

"What's wrong with it?" she demanded, not even waiting until Kat was out of earshot. She never waited.

"Nothing," he said. "It's beautiful. I'm just overwhelmed that you and Kat managed to keep a secret such as this."

"It took almost a whole year," Kat said, studying the painting. "I had to go for sittings every week." Dale's stomach clutched a little as he tried to figure out the cost of such an extravagance. (He was still working for his father then, and earning less than he might, for Glen was receiving the exact same salary for doing nothing.) It wasn't that he begrudged Chloe the money, just that such an expensive gift demanded to be hung in a prominent place, where everyone would see it.

"It's beautiful," he said, adding, with far more sincerity, "*You're* beautiful. But you're even more beautiful in real life than you are in this picture."

A week later, on New Year's Day, Chloe looked up from her checkbook and said, "I need ten thousand dollars."

"What on earth for?"

"The painting. I put the deposit on my credit card and carried the balance month by month, so you wouldn't know. But now that you've got it, I can pay it off."

"That painting cost ten thousand dollars?"

"She sometimes gets as much as fifteen thousand. It was a deal."

"And you carried ten thousand dollars on your credit card for twelve months, incurring finance charges?"

"Don't be stingy. It was only, like, a hundred or two hundred a month. I cut some things out to make up for it."

"Such as . . . ?"

"Things. What do you care? It was for you. It was all for you."

Chloe began to cry. They had been married long enough by then that the effect of these lusty tearfests, as Dale thought of them, was not as great as it once was. Still, he hated to see Chloe cry, if only because she seemed so dangerous and out of control.

"I wasn't being critical, Chloe. Or ungrateful. It's just that . . . ten thousand dollars is a lot of money for a painting, and the finance charges probably added another thousand dollars to the cost."

"It's a work of art. It's one of a kind. You can't put a price on things like that."

"And yet someone did." He thought his droll remark might undercut the tension in the room, but Chloe's fury only escalated.

"What's that supposed to mean?"

"Nothing. It was a lovely idea. I just think that whenever you consider spending that much money — whether it's for a gift for me or something for the house — we should talk about it."

"You don't like it," she wailed.

And because this was back when Dale still lied to spare his wife's feelings, he swore that he did. But Chloe was not stupid. She realized that she had erred, made one of those mistakes in judgment that revealed the gap between her roots and her aspirations. Brought up in Colorado, in hardscrabble circumstances, Chloe was terrified of being seen as tacky or déclassé. Her solution had been to study newspapers and certain magazines, then throw money at the things she thought could transform her into a natural-born member of the upper middle class. Nine times out of ten, she got it right, winning praise for her clothes, her hair, and especially the house. But every now and then she suffered a costly misstep, a bitter reminder that she was faking it. Since the divorce it had been a relief to hear of such things secondhand, usually through Kat. Once, just once, Dale had stepped in and warned Chloe that aboveground swimming pools were banned by Glendale's covenants. (And how glad he was to have that excuse, rather than be faced with trying to explain to Chloe the real reasons they were undesirable.) Otherwise he no longer had to pay the price, figuratively or literally, for Chloe's errors in judgment.

"I told you to wait in the hall," Chloe said, coming into the kitchen as if she had been looking for him everywhere, mail in her hand.

"I always liked the view from here." He pointed to the huge picture window in the kitchen's dining alcove. It framed a deceptively bucolic scene — a meadow sloping down toward a creek, the fringe of trees that Kat had insisted on calling "the woods." This house was probably the only place in Glendale where a man could look out a window and see something other than another house. Although developing the property would have meant a big windfall, he had always been secretly glad that the Muhlys and the Snyders wouldn't sell. Kat would have grieved so to see this view spoiled. Kat. *Kat.* He should have realized that just coming to this house would be like entering a minefield. She was everywhere, even in this redone kitchen. He felt sorry for Chloe, alone here with so many ghosts and echoes. It would drive him mad. Madder.

"Will this do?"

The photograph Chloe had chosen was a class portrait, possibly Kat's yearbook shot. Dale would have preferred something that wasn't so obviously airbrushed; the very fact of alteration seemed to suggest that Kat had needed it, which she had not. But the photo was suitable, he supposed. He felt a sudden desire to reach out to Chloe, to find some kind of rapprochement. They had lost their daughter. They were in this together. They would need each other, going forward, to survive. Two people, left alone by some cataclysm, just like Kat's poem for graduation.

"She looked more like you every year."

"Really? All I see is my hair. Her face is yours — actually —" She stopped, unusual for Chloe, who never worried about how her words landed.

"What?"

"She looks like Glen to me. I know you don't like to hear that, but it's true. His face is just a little rounder. Gentler."

"My brother's face," Dale said, "has not been hampered by thought or stress. Instead of getting Botox, maybe more women should just smoke marijuana every day of their lives. While living off their parents, of course."

"You're too hard on Glen," Chloe said. "Always have been. It wasn't easy being your brother. Not just your brother but your *twin,* for God's sake. I wouldn't wish it on my worst enemy."

But I'm your worst enemy.

"I don't see how being my brother was such a disadvantage. I was the one who was told I couldn't go to Stanford because my father thought it was unfair for me to go to private school across the country while Glen was at College Park."

"And you let Glen know just how much you resented him for it."

"You two always were thick as thieves."

"Thick as *losers,* you mean. That's what we had in common. We were the only underachievers in the bunch. Even your mom, sweet as she was, made me feel scattered and useless."

"You raised Kat, and she was lovely. If you never did another thing, Chloe, what you did with our daughter would be a greater accomplishment than most people ever know in their lives."

To his astonishment, Chloe put her arms around him and began to cry, but not in the frightening, rage-filled way he remembered. She cried silently, her body heaving with tears, and he started to cry, too. He had cried frequently over the past three days, but this was different somehow. The grief was powerful yet pure. For a moment he was free of the desire to redress or avenge, to somehow fix what had happened.

But just as quickly Chloe broke the embrace, as if embarrassed to have dropped her guard in front of Dale. Disoriented, she began fanning herself with the envelopes she still clutched in one hand, then patted her cheeks with them.

"Oh, shit, look at me — I'm trying to dry my eyes with the mail." She sat at the table and slid a letter opener through one. "That reminds me — you didn't pay child support this month."

"I'm sorry. I had meant to bring the check Friday night, when I came to take Kat out to dinner." Despite the traditional every-other-weekend custody arrangement, Kat seldom spent full weekends with her father anymore, given the demanding social life of a high-school senior. So Dale came out every Friday for dinner and talked to her by phone almost every evening.

"Do you have your checkbook with you now?"

"No — why?"

"For the check."

"What check?"

Chloe's voice was patient, practical. "The June child support."

"I've never examined this part of our separation agreement, but I have to think that child support ceases when the child is *dead,* Chloe."

"The check was due on the first. I agreed you could bring it out Friday, the fourth, rather than risk it getting delayed in the mail. But you owed me that money as of the first."

"I cannot believe you are busting my balls this way. Our daughter is dead, and all you care about is extracting more money from me."

"I just want what I'm entitled to. I'm sorry I don't have the option of being so pure in my grief, Dale. But I have bills." She waved the envelopes at him, then began tossing them at his feet one by one. "Utility. Water. Credit card — no, wait, that's a new credit card *application,* because that's one part of the world that finds a forty-five-year-old woman desirable: credit card companies. Oh, the Glendale Association — for the services and clubs I don't even use. And — what the fuck is this?"

"Your fur-storage bill?"

"Shut up, Dale. This is . . . this is . . ." She flapped it weakly, but all Dale saw was a plain white envelope, addressed in an elaborate handwriting, almost like calligraphy.

"Maybe it's a note of condolence," he said.

"It's for Kat."

He took it from Chloe, turning it over in his hand. "I'm sure it's some school thing. It's postmarked Friday morning. It was mailed . . . before. Certainly before the sender knew."

When Dale opened it, a single page fell out: *"I ask only that the truth be told."* The word "only" had been crossed out with a single pen stroke, and it was signed in the same blue ink: *"Love, Perri."*

19

Alexa had neither office nor classroom in Glendale, a situation attributed to her lack of seniority, although she suspected Barbara Paulson's resentment of her was the real reason. For all Glendale's overcrowding issues, it should have been possible to carve out a space for her things — a desk, a cupboard, a filing cabinet — if not an actual classroom. Instead she was relegated to floater status, ferrying her papers and supplies on a wheeled cart, meeting with students wherever a quiet corner could be found. "My door is always open to you," Alexa told her students with what she hoped came across as wry acceptance of a bad situation. "That is, my door is always open, assuming you can find it."

This morning she established a temporary beachhead in the dressing room behind the auditorium to begin gathering her thoughts about the assembly she had volunteered to organize. Had Barbara tricked her into taking on this extra chore? Alexa was no longer sure. All she knew was that she had found herself insisting that she had the necessary background, with her under-graduate work in rhetoric and her post-graduate degrees in psychology and education.

"Oh, I wouldn't *dream* of imposing on you," Barbara had said. "Besides, I really don't have the authority to assign you extra work — as you often remind me."

"It wouldn't be an imposition," Alexa had said. She was still remembering last year's assembly in the wake of a car acci-dent that had killed three popular athletes, how the outside grief counselors had mis-handled it.

"If you insist."

Barbara's bland tone couldn't quite con-ceal her smugness. Over the past two years, Alexa had been quick to remind Barbara that the Girl Talk! Empowerment Project had a specific purpose, and that Alexa had to account for her activities to both the state and the nonprofit that underwrote her grant. Yes, it made her sound a little petulant at times, but Barbara would have exploited her otherwise. If Barbara had her way, Alexa would have ended up pulling cafeteria duty and Lord knows what else.

Alexa knew she looked privileged and protected to the rest of the staff, holding what were derisively known as her "hen sessions," with blocks of time kept open for one-on-one counseling with students. Sometimes she dreamed of placing a sign on her desk — in her fantasies she had a desk — a sign that said IT ONLY LOOKS LIKE I'M NOT WORKING.

She picked up the in-house phone and dialed the office, thinking, as she had frequently over the past three days, about the in-house call that had started everything on Friday. Well, not *started,* exactly. The shots had been the signal, the clarion call, but even the shots were a reaction to something, something as yet unknown. What had motivated Perri to do such a thing? The school today was rife with rumors, stories so wild that they seemed more like Internet fanfic inspired by one of those prime-time teenage soap operas. Jealousy was the common element in all the stories. Perri must have wanted something that Kat had, or resented her. Her blond good looks? Perri was pretty enough, in her angular way. Her future? But Perri's admission to Northwestern's theater school was as prestigious as Kat's early acceptance to Stanford.

Could it be a boy? Neither girl had anyone steady as of late. Perri, solo since her on-again, off-again boyfriend graduated the year before, had insisted on taking Dannon as her date to the senior prom, prompting much nasty talk. Kat had attended the dance with a soccer player, a handsome, loose-limbed boy named Bradley, but it appeared to be more a relationship of convenience, like two film stars walking the red carpet at a premiere. Kat and Bradley, both outstanding students, needed suitable partners to navigate the final rites of high school. There hadn't been a trace of a real romance there.

Besides, Perri truly had no use for jocks like Bradley. While some of the drama-geek girls had chosen that path as a consolation prize, Perri's indifference to Glendale's popular crowd had always seemed sincere. Her friendship with Kat and Josie guaranteed her acceptance by the jocks and the preps, but she had never pursued those kids. Her humor was a bit waspish, and Alexa had encouraged her to curb the more scathing comments, a concept that Perri had embraced this past year with her usual overkill. Once she stopped being so vicious about the high school's unfortunates, she vented her spleen on those who were simply doing what she had once done — coining cruel nicknames, making devastating critiques of wardrobes and bodies. And where she had once been carefully neutral about the diva crowd, perhaps in deference to Kat's friends within it, she had become openly disdainful the past year, which had only encouraged their enmity and gossip.

But beneath her lippy bravado, Perri yearned for adult approval. Her exhausting, articulate arguments on every topic under the sun were not meant to challenge the status quo, simply to persuade the grown-ups around her that she was an original thinker. Tightly wound, yes. Almost too empathic, with an easily aroused compassion for anything and everyone. *Yet never violent,* Alexa thought, although Perri had been increasingly conflicted about the ethical dilemmas posed by those who were. Events in the Middle East had been particularly hard for Perri to synthesize over the past year. Was war ever right? Did violence ever accomplish anything? Alexa had watched Perri struggle with these ideas — her heart yearning to say no, even as her head was insisting that pacifism had a spotty historical track record.

The phone buzzed and buzzed and

buzzed, but no one picked up. Anita Whitehead had called in sick this morning, claiming she had a doctor's note to stay home indefinitely. The events of the past few days had been much too traumatic for her. (As if Anita were the only one who had suffered, as if one needed Anita's hypersensitive hypochondria to be affected by what had happened.) Where were the other secretaries? Where was Barbara? Probably in the seventy-fifth meeting of the morning. It would be wrong to say that Barbara was enjoying herself, but she had an unusually high color, as if flushed with usefulness in the wake of the tragedy.

There was a knock on the dressing room door, and the unexpected sound made Alexa jump. Everyone was on edge today, naturally. The door was pushed open before she could issue an invitation, and a round-faced man, stocky in a comfortable way, came into the dressing room.

"Ms. Cunningham? I'm Sergeant Lenhardt, Baltimore County Homicide. Mrs. Paulson said I could find you here."

"You were here on Friday, right?" Alexa was proud of her memory for faces. "Don't you have a partner?"

He had a slow, lazy smile. "Yeah, ladies always remember Kevin."

"No, that's not what I meant at all." She resented the suggestion that she had been focused on something as trivial as a man's looks in the midst of a crisis. Besides, the younger cop had been *too* handsome, the kind of cocky stud that Alexa avoided on principle. "It's just that I thought you guys always worked in tandem."

"We do tend to travel in pairs," the sergeant conceded. "But it happens that the high school is more or less en route for me. I live up near the state line. Detective Infante has to come from the other direction, so he's going to meet me here for the assembly."

"You planned on attending?"

He eased himself into the chair one over from Alexa's at the long counter beneath the makeup mirrors and rotated on its wheeled base, taking in the room. "We didn't have anything like this at my high school. When we did shows, we had to get dressed in the wings or the boys' lavatory."

"Oh, it's pretty standard stuff for schools these days," Alexa said, wondering at her own reflexive defense of Glendale. Among her friends she was quick to mock how overdone the school was in the physical details, how lacking in basic amenities — such as space for its faculty. "But the auditorium is large, large enough to hold the entire student body. Feel free to sit in the back or to watch from the wings."

"Actually, I was hoping I might speak. Me, or my partner, if you think the kids would be more responsive to him."

"He's *not* my type," Alexa shot back, then blushed.

"I was just thinking, him being so handsome and all. And he's younger, you know, closer to their age." Again that slow easy smile. "But I'm happy to hear he's not everyone's type. We go to lunch, the waitresses swirl around him, offering seconds and specials and thises and thats. Me, I sit there pointing at my empty coffee cup until someone takes pity on me and pours me a refill. Even then it turns out to be decaf."

Alexa doubted this. The sergeant clearly had his own kind of charm, and he wasn't unaware of it. She could imagine him as a shopping-mall Santa, a good one, who never made children cry. Not that he was fat, although his middle was a little bulky. There was just something in his demeanor that made it seem possible, attractive even, to whisper in his ear.

"I don't understand why either of you wants to address the students."

"The usual stuff. Remind kids that they should come forward with anything they know. With the promise of confidentiality, of course."

"Are you hoping to find out something about the motive?"

"Not really."

"Excuse me?"

"Motives can be interesting. And when you don't have anything, they're a good place to start. But they're not how you close cases, much less get convictions. I prefer eyewitnesses, hard physical evidence."

"It's pretty obvious what happened, right? Perri killed Kat, shot Josie, and then tried to kill herself."

"That's what everyone seems to think, yes."

"But you don't?"

"I'm not saying that."

"Then what do you think the students could tell you, if you already have an eyewitness and physical evidence?"

"I'm an open-minded guy. That's my stock-in-trade."

He rested one arm on the counter, his gaze unnervingly steady. Alexa's eyes slid away, toward her own reflection. At twenty-eight she still looked twenty-two, although she worried about the way she might age. Time was unkind to blue-eyed blondes, judging by her mother. *Were you always pretty?* the girls asked, wistful and resentful at the same time, as if someone who was pretty in high school could never understand them. *Not in my head,* Alexa replied, and it was a good answer, true even. In high school she had not understood how blessed she was. No girl did.

"It's a bad idea," she said.

"Being open-minded?"

"Talking to the kids at the assembly."

"Why?"

"Two reasons. One is that the anti-snitch culture is alive and well in high school. Once you ask kids to talk to you, some will feel pressure to do anything *but*. The kids who do come forward will most likely be the drama queens and kings, desperate for attention. Or looking for a reason to get out of class for an hour."

"Interesting," he said. "I hadn't thought about that. So should I go about it a different way? Are there any individuals I should seek out?"

She thought of Eve but hurriedly pushed the girl out of her thoughts, as if fearful that this policeman could read her mind. Eve was hers.

"Well, Josie Patel, obviously. She's the only eyewitness, right?"

"Right," the sergeant said in his agreeable tone, so why did Alexa have the feeling he wasn't really agreeing with her? "Still, I'd like to speak at this confab. Just for two minutes, maybe at the very beginning. Then you can get down to the serious business at hand."

"You sound a little . . . sarcastic." Like her brother, the day before. She was tired of people making fun of what she did.

"Do I? I don't mean to. I think grief counseling is a good thing. Posttraumatic stress, all that stuff. They talk a lot about it in my shop."

"Have you . . . ?"

"Oh, it's not for me."

"No, I wasn't asking if you've had it, just if — Well, you must have seen a lot. As a detective."

"I'm in homicide. My whole life is posttrauma. But it's not what I've seen that's likely to bother me. It's what I've *heard*. The confessions. The rationalizations. The lack of rationalizations. You can't believe how thoughtlessly some lives are ended, how little goes into the decision. Makes me sad."

Me, too, she wanted to say, yet she knew

it was inane, a guidance counselor claiming kinship with a homicide detective. Still, it was amazing, the stories that teenage girls confided, once they felt safe. Their confused notions of sex, the things they were willing to do for the tiniest scrap of male attention, the viciousness of other girls.

"Look, you really shouldn't go before the assembly. You're just going to end up trying to sort a lot of chaff from the wheat, the attention hogs and liars."

"Everybody lies. It's the cardinal rule of homicide investigations."

Alexa blushed, feeling that he had seen through her own omissions, her refusal to mention Eve. But there was no way she could turn Eve over to police. The girl would never trust her again.

His cell phone rang, a strangely straightforward ring to Alexa's ears, inured to the elaborate tones that the kids downloaded. ABBA was big, for some reason. "Dancing Queen" and "Waterloo" always seemed to be coming out of someone's purse or backpack these days. There also was a lot of hip-hop, at least among the boys, a hilarious affectation at Glendale, where only 5 percent of the student body was African-American and almost everyone was well-to-do.

The sergeant took the call, his mono-syllabic responses revealing little about the information conveyed. *Really? Do we need a lab tech? Okay. Okay. Okay.*

"I guess it's all moot for now," he said, snapping the phone shut and placing it back on his belt. "Something — well, maybe nothing, really, but it takes priority. You could ask for us, though, couldn't you? Ask the kids to call me or my partner, give out our numbers. In whatever way you think would elicit the best responses."

He hit the word "elicit" hard, as if he expected her to be surprised by the usage. As if she thought he was stupid, when she was now quite sure he was anything but.

"I'll do my best," she promised.

"Good girl."

She disliked him for that — in part because it was so patronizing, as if he were old enough to be her father, and maybe he was, but he should treat her as the professional she was, his equal.

And in part because, having heard it, she wanted to hear it again, wanted this man's approval.

Wanted, in fact, an excuse to talk to him again. Because while his partner was not her type, Lenhardt definitely could be. Was he married? She hadn't noticed a ring. Not that all men wore rings. Her father certainly hadn't. Besides, she just wanted to talk to this man, get to know him better. There was nothing illicit about that.

20

Peter knew it was a bad idea to go to the high school Monday morning, but he just couldn't help himself. He was bored out of his mind. Television was all girly stuff, even on pay cable — clearly no self-respecting man was supposed to be watching television before noon. The Glendale pool didn't have weekday hours until later in the summer, and the early-June days were too cool for swimming anyway. Besides, he wasn't sure how the producers would feel about him tanning. Guy Pearce was a pretty pale guy, although there was a hint of olive in his complexion. With all those self-tanners on the market, Peter could always go darker fast if need be, whereas if he overtanned, there was no makeup in the world that could take it down. Too bad, because Peter tanned beautifully.

A year ago, even as recently as Christmas, Peter might have found some of his old compadres hanging around Glendale, but college graduation had changed that dynamic. People had jobs or internships, or else they were doing big trips before they plunged into grad school. There were no students at the high school who knew him, although the real drama geeks might remember him from his community-theater work.

But his drama teacher was still on the faculty, and Peter couldn't resist going up there, sharing his big news. Old Giff would be so happy for him. Really, it would be a favor to him, letting him be the first to know that one of his former students was succeeding at such a high level.

Vans from the local television stations were parked on the shoulder along Glendale Circle, and Peter had a hunch some security guy would be posted at the front door, making sure that all visitors reported to the office. But these were his old stomping grounds. He knew tricks that no reporter, no stranger, ever could. Instead of heading to the front doors, he ambled to one of the breezeways, losing himself in the crowd of students during a class change. The kids glanced his way — they weren't fooled by the twenty-two-year-old impostor among them — but didn't challenge him, just kept up their own manic chatter.

It took him a second to tune in to their frequency, and when he did, he realized that all the buzzing was about the shooting. Of course.

Old Giff was sitting in a chair on the stage, and in the split second before he realized he was being observed, he reminded Peter of a particularly poignant Malvolio from a Lincoln Center production of *Twelfth Night*, and it wasn't just because he wore bright yellow trousers. Giff had a rubbery, comic countenance, the kind made for Neil Simon's earlier plays, but left to its own devices, Old Giff's face sagged into melancholic lines and folds. He looked lonely and unloved, and in full knowledge of the fact that he was lonely and unloved. In high school Peter had refused to think about Giff's sexuality, not that he had a problem with people being gay or whatever. Peter had even threatened to beat up an oafish freshman who threw the word "faggot" around a little too carelessly. It was just that if he conceded Giff was gay, then he would have to wonder if the older man's devotion to him was based on Peter's talent or some latent attraction.

But *of course* he was gay, Peter thought now.

"Lasko!" the teacher cried out, his face

truly lighting up. "What a welcome surprise at such a sad, sad time. Did you come back for Kat's funeral?"

The question shamed Peter a little. But it wasn't his fault that he had planned his trip before Kat was killed, he reminded himself.

"Yeah," he said. "Of course."

"Isn't it horrible?"

"Horrible doesn't begin to approach it. What happened anyway?"

"No one knows. Perri lost her mind, I guess. Lord, I feel terrible about it. She was in my homeroom, you know."

"Hey, just because she was your student doesn't mean you could have seen it coming."

The stage had been set with chairs, and Giff began loading them onto a wheeled cart.

"I'm not being melodramatic." Giff allowed himself a half smile at his choice of words. "Perri was very angry with me over something that happened last fall. She and a few other students persuaded me to stage *Anyone Can Whistle* as our fall musical. I cast her and Kat in the leads, and we started rehearsing."

"That's pretty cool, actually. Doing a show like that at the high-school level."

"Well, it's dated, and the problems in the book have never been resolved, but it feels powerful and sophisticated to high-school students. And the chorus is huge, just utterly expandable, which is always a good thing for us."

"So what was Perri's beef, if she got the play she wanted and the part she wanted?"

"Three weeks in, we had to give up on *Anyone Can Whistle* and sub in *Oklahoma!* There were some complications with the rights — turns out that Everyman wanted to do it. You know an Equity company within a certain-mile radius had bumping rights. To be fair, I told the leads they could have comparable parts — Kat as Laurey, Perri as Ado Annie."

"Most girls would kill to be Ado Annie." Peter regretted the wording, but Old Giff didn't seem to notice.

"That's what I thought. But Perri wanted no part of it. She accused me of selling out, of bowing to pressure from Kat's father, so his daughter could have a bigger part."

"Crazy." The word echoed a little in the empty auditorium, and Peter realized he had sounded insensitive.

"Well, between us, a lot of parents *were* upset, once they began reading the script.

The Everyman Theater gave me a graceful way out of a tight spot. The mental institution! I mean, half the kids in this place are on Prozac or Wellbutrin. It's a kind of sensitive topic. And when Hartigan read the lyrics to his daughter's little seduction number, 'Come Play Wiz Me' — well, the guy was on the phone trying to rewrite Stephen Sondheim. And my Hapgood was no good. Now, you — you would have been extraordinary in the role. Sexy *and* a good singer."

While Peter had come here in hopes that his old drama teacher would gush over him, this was more affection than he had bargained for.

"Do you honestly think choosing *Oklahoma!* over *Anyone Can Whistle* is a reason to shoot somebody?"

Giff rubbed his cheeks, massaging them in circles, forward and back. "People have killed over the cheerleading squad, why not the school musical? But — no, no, I don't think this is a case of cause and effect. Perri may have had some resentment of Kat. You know I always saw my classes as —"

"A repertory company, like the Old Abbey," Peter finished. It was one of Old Giff's more repeated riffs, and Giff repeated a lot of his riffs. Yet Peter had never been relegated to spear-carrying. He had been too good to waste on the chorus, for even a single production.

"Yes, exactly. And Perri had played by the rules, taking parts large and small, doing a lot of behind-the-scenes work. The year after she was the lead in *The Lark*, she did chorus in *Brigadoon* with no complaint. It was one thing to cancel *Whistle* — I think even Perri knew it was a stretch — but to see Kat, who had never auditioned for a school play, waltz in and end up with a plum lead in a show that her father had lobbied for . . . well, I'm sure it stuck in Perri's craw. She didn't even try out for the spring play this year — *Our Town*, which I chose because I thought she would be a wonderful Emily. She was mad at me. She was mad at everyone, it seemed, this past year."

"Well, that explains it, doesn't it?" Peter didn't see how he could ever lead the conversation back to himself now, not in a graceful way.

"Maybe," Giff said, rubbing his cheeks again. "Maybe. You know what you should do?"

"What?"

"You should speak — or sing, yes, sing

351

— at today's assembly. We should pick an appropriate song. For Kat."

"I don't know . . ." Peter was thinking of the songs he had sung to Kat three years ago, made-up songs that he would be mortified to re-create for anyone, ever.

"Not a show tune, just something sweet and simple. A hymn — well, not a *hymn*-hymn, someone would complain, and it would be so Madalyn Murray O'Hair all over again. But you should sing. Or speak."

"I don't think so, Giff."

"Oh, you must. You must, Peter. For me. For Kat."

And so it happened that Peter Lasko stood before the assembled student body of Glendale High School after a series of presentations — by the principal, by the county executive, by a pretty young guidance counselor who encouraged students to come talk to her about anything, absolutely anything, with the promise of absolute confidentiality.

Like any actor worth a damn, he had stage fright, but he'd never had it in such overwhelming proportions before. Willing his legs not to shake, Peter clasped his arms across his chest and leaned into the mike, singing the song that Giff, the principal, and the guidance counselor had finally agreed was appropriate: "You'll Never Walk Alone." It was, ironically, a show tune *and* a hymn. Peter sang in a clear, unaffected tenor, although it is doubtful that anyone heard the final, powerful build, for the girls in the auditorium began to cry so hard and so lustily that they drowned him out, almost as if he were starring in *Bye Bye Birdie*. Suffer indeed.

Peter, who had been Billy Bigelow in *Carousel*, realized he'd never had a chance to sing this particular song before, given that it's first performed over Billy's dead body. And in the reprise, at the play's end, Bill just stands to the side, a ghost, praying for his daughter to hear the choir's words and heed them, to know that she is loved, that he would always be there for her even if he was dead.

The last note, while not the highest, was a bitch, even transposed to a friendlier key for his tenor range, but Peter nailed it. *You'll never walk alone. You'll never walk A-LOOOOOOOOOOOOOOOOOOONE.*

He absolutely nailed it, not that anyone heard.

21

The Kahns were adamant that they did not want to speak to the police in Perri's room, but neither did they want to leave her for even a few minutes. Middle-class people, used to having rights, they assumed this ended the discussion. They couldn't leave their daughter, they didn't want to be interviewed in front of their daughter, so the police would have to come back later.

But they were also reasonable people, and when it was explained that the conversation could not be postponed, they agreed to take turns, meeting with Lenhardt and Infante in the hospital's food court one at a time. Lenhardt allowed them to think he was accommodating them, but it was what he had wanted all along, getting each parent alone. He was surprised they didn't insist on calling their high-priced lawyer, but it probably didn't occur to them that they needed legal advice. Good.

First came the father, Zachary Kahn, although his wife called him Zip. Lenhardt began by asking about that, a way of settling in, as if he were making small talk with the father of one of Jessica's or Jason's friends.

"An old nickname," the man explained, grasping his cup of black coffee in two hands as if it were a winter day and he was trying to warm himself. "I gave it to myself, in my twenties. I wanted a nickname, and I liked that comic Zippy the Pinhead, so I anointed myself Zip. Twenty years later I'm still Zip. The follies of youth."

"I always wanted a nickname, too. But my mom insisted that people call me Harold. Not Harry or Hal. Now I can't bear it when someone shortens my name straight off, without even asking."

Zip Kahn — what an unfortunate name to carry into adulthood — looked as if he wanted to say something normal, something expected, except he no longer knew what normal was. He and his wife had been at the hospital for almost seventy-two hours, going home only to shower. Of course Lenhardt couldn't know what the guy looked like on a typical day, but there were traces of energy and vitality. Zip was stocky and athletic-looking, with a round face and an admirably thick crop of hair, the kind that never fell out and barely grayed.

"As I told you Friday, we traced the gun," Lenhardt said, plunging in. "To Michael Delacorte."

"Right. Perri baby-sat for the Delacortes." He seemed to think this fact explained and closed the discussion.

"Now that we've checked it out, we don't see any of the other girls having access to that gun. But I also have to assume you didn't know it was in your daughter's possession."

Like a boxer getting a second wind, the guy seemed to sharpen through sheer will. "How can you be so sure the gun was ever in her possession? Have you been able to make that connection with certainty? Opportunity doesn't equal certainty."

Eddie Dixon had prepared the parents well, then.

"Your daughter worked for them. The other girls didn't."

"And Dale Hartigan was pals with Stewart Delacorte. For all you know, *he* took the gun, and his daughter took it from him, and that's how it came to be at the school."

Yeah, right. "We'll ask him about that. Believe me. We'll ask him."

"Okay, then." Said emphatically, as if something important had been settled. Lenhardt did not want to be unkind to the man, but he needed to tug him gently back to reality, away from the paranoid rationalizations he was using to comfort himself.

"Now, as you know, your daughter's hands were tested for gun residue, but the weapon was a .22, which almost never leaves enough barium or antimony to detect."

He could have said "trace evidence," but he wanted to let the father know he was on top of the technical stuff.

"They bagged her hands. They put paper bags on her hands, and they wouldn't take them off, not for hours. I wanted to hold my daughter's hand, and I couldn't. Can you imagine what that's like?"

"I'm sorry," Lenhardt said. With a look he tossed the interview to Infante. It wasn't a routine with them, it wasn't good cop–bad cop, just a rhythm born of practice. Lenhardt could imagine all too well what it would be like, seeing his daughter hurt, not being able to hold her hand.

"What we didn't do on Friday was get fingerprints. We're here today to do that, and we're asking only as a courtesy," Infante said. "The gun was taken from the home of a family for whom she worked. If her fingerprints are on the gun, we have to proceed on certain assumptions."

They really wanted the fingerprints so they could ascertain the letter had been written and mailed by Perri, but Lenhardt and Infante had agreed between themselves not to mention the letter at the top of the conversation and, no matter what, not to reveal that it raised far more questions than it answered.

"I would think," Zip Kahn said, growing more defiant, "that you would want to do quite the opposite. If you investigate on the basis of a narrow hypothesis, you end up finding what you were looking for. That's human nature. You need to collect the facts with minds open to any possibility."

"There is a witness," Infante reminded him. "A girl who knows your daughter quite well, a girl who was there and has stated that Perri brought the gun to school and shot Kat Hartigan."

"I've heard the Patels obtained a lawyer. Is that something all witnesses do? In fact, they've hired an excellent criminal defense attorney, Gloria Bustamante, someone who has a great deal of expertise in homicide. Why does Josie Patel need a lawyer?"

Damn Eddie Dixon. He was just *too*

plugged in, Lenhardt thought. And if Dixon knew the Patels had hired Busta-mante, he might know why as well.

"A letter arrived at the Hartigan house today," Infante said. He was always coldly patient in an interview, unless the person opposite him required out-and-out bul-lying. Infante played it like a Department of Motor Vehicles bureaucrat, someone who couldn't be moved under any circum-stances.

"Which *one?* The house in Glendale or the little love nest that he set up in Balti-more with his young girlfriend?"

His resentment was palpable, and it in-terested Lenhardt. Was Zip Kahn trying to suggest that Dale Hartigan deserved to have a dead daughter, because he had left his wife, while the still-together Kahns should not be penalized? Or was he bitter in the way some men were when they saw another guy get out? In Lenhardt's experi-ence, the only outsiders who begrudged a person the end of a marriage were those secretly wistful about their own.

Even if you were happy in your marriage, as Lenhardt was, it could give you a pang, seeing a guy your age with someone new, someone young. There had been a Christ-mas party last year, and he had been reminded of the kinds of girls that young cops can get — the pretty young emergency-room nurses, the good-time party girls, even an occasional assistant state's attorney. Infante's girl-of-the-moment was enough to give a man a coronary, with long black hair and big fake tits, not that Lenhardt deducted points for surgical enhancement. These were the girls that Lenhardt had once gotten, part of the reason he hadn't married again until he was in his forties. And Marcia, twelve years younger, was the best of the best — cute, down to earth. Plenty of his colleagues still gave her approving looks. But it wasn't the young guys and the young girls that had unnerved him at the party. What had been weird was seeing a guy his age, a robbery detective, show up with this total piece. Lenhardt could live with Infante's beautiful girls, but it had been strange seeing fifty-two-year-old Fred Duda with a high-assed waitress.

"The envelope was addressed to Kat Hartigan," Infante continued in his robotic voice. "It came to the house where she lived with her mother. Mrs. Hartigan says the handwriting looks like your daughter's."

"So what does the letter say?"

"It's not so much what it said," Lenhardt put in, all too aware that the one-line letter could be a boon to a smart defense attorney. "It's that we want to establish it isn't a forgery. So between that and the nonconclusive tests on your daughter's hand, we decided we should get her fingerprints sooner rather than later. Really, we should have done it earlier, but . . ."

He didn't finish the thought, that they hadn't worried about fingerprints because Perri Kahn was comatose, and not going anywhere.

Kahn made a move as if to crumple the coffee cup in his hands, realizing just in time it was still full. "That's shitty," he said. "That's just plain shitty. You don't need to do that now. My daughter might not live. Do you know that? So maybe none of this matters anyway."

"But if your daughter *didn't* send the letter, and her fingerprints don't match any of the latents lifted from the gun, we need to know that sooner rather than later. Right? Like you said, we have to be open to every possibility."

"Why? What does it say? Was it a threat?"

"It was kind of . . . obscure in its intent. In and of itself, the letter tells us nothing.

361

That's why we need to check the envelope against your daughter's fingerprints."

"Do what you have to do," Zip Kahn said. "And go fuck yourself."

Mrs. Kahn came down fifteen minutes later. She was a large woman, but she carried herself with the confidence of someone who had once been thin and attractive.

"Perri was her normal self these past few months," Eloise Kahn began before either Lenhardt or Infante had a chance to ask her a single question.

"What was normal for Perri?" Lenhardt asked.

"She was like any teenager, moody and rebellious, nothing more. In fact, it makes sense for a high-school senior to get a little irritable. It's a way of preparing for the transition to college."

"Had she quarreled with Kat over anything, to your knowledge?"

"Girls don't really do that," Eloise Kahn said. "They just . . . drift apart, for whatever reason. Kat and Perri were heading in different directions. Their differences hadn't mattered as much when they were younger, but that started to change, and it became harder to overlook the ways in which they were incompatible."

"Differences?"

"Kat was . . . well, so mainstream in her attitudes and aspirations. I don't mean to be unkind. . . ."

In Lenhardt's experience, people said they didn't wish to be unkind only when they intended to be extremely unkind but wanted dispensation for their cruelty.

"Kat became more . . . well, dilettantish after her parents' divorce. Kat was a charming little girl, but as a teenager all she cared about were the most superficial things. Cheerleading, grades for grades' sake, but not knowledge. She had a gorgeous soprano voice, but she didn't want to do anything with it — until she realized that appearing in a school play might round out her college applications. She wanted to get top grades and go to a top college because her father had been preparing her for that since she was small. I don't know what you've heard, but Perri was the one who tired of Kat, not the other way around."

"We haven't really gotten into that," Lenhardt said. "No one's told us much of anything about the girls' relationship. We've been giving the Hartigans a little space. Her mom said she knew the girls weren't close anymore, but Kat hadn't confided in her."

"Oh." Mrs. Kahn looked thoughtful, as if considering whether she was at an advantage or a disadvantage, getting to tell this part of the story before anyone else. "Well, some people assumed it was the other way, that Kat and Josie had dropped Perri because she wasn't a cheerleader who dated jocks. The thing is, Perri has very high standards for herself and her friends. Always has."

"Who were her friends? Besides Kat Hartigan and the Patel girl?"

This question seemed to pain the mother, and she stammered a bit. "There wasn't . . . after Kat and Josie. A lot of kids from drama class, of course. There's this one boy — not a boyfriend. Just a friend. But very sweet."

"What's his name?"

"Dannon Estes, poor thing. His mother . . . well, honest to God, I think she named him after a cup of yogurt. Literally."

"That so?" Lenhardt was making a mental note to get to know Dannon Estes.

"His mother is a little *unusual,*" Eloise Kahn said, still in the vein of not meaning to be unkind, yet managing it with flying colors. "Sort of a hippie type, but married to the straightest arrow you could imagine. Her second husband, Dannon's stepfather, and not a great fit, based on what Dannon tells me. The boy has practically lived at our house this past year."

"Huh." His neutral, noncommittal noise was intended to keep her talking. Sometimes people could be helpful when they got revved up about inconsequential things.

"It's funny how much you can determine about someone based on the children's names. Social class, education. I named Perri after a writer. A wonderful writer who's also a doctor. I thought it would be a good omen, sort of like christening her left and her right brain at the same time. And she turned out to be good at both things — not writing and science per se, but she had a creative side — drawing, drama, writing. Yet she was great at math. She loved geometry. Have you ever heard of a teenage girl — a normal one, I mean — who loved geometry? Perri used to make up her own theorems for extra credit."

Eloise Kahn's words, which had been coming in a great rush, halted abruptly. Lenhardt wondered if she was thinking about whether her daughter would ever again do anything for extra credit. Perri

365

Kahn had one of those injuries that flum-moxed doctors, as brain injuries sometimes do. Lenhardt had seen a case, a would-be suicide, who fired a gun straight into his temple and woke up four weeks later, functions virtually unaffected. Yet the shot from the .22 had cut a cruel path through Perri Kahn's face and brain. What would be the best scenario for Perri's parents? Alive and in prison? Brain-dead and here? Dead-dead? Could a parent ever wish for a child's death, under any circumstances?

"Sergeant?"

"Yes, Mrs. Kahn?"

"You believe me, right?"

"About . . . ?"

"That we really didn't see anything in Perri's behavior? That there really wasn't anything to observe or notice? She's a good kid. Yes, I know every parent says that. The parents of serial killers say that every time. But Perri is truly *good*. Principled. All we ever asked her to do is stand up for what she thought was right, not just go along with the herd. She wasn't up in her room playing violent computer games. She didn't do drugs or drink. She's a little high-strung. Passionate, sure, but that's how she was raised to be. The fact is, we're very proud of her."

"I'm sure you didn't notice anything out of the ordinary," Lenhardt said, and Mrs. Kahn accepted it as the benediction she needed, although his wording had been carefully noncommittal.

As soon as Eloise Kahn boarded the elevator to Shock Trauma, Lenhardt began making a list. "We'll want a warrant to search her room, by tomorrow if possible. I hope the parents haven't thought to mess with it. And we'll want to seize the computer, check to see if the full body of the letter is on it."

"Wouldn't it be great," Infante said, "if she kept an online diary like so many kids now, one where she conveniently wrote all about this in great detail, so we'd know exactly what was going on?"

"We never get that lucky. But there might be e-mails, or some other kinds of records."

"We need to check the phone."

"Phone records, sure."

"Not just the landline," Infante said. "The cell phone, assuming she has one, and I bet she does, although it wasn't at the scene. Probably in her car or something."

"Yeah, maybe the list of incoming and

outgoing calls will show something."

"And the text messages. Those live forever, depending on the provider. These kids are crazy for text messaging."

"They are?" Lenhardt was refusing to give his kids cell phones until they were in high school and restricted their IM use on the computer, despite Jessica's contention that this made him the cruelest, meanest father in the universe.

Infante grinned knowingly. "That girl I brought to the departmental Christmas party? She was nineteen."

"That's barely legal."

"Hey, same age difference as you and Marcia. Anyway, it seemed like the only time she ever put her phone down and stopped texting her friends was when we were in bed."

"Well, yeah," Lenhardt said. "Everyone knows that's nothing to call home about."

22

"That was soooooooo queer," Lila said.

"Definitely," Val agreed, cupping her hands around her cigarette to light it. The breeze was surprisingly stiff this afternoon, even here where it was buffered by a stand of evergreens. "He, like, wouldn't make it past the first round on *American Idol*."

Eve kept her head down, worried that Lila and Val would see that she did not agree. She tried to think whatever they did. It seemed to her a reasonable price for their friendship, sharing their opinions. But she couldn't believe they hadn't been moved by Peter Lasko's performance.

"I mean, he was just swimming in Lake Me, he was so in love with himself," Lila continued.

"He is hot, though." Shit, had she really said that out loud? "I mean, if he wasn't singing such a stupid song, he could be hot. Don't you think? He's going to be in this movie and all."

"Yeah," Val said. "We all heard Old Giff huff and puff about that. But I just figured he was trying to show us that getting killed wasn't the only way to get famous at Glendale High School."

Lila rewarded Val with the laugh that line demanded, but Eve couldn't quite muster one.

"I'm not saying it's a big deal," she said carefully, ready to abandon the conversation if it was clear Val and Lila were united against her. "But it's cool. And he is good-looking."

"Lasko's okay-looking," Lila admitted, a little cautiously, as if she, too, craved Val's approval. It was funny about Val. She wasn't pretty or attractive. In fact, she was kind of heavyset, with bad skin and mud-brown hair. She wasn't accomplished at the things that mattered, like sports or music or classwork. Yet lots of people at school wanted to be on her good side, not just Eve and Lila. She had some kind of weird authority. "But why did he have to sing such a queer song? I mean, there have to be a million better things to sing. Even . . . 'Wind Beneath My Wings.' That would have been okay."

"But that would have been more about Kat," Val pointed out. "I think they wanted him to sing something for us. Like a stupid song could make us feel better."

"Do you feel bad?" Eve's question sounded odd even to her ears, so she tried rephrasing it. "I mean, of course we all feel bad, but do you feel *especially* bad? It's not like we really knew her."

"She was a little stuck-up," Lila said. "But not as stuck-up as she might have been, given how rich her dad was. And she didn't cut on people. She wasn't really a diva that way, although the divas liked to hang with her. She got along with everybody. She was, like, above the divas."

"Yeah, but it's easier to be nice when you're rich," Val said. "Because when you're rich, you have nice clothes and a car of your own, and you can afford to be nice, because no one has anything you want. She had everything."

"She didn't have a boyfriend," Eve said. It was one of the things that amazed her about Kat, the fact that she could have any boy in school yet didn't seem to want any of them. "I heard she told her parents she'd rather take the money they were going to give her for after-prom and donate it to a homeless shelter."

"That's because Kat was scared to spend the night in a hotel," Lila said. "A curfew is a cocktease's best friend."

"Was she, had she . . . ?" Eve was unsure how to phrase the question.

"She was a *virgin*," Lila said dismissively.

Eve was, too. A virgin, that is. Val and Lila never pressed her directly on that subject, but she suspected they knew she had never gone further than she did that day on the bus — had never gone that far again, truth be told. A lot of boys had come around at first, of course, but when Eve showed no inclination to repeat her performance, they gave up on her. Ms. Cunningham had given her a book, a slender but odd story about a school in Scotland, called *The Prime of Miss Jean Brodie*. "Nothing changes," she had told Eve. "The girls in this book could be smoking with you out in the woods." (That was Ms. Cunningham's style, letting the students know she was privy to all their secrets but didn't care. She thought she was so cool, so hip.) The thing is, Eve didn't see how these girls in the book were anything like her. There was one girl who was described as being famous for sex, although she wasn't actually having sex. She was just very pretty and posed naked for a painter. Eve supposed that was her and was flattered, but she didn't really know what else to do with the book, other than write an extra-credit report for English, which pulled her up to a C-plus.

"If one of us was shot, do you think it would be as big a deal? Like, would they let everybody out of school to go to our memorial service?"

Val and Lila shook their heads in unison. "Definitely not," Val said. "Although I think what's really freaking them out is that it was Perri Kahn who shot her. If you had brought a gun to school, Muhly" — Val always used their surnames — "they wouldn't have been shocked at all. Or any of us. Because we're skeezers. If you ask me, the real surprise is that it doesn't happen every day. I can think of at least a dozen girls I'd like to kill."

"Including Kat?" Eve asked.

Val exhaled noisily. "No. Not her. She was okay. She wouldn't even make my top twenty."

Eve thought about her secret. Val and Lila could definitely be trusted. But she had promised. She must tell no one. *No one*. If only Val and Lila had been here Friday morning, if they had not been late — but they were, there was no undoing it.

Instead she asked, "Are you going to talk

to Ms. Cunningham? One-on-one, I mean, like she encouraged us to?"

"Of course not," Val said, as if insulted by the very suggestion.

Eve fingered the paper slip in her pocket, the one given to her at homeroom that morning, the one that she was trying to ignore. "Ms. Cunningham keeps bugging me to talk to her."

"That's what you get," Lila said, "for yakking to her on Friday like a little brown-noser. What were you thinking?"

"I dunno. I was bored. Besides, she's okay, Ms. Cunningham."

"Never trust a guidance counselor," Val said. "They live to get inside your head. Her more than most of them. She thinks she's, like, decoded us. Guidance counselors are supposed to help us get into college, not play shrink. I don't need Ms. Cunningham to explain to me how girls are mean to each other because they're competing for boys. I need her to tell me how I can get my SATs over 1250."

"What's your reach school?" Lila asked.

"McDaniels, can you believe it? If I'm *lucky*, I'll get to spend four years in beautiful downtown Westminster, Maryland."

"Dickinson," Lila said. They looked expectantly at Eve.

"My parents say I have to live at home, wherever I get in."

"Wow."

Val's sincere and sorrowful shock proved to Eve just how dire her situation was. It was one thing to joke about community college as one's only option, another for it to be true. Theoretically, Eve's parents had told her she could go anywhere in the metropolitan Baltimore area, and that included Johns Hopkins and Goucher. But even Towson University or Villa Julie were not sure things for Eve, with her middling grades and test scores. She thought she might be able to do an end run, get into Maryland College Institute of Art on the basis of her work in jewelry making and ceramics. But her father might decree that an art school didn't count as a real college, even though it had regular classes, like English and math. Or he might say she hadn't banked enough in her college fund. Eve's chest felt a little tight. She was seventeen, only a junior. She hadn't even gotten her driver's license yet, because her parents kept putting off the mandated forty hours of supervised practice, and she was expected to make this decision that was going to rule the rest of her life. How weird was that?

They heard the bell ring, announcing the change for the last period of the day. Eve had to be all the way back at the south wing for history, an impossible distance even when she actually showed up for her PE class, instead of crouching and smoking in the woods. But the teachers were being extra lenient today. Between the end of school and the shooting, tardiness and cuts weren't going to draw too much attention.

She stood up, brushing the dirt from her jeans. What would it be like, she wondered, to cut class and meet a boy, instead of just smoking cigarettes with Val and Lila? She didn't want to give them up, but it would be nice to have their companionship *and* a boyfriend. A boy who really liked her, a boy who wouldn't think of her as the girl on the bus, who might not even know about that. Someone who looked like Peter Lasko, with his dark hair and green eyes. She hoped he was doing okay. He would probably go to the funeral, being Kat's former boyfriend and all. She wondered if he would sing again.

"Are either of you going to the memorial service?" she asked her friends.

"Sure," Val said. "It means missing the last three periods."

"We could say we're going, then just cut," Lila said.

Eve waited to see what Val would decide. The thing was, she wanted to go to the funeral, although she couldn't say why. It just seemed like one of the few all-school events where everyone was truly welcome, where everyone belonged. Unlike pep rallies, for example.

"That would be in bad taste," Val decreed. "If we say we're going to go, we should go. I'll get permission to drive us there, though, instead of going on the buses. Then we can hang out in Baltimore after. Who's going to complain?"

Eve thought of her dour father, who objected if she was even a minute late for supper, which they ate at six o'clock sharp. But it was Kat Hartigan's funeral. Her mother would explain to him that such a circumstance merited an exception.

Tuesday

23

Back when Lenhardt was coming up, he had a sergeant, Steve Waters, who was about as good a murder police as anyone he had ever known. Waters was unflappable, nothing got to him. Except for one suspect, who was brilliant in his stupidity. Although the guy's story was implausible, it wasn't impossible, and he stuck to it with unwavering conviction, refusing every opportunity to change it even a bit. Waters finally lost it, just lost it, screaming into the guy's face, then running out of the interrogation room and punching a Coke machine, accomplishing nothing but a broken hand.

It was a funny story — when it was happening to someone else.

Not so funny when the stubborn subject with the monotone voice was key to one's own case. Less funny when one considered she was a teenage girl. Josie Patel wasn't a genius. She wasn't even a particularly skilled liar. But two hours into his second interview with her, Lenhardt was more than ready to assault a vending machine. Whenever challenged on her inconsistencies, she simply said, "Well, that's the way I *remember* it. But it happened so fast."

"Tell me again. Tell me what you do remember."

And she did. She told it again and again and again, and she always told it the same way. Perri Kahn came into the bathroom where Josie and Kat were primping. "Why there?" Don't know, Kat said she wanted to go there. "Why?" She didn't say. Perri Kahn came in, shot Kat, shot Josie in the foot during a brief struggle, shot herself in the head.

"Was — is — Perri right-handed or left-handed?"

"Right-handed."

"Yet the injury is to your right foot."

She didn't jump in, the way some subjects might. Where an adult man or woman might feel obligated to explain or account, she offered nothing. She didn't have the nervous citizen's tendency to be helpful or the too-smart perp's compulsion to explain. She was, in fact, like a kid stuck on a teacher's question, a kid who just stared back, waiting for the teacher to provide the answer out of frustration.

"See, Perri Kahn was right-handed. She'd be more apt to shoot you in your *left* foot. And she's tall, which should have affected the trajectory. But your X-rays show a pretty straight entry, before the bullet glanced off this one bone here."

He held up the X-ray, and not for the first time. Josie inspected it with interest but said nothing.

Gloria Bustamante, never particularly patient, was beginning to boil over. "Are you suggesting my client shot herself in the foot? That's ridiculous. She has an athletic scholarship to the University of Maryland, College Park, which such an injury could void."

Lenhardt chose not to respond to Gloria's challenge, keeping his focus on Josie. Gloria had to be in the room, but nothing required him to acknowledge her.

"As you know, Josie, we took your blood today. We've also taken your fingerprints. Are those going to match any of the prints we found on the gun?"

"But I told you," Josie said, "I tried to grab the gun. I almost got it, too. So of course my fingerprints are on it."

"And you were shot while you and Perri struggled?"

"No. I tried to grab the gun. I almost got

it. She yanked it back, out of my reach. *Then* she shot me."

"So when the gun went off, your hand wasn't anywhere near it?"

Josie nodded, even as her lawyer smirked. Gloria knew it was a .22, so even if they had tested Josie, it wouldn't have mattered. They could never prove she had fired the gun, and she had a somewhat plausible explanation for why her finger-prints were on it. The only reason he had asked her to submit to a test was to see how panicky she would get at the sugges-tion. *Very,* in Lenhardt's opinion.

"Did you see Perri shoot herself?"

The girl nodded, her eyes beginning to fill with tears. She always misted up at this point in the story.

"Show me where she held the gun, Josie."

She started to shake her head, as if the scene were too graphic to confront in her memory, but then relented. "Here." She aimed at her own temple with an out-stretched index finger.

"Yet the bullet goes into her *cheek,* an upward angle."

Josie Patel nodded.

"You see, what you're saying doesn't match."

"It's how I remember it," she said. "I'm not saying my memory is perfect, though. I could be wrong about stuff. Ms. Cunningham once told us that about sixty percent of all eyewitness identifications are false."

"Ms. Cunningham?" Lenhardt echoed, even as his brain provided the information a beat late — *the fluffy little blonde.*

"She's a guidance counselor, but she also teaches a couple of classes on — well, I'm not sure what they're on, really. Language. Communication. I just did the mandatory sessions, but Perri did two independent studies with her."

This was the longest unbroken sentence the girl had uttered so far, and the only new piece of information. Worthless, but new.

"Tell me again, Josie. Tell me again."

And she did, in just the same way, in almost the exact same words. It was not that she was rehearsed, although there was a rote quality to her statements. It was more that she had a teenager's knack for stonewalling and the shrewdness not to overreach. If she had come in without a lawyer, Lenhardt knew he could have broken her down, told her made-up stories about Perri Kahn regaining consciousness and asking for Josie Patel's forgiveness. Or he could show her the letter, which was in fact from Perri Kahn, and bluff her, say they knew the "truth" to which Perri alluded. Heck, he'd use the old trick of pretending the photocopier was a lie detector machine, although that had lost some of its punch since it had been re-created on national television. Under Gloria Bustamante's eagle eyes, he didn't dare try such tricks.

"Josie, was there someone else there? In the stall?" He had asked this before, of course.

"No. It was just the three of us."

Her response, although also consistent, always seemed a fraction too quick, like someone slamming a door shut. Okay, he'd let that go for now. He had been promised fast results on the blood, so he'd pull her back in a day or two on that pretext. He thought about telling her that they thought a fourth girl might have been there, watching everything unfold from behind that locked stall door, but he didn't want Gloria to get that bit between her teeth. At this point rumors of a fourth girl only helped Perri Kahn's lawyer.

"Tell me again, Josie. Start to finish."

"Sergeant, please." Gloria was antsy, probably crazed for a cigarette. Or a drink, although she might have spiked her Mountain Dew with vodka. Too bad the girl didn't smoke. Nicotine deprivation had its merits in interrogation. "This is beginning to border on abusive. Besides, you promised us that if Josie came in to speak to you today, you'd make sure she had time to get to Kat's funeral."

"Well, I just don't feel comfortable hanging a charge on a comatose girl unless I feel ironclad about the details. And it would be just Perri, right? She did all this by herself?"

"Yes." This time there was a spontaneous note of surprise in the girl's voice, even resentment, as if she couldn't imagine why anyone would think she was a coconspirator. But that was the scenario that made the most sense to Lenhardt — two girls luring a third to the bathroom, setting her up. Maybe this Josie girl had started out thinking it was all a prank but didn't know how to admit she had been duped without being implicated. Maybe she was counting on the other girl dying and all this going away. It wasn't a bad bet.

Still, how to explain that blood trail that led away from the door, as if this one had locked it *after* the fact? Or that Perri Kahn's injury was consistent with being self-inflicted? If anything, the off-the-mark entry wound could have been the result of someone trying to grab the gun away from her. Only Josie Patel, by her testimony, couldn't do that, because she was lying on the floor with a bullet in her foot, writhing in pain. She had grabbed it earlier, to no avail.

"Josie, what is 'the truth'?"

"I'm telling you the truth."

"No, the truth that Perri wanted Kat to tell. What was that?"

She looked at her lawyer. "I don't know what you're talking about."

"You can go," he said. "For now."

The girl gathered her crutches. She used them with almost theatrical ease, but then, she was a gymnast, as Gloria kept reminding Lenhardt. A gymnast whose college scholarship was now on the line. "Who would jeopardize her admission to one of the state's best schools?" Gloria had asked repeatedly.

Someone who thought it was the only way to avoid a homicide charge, Lenhardt had answered, watching Josie Patel's eyes widen nervously. For one moment she had seemed tempted to speak, but she had restrained herself.

Now, as he watched her make her way to the door, he soaked in every detail. She was pretty, but more in a little-girl way than an overripe-teenager way, with the kind of face and figure that would keep her getting carded well into her twenties. She was wearing a short, full skirt and one of those odd, lacy tops. On a fuller-figured girl, it might have been a little sleazy, like those girl singers who cavorted on television, much to Lenhardt's horror, although he tried to refrain from commenting in front of his daughter. He didn't want to make that stuff more desirable by coming out against it. No, this girl looked fresh and sweet, the kind of girl you'd be proud to have as your daughter.

She wore only one shoe, of course — a pink suede slip-on, sort of like an athletic shoe, but not. Jessica had a similar pair, although he was sure there was some subtle distinction he was failing to make.

Only one shoe. That's what was missing from this little Cinderella story — footwear. Where were this girl's shoes? Why hadn't they been recovered at the scene? If you got shot in the foot, you should have a bloody shoe to show for it, right? He checked his notes. The girl said she had propped her injured foot on a knapsack, but she had never said anything about removing her shoes.

The girl caught his gaze.

"I was just wondering what brand those were," Lenhardt said, "because I think my daughter would like a pair."

"Pumas. You can get them at Hecht's."

"Hecht's." He nodded. "Good to know."

Infante, who had watched through the one-way glass, came in after she cleared the hallway. Of course, Gloria had known people were watching and had probably told her client as much. But Lenhardt had still thought the girl might be a better interview if she didn't feel outnumbered. He had wanted her to relax, maybe even get a little cocky and trip herself up.

"The shoes," he told Infante. "Why would she hide her shoes from us? How did she hide them?"

"A paramedic might have stolen them if they were really nice. I mean, if they steal jewelry, they'd steal shoes, too. Right?"

"But only if they weren't damaged. And if they weren't damaged . . . well, explain that. How does someone have the forethought to remove one's footwear before they're ruined by a gunshot?"

"I don't know," Infante lisped, his voice girlishly high. "I'm not sure. It happened so fast. That's the way I remember it."

Then, switching to his regular voice: "You know, the cell phones are missing, too. The Hartigans and the Kahns both confirmed that their daughters had phones on them, but they weren't at the scene. If she hid those with her shoes, she was one busy little girl before those paramedics arrived."

"The phones don't bug me so much. We can get records from the service providers. But the shoes — I sure would like to find them."

24

The lot in Loudon Cemetery was desirable, assuming such a term can ever be used for a burial site. Remote, but not too remote, near a line of willow trees. It looked especially nice on this June afternoon, banked by displays of yellow roses, pale and pastel as ordered, with rows of white folding chairs facing the freshly dug hole.

School secretary Anita Whitehead walked around these chairs, trying to pick out an appropriate spot. She preferred an aisle, of course, so she could slip out the second it ended and avoid the congestion along the cemetery's narrow drives, but the aisle seat in the last row seemed antisocial somehow. Perhaps two up? No, the far seat on the front row would be best, providing the access she needed without seeming presumptuous.

But as she settled herself in the less-than-comfortable chair, she was confronted by some undertaker type.

"We've been asked to reserve the seats for family and their closest friends, so if you could wait until —"

"I got here *early.*" Anita could see how it might be a problem if she had arrived late, expecting special treatment, but this was just the typical unfairness that Anita faced everywhere she went.

"I understand, but if you could just wait, miss, until everyone has arrived, and then we'll be able to accommodate you."

"I have a *condition,*" Anita said. "I can't be on my feet, especially on such a warm day."

"It's just that I have a list —" The undertaker, or funeral director, or whatever such people wanted to be called, was very creepy, in Anita's opinion. He was a normal-enough-looking fellow, but that was exactly what made him suspect to Anita. A funeral director should be pale and thin, ghostly-looking. This one was tanned and vigorous, with a broad chest and a gap between his front teeth. How did someone who worked with dead people get to be so healthy, not to mention cheerful? He was all wrong.

"Look, I'm just going to sit for now, and if you don't have enough places, you let me know, okay?" She settled herself with as much dignity as possible. She had no intention of moving, ever. She was on sick leave, after all, her nerves so frayed by the shooting that she might have to go on permanent disability. She had gone to a lot of trouble, driving all the way here from her house, and that was no small thing. Anita was surprised, disappointed even, that the Hartigans, so obviously wealthy, would bury one of theirs in this seedy neighborhood. She was pretty sure she had passed a drug corner or two on her way in, and some black boys had stared into her car at a stoplight. Nonchalantly, she had lifted her left elbow and propped her arm on the edge of her door, as if resting it there. That had given her a chance to lock the door, without hurting the boys' feelings. Better safe than sorry.

Wherever you go, there you are. The nonsense sentence jolted into Dale's consciousness as if it were another pothole along Frederick Road, whose neglected surface made even the funeral home's town car bounce and rock. It was a line from a film, although Dale wasn't sure which film, or if he had the wording exact. But he recognized it as stoner humor, hilarious if you were high. And

Dale had been high a lot in high school.

Then one day, when he and Glen were seniors, he had watched Glen make the most ungodly mix of melted chocolate, butter, raw eggs, and flour. "It's brownie mix," Glen had said, proffering the bowl. "You left out the sugar, Glen." "Oh. Yeah. I thought it tasted kind of bitter." Dale had sworn off pot from that day on, while Glen had pretty much majored in marijuana. He had probably smoked a bowl this very morning, judging by his eyes — and how Dale envied him for that. Maybe *that* would blunt the pain. Alcohol clearly didn't work, although he had given it every chance. Alcohol and Ambien and Tylenol PM, all worthless. He had even tossed down a couple of Percocet, left over from Susannah's dental surgery two years ago, but the painkillers were helpless in his body. They needed a literal inflammation, something they could dull and still.

"The old house," Glen said. They were passing a section of rowhouses with Tudor touches that had been intended to make them distinctive but only served to make them odd and cheap-looking. "We're going by the old house, Dad."

Susannah, always gratifyingly interested in Dale's past, made a point of craning her neck and looking at the house before it was out of sight, but Thornton Hartigan didn't even turn his head to the side.

"Those houses," he said, "were pieces of shit."

The Hartigans had lived here on Frederick Road in their leanest years, back when it was still unclear if Thornton's decision to start amassing property in north Baltimore County would accomplish anything more than his complete and total ruin. The place was tiny even by rowhouse standards, two bedrooms and a single bath. Dale and Glen had been literally on top of each other, in a rickety bunk bed, the kind that would now be banned by several federal and state regulatory agencies. The household air was thick with the smells of a family whose resources were stretched thin — onions, potatoes, bacon fat. "The wolf is at our door, Martha," Thornton had said one night, unaware that the boys were listening from the top of the stairs. The brothers had spent weeks trying to catch a glimpse of that elusive animal. Yet the little house was cozy — one of the advantages of a middle rowhouse, less light but more warmth — and Dale remembered those lean years as a happy time. Did children ever really know if their households are happy, or only if *they* are happy? Is there a difference? He thought his pretty stone farmhouse was one of the unhappiest places on earth during those last few years with Chloe, but Kat would have given anything to maintain the status quo.

Naturally Dale had thought quite a bit about whether it was an advantage for a kid to know hard times before being catapulted into good ones. Conventional wisdom held that it was better for children not to be given everything. Yet his own brother, Glen, who had been fifteen when their father finally hit, was as wrecked as any lifetime trust-funder, while Kat had always been sweet and modest. He was not romanticizing his daughter, Dale insisted to himself, as the limousine turned into Loudon Park. Kat had a natural goodness from the day she was born, a capacity for sharing and a marked lack of interest in material things. He liked to believe it was because he and Chloe, whatever their faults as people, had imparted to their daughter the sure message that they would take care of her, that her needs would always be paramount to them.

Of course, most parents think they're doing the same thing. Dale's dad probably credited his ways with instilling Dale's work ethic. It would never occur to him to ponder the fact that the son he had ignored at the best times, bullied at the worst, had turned out to be the successful one, while Glen, indulged and bailed out at every turn, was a mess. When Dale had tried to make this point to his father — and he had, in a roundabout way, a time or two in his twenties — he was treated to the Hartigan legend, as Dale thought of it. How Glen, as the second twin by three minutes, had briefly been deprived of oxygen, which meant his mere normalcy was an achievement to be celebrated. Dale wasn't even sure if this story were true, and his mother had always been tactfully vague on the subject. At any rate, it seemed to Dale that Glen had been given unconditional love, whereas he'd had to earn the love portioned out to him.

The result was that people respected Dale but they *loved* Glen, a chicken-or-the-egg conundrum, in Dale's opinion. Was Glen loved because he was charming, or was Glen charming because he had been heaped with so much selfless love from the day he was born? Dale would probably be a pretty collegial fellow, too, if he had been cosseted and cotton-wrapped the way Glen was.

Kat, in fact, was one of the few people who hadn't been beguiled by Glen's easy-going nature. Oh, she loved him — he was her uncle, after all, and he tried to be doting, although he seldom followed through on his best intentions. His big talk of trips or projects, such as keeping a horse for her on his acreage, tended to peter out pretty quickly. Kat had realized early on that Glen was not reliable, and it was the one thing Kat required in the people around her — constancy, dependability. This was the key difference between Chloe and Glen, kindred spirits in so many respects. Chloe, no matter how scattered and crazy she might be with Dale, was someone Kat could count on. Even in the wake of Kat's death, Chloe was meeting every expectation as a mother.

And so she was here, suitably dressed and behaving herself, holding Glen's hand. What was it like, holding hands with his brother? Did it feel like Dale's hand? Even when a twin was fraternal, even when you had spent most of your life making sure the physical resemblance was the only resemblance, it was hard not to think such thoughts.

Peter had thought he could skip the funeral, but when his parents got home

Monday night, his mother insisted they go as a family. His mom was a little too much in awe of the Hartigans, in Peter's opinion, but she had also been genuinely fond of Kat. She was one of the few people who thought Kat looked better before she lost weight, who was always trying to load her up with frijoles, plantains, and arroz con pollo.

Still, the Laskos hung back once they arrived, determined not to be presumptuous. Mrs. Hartigan motioned to them and insisted they take seats in the second row. His eyes on the ground, Peter stuck out his hand to the dark-haired man at her side, muttering, "I'm so sorry, Mr. Hartigan," only to have Kat's mom correct him. "This is Kat's uncle, Glen. Her father's over there, with the young redhead."

Mr. Hartigan, the real one, had given his ex-wife a sharp look — she hadn't tried to mute her voice in any way — then taken Peter's hand with a loose, quick shake that reminded Peter just how much contempt the man had for him. *Because I dated your daughter? Or because I stopped?* To this day he still wasn't sure what Dale Hartigan had wanted from him.

Dale noticed Peter's error with his

brother — but also saw how quickly he recovered from it. The young man had developed some poise in the last three years, but he still radiated that desperate like-me vibe. That same quality probably explained his success as an actor. It could be a useful quality, Dale thought, watching Josie Patel swing along on her crutches.

She was prettier than Dale remembered, but perhaps he simply hadn't seen her since she passed through her awkward stage. Josie had been, well, monkeyish as a child, small and tanned, her nose a little large for her face, her cheeks pinched. She was still tiny, but the cheeks had filled in and the nose had receded, and there was no denying that the light-colored eyes gave her face an almost mystical cast. She made her way carefully along the front row, only to find that every chair was filled.

Susannah, who had the usual forethought to include Josie among those who would be seated for this brief memorial service, looked puzzled. She craned her neck, searching for the impostor among them. "What's that?" she whispered, pointing to an impossibly large woman with a strange red rash visible on her bare arms and legs. The woman was at the end of the front row, on the other side of Chloe, who had engineered the seating so Glen, Thornton, and Susannah were between her and Dale.

"I haven't the faintest idea," he began, and that was all Susannah needed to confront the woman. He couldn't hear Susannah's whispered exhortations, but everyone was treated to the woman's vehement protests. Finally Susannah's gentle voice rose in frustration: "The girl is on crutches. She was Kat's best friend. You can't possibly expect her to stand."

The large woman moved, although not without quite a bit of muttering, and it seemed at first that she might leave the cemetery altogether, as if this would prove she was the wronged party. Instead she settled for forcing her way into the front row of those standing.

Josie swung toward her seat, murmuring "I'm sorry" over and over. But for what? For the little scene over the seat, which was not her fault? Or for Kat's death, which also was not her fault? Or was it? What the fuck did that one-line letter mean anyway? What truth did Perri want Kat to tell; what secret hung between them? Dale had sources inside the police department. He knew that Josie had been evasive with the detectives, obstructionist even. But why would Josie lie? Chloe insisted Josie had adored Kat.

Once Josie was settled in her seat, Chloe turned and held the girl's hands in hers. Even from the other end of the row, Dale could see she was gripping them much too tightly, and her voice was inappropriately loud for this somber setting.

"I always thought," she said, "that Kat would be safe with you."

If he had been next to Chloe, he would have whispered some reprimand out of the side of his mouth or put a restraining hand on his ex-wife's arms.

But Josie, tears in her eyes, merely said, "I did, too."

Sergeant Lenhardt and Detective Infante stood on the other side of the drive, apart from the crowd, but in a spot where they were clearly visible to Josie. It was a cheap trick, but cheap tricks can work. *We're watching you. We're going to talk to you again and again and again.* Mr. Patel, seated behind his daughter, glared at them but did not try to approach or chase them away. How could he?

"Are these high-school girls," Infante asked, "or strippers on a break from Northpoint Boulevard?"

"Pervert," Lenhardt said, but Infante had a point. The girls' idea of funeral wear was strangely provocative — short, tight black skirts with tops that hugged their bodies, leaving a strip of stomach bare. Perhaps it was a trick of memory, but he did not remember girls looking like this when he was in high school during an allegedly permissive time. The girls at Northern High School had worn low-slung jeans and gone braless, yet they had still been fresh, wholesome-looking even, with long, shiny hair and very little makeup. He would die before he let Jessica out of the house looking like this. Even as he made that vow, he knew he would be helpless to do anything about it. If this was how girls dressed, this was how girls dressed, and trying to force a kid to behave differently would be disastrous. Maybe, he tried telling himself, these getups were proof of just how innocent these girls were. Only a child who hadn't made the connection between her body and sex could parade herself this way.

Infante nudged him, directing his attention to a short, compact beauty with her breasts pushed up into an impressive swell in her scoop-neck black top, a big gold *E* nestled in her cleavage.

"I never wanted to be a necklace before," Infante said. "But I'm beginning to see the possibilities."

"Hey," Lenhardt said, more sharply than he had intended. He usually didn't mind Infante's on-the-prowl shtick, but these girls weren't even legal. "Keep your gaze fixed on the Patels. We're here to eyefuck, emphasis on *eye.*"

Eve was proud of her necklace, and she had borrowed a scoop-neck T-shirt from Lila to show it off, not realizing how much smaller Lila was across the chest. It had been hard deciding between a genuine gold letter and a super big one that was just plated. Val was the one who said she should go big because the necklace wouldn't stay in style long, so Eve should get the most bang for her buck, not waste her money on real gold.

"Just make sure you paint the back with clear fingernail polish," Val had advised. "Otherwise it'll turn your skin green."

It was funny how Val knew such things, because she didn't give a damn about style or fashion for her own self. But that was the great thing about Val: She didn't insist that everyone be like her. She just wanted the people around her to be honest, without affectations. It was okay by Val if you got caught up with wanting trendy stuff. Val wasn't completely immune to such desires herself; she was, like, in love with her iPod. But somehow she kept it in perspective. Lila could be a little bitchy and, if she liked a guy, crazy competitive. Val was always mellow, always accepting. The only thing she despised was hypocrites. Hypocrites and liars.

The problem was, *not* lying was harder than it sounded, especially for someone like Eve, who felt as if she had been set up to deceive people. When she had started liking boys — and Eve had started liking boys young, back in fifth grade — it had been inconceivable that she could speak of this fact to her parents. They were so old, for one thing, and so stiff. Not only could she not tell them how much she liked boys or how often she thought about them, she found herself taking it to the extreme, insisting she had no interest in them whatsoever. If she told her parents that she liked boys, she might then have to admit they didn't like her back.

It seemed to Eve that she told big lies only when she was trying to keep some part of herself hidden. She would start out with nothing more than a desire to conceal, to protect, and it somehow ended up being a lie. That's why she had to continue dodging Ms. Cunningham. She'd end up telling some enormous lie to protect her secret, and it would be just like last spring all over again. Of course, the weird part about last spring was that she had tried to tell the truth about the car accident, but everyone thought it was a lie, so it had the same effect. Even Val had cautioned her not to spread stories, told her she would not put up with a friend who was a gossip.

That was when Eve had first realized that the dead lived by different rules. Well, not lived — the dead being dead — but the reputations they left behind were definitely changed for the better. Eve wondered what kind of rep she would have if she should die.

Kat's crowd — mostly preps, although there were cheerleaders and jocks sprinkled among them, and even some drama geeks — were grouped at the front of those standing. Sniffling, holding each other, the girls presented a pretty tableau of grief. But Alexa couldn't help thinking they knew this, which undercut the effect in her mind. It was as if they were enacting a scene from a music video. *Pose, pose,*

*pose. This is what grief looks like. Hair
flip, clutch, hair flip.*

It worried Alexa, these unguarded waves
of hostility toward the girls she was com-
mitted to helping. But ten years out of high
school, she still had mixed feelings about
the popular kids. Because Alexa was pretty
and slender, the girls at Glendale had projected on her the mantle of a once popular
girl, and after a few token protests, she had
allowed that false impression to stand. She
should have been popular in high school.
She was pretty enough. She did well in her
studies without being a competitive grind.
But she simply did not have the money to
keep up with the upper-middle-class kids
who dominated her school. Part-time jobs
at the Gap and Banana Republic had
helped Alexa hold her own in terms of
clothes, but some things — a car, for instance — could not be faked in a single-
parent household where the child-support
checks seldom arrived. While her brother
was home, they had kept up appearances,
just barely. Once he left, the house had
rotted quietly around them. Today location
alone meant that the ugly old Cape Cod
was worth almost four hundred thousand
dollars, and Alexa had encouraged her
mother to sell it, buy a little condo, and

sock away the equity. But her mother refused to budge. It was as if she still expected Alexa's father to show up for the
scolding she had never been able to give
him. Alexa wasn't even sure if her father
was alive, although she sometimes studied
those lists of unclaimed property. It would
be so like him to die without a will, failing
to care for his children in his death as he'd
failed to care for them in life.

Do you realize Kat is dead? she wanted
to scream at the girls. (The boys, sullen
and uncommunicative, were less appalling
to her.) *Dead because of you, because of
the inadequacies bred in girls like Perri,
who are driven insane by the no-win
games you play. You killed Kat.*

But she was being ridiculous, venting her
anger toward Barbara on these innocent
girls. Just an hour before she was to leave
for the funeral, Barbara had convened yet
another meeting, one for Perri's teachers.
They had been told, in no uncertain terms,
to sit on Perri's grades. The logic, if one
could call Barbara's twisted thinking logic,
was that Perri's diploma couldn't be
awarded if her records were incomplete.
And it turned out that the Kahns were
keen for their daughter's name to be called
from the stage Thursday night, arguing

that she was not under indictment, so how could her diploma be withheld? Meanwhile Dale Hartigan was just as intent for Perri's name to go unspoken, and Barbara had tended to do things Dale Hartigan's way even before he had the moral advantage of a dead child.

"You know how it is when parents take notions about graduation into their heads," Barbara had told Perri's teachers. "We've already had to forgo the traditional valedictorian address because — well, you know how insane it got. So the easiest thing to do is just say she had incompletes in a subject or two. Surely she must have owed some of you work."

Only it turned out she hadn't — except to Alexa and the trig teacher, Maureen Downey, who had given seniors a take-home. Maureen couldn't remember if Perri had turned it in or not, but she was happy to obey Barbara's orders even if she did find the test among her papers. Alexa, however, wanted no part of it.

"It's a cover-up," she began, only to be shushed by Barbara. Literally shushed, a finger held to her lips, as if Alexa were some troublesome child.

"Think of it this way," the principal said. "Perri violated school policy by bringing a firearm onto school property. That's automatic expulsion. So even if she did submit those final papers to you both, she would be barred from the ceremony."

"But it still hasn't been established that Perri brought the gun to school," Alexa had said, feeling dangerously close to tears. The other teachers seemed embarrassed for her, except for Ted Gifford, who appeared just as upset.

"Did she turn in her work to you?"

"I'm not sure." Alexa still had not gone through all her final papers, given that the teachers had until the end of the day Wednesday to submit seniors' grades.

"Then it's moot anyway. She's shy two credits. Even under normal circumstances, she wouldn't have walked."

She *had* seen Perri's final paper, Alexa decided now. Hadn't it been in her box that Friday morning? She tried to re-create the scene in her mind, but those moments of normalcy could not be brought back. She had been sorting papers, reading Barbara's memo — and then Anita had started to scream.

Anita, who was here at the funeral, despite being out of work on a doctor's note. The gall, as Alexa's mother would say. The unmitigated gall.

★ ★ ★

Peter pulled at his collar. He hadn't worn a tie, offstage, for a long, long time, and the day was vicious hot. He was such a bonehead, lurching at Kat's uncle that way, but the resemblance was pretty strong and he hadn't seen Mr. Hartigan for almost three years. Peter had spent far more time with Mrs. Hartigan, who honestly liked him, and the feeling was pretty mutual. A hot mom, a total MILF. Oh, shit, that was probably the kind of thought that got you struck by lightning, standing at your ex-girlfriend's grave and thinking about how sexy her mom was. *I didn't mean it,* he assured God. *It was just an observation.* Besides, anyone could see that Kat's mom was appealing. Mr. Hartigan's girlfriend was nice, too, but Peter preferred Mrs. Hartigan. Her eyes had that little downward droop, so sad and sexy, and her hair was always slipping out of this semi-topknot she wore. There was something about Mrs. Hartigan that made it very easy to imagine her naked, as if her clothes would give way as easily as her hair, sliding to the floor, and there she would be. No, wait, this was really wrong. He had to stop thinking like this. Listen to the minister. Focus on the words. "We" . . . "Kat" . . .

"special" . . . "extraordinary" . . . "before her time."

Bit by bit the words assembled themselves into sentences, and Peter willed himself into an appropriate state of grieving.

Josie stole a quick glance over her shoulder, curious to see who had shown up. Peter Lasko was beet red — it looked almost like sunburn, but she had seen him just yesterday at the assembly and he hadn't been red then. One nice thing about her darker skin — it was very hard to detect a blush. When Josie was nervous or embarrassed, her cheeks flared prettily, two spots of pink on the bone, perfect as a painted doll's, but only her parents recognized her color as embarrassment or nervousness. The police officers, for example, hadn't noticed she was blushing at all, especially when they kept asking her about that stupid Tampax.

Josie could tell by the heat in her face that she was blushing now, in her own way. Why had she said that thing to Mrs. Hartigan? Had anyone overheard? When her lawyer had told her that the cops wanted her cell phone to review her text messages from the day of the shooting, Josie had kept calm, handing over her phone as if she didn't think it was any big deal — and it wasn't. But that meant they were going to look for Kat's and Perri's phones, too. What if they found them? And why had that cop been asking about her Pumas? She had thought she could keep her sandals, wear them again, but maybe not. She shouldn't have improvised. Definitely not her strong suit. She should have stuck to the plan.

She had never missed Kat or Perri more. Kat would have soothed her, told her it was all going to be all right, while Perri would have had a strategy to deal with those police officers, something far more inventive than just droning "I don't know" or "I don't remember" over and over. She felt so lost without them.

"Ashes to ashes," the minister said, sprinkling dirt on Kat's casket. "Dust to dust." On the second "ashes," Anita Whitehead launched herself down the path, eager to get to her car before anyone else, not caring if her sandals sounded flat and loud on the asphalt path. She wasn't going to get stuck in some traffic jam getting out of here. She had put herself out enough for these people. Just watch her get carjacked in this horrible neighborhood, and then wouldn't they be sorry?

She hated to say, she really did, but last year's funeral was so much better.

eleventh grade

25

In the spring of the girls' junior year, three soccer players had been killed in a one-car accident on Old Town Road. The boys had all been stars on the team, which had made it to regionals that year, and the two juniors, Seth Raskin and Chip Vasilarakis, were their longtime classmates, going all the way back to first grade — third grade for Josie, of course. The third was Seth's little brother, Kenny, who was not as fortunate in his looks. The older brother's enigmatic grin became a goofy, overtoothed leer in Kenny's face, the long, lean body compacted into a much shorter frame, so Kenny was sometimes called "Munchkin" or even "Runtkin."

But Kenny had been so good-natured and quick to laugh at himself that he was the most popular of the three. The news that he was behind the wheel of the Raskins' SUV, playing the part of designated driver when he had only a provisional license, had been especially hard on everyone in Glendale. Parents such as Josie's, assuming that their children were safely out of earshot, said as much. They would actually feel better if Kenny had been drunk, the Patels agreed, but blood tests made it clear that he'd had only a trace of alcohol in his system, whereas Seth and Chip had been just barely over the legal limit. But they also had failed to fasten their seat belts, so they were thrown from the Cadillac Escalade when it rolled.

"I know people misuse the term 'irony' all the time," Josie's mother had told her dad, making the mistake of thinking that Josie was too absorbed in the family room computer to pay attention to the adult conversation on the other side of the kitchen counter. "But this is *truly* ironic. Those boys might still be alive if one of the more experienced drivers had been behind the wheel. They were drunker, but they were probably better drivers. Kenny lost control on a curve, overcorrected, and flipped the SUV."

"Maybe we should slow down with Josie," her father said. "She needs forty hours of on-road practice before she gets her license. We could put it off until next spring. And I really think the county ought to rethink the Senior Ramble. All those

420

new drivers on the roads at one time . . ."

"That's not *fair,*" Josie had protested, turning away from her mother's computer, where she and Kat had been IM'ing about the tragedy. "It's bad enough that I'm the last one to get my license because I have an August birthday. I have to get my driver's license this summer. How else am I supposed to get anywhere? Do you want to drive me everywhere forever?"

"Only until you're fifty," her father had said, coming over and ruffling her short curls.

"If we had stayed in the city," her mother said, "this wouldn't be as much of an issue."

"Yeah, then all we'd have to worry about is whether Josie was going to be stabbed in the girls' room."

Given all the attention demanded by the three deaths, it was perhaps understandable that few Glendale parents noticed, much less cared, that there had been an incident of vandalism on a local farm the same weekend. Vandalism was, unfortunately, all too common in this part of the county. The stock ponds on farmland were a longtime lure. But this had gone far beyond mere mischief. Three pigs had been poisoned at the home of Cyrus Snyder.

Under different circumstances such a crime might have been the talk of the north county. But the Glendale families bristled at the idea that the death of three boys should be mentioned in the same breath as the slaughter of three pigs. It was disrespectful to two families who had suffered a real loss.

Then an unthinkable rumor began, and the two stories merged in a way that no one could have predicted. Josie heard it first at a cheerleading practice that Kat had missed because she was being tutored for the AP tests. As soon as she got home, she IM'ed Kat, eager to be the first to tell her the latest gossip.

J: have u heard?

K: ?

J: S, C and K = incident at Snyder farm. Blood on clothes not theirs. May be PIG blood.

K: NO.

J: Yes.

K: That's just stupid gossip. Don't spread it. U know what Ms. Cunningham says.

J: Perri calls her Ms. Cunnilingus. Cuz she's all about the mouth.

K: :O! Gross!

J: Audrey sez her mom heard from someone at school.

K: Audrey is an idiot. Gotta go — c u later.

Later Josie remembered that Kat had dated Seth once or twice, back in sophomore year, her rebound relationship after Peter Lasko. Like most of the boys Kat dated since that summer with Peter, Seth had ended up being more of a friend, but a devoted one. Josie had pretended to like him, because life was easier that way. It didn't pay to be too obviously at war with any of the jocks. But Seth had always creeped her out. Where other girls saw his silent style as cool — still waters running deep — Josie had sensed a real meanness in him. And everyone knew Chip was a thug.

But Kenny — well, Kenny had always reminded her of herself, and not just because they were both short. His energy, his bounciness, his clownishness, were not unlike hers. He was the kind of boy who tried hard to please others. In the same situation, if Kat had been drinking — or Perri, although Perri was uninterested in alcohol, perhaps because her parents had given her permission to drink as long as she promised to call them should she ever need a ride — there was no doubt in Josie's mind that she would take the wheel.

The rumors about the accident continued to whip through Glendale with the same hit-or-miss velocity of the breezes that cut through the courtyard at the high school. Everyone's information seemed to be fourth- or fifth-hand; each new piece of gossip had the life span of a soap bubble. People did not seem to care if the boys had really done what they were suspected of doing. Their primary concern was whether it was fair to pursue such an inquiry in the wake of their deaths. People were people and pigs were pigs; their lives should not be equated in any way.

The gossip spun 'round and 'round like a child in a tantrum, reckless, indifferent to its own strength. The Snyders wanted an investigation. The Glendale families wanted the controversy buried with the boys. The matter was resolved in an unexpected way when an anonymous benefactor stepped in and made restitution to Cyrus Snyder. The police dropped the inquiry — after all, there was no one to charge, and the murder of a pig, unlike the murder of a person, was not a statistic that demanded a clearance. In the end no one in Glendale really knew if the boys' clothes had been tested for the presence of nonhuman blood, as rumor had it. Or if a bag of poison had been recovered from the wreckage of the car. It probably wasn't true either that Kenny Raskin, dying slowly behind the wheel of his overturned SUV, had attempted to make a full confession to the firefighters attempting to extract him. His injuries had been much too severe for him to speak.

Once everything settled down, Alexa Cunningham tried to use the tragedy as a learning exercise, explaining to her students that spreading such rumors was irresponsible and cruel, that people could even be sued for making false allegations about private citizens.

"In your history class," she had told her girls, "you are taught the difference between primary and secondary sources. In the media there are distinctions among knowing something first-, second-, and third-hand. Primary, or firsthand, refers to things you have observed. The moment you rely on someone else's account of an event, no matter how authoritative, you open yourself up to errors. Even in retelling the details of an event that you have seen, you may make mistakes, large or small. Memory is imperfect."

She told them about the fallibility of eye-witnesses in criminal cases, reading from a piece in the *New Yorker*. She put them through an exercise, asking half of the students to leave the room while the others watched Ms. Cunningham and the history teacher, Mr. Nathanson, act out a skit. The other students were then summoned back to the room and paired with those who had seen the skit. Based on the retelling, they had to write short reports about what happened.

"It's like Telephone," Ms. Cunningham had concluded after sharing some of the funnier errors with the students. "Only it's not a harmless game. Misinformation can ruin a person's life."

A girl's voice called from the back of the room, "But what if a story is true? Can someone sue you for telling the truth?"

A few girls gasped, but it was a fake shock, a form of mockery. The girl who had asked the question was Eve Muhly, and everyone knew that the stories about *her* were true. Who was she going to sue, when sixty other sophomores had seen exactly what she did?

"The point of this exercise is just how hard it is to know the truth of anything. If you don't have firsthand information from primary sources, you shouldn't gossip about it."

"What if you talked to the victim?" Eve persisted. "Because I did."

"I didn't know," Ms. Cunningham said, "that you were a pig whisperer, Eve."

Everyone laughed, and Ms. Cunningham looked uncomfortable at the success of her joke, clearly aware that she had been less than teacherlike in her demeanor. But Eve didn't seem to be the least bit perturbed.

"I mean the Snyder family. We live next to them. My dad went over there after he heard what happened. Would my dad count as a firsthand source?"

"No, he would be secondhand, unless he told you about something he observed directly, not what Mr. Snyder told him. But really, Eve, the point is not to talk anymore about this horrible incident, the point is —"

"My dad saw it. So it's firsthand. He saw the letter with his own eyes."

"Eve —"

"They used blood to write a note. It said, 'We're coming for your pig daughter this summer.' "

This gasp was real. This information was new, and quite provocative. Binnie Snyder was not as pink and red-eyed as she had been in grade school, but she was still an odd girl with carroty hair, a girl so advanced in mathematics that she took extra classes at Johns Hopkins. When she spoke in class — and she spoke often — her voice was too loud and strangely inflected. And she still had a way of squinching up her face when thinking hard. "Pig" would have been unkind, but not altogether untrue.

"I think," Ms. Cunningham said, "that we're getting off topic."

Josie, who was there for the session, could not wait to tell Kat and Perri about this development. She raced to find them as soon as class was over, risking a tardy slip for English. She reasoned that it was okay to tell Kat about Eve's information because she wasn't saying it was Seth, Chip, and Kenny, whose guilt could not be established. The point was that the perpetrators, whoever they were, were so much more evil than anyone had realized.

But Kat had shook her head, refusing to believe the story even in its generalities.

"Eve Muhly is a slut," she said, shocking Josie, who had never heard Kat speak so cruelly of anyone. "And a liar. Everyone knows that. She's just making stuff up to get back at the people who talked about *her.*"

"Don't use 'slut' just to criticize some girl you don't like," Perri said, her voice a dead-on imitation of Ms. Cunningham's. She switched to her real voice. "Seriously, if anyone is a slut in this scenario, it's Chip. He went after girls the same way he scored goals in soccer. But everyone thought he was cool, whereas Eve gets in trouble for giving one blow job."

"He's *dead*," Kat protested.

"And when he was alive, he wasn't very nice. People don't become something other than what they were just because they had the misfortune to die."

"Okay, Chip wasn't the greatest guy. But Seth was our *friend*," Kat said. "And everyone loved Kenny. We've known them both since we were five years old, Perri."

That gap, seldom alluded to, always made Josie feel a twinge of jealousy and insignificance. She hated being reminded of Kat and Perri's longer history, the three-year difference she could never make up. The three could be friends for eighty years, and yet Kat and Perri would then be friends for eighty-three.

"But what if they really did it?" Perri persisted. "How would you feel about them then?"

"I'm not going to speculate about

someone who's dead."

"Why not?"

"It's mean, it's harmful."

"To whom? They're dead and it's not like their parents are standing here."

Josie had watched them, anxious, filled with regret that she had brought them what she considered nothing more than a juicy story, only to start this near fight. Ms. Cunningham was right about the destructive power of gossip.

Kat and Perri glared at each other. It all seemed so much angrier, so much more personal, than it had any right to be. But Kat had no talent for anger, and she broke first.

"I can't be sure of anything. I don't know, and you don't know, and Eve Muhly *definitely* doesn't know. She was, like, borderline retarded when we were kids, remember? I can't believe you're taking her side."

"I'm not. I'm just being open-minded. There are *infinite* possibilities here."

"If someone said anything horrible about you or Josie, accused you of doing something disgusting, wouldn't you want me to defend you?"

Josie waited, as curious about this answer as Kat.

"It depends," Perri said. "What if I really did it?"

Part Five

there won't be trumpets

Wednesday

26

Infante liked to say he could smell crazy on a woman — the better to run right toward it. But even Infante seemed skittish around the gorgeous redhead who had shown up at headquarters this morning offering her full cooperation in the Hartigan case. Yet thirty minutes into the conversation, she had managed not to answer a single direct question. *This horse has led herself to water,* Lenhardt thought in exasperation, *but she still doesn't want to drink.*

The woman was Michael Delacorte — estranged wife, registered owner of a murder weapon, Perri Kahn's former employer. So far she had explained how she came to marry Stewart Delacorte (much too quickly), and the travails of their two-year-old son (rare genetic disorder), which had helped her focus, after much searching (yoga, Buddhism, ceramics) for meaning in her life. The epiphany that she needed to leave her husband arrived, coincidentally, the same week as the news of the SEC investigation into his business affairs.

"I realize now that I was put here to care for my son, that my purpose in life was right there in front of me," she said, smacking the table so forcefully that her tennis bracelet slid up and down her skinny forearm each time her palm landed. Lenhardt had never understood the origin of that name, tennis bracelet, but he knew that his wife would like one. "Oh, you have no idea how wonderful it is to realize that one's life has true *meaning*."

Mrs. Delacorte smacked her hands a few more times, and Infante twitched, just a little, as each blow landed. She had a cat's face, a dancer's body, and, by all appearances, a plastic surgeon's breasts, high and molded. Lenhardt prided himself on being able to tell. His wife had explained it to him one day, how the artificial ones always pointed straight ahead.

"About Perri Kahn," he began, and it was far from the first time that he had tried to introduce the girl's name into the conversation. But Mrs. Delacorte was not interested in approaching anything that might be called a point.

"Yes, exactly. Exactly."

"Exactly?" Infante seemed to be echoing

a word here and there, just to keep himself alert.

"You see, before I really understood my situation, before I accepted the fact that this was part of a higher plan, what my real calling was, Perri used to baby-sit for me every Thursday. I was in denial. I felt I just couldn't survive if I didn't have a day, once a week, where I knew I was going to get out of the house. I mean, I had a nanny, of course, but the nanny had Thursdays off, and I just needed a day that was all for me."

Lenhardt tried to digest this concept, a woman with full-time help who needed part-time help so she wouldn't feel trapped. Well, rich people had different expectations, he told himself, although he would bet anything that Mrs. Delacorte hadn't been rich before she met her husband.

"In May I finally saw that I had to leave. I was very aboveboard about it. I told Stewart that I wanted out, that I wouldn't seek anything more than was fair, under the law. Although, of course, support would have to be calculated differently with a special-needs child. I'm going to need help as long as he —" Her breath caught. "As long as he lives."

Lenhardt's heart softened toward the woman, silly and ditzy and spoiled as she was. She had a child with a fatal condition. She had earned her craziness.

"About the gun?" he asked, reasoning it was a kindness to distract her from what had to be a painful subject. "Did you know it was missing?"

"That's what I've been trying to explain to you — I left earlier than I planned *because* I noticed it was missing, and I assumed Stewart had taken it. I was terrified. I thought he was going to kill me as I slept. That's why I had to get out so quickly."

"But you never asked him directly if he had taken the gun?"

"No. I just plotted my escape." She gave a strange little laugh, like one that an actress in an old-fashioned radio play might have used. "I mean, I had been thinking about leaving for a while, but when my gun disappeared, I knew I had to get out sooner rather than later. I found a new place for the baby and me, then hired a moving crew that could get me packed and out in twelve hours." She laughed in the same fashion. "I guess there were some advantages to the hours he worked after all."

"Back to the gun — you noticed it missing in May, but you never asked your husband about it."

"No."

"Did you mention it to anyone?"

"No."

"And was Perri Kahn still working for you when the gun disappeared?"

"I don't know when the gun disappeared. I only know I *noticed* that it was gone in mid-May, when I started packing and I couldn't find it."

Great, now she was suddenly Ms. Precise. Lenhardt pictured her in front of a grand jury, dithering for two hours and then taking pains to make clear how hard it was to know exactly when the gun had gone missing.

"You said you realized the gun was gone and started packing to leave. Then you said you were packing to leave, and it was only then that you realized it was gone."

"Same difference."

Actually, the two things weren't the same at all, but Lenhardt decided to drop the subject, for now.

"How long did Perri Kahn work for you?"

"She started last fall and continued through mid-May, when I moved out. But until then she came every week. She was reliable for a high-school girl."

This was a promising detail. Juries did not necessarily reject coincidence. In fact, they were quite happy to draw inferences from mere opportunity. Perri Kahn had worked in a home where a gun went missing, and that gun was later used in the commission of a crime where Perri Kahn was present, so it was logical to assume that Perri Kahn had taken the gun and used it. But a good defense attorney could make a person doubt that logic.

"You see, Mrs. Delacorte —"

"Michael, please! I hate that name. I can't wait to be rid of it. I hate anything that reminds me of him. Except for Malcolm, of course. But Malcolm doesn't remind me of his father."

"Michael, sure." Lenhardt wondered again at the parents who gave a newborn girl that name. It was okay, since she had turned out gorgeous. But what if she had been broad-shouldered and hulking? Then the name would have been a death sentence. "What you've told us is a help. But it's better if we can prove that Perri at least was aware of your gun. Did you ever mention it to her? Show it to her?"

"No, no, no, *no*."

Infante had slid down in his chair, his posture so bad that his chin was almost on the table. Lenhardt realized that his own shoulders were hunched and rounded, and it was only 10:00 a.m. Mrs. Delacorte — Michael — was exhausting, a reminder of the old adage that no matter how beautiful a woman was, someone, somewhere, was tired of her.

"So you can't help us link Perri to your gun?"

"Oh, no. *That* I can definitely do." She pulled a slender silver rectangle from her purse. "About ten days ago, I found this."

"It's a camera," Infante said. Lenhardt had thought it was a cigarette case.

"I know that. But look at the photos."

Infante, the more technologically inclined of the two of them, took the camera and began scrolling through the display. "Baby in high chair. Baby at zoo. Baby at zoo."

"Oh, I forgot there were some photographs of Malcolm there."

Lenhardt looked over Infante's shoulder. The boy was huge, plump and pink-cheeked and smiling. If Lenhardt didn't know otherwise, he would have assumed he was freakishly healthy, not a child whose very DNA was wired against him.

"Baby, baby — *whoa!*"

It was a photograph of a thin, dark-haired girl, wearing an emerald green bra and panties while holding a gun, by all appearances the same .22 recovered at the scene.

"Perri," Mrs. Delacorte said. "In *my* underwear."

"Who took these photos?"

"Now, that," she said, "is the ten-million-dollar question."

Lenhardt almost literally braced himself on the table between them. He hadn't liked Delacorte, but he hadn't picked up a pervert vibe from the guy. Okay, the girl was eighteen, technically legal, not pedophile stuff, but it still disgusted him. Maybe Jessica would be better off getting a mall job when she was old enough to work. Even if the father of the house wasn't some sicko, Lenhardt wasn't sure he wanted Jessica free to roam another household. Look what this one girl had found — lingerie, a digital camera, a gun. And that's just what they knew so far. There could have been more. Unlocked liquor cabinets, drugs, legal or not. How could he control for that? Lenhardt's wife didn't know it, but before he allowed Jessica to go on sleepovers, he ran the parents through all the state and national criminal checks.

"So enlighten us," Lenhardt said. "Because we don't have ten million dollars, and we don't have all the time in the world."

"Maybe my husband didn't always work late. Maybe he sneaked home early on some Thursday afternoons."

"Maybe?"

"I mean, I can't prove anything, which is utterly, utterly unfortunate," Mrs. Delacorte continued. "You see, with a digital camera, there's just no way to establish what my lawyer calls 'provenance.' Date and time — yes. This photo was taken on May third. But can I prove who clicked the shutter? No."

"What?" Infante said, although he knew full well what the woman meant. He was just having trouble catching up, now that she was finally on topic.

"There's no way to prove who took the photos. It's my camera, after all. Besides, digital photos can be altered. They were of no use to my lawyer."

"But your husband —"

"Oh, he would just deny everything. I haven't even bothered to show this to him. The only person who can tell us what happened is Perri, and she's probably going to die, which is too bad."

"Too bad that she might die or too bad

that she can't talk?"

"Why, both, of course."

Had the husband's surprise about the gun and his ignorance about the baby-sitter been genuine? Lenhardt thought so at the time. In fact, the guy had seemed unnerved to learn that his wife had a weapon, and now that Lenhardt had met her, he could see his point. Discovering in hindsight that you had dared to close your eyes when this lunatic had a gun at hand was no small thing.

"Does it have a timer?" Infante asked of the camera, turning it around and examining it. "Can it be set so someone can take a photo of herself?"

"I'm not big on reading instructions," Mrs. Delacorte said airily. That must be one of the perquisites of beauty, Lenhardt thought, not reading instructions because someone else would do such things for you — read your instructions, carry your packages, waive your speeding tickets, assemble your furniture. Then again, Mrs. Delacorte probably didn't have the kind of furniture that needed to be assembled. At least, not during her marriage to Mr. Delacorte.

"You said you found this ten days ago. The shooting happened *five* days ago."

"Ten days, five days, whatever." She

didn't get the point he was making, didn't get it at all. "I needed to consult my lawyer, of course. He's the one who told me it would be impossible to prove that Stewart took them, so we shouldn't show it to Stewart's lawyer."

"I'm just not sure," Lenhardt said, "why *that* was your primary concern. You knew about the shooting, right? And that your old baby-sitter was involved? Didn't you think the police would want to know you had a dated, timed photograph of her with the gun that she apparently used?"

"Well . . . there are liability issues. Right?" She sounded like someone guessing on a multiple-choice test, throwing out a term she had heard but not quite understood. "I mean, yes, I found the photo, but I didn't see any urgency."

"The law requires that you report a stolen firearm ASAP. You had a photo of an eighteen-year-old girl posing with your gun, a gun you knew had been missing for several weeks. If you'd come in here last week instead of today —"

"But I couldn't know, from a photo, what she planned to do. It was taken in my home — I recognize the maple drawers of my walk-in closet — so I don't even know for a fact that she *took* the gun. I thought she was just acting, playing a part. Acting for someone else's benefit, don't you think? She probably meant to erase it and forgot, or didn't realize there was one photo left on the camera."

"We don't sit here and make up stuff that might be true," Lenhardt said, angry and out of patience. "We try to establish what is factual, what really happened."

"What if my husband asked Perri to do it? I saw that on a *Law & Order* once." The way this woman's brain worked, it was like those science fiction movies Jason loved so much, where people moved in defiance of gravity. Up, down, sideways.

"Excuse me?"

"A man was having an affair with his stepdaughter, and he convinced her to shoot her own mother. Only maybe . . . I think there was another twist, and it turned out it was the girl's idea. Or, no, that was the one about the private school —"

"Mrs. Delacorte, we've never even established that your husband knew the Kahn girl, much less the victim. He couldn't even pick Perri's name out of a list or describe her to us."

"He knew Dale Hartigan."

But Delacorte had readily admitted as

446

much to Lenhardt.

"I know. I talked to your husband Sunday."

Her worried look told him that she hadn't known that. "You can't believe a word he says. He's the most horrible liar."

"Be that as it may, to your knowledge, your husband doesn't know the victim, has a cordial relationship with her father — or did, at least, before this happened — and may never have even spoken to your babysitter. Meanwhile this is your digital camera, your gun."

"Your underwear," Infante put in. "I mean — that's what you said."

Mrs. Delacorte nodded, as if she had been complimented. "Yes. And I'm just trying to be helpful. You are free to use this information in any way you deem necessary if it will help you in your investigation of this horrible tragedy. Give it to the state's attorney, even release it to the press."

Release it to the press? To what purpose? To what publication? Lenhardt finally understood why this good citizen had come forward.

"And, maybe, it would help you, too, to have this photo in circulation? I mean, it's not admissible in your divorce, but if it were part of a homicide investigation, someone might leak it to the *Beacon-Light*. What can't be proven in court can still be potent in a divorce."

She lifted her chin, a grand-lady mannerism that didn't really suit her. "I have nothing to be ashamed of."

"But you hope that your husband does, even if you can't prove it. Me, I'm now more convinced than ever that your husband doesn't know anything about this. How do we know that *you* didn't take this photo, just to cause all this trouble? Took the photo, then gave Perri Kahn the gun, as a parting gift, to do with as she pleased?"

"That's just ridiculous. I'm not exactly inclined that way." Toward women? Toward blackmail? Toward arming adolescents? Lenhardt waited, but Mrs. Delacorte didn't elaborate. Instead she rose and held out her hand for the camera, but Infante shook his head, closing his fist around it. She left the room with the same rushed flutter with which she had arrived.

"Tempting," Lenhardt said.

"Her?"

"No, erasing this photo just to get back at her. But at least we have it for now and the time stamp is a good break for us."

"I'm sure she's downloaded a few versions for her own files, not to mention her lawyer's. Someone took it, by the way. The composition is too sure for it to be a set-and-run-around."

"You sound as if you have some experience in the field."

Infante smiled. "Digital technology has changed the world. Why do you think all these girls keep getting caught doing stupid shit on home video? It's the false sense of security created by an image that can be instantly wiped out. They forget the flip side — that it can just as easily be uploaded to the Internet. Hell, you can send photos like this on a cell phone now."

"So does it matter?"

"Only in a long-term relationship. Because then there are all sorts of trust issues if other people see it."

"No, I mean, does the *photo* matter? Should we care who took it? If there's a person on the other side of the camera, then there's someone who knew she had access to a gun. All the research says a school shooter almost always tells someone before bringing a gun to school. If she vamped with the gun in front of someone, maybe she also told her photographer what she was thinking. Maybe she had an *accomplice*."

"The Patel girl," Infante said, taking the camera from him. "Only if this was some sort of conspiracy between them, how does Perri Kahn end up near death in Shock Trauma while Josie Patel is hobbling around with an injury that could sideline her scholarship?"

"Some sort of bizarre suicide pact?" But Lenhardt had never heard of two girls, much less three, planning such a thing. A girl and a boy, yes. But two girls with a handgun — very strange.

Infante held the photo out at arm's length, then shook his head.

"What?"

"She's got no shape at all. What a waste of underwear."

Lenhardt considered the way men would start judging his daughter, the way they probably did already, young as she was. He thought of boys in schoolrooms, ranking girls, noticing which ones were developing and which ones weren't — and punishing them all. He envisioned men watching his daughter walk down the street in a few years, reducing her to her parts. He thought of the creeps who got excited looking at little kids, guys who would get off at the sight of Malcolm Delacorte, the monster baby, taking a bath. The night had

450

a thousand eyes, as the old song had it. Somewhere — at church, on an athletic field, in a shopping mall — his daughter had already been assessed by someone. Assessed and found wanting.

Or, worse yet, found desirable.

"You're such an *asshole*, Infante."

27

In the thirty-five years since Thornton Hartigan had first fixed his gaze on the farms and undeveloped acres that would become Glendale, civilization had marched toward the area just as he had prophesied. Roads were wider and smoother. Several large grocery chains now vied for customers, and there were two Starbucks. The nearest mall, after a flirtation with bankruptcy, was retooling itself as an upscale shopping destination. Just adjacent there was a multiplex with stadium seating and enough screens to allow the occasional art film to lose money.

But decent restaurants continued to elude this part of the valley. The usual suspects — the fried-cheese franchises, as Dale thought of them — were represented. But the only high-end places were old-fashioned relics, throwbacks to a day when people took Sunday drives in order to stuff themselves on crab imperial. When Dale had lived here, the lack of good restaurants had not bothered him so much, but after four years in the city, when Baltimore was suddenly enjoying a mild culinary renaissance, he was spoiled. Dale regretted every meal he was forced to consume in Glendale. And given that he had come out every week, sometimes twice a week, for dinner with Kat, he had logged more than his share of time at Applebee's and Chili's and Bertucci's. He knew it was decadent, caring so much about food. An educated palate actually increased one's ratio of disappointments, for as one grew more sophisticated, fewer meals met one's expectations. Still, Dale could not bear eating crap.

Which was how he rationalized making Peter Lasko come to meet him in the city for breakfast at the Blue Moon Café in Fells Point, one of Dale's favorites. The fare was wonderful, old-fashioned comfort food with a twist. But Dale also wanted a meeting on his own turf, a place where the waitresses knew and fussed over him. Three years ago, when he had tracked Peter down at the Glendale pool and taken him out for a sandwich at the local Dairy Queen, he had felt old and pasty, out of place among all those tanned young people. He wasn't going to make that mistake again.

Yet it was apparent from the moment Peter Lasko sat down that waitresses did not need to know him to pay special attention. Apparently he was that good-looking, although Dale would never be able to see it.

"Nice," the boy said, glancing around the narrow rowhouse. *Man,* Dale corrected himself. He was a man now. Technically. Old enough to drink and vote, and more than old enough to go to war, although the Peter Laskos of the world didn't have to worry about that.

"You can't get in here on the weekends," Dale said. "But I think it would lose a lot of its charm if it expanded to a larger space. It has only one flaw." He lowered his voice. "The coffee's the usual overscorched brew. That's why I bring my own, from the Daily Grind." He tapped his thermal cup. "Technically not allowed. But I'm a favored customer."

"Outlaw coffee, huh?" Kat had made a similar joke about her father's fussiness when he brought her here. Shit — Dale again felt the waves of grief, not unlike nausea, except these seemed to get stuck in his throat and stay there. He did not want to break down. Not here, not in front of this boy.

"I hear," he said, moving to a subject that he knew the boy would like, "that you've scored quite a success for yourself, right out of the gate. A major motion picture."

"Well, it's a Miramax film. They don't carry the artistic cred they once did, but it's still a big deal. Of course, I'm not the star, far from it. But it's twelve days' work, and I play the star's brother."

He threw out a name that meant nothing to Dale, who nevertheless widened his eyes as if impressed. Dale couldn't remember the last time he had been to a movie theater, or even watched a film straight through on cable. Who had two hours to sit in one place doing only one thing? That was one of the unexpected sides of Susannah, her devotion to certain programs, and, stranger still, her belief that they connected her to others. Television was church for her generation. She and Kat had bonded over that HBO show *Sex and the City*, which Dale found appalling. It was porno without the money shots, although the girls incongruously kept their bras on while fucking.

"Will you film around here or in Pennsylvania?"

"Toronto. More bang for the Canadian buck. Besides, even though it's called *Susquehanna Falls*, it's supposed to be set in some vaguely generic city, like in *Miller's Crossing*. We don't want the audience to know exactly where they are, or even what year it's set in. The sense of dislocation is key to the experience."

Dale imagined a director or writer or someone else connected to the movie saying these exact words to the boy, who had absorbed them earnestly and now repeated them on faith. Yes, he was just the kid for the job Dale had in mind.

"So you've got the world by the balls and you decided to kill some time in little old Glendale?"

"I had four weeks off. It's not really enough time to do anything. Besides —" There was that raffish grin again. "The money hasn't started rolling in yet. My rent in New York is manageable, but it's an expensive city, just sucks the ducats out of your pocket, so I went ahead and sublet my place. And my mom's the best cook I know."

Ducats. Even Dale was pretty sure this was outmoded slang. Kid would probably be talking about "benjamins" in a minute, or drawling *a-ight,* as if he were some street-corner drug dealer. Dale knew he was being cruel, but such outward pettiness helped keep other, darker feelings at bay. It was easier to feel contempt than think about Kat. Easy yet unnatural, too.

"Do I know your parents? What does your father do?"

"He's at Procter & Gamble, manages people or something. I've always been a little hazy on the details."

The conversation stalled out, but their food arrived before the awkwardness became too obvious, allowing them to busy themselves with forks and salt shakers. Dale was having one of the Blue Moon's specialties, the huevos rancheros, and he had assumed that a twenty-two-year-old boy would order something even heavier — the chocolate chip pancakes or Belgian waffles. But Peter was eating an egg-white omelet, no toast, minus the hash browns.

"They hired me for my lean and hungry look," he said when he caught Dale eyeing his plate. "I'm not doing low-carb, exactly, but when I'm away from my mom's table, I try to keep it light. I can say no to a waitress, but I can't say no to my mom."

"Yes, it's hard to say no to one's mom, no matter one's age."

"Does your mom still expect you to eat

when you see her?"

"My mother passed away ten years ago."

He lowered his head, embarrassed. "Oh, yeah, I should have noticed. I mean, yesterday, in the cemetery . . . I mean — sorry."

"It's part of the natural order of things, losing one's parent. Sad, but logical. Losing one's child, however . . ." Such clichés were inextricable from grief, Dale was discovering.

"I know, it must be awful. I still can't believe it's Kat. *Everyone* liked her."

"Well, someone clearly didn't." He let that sink in. "Did you know Perri very well?"

"Not at all. I mean, I must have met her, the summer I dated Kat. I think she was in *Carousel*. But she wasn't, like, someone I talked to. Her older brother was ahead of me in school, but I knew him a little better. Dwight."

No matter how things end, they have a child left, Dale thought. *It's so unfair. And the Patels have all three of theirs.* Again he felt that impulse to pound the table, to throw his own untouched plate across the room, to succumb to a tantrum.

But all he said was, "So you stay plugged into Glendale, after all these years?"

"It's home," Peter said with a shrug. "You hear stuff, almost without trying. Truth is, I feel a lot closer to my college friends than my high-school ones. I mean, I have so much more in common with them. Whereas in high school, it was just, you know, being in the same place."

"Propinquity."

"Sir?"

"The mere fact of being in close physical quarters. It's that way for most people. I seldom see my high-school friends outside reunions. And I wouldn't even go to those if I still didn't live in the area. My brother never goes." *Because he doesn't want everyone to see how Mr. Most Popular turned out.* Those whom the gods would destroy they first elect most popular. Then again, Kat was most popular. Most popular, first in her class, prom queen. *Yes — and she was dead.*

"Yeah," said Peter, clearly just being agreeable, but Dale started, thinking the boy was affirming Dale's unvoiced thoughts.

"The thing that bothers me," Dale said, growing impatient, as he always did, with the small talk endemic to business, "is the idea that I might never know *why* this happened. If Perri doesn't recover, we won't find out. Even if she does, it will probably turn into some variation on the insanity defense. Either way we lose. And not just my family. I think everyone in Glendale has a stake in what happened."

"I just assumed Perri was jealous or something."

"But do you *know* that? Is it based on something someone said, or is it just your conjecture?"

"Um, well . . . I don't really know anything. Giff, the drama teacher, said Perri was really burned when they subbed *Oklahoma!* for *Anyone Can Whistle*. Even though he said Perri could be Ado Annie, which is the kind of part that actors salivate for."

"What did any of this have to do with Kat? I mean, I know she had the lead in *Oklahoma!*, but why would Perri care about that, especially if the drama teacher told her the other part could be hers?"

"Beats me. Girls get crazy over weird shi— stuff. But, Mr. Hartigan, won't the police figure this all out? I mean, isn't it their job?"

Dale took a gulp of his coffee, willing himself to slow down, reel the boy in gently. This was the part Susannah played in his company, the gentle, gracious hostess. But he couldn't use Susannah for this bit of liaison, for Susannah would not have approved of what he was doing.

"It should be. But I'm hearing about, um, some irregularities in the investigation. They're nice fellows, very professional. But it's a job to them, nothing more. They'll be satisfied with far less than I ever will — a straightforward exegesis of bullet trajectories, where everyone was standing."

Vocabulary was clearly not the boy's strong point. How had he ever gotten into NYU? Oh, yes, the Cuban mom. "Well, what about Josie Patel? Can't she tell you what you need to know?"

"As I understand it, Josie's story doesn't exactly track." Dale hated to admit it, but his father had been right, calling in all those political markers, making sure they were kept up to speed on the investigation. It was like getting private title insurance — the lender's interests and your interests overlapped only up to a point, and then you were on your own. "And her parents have hired a lawyer now."

He made eye contact with the boy and held it. Why did women think he was handsome? Yes, his features were even, his skin pleasingly smooth, his eyes puppy-doggish, his hair floppy in the retro style that girls seemed to like. But those lovely eyes were a little vacant, his manner as floppy as his hair.

"Do you know Josie, Peter?"

"A little. She and Kat were tight. She did flip-flaps in the opening of *Carousel,* the one where I played Billy Bigelow."

"Right," Dale said, although he certainly hadn't seen the show. Kat wasn't in that one. He remembered Kat's asking him to go with her, however, to see Josie and Perri. And Peter, he realized now. She had wanted her father to see her boyfriend as something other than the predatory college creep he was. Whatever regrets he had about Kat, he would never feel bad about getting this kid out of her life. He was just sorry that Peter hadn't finessed it better.

"You know, Peter, the people who loved Kat — we need each other more than ever right now. And we have to pursue the truth as . . . a memorial to her. We owe her that much, don't you think?"

The boy wasn't the sharpest crayon in the box, and the seconds passed. Finally, *finally,* however, Peter said, "I could talk to her. Josie, I mean. If you think it would help."

"Really?" Dale replied, as if the idea had never occurred to him. "Why — of course, that was never my intent, but if you did find out something, it would be . . . a comfort to me. Whatever you found out. From anyone, not just Josie. I mean, you have a lot of influence with that high-school crowd. People who wouldn't dream of talking to the police might talk to you."

Peter brushed his hair out of his eyes, sat up a little straighter. Dale could not say for sure, but he believed that what he saw then was the dreamy aspect of an actor trying on a part.

"Yeah," he said. "Yeah. I could definitely do that."

Dale pushed his business card across the table. "Between us. I know I can trust you."

"Because . . ."

"Because you're an honorable sort." No point in reminding Peter how dishonorable he had been, how abruptly he had dropped Kat three years ago, when he thought there might be some advantage in it for him.

"You know, I kind of loved her. Kat, I mean. I really did. But we were young, like you said."

"I'm sure you did care for her." *I'm sure you think you did.*

"I really want to help, in any way I can. Josie, anybody. I'll talk to anybody."

The boy felt guilty, Dale realized with a thrill. Guilty and obligated — as well he should. If he had really loved Kat, Dale wouldn't have been able to scare him away. He hated him now, just a little, for doing exactly what Dale had wanted. Even if it had been in his daughter's best interest, it had hurt her. Even Dale could see that.

"That's great, Peter. Once you do, check in with me on my cell. I'll be interested in hearing what Josie has to say when she can talk to a friend, instead of strangers. Now — you sure you don't want a Blue Moon cinnamon roll? They're homemade."

The boy puffed out his cheeks and shook his head in regret. Only he wasn't really regretful, Dale realized. Peter Lasko was glad to give up cinnamon rolls for the privilege of being handsome and buff. There would be time enough, to paraphrase Prufrock, for cinnamon rolls and whatever small treats he denied himself now. The waitress topped off Peter's coffee, although it was barely down an inch, brushing her breasts against his arm as she leaned forward.

Dale's water glass was empty, but no one seemed to care. And all the water he had downed in between gulps of his private coffee now seemed lodged somewhere in his chest. These days it was as if he could never get enough air, as if he were always in danger of suffocating.

28

A floater couldn't help losing things, Alexa told herself, pawing through a sheaf of papers for the second time, still trying to find the paper she was now sure that Perri Kahn had submitted just minutes before she had gone to the girls' restroom to confront Kat. If the paper didn't exist, she couldn't give Perri a final grade and challenge Barbara on her refusal to grant the girl a diploma. Maybe it never existed, but Alexa had convinced herself that it did, that she'd held it in her hand the very moment the phone rang, a stapled sheaf of off-white typing paper in one of the distinctive fonts that Perri preferred. But the papers had been dropped, and the soda had spilled, and everything had been gathered up in such a rush —

She lifted her head at the sound of a student *clop-clop-clopping* down the hall, a would-be stealthy Billy Goat Gruff, trying to muffle the sound of her Dr. Scholl's. It was Eve, trotting toward the exit, shoulders squared. Alexa called the girl's name once, twice, three times before she finally turned around.

"Oh?" Eve said. "Were you talking to me?"

Several sarcastic replies occurred to her, but Alexa had learned that sarcasm didn't work on these girls. "Got a minute? I want to talk to you."

"I'm on a bathroom pass from health," Eve began, but Alexa knew she was headed for her usual cigarette break in the trees, with Val and Lila.

"I'll write you a note. Let's talk."

Alexa had a classroom for this period, but no real class. This had been her independent study session, and the five girls had all finished their work for the year, except for Jocelyn Smith, who had been given an extension for mental-health reasons. She said, and a family doctor agreed, that Jocelyn had been traumatized by the shooting. Alexa was reasonably sure that Jocelyn had just found an unimpeachable excuse for not finishing her work.

Alexa sat in one of the chairs in the front row, feeling that a desk was too much of a barrier to intimacy in a conversation. She was always attentive to such seemingly insignificant issues. When she was holding a class, her preferred configuration was a circle, although some teachers bitched if she forgot to have the students put the chairs back in their rigid little rows. And she insisted on a true circle, not one of those horseshoe-shaped parabolas, which maintained the teacher as focal point. Ladies of the Round Table, she had once dubbed this circle, although one of her students had quickly pointed out that the Arthurian ideal had not survived. "It was torn apart by a woman, in fact."

Perri had made that contribution although her knowledge of King Arthur almost certainly came by way of *Camelot* as opposed to *The Once and Future King*. Alexa had countered with the story of the Paris peace talks and the argument over the table's shape, an anecdote that one of her history professors had loved. But she might as well have been talking about a time as remote as King Arthur's, given the girls' furrowed brows. At the end of her story, there was a confused silence, and then one girl asked, "Did you march against the war and stuff?"

Alexa had to inform the girls that she had been born after the Vietnam war ended, a fact they seemed to find suspect. No matter how young you were, no matter how young you looked, students thought you were ancient, a witness to everything that had happened in the previous century.

"How are you, Eve?" No reproach in her tone, no reminder that the girl had been ducking her for three days.

"Good."

"Good?"

Eve frowned. "I mean, good under the circumstances."

"I imagine it's hard for students to concentrate these days — not that June was ever known as a month for students to focus."

"I'm *okay.*" Said firmly now, in the manner of someone trying to get rid of a telemarketer.

"How are things at home these days?"

Eve squirmed a little in her chair. Her embarrassment about her parents was far more acute than the average adolescent's. When Mr. and Mrs. Muhly had been summoned to school for that infamous meeting, Eve's main concern had been that people would see just how old her parents were, and that would be held against her in a way that made the blow job on the bus utterly secondary. They were old, at least her father was, and her mother had disastrously retro taste.

"Fine," Eve said at last. "Fine."

Frustrated, Alexa decided to go straight to the matter. Directness was a risky tactic with a girl like Eve, but she hoped her reputation for being truthful and loyal would pay off here. And Eve *owed* her.

"Did you ever figure out who spoke to you that day? Who you overheard talking about the girls' room and the gunshot?"

"Nope." She was swinging her head so hard that her fine dark hair lashed at her cheeks.

"It could be important. You might know something crucial to the investigation and not even know you know it."

She had expected Eve to look intrigued, but the girl just glowered, as if having vital information were an unfair burden.

"The thing is . . . there are so many rumors going around. The Kahns have a lawyer. Josie Patel's family has hired a lawyer. Even Mr. Hartigan has a lawyer. I've heard that Perri wrote Kat some sort of letter, too."

Eve's face was now a classic teenager's mask, her eyes focused on some spot over Alexa's right shoulder.

"So the girl you *overheard* . . ." Alexa, no slouch at nuance in conversation, gave this word the most subtle rendering she could, something well short of the arch invisible quote marks used by doubters, but a tone shot through with light challenge. "The girl you overheard . . . well, maybe it's the age-old case of someone saying she heard something happened to a friend, when it was really her. This girl, I mean."

It was you, Eve. Admit it was you.

"And maybe she didn't just hear something. Maybe she saw something."

"I wasn't there," Eve said, her words coming with painful slowness. "I wasn't anywhere near there."

"But the girl who spoke to you . . . ?"

"The girl I overheard." Eve's smile was triumphant.

Alexa found herself thinking of one of the few happy memories she had of her father, when he had told her she could win ten dollars by playing the "No" game. He explained the rules at great, ponderous length, speaking for almost ten minutes. She must answer "No" to every question, whether it was the truthful answer or not. "No" was the only answer permitted. The game would go on as long as she was successful. It might go on for hours. Did she understand? "NO," Alexa had roared, and her father had laughed. But he had also tried to renege on the promise of the ten-dollar payment. No matter. Alexa was sure her five-year-old face had looked much as Eve's did just now. Victorious, but a little fearful, too, as if there would be consequences for winning this point.

She was trying to figure out what to ask the girl next when Jocelyn Smith appeared in the doorway, her features working as if she were a silent-screen actress.

"Ms. Cunningham, Ms. Cunningham? About my paper?"

"It's okay, Jocelyn. I already told you it's okay. You got the extension."

"But it's not about finishing it late. It's about finishing *ever*. I have horseback-riding camp this summer, and then a killer schedule in the fall, and my parents pointed out that if I have an incomplete going into the fall, it could totally screw up my transcripts on my college applications. . . ."

She was now in a state of near hysteria, admittedly a place never far away where Jocelyn was concerned. Alexa couldn't help being annoyed by the girl's selfishness. True, this was Jocelyn's independent-study hour, when Alexa was supposed to be available to her, but hadn't she noticed Eve sitting here? For all Jocelyn knew, Eve also was doing an independent study with

Alexa and Jocelyn was stealing her time, her attention. But Jocelyn never worried about such things.

"Hold it a sec, Jocelyn. I'll talk to you in the hall."

She closed the door behind her, signaling that she was not through with Eve.

Eve, left alone in the classroom, found herself reaching almost automatically for Alexa's cart. Her father spoke of people who stole as having sticky fingers, and while Eve understood the metaphor, it didn't apply in her situation. Her fingers never felt drier or cooler than when moving through property that wasn't hers.

Her parents had made her a thief, she reasoned. They would not buy her the things she needed nor allow her the part-time job that might subsidize such purchases, so she had learned to get what she wanted — what she needed — by seizing opportunities. Left alone to tend the produce stand, for example, she gouged the more gullible types, claiming that ordinary beefsteak tomatoes were a rare hybrid or that the corn was true Silver Queen. (Her father's corn was actually better, but people thought they wanted Silver Queen.) And she was always on the prowl for untended money, because only a fool would boost things at the mall, although items without price tags were ripe for the taking. Once pocketed, these things were guaranteed, for how could someone prove you took it? Or you could pull a little switcheroo. That's how she had gotten her big gold *E*, by switching price tags.

But money was the best. So her fingers moved through Alexa's cart, looking for a billfold. Never take it all, was Eve's motto. People noticed when everything was missing. But when it was one twenty-dollar bill out of three, the marks tended to blame themselves, assuming they had lost track of some minor purchase. This assumption worked with everyone but her father, who knew to the nickel how much money he had. That had been a hard lesson, but once learned, it was never forgotten. Eve didn't make the same mistake twice.

But Ms. Cunningham, while so stupid in some ways, had taken her purse with her when she stepped out of the classroom. Really, Eve should be insulted. Did Ms. Cunningham think she was a thief? (Okay, she was, but Ms. Cunningham didn't *know* that.) Would she have taken her purse with her if, say, Perri had been here? Perri, who had brought a gun to school, who had proved to be much more unpredictable than anyone knew? What about Kat Hartigan? But if Kat Hartigan had been a dog, you could have left her alone with a steak and she wouldn't budge. No — Kat would sit and wait, and someone would bring the steak to her. That was the beauty of being Kat Hartigan. Everything offered up, everything done for her. All she had to do was exist.

Out in the hall, Jocelyn was now sobbing, the sobs growing fainter, as if Ms. Cunningham were trying to walk her away from this corridor, where several classes were in session. Ms. Cunningham probably thought she was doing Jocelyn a kindness, but Jocelyn cried precisely so she would get attention. Being deprived of an audience, Eve thought, was the opposite of what Jocelyn wanted.

There was a folder at the bottom of the cart, marked "Independent Study." Eve opened it. The first paper, by Paige Hawthorne, had the word "pornography" in the title but also the word "semiotics," which canceled out the promises of the first word. She tried to skip to the end, to see if it got juicier, but the final pages were sticky, almost as if something had been spilled on them, and when Eve finally got the last page to pull away, it was a different font, a different topic. A paper by Perri. Again it had a promising title but a dull treatment, and she skipped to the end. But instead of finding a great summing-up, she found a letter. A handwritten letter to Kat, stapled to the term paper.

Oh, fuck, oh, fuck, oh, fuck. Fuck. No wonder Ms. Cunningham wouldn't leave her alone. If she had read this, she *knew*. Not everything, but more than she should. How had she gotten this letter? She had enough information to put it together, and now Eve would be accused of not keeping the secret, which she absolutely had. It was so unfair.

Wait, Muhly. (The voice in her mind was Val's, calm and cool.) *Wait*. The paper wasn't marked, not anywhere, and perfect as Perri was, not even she could turn in a term paper that didn't merit one correction. It had been stapled to the back of Perri's paper, which had been stuck to Paige's paper until Eve had pulled it away. Maybe Ms. Cunningham hadn't seen it. And even if she had, and it disappeared, then what could she prove? All Eve had to do was make this letter disappear, and then Ms. Cunningham couldn't do anything.

Eve took the whole batch — Paige Hawthorne's paper, Perri's, the letter — reasoning that this caper should be played according to reverse logic: The more missing, the less suspicious it would be. No, better, an entire *folder*. She would take the folder, secure it inside her oversize binder and —

"I'm so sorry about that interruption, Eve. Jocelyn was very upset."

"No problem. But I really should get to class. I have . . . a paper due."

"For health? So late in the semester?"

"I'm behind. It's on STDs — sexually transmitted diseases. Did you know that babies can be born with that stuff, even though they never had sex?"

"Well, they can be infected by their mother in utero —"

"They can be born *blind*."

"All the more reason to use a condom."

"Then there's no baby at all."

"Exactly, Eve. Exactly."

Teachers were always bringing up condoms to Eve in this roundabout way, which amused and disappointed her. Even the teachers, even Ms. Cunningham for all her disavowal of gossip, thought she was a slut. Whereas her only true sexual adventure was that time on the bus, almost two years behind her now. Eve wanted a boyfriend, although no one really had them anymore. The problem was, the boys all thought she knew so much more than she did. Virginity, once gone, could never be reclaimed, a point that was made repeatedly in health class. But it was worse, Eve thought, to be a virgin and have everyone think you were this superslut who knew how to do everything. The only way she could keep her reputation intact was to stay out of the fray completely.

She almost wished she could be who she used to be. She loved hanging with Val and Lila and had no affection for her old outcast status. She was proud to be a skeezer. Still, there was something about the girl who had gotten on the bus to Philadelphia that day, the girl in her mom's crocheted vest, with her uncool lunch of preserves on lumpy homemade bread. The girl who had taken second place in the juvenile fudge division the year before. She was *nice,* that girl. Nice and maybe even pretty. Talk to her. Get to know her. You'll be surprised by how much fun she can be.

Yet Eve had abandoned that girl at the first opportunity, finally seeing her as everyone else did — out of it, stupid, queer, a social liability. It was bad enough dropping an old friend for such reasons, but you could take the friend back or make it up to her in other ways. Once you dropped yourself, you could never go back.

29

Josie was lying on the sofa in the family room, clicking idly through the channels. This mundane afternoon activity was almost exotic to her, given how many extra-curriculars she had pursued over the years. She had started with soccer as a six-year-old, then gymnastics, which had led to both the-ater and cheerleading. The last had meant not only practices and games but also end-less fund-raising activities.

Josie had never much cared for the "spirit" part of cheerleading — the car washes, the bake sales, the pep rallies. In fact, Josie didn't really care if the Glendale Panthers won or lost. She liked leaping into the air, pooling her hoarse voice with the others, the crowd roaring back at their command, completely in their control. She loved her purple-and-white uniform, the way the pleats brushed her thighs as she walked through the halls, but she barely noticed if the boys in purple and white heeded the exhortations to fight, fight, fight. At dinner Josie sometimes had to think for a moment when her father asked her the score. The only way she could remember was by recalling what *she* had done, in the final moments. Had she jumped up and down squealing or stood in pretend dejection, hands on hips? Some of the girls cried over games, shed actual tears, but Josie never did.

She studied her bandaged foot, propped up on a pillow. Although she was not quite five-two, her right foot looked very, very faraway and alien, as if it were not truly attached to the rest of her body. The prognosis was uncertain, the doctor had said when she left the hospital. So many bones and nerves in feet, so many possible outcomes. She would definitely walk again, probably do everything again. Yet she was cautioned to be patient and let the foot heal before she started pressing it, testing its flexibility and strength.

"When you come off the crutches," the doctor said, "it may even take time for your leg to believe it can come all the way down to the floor. It's almost as if your foot needs to learn to trust itself again, to remember that it really does have the capacity to make contact with the ground, to support you."

Her mother's car pulled into the garage. Josie could tell it was her mother because the muffler on the Honda Accord was beginning to go. She could hear her mother coming from a block away sometimes. Her parents kept saying the Honda would be Josie's car when she went to college, a car being pretty much a necessity at the University of Maryland. Josie hoped they would get the muffler fixed first.

"You're home early," Josie said as her mother came through the door from the garage, burdened with purse, tote, and two bags of groceries.

"My boss is cutting me some slack right now. No one likes the idea of you here alone, hobbling around by yourself."

"Matt and Tim are here somewhere," Josie said, even as part of her mind focused on that one word, "alone." "Although maybe Marta took them out."

Josie had never been expected to care for her younger brothers. When she did baby-sit, her parents paid her the going rate — not as much as Marta, of course, but what other teenagers made to baby-sit.

"Besides, I have some good news. *Enormous* news."

"Hmmmmm?" Josie was still flicking through the channels, looking for something decent. *TRL* was on, but Josie hadn't watched that since she was fourteen or fifteen. She was in the mood for something quasi-real yet not truly real, and not too mean-spirited. The show where they redid a dowdy woman's wardrobe would be good, or something competitive, as long as it didn't involve eating gross stuff.

"Mr. Hartigan called me today —"

Josie's stomach clutched a little.

"Remember the scholarship his family endowed for the school? Well, it's going to be the Kat Hartigan Memorial Scholarship now."

"Hmmmm." Josie had landed on the show about people who had too much stuff and their makeover included a garage sale where they were forced to divest themselves of their clutter. A very large woman was swearing she couldn't give up a single *Aladdin* toy. She had seventeen Princess Jasmines alone.

"And *you're* going to be the first recipient."

Josie muted the television. "Why?"

"Well, he didn't say. But you were her best friend. You tried to take the gun from Perri. And you stayed with her. Mr. Hartigan said that meant a lot to him, that you wouldn't leave her."

"Is that going to be the requirement every year? Hanging out with a dead body? Because there are plenty of kids at Glendale who would kill someone if that's the case. Kill someone and just sit there waiting for the paramedics."

Her mother's face puckered, the way it did whenever someone didn't share her excitement or enthusiasm. "I thought you'd be happier. We've all been so worried about your scholarship, the implications of the injury. If you *can't* . . . well, then you can't. College Park said they'd hold the spot for you, at least for the first year, but they can't offer any financial aid if you can't participate in the program. This solves everything. You should be happy."

"I *am* happy," Josie said, bursting into tears.

"Oh, Josie baby." Her mother started to sit on the sofa, but she didn't want to crowd Josie's foot, so she knelt on the carpet, looking for a way to put her arms around her, only Josie wouldn't quite yield. Instead she allowed her mother to pat her all over, smoothing her hair away from her face, rubbing her shoulders.

"I wasn't thinking. Of course it's bittersweet. Maybe just bitter. I shouldn't expect you to be jumping for joy."

"I can't jump for anything," Josie muttered, knowing that the halfhearted joke would calm her mother.

"It is a relief. I can tell you now, honey, your father and I weren't sure what we were going to do. I mean, we would have found a way — a second mortgage maybe, although we already have a second mortgage — something. But this is truly a godsend."

"You don't think I'm going to get better, do you? If it was just this year, it wouldn't be a big deal. But you think I'm never going to be able to join the cheerleading squad at College Park."

"No. *No.* I'm sure you'll be fine. But this way you don't have to even consider deferring your acceptance. Assuming," she added, "it's even that bad. I didn't think you'd enjoy delaying a year, with all your friends gone."

They're already gone, Josie wanted to say, but her tears were slowing. She would get to go to college, no matter what. Even if her foot were permanently damaged, she would still get to leave. Her mother was right: She wouldn't want to stay in Glendale one more day than necessary. She had to get out, go somewhere, anywhere.

"Now, remember, it's a secret," her

mother said, rising from the floor, her hose generating a little electric shock that raised the hairs on Josie's arm. "We mustn't tell anyone until it's announced at graduation."

Josie knew that her mother was not much good at keeping secrets, not happy ones. She would probably call Grammy and Grampa in Janesville tonight, and the news would be all over Janesville, Wisconsin, before it was announced at graduation.

Then again, only family members could appreciate the story, for only the family knew that Josie's college education had been saved for the *second* time. Her mother, gregarious and talkative as she was, had told very few people just how bleak Josie's college prospects were. For it was her mother who had squandered Josie's college savings in a desperate game of catch-up, trying to save in three years what she should have been saving since Josie was born, only to end up with a paltry few thousand.

The Patels had started a small fund when Josie was in third grade, but it had stayed small, in part because her mother had a bad habit of mentally assigning the fund various abstract savings without actually putting them there. "All the money we save by not sending Josie to private school can go to the fund," she had said when they had moved to Glendale. But she had allocated those same savings to the kitchen renovation, and her Honda Accord, and the trip the family had taken to India when Josie was twelve, and the fees paid for Josie's gymnastics lessons, not to mention Josie's orthodontia. Meanwhile her brothers had come along, and they needed college funds, too, so the nonexistent savings were now divided by three. One didn't need to be a math genius to know that zero divided by three kept ending up zero.

When Josie was thirteen, a stock adviser had done the math for her mom, explained the mysteries of compound interest, and said the boys still had a chance but only a high-risk strategy would work for Josie. He recommended that Mrs. Patel take out a second mortgage and invest that money. He pushed Josie's mom toward telecommunication stocks, including WorldCom. For a brief, giddy period, it looked as if they would be okay. But it was very brief.

Josie still remembered the shock of finding out that all those headlines about people somewhere in Alabama actually affected *her,* that a corporation's accounting fraud had dovetailed with her mother's incompetence to deprive her of the funds for a college education. By junior year her fund had dwindled to three thousand dollars, barely enough to pay tuition for a single semester at the University of Maryland — and Josie did not have the grades to get into College Park. The chances for a National Merit Scholarship were long gone, not that Josie would have had much of a shot, even with a tutor, and the Patels earned too much for Josie to qualify for a needs-based scholarship. "On *paper,*" her father said, his voice despairing, looking at how much they still owed on the second mortgage. "On paper, we're very well-off."

Forced to confront for the first time the financial sacrifices her parents had made over the years, Josie felt guilty and resentful. She had not asked to move to Glendale. It wasn't her fault her teeth came in crooked. She had never wanted gymnastics lessons. Well, no, she had wanted those.

Even as Josie stewed, her mother schemed. Nothing motivated Susie Patel as much as Vik Patel's disappointment. After researching Title IX scholarships and deciding that Josie was too late for lacrosse and too small for rowing, she had found out that College Park was offering athletic scholarships to *cheerleaders*. It was an odd kind of cheerleading, to be sure, in that the qualified students spent all their time competing while a different group of young men and women cheered for the UM Terrapins. ("Fear the turtle!" was the school's well-known slogan.) The program was, in short, what Josie had always wanted — a chance to fly and soar on her own, no longer a sideshow to the main event but the event itself. Josie wasn't crazy about staying in-state, but at least College Park was prestigious now, taking only the top Maryland graduates. No one had to know how close she had come to attending a truly crappy school.

She called to her mother, who was now puttering in the kitchen, "Do I have to, like, make a speech when they give it to me?"

"I don't think so. Is that what's bothering you? You've never minded being the center of attention."

Josie thought of herself at the top of the pyramid, airborne in the night sky at football games, flying as Michael in *Peter Pan*. Yes, she had enjoyed the attention, but what she had really liked was the feeling that she had complete mastery over her body. It was the one thing she could always control.

"Not talking, though. I don't like to talk in front of people."

"Well, I'll make sure you won't have to talk. Just say thank you and get off." Her mother returned to the sofa to rumple Josie's curls. "You have the prettiest hair. I would have killed for hair like this when I was your age. I think I fell in love with your father because of this hair."

"Mom." It was far from the first time her mother had shared this anecdote, but it never ceased to embarrass Josie, this vision of her father not as her father but as a boy, someone with hair that a girl could love. And not just any girl, but her mother. She did not like to think of her parents that way. These images had made her adamant in her rejection of Grinnell College, although her double-legacy status might have secured her a place in a school that would otherwise be a huge reach for her. She did not want to walk where her parents had walked, sleep in the dorms where they had slept, much less daydream in the classrooms where her father had impressed teachers with his budding genius and her mother had beamed at him, happy just to bask in his glow.

"Wow, I think you got five syllables into that 'Mom,' a new personal best for you."

This was Josie's cue to say it again, holding the final syllable so it sounded like the "om" chant in a yoga class. But her heart wasn't in it today.

"It's expected, you know," her mother said after realizing that Josie wasn't up for their usual game. "Being sad. You might be sad for a long time."

Like the rest of my life?

"It's not just being . . . sad," she said. "It's . . ." But there was no way to finish the thought. She felt sad and guilty, yet resentful of the guilt, convinced she didn't deserve it. None of this was her idea.

She picked up the remote control, began working her way up and down the channels again. Her parents had only basic cable, so there wasn't as much to see as there had been at Kat's, for example, where the Hartigans had all the movie channels, ten for HBO alone. Perri's parents didn't even have cable, and they limited their children's "screen time," as they called it, which had just made Perri crazed on the subject, plopping in front of Kat's set for hours at a time, surrendering her vivid imagination to much lesser ones. Kat and Josie had to flatter her outrageously to get her away from the television, but Perri had grown out of it. Eventually. That was the way it was with Perri. Her manias were like the flu bugs that knocked her flat every winter. You just had to let them run their course.

Josie preferred the local stations anyway, with their cheesy ads for cars and copiers and insurance. This time of day, these channels were filled with shows about judges — sarcastic, adamant, bossy judges, who cut so quickly to the heart of the matter, making questions of right and wrong look so simple. You — pay the rent. You — fix his car. You — replace the dress. The gavel banged and the losers bitched once outside the courtroom, but the judge's decisions were final.

30

Dannon Estes could tell he made the detectives uncomfortable. Some people have gaydar, but Dannon had gay-*hating*-dar. Not that these guys were haters. Their reactions were more subtle than that. The younger one, who reminded Dannon of Alec Baldwin — circa *Married to the Mob*, moving through that hot-tub mist, back before he had gone totally to seed — had the general air of bafflement common to the hyperhets. *What? You don't like tits? You don't like pussy? What's that about?*

The older guy, the fatherly one — now, he was the type who felt sorry for Dannon. His stepfather had much the same air when he was forced to spend time with him, as if Dannon were missing a limb or something. Disabled, or *differently abled,* as Glendale students were encouraged to say.

Then again, Dannon had made a point of informing these police officers he was gay, singing it out loud and proud. He couldn't really blame them for being focused on it, given that it was the first thing he had told them about himself.

"We understand you went to the prom with Perri Kahn," the older guy had started, and Dannon had promptly interrupted him.

"Just as friends. I'm gay. But I suppose Mrs. Kahn told you that."

"Um, no, that didn't really come up." The older guy was so clearly lying, determined to ignore the fact. You would think that Dannon had farted or something. "But you *were* friends, right?"

"Right."

"Good friends?"

"Pretty good, but just the past year." Dannon, used to the fierce precision of the Glendale divas, would never be caught embroidering his social status in any way. That was one of the school's deadly sins, an offense for which one would be taunted and punished. "We knew each other from theater stuff, going way back, but we didn't start hanging out together until last fall."

"Would you say you were close?"

"I suppose so." *I hoped so. I only built the past year of my life on that concept — being Perri Kahn's new best friend.*

"She tell you anything about her . . . plans?"

"How do you mean?" Shit, that was the wrong way to say it. "No, she didn't tell me she had planned anything."

"But she told you *something*."

"Not really." Technically true. She hadn't *told* him anything.

"You know, it's just unusual for a thing like this to happen without anyone having an inkling."

Inkling. What a funny word. If Perri had been here, they would have exchanged a look or stifled their laughter. *Inkling*. It was like the riff from *The Sunshine Boys*, the whole laundry list of what words were funny, what words weren't. Pickle, cucumber . . .

"No, I didn't have an *inkling*."

"Back at Columbine," the handsome cop put in, "there was a Website and everything. And in some other school shootings, kids told people what they were going to do, showed off the gun, told people when it was going to go down."

"Yeah, only this wasn't Columbine," Dannon said. He was feeling strangely fearless. He had always been a behind-the-scenes guy, but maybe he was a better actor than he realized. "I mean, that's what

Ms. Paulson keeps telling us. Columbine was, like, about the school's social hierarchy. This was something private among three friends that just happened to play out on school property."

"But why?"

He shook his head. "I honestly don't know." And this was true, too. Perri had never explained her anger. Was it because she didn't completely trust him? Then again, to the extent that she had confided in him, he had betrayed her, so perhaps she was shrewd enough to realize that Dannon didn't deserve her trust.

"Was she unhappy? Did she speak of suicide? Did she have some kind of grudge toward the dead girl?"

He should never have agreed to speak to these men. Now that he was in too deep to turn back, he should just keep feigning ignorance. But Dannon had never been able to shake his own fascination with the story of the imperious three, broken at last.

"Perri *never* spoke of it. To me. To anyone."

"The shooting?"

"No. I mean, yes — she never said she was going to shoot anybody. But she also never told me why she had stopped talking to Kat."

The policemen didn't say anything. Dannon understood that their silence was deliberate, one intended to make him feel uncomfortable. Old Giff had once expounded on the possibilities of stillness, citing Kevin Spacey's *The Iceman Cometh*, how powerful a pause could be after so much steady, constant talk, talk, talk. Despite this insight into his own manipulation, Dannon just couldn't shut up. He loved to speak of Perri, relished the fact that he knew her, that he had something to offer.

"There was a lot of speculation over the past year. The divas —"

"Excuse me?"

"The bitchy popular girls. Anyway, they were always a little antagonistic toward Perri because she didn't follow their dictates, you know? She wasn't scared of them. But she was friends with Kat, who was, like, the queen of the school, so they left Perri alone. Until she and Kat stopped hanging out together, and then they started all these rumors."

"Such as?"

"They were *rumors*. Bogus."

"Still, it might have bothered Perri. Being gossiped about."

"It didn't. She was above that stuff."

"Dannon." The older cop was so much like his stepfather it was freaky. Like, right now, the way he placed his hands on his knees when he was trying to show he was very, very serious about something. His stepfather did that all the time. Hands on knees, Bill was getting serious. "Dannon, what did the girls — the divas — say about Perri?"

"They said she was gay, that she had fallen in love with Kat, and Kat had dropped her."

"And that wasn't true?"

"No." He laughed, although he was sure that made him look weird, laughing. "If I'm sure of anything, it's that Perri Kahn was *not* gay."

"But did Kat say those things, too?"

"The only things Kat Hartigan said to me during almost ten years of school were 'Hiiiiiiiiiiiiiiiiiiiiiiiiiiiiii!' and 'Looking *good,* Dannon.' "

The older detective smiled at Dannon's imitation of Kat, but he couldn't know just how pitch-perfect it was. Dannon was an excellent mimic. He had cracked Perri up, imitating Kat and their principal and the diva crowd, among others.

"That's basically what Kat Hartigan said to everyone. And that's why she was popular. She was nice. Not two-faced. But kind of bland, too. Perri said she was banal."

"And that's why they weren't friends anymore? Because Kat was boring?"

"*Banal.*" It was such an excellent word; Dannon couldn't imagine settling for boring old "boring" when one could say "banal" instead. Maybe the cop didn't know what it meant. "She said Kat was banal, and she had a point. No one can be that nice, you know? But Kat would never spread a rumor — not about Perri, not about anyone. Not her style. Then again, she didn't stop it either."

"What do you mean?"

"All she had to do was say why Perri was mad at her, instead of letting people gossip. She had that kind of power. But she wouldn't."

"And this made Perri angry, her refusal to stop the rumor?"

Dannon allowed himself a melodramatic sigh, only to be surprised by the surge of real emotion beneath it. "Perri didn't give a shit what people said about her. She was *beyond* that."

"Did you know she had a gun?"

Shit. He thought they had moved past that topic. "Um . . ."

"It wouldn't be a crime, it doesn't implicate you in any way. But we do want to establish without a doubt that Perri was the one who brought the gun to school. Did she show you the gun? Did she mention having one or how she came to get it?"

This was a trap. It had to be a trap. If he said yes, there would be more questions, questions he honestly couldn't answer, but who would believe his ignorance of Perri's plans once he admitted she had shown him the gun? And if he said yes and the Kahns found out he had known about the gun, they would never forgive him. Oh, he had tried to be strategic, tried to have it all ways — be a friend to Perri, keep her confidences while trying to protect her against her own self-destructive impulses. He was so smart he was stupid.

"Mom? Ma?"

His mother, who had been hovering nearby, appeared instantly. Dannon had many beefs with his mom, starting with his name — a gay boy should not be saddled with the brand name for a product that's famous for having fruit on the bottom — and continuing through her marriage to his humorless idiot of a stepdad. But, ultimately, she was always there for him, in a way that no one else was. She might not believe *in* him the way Eloise Kahn did, but she always believed him, taking his side against everyone. Except his stepfather.

"What is it, honey?"

"I don't want to talk to the police anymore. Do I have to?"

The good-looking one, Infante, stood. He was over six feet, and his five o'clock shadow gave him a menacing look, but his intent was clearly to charm. *Hey, flirt with me,* Dannon wanted to say. *She's taken, but I'm totally available.*

"It's always better for people to cooperate, ma'am. It's a mistake for innocent people *not* to talk. Makes them look guilty."

"Dannon isn't guilty of anything."

"So he should talk to us, don't you think?" The detective continued to try to ply his handsomeness, but Dannon's mother was indifferent to conventional charm tactics. She had said no to a lot of men before her second husband came along, and his main charm seemed to be his earning power. "You can sit in, ma'am, if it would make you feel better."

"I don't want to talk to them at all, Mom. I . . . I . . . ." Dannon clutched his stomach, groaning. Oh, yes, he had missed his calling, staying behind the scenes. "I'm having that stomach thing again. You know how I get. I gotta go. I gotta go, or I'm going to shit my pants right here."

He ran from the room, dashing into the powder room in the hall, where he didn't turn on the light because it would trigger the exhaust fan, and he wanted to hear what was going on in the living room.

"He does have a sensitive tummy," his mother said. "Always has. Dannon's very sensitive. But I'm sure he doesn't know anything about what happened at the school, close as he and Perri were. If he did, he would have confided in me. Dannon tells me everything."

I did once, Mom. When had he stopped? Upon her remarriage? When he had finally come out, at least to himself? No, earlier than that, back in middle school, when a cruel girl had mocked him for having boobs. A girl who happened to be named Perri Kahn. That had been the day that Dannon realized there were things in his life his mother could not fix and that confiding such problems in her would only serve to make her feel sad and ineffectual. He had sucked it up, endured what a fat gay boy had to endure, made it through middle school and into high school, which was marginally kinder. By high school the groups had solidified, the territory had been meted out, and the warfare had subsided. High school had been fine for everyone but the most obvious misfits, the ones who courted trouble. Dannon kept his head down, his profile low.

And then one day Perri Kahn had arrived in his life — a whirlwind, a benediction. At first he thought it was only because she needed an ally to get Old Giff to pick *Anyone Can Whistle* as the fall musical. When that battle was fought and won and then lost, he assumed that Perri was still hanging with him because she had divined his talent for eavesdropping and wanted to know things he might have heard or overheard, in places she could never go. But no, she was a genuine friend.

He had never had the nerve to mention how mean she had been, back in middle school. He was scared that she had forgotten he was once an object of scorn; reminded, she might drop him rather than confront her own cruelty. He accepted Perri as she believed herself now to be, a disciple of fairness, bordering on self-righteous. Perhaps Perri had sought him out as a penance. She had been trying to set a lot of things right in these past few months, reaching out to all sorts of people she had once wronged. But he was the only one she had befriended. He was the one she had hung out with — not Skeevy Eve Muhly, not Fiona Steiff, not Binnie-the-Albino Snyder. Just him, Dannon. Only he was sufficiently cool enough to be Perri Kahn's friend, and he would protect her as long as he could.

Just a little rumpus, she had promised him, holding the gun to her cheek. *No big deal.*

"He knows something," Lenhardt said as they headed out of the cul-de-sac and onto one of the long, looping drives that ran along the spine of Old Town Road. "He didn't have the balls to lie to us, so he bolted. But he wasn't smooth enough to cover his panic."

"Smooth? By his own testimony, he literally almost shit himself."

"Would you have known? If we hadn't known going in, if he hadn't made a point of telling us?"

"Known what?"

"That he was a fag."

"Oh, yeah, he'd suck a dick."

Lenhardt had felt sorry for the kid. Not because he was gay per se, but because he was so obviously, painfully gay, a pudgy little stereotype who might as well lisp through life with a "Kick Me" sign affixed to his back. It was one thing to be swishy and arch within the safe boundaries of Glendale High School, with its "No Hate Zone" sign in the front hall. College would be another version of the same bubble world. Eventually, however, this kid was going to take up residence on a planet where everyone didn't get all warm and fuzzy at the sight of some gay guy, inviting him in and asking him to play fairy godfather with their lives — redo the furniture, restock the fridge, rearrange the closet.

His cell phone buzzed, and the caller ID showed a name that didn't register, not at first: A.CUNNING.

"Lenhardt."

"Sergeant? It's Alexa Cunningham from Glendale High School. There are some things going on here, odd things. A theft . . . well, I'm not sure how to explain it over the phone. It's terribly complicated. But it just struck me that it could be key to your investigation. Could you meet with me?"

He sighed, looking at his wristwatch. He had promised to try to make Jessica's swim meet tonight.

"Could this wait until tomorrow?"

"I don't think so."

"Should I come up to the school?"

"No, I think it's better if I'm not seen talking to you, as what I'm doing might be considered insubordinate. Is there some place we could meet, sort of off the beaten track?"

"There's a place on Joppa, called Wagner's. Can you swing by there about five?"

"Absolutely."

He studied his phone. He could call his wife and tell her he was a likely no-show at the meet, or he could not call and hope the gods were merciful, that he would slide in toward the end and never be missed.

He did the chickenshit thing and left the message on the home phone, knowing that no one was there to pick up.

31

It was his mom's idea to cut flowers from her garden when Peter said he was thinking about visiting Josie Patel, see how she was holding up. "This is so thoughtful of you," she said, arranging the purplish flowers in bright tissue paper. Peter was a little humbled by his mother's pride, given that he wouldn't have dreamed of making such a visit without Dale Hartigan's encouragement. Peter had never been particularly fond of Josie, and he liked to think he was not a hypocrite. Show business required so much phoniness that he worked hard not to make it a habit in his real life, insofar as it was possible.

To Peter, Josie Patel was nothing more than Kat's pesky shadow, and there had been countless times that he had wished he could shut her in a drawer, just as Mrs. Darling had captured Peter Pan's dark twin. The summer that Peter and Kat had dated, Josie had come to the pool with Kat every day, then gone to movies and restaurants with them, even to the parties where she was clearly out of place. Because while Kat looked so much older than she was — Peter had no idea she was fifteen until he was already head over heels — Josie looked like a middle-schooler.

Perri had tagged along, too, once or twice, but she was smart enough to realize she wasn't wanted. Josie never seemed to get that. Or if she did, she didn't care. She rode in his backseat, the little chaperone, and he began to suspect that it was at Kat's invitation. Then there came a July day when Josie simply stopped coming along, and Peter understood that this was Kat's signal that she was ready to be alone with him, to allow more than the tentative good-night kisses she had allotted up to that point. They spent the rest of the summer looking for empty houses, hidden spots along the Prettyboy Reservoir, anywhere that Kat could cocktease him into oblivion.

Mrs. Patel answered the door. Not exactly a hot mom, not like Mrs. Hartigan, but pretty in a worn way.

"Mrs. Patel? I'm Peter Lasko. I know Josie through Kat, and . . . well, I wanted to pay her a visit."

"What beautiful irises," she said. Peter, used to compliments, thought for a moment that she was referencing his eyes. Then he remembered the purple flowers that his mother had chosen. So that's what they were, irises.

"I wasn't sure if it was right to bring flowers — she's not sick, exactly. But everyone likes flowers, right?"

"And Josie loves purple. Let me get a vase for those while you go up to her room."

The Patels' home was in one of the older sections of Glendale, built almost thirty years ago, and it looked a little tired to Peter. The stairwell was scuffed in places, the carpet dingy from foot traffic, and there were lots of boy toys scattered about, trucks and cars. He knew instinctively that Josie's room would be to the right of the staircase, at the opposite end of the hall from the master bedroom. The door was ajar, but he knocked anyway, waiting for Josie to look up from her computer. Her crutches were leaning against the desk, and her right foot, the injured one, was propped up on a pillow on another chair.

"Hey," he said. "You online?"

She turned quickly, her right arm knocking her crutches to the floor, then poked a key, losing what was on her screen. But that was instinctive. Peter always closed whatever was on his computer when someone walked into the room, even Colin, even if it was innocuous as the Television Without Pity boards or ESPN.com. Being caught at your computer was like hearing someone rattle the stall door in a public bathroom. Even if the door was latched, even if you were dressed, it spooked you a little.

"It's you," she said, not particularly surprised to see him. Not surprised and not happy either.

Peter took a seat on the bed, which was covered with a pink plaid spread. Girls' bedrooms always struck him as odd and a little overdone, with so much emphasis on self-expression. It was as if every object, every decorating touch, had to convey some deeper meaning. Sure, guys stuck up posters, too, but it wasn't like the announcement of a personal philosophy.

"I wanted to see you," Peter said, offering the explanation that seemed expected of him, "because you're probably one of the few people around here who feels worse than I do these days."

"Why do you feel bad? Because you never apologized to Kat for the way you dumped her that summer and now you never can?"

"I *didn't* —" It was automatic to defend oneself, but not productive, not in this situation. He was supposed to be winning Josie over, gaining her trust. He sighed so his shoulders sagged. "I never meant to be a jerk."

"Well, you were. You broke her heart."

"Really?" He had never known that. Kat had never reproached him in any way after he stopped calling.

"The way you did it. No call, no explanation."

"I went back to college. I really shouldn't have been messing around with her at all, if you think about it."

"She never really got over you just dropping her. She was in love with you."

No she wasn't, he wanted to protest. No one at fifteen was ever in love, outside Romeo and Juliet, and maybe not even them. Old Giff used to argue that the star-crossed lovers simply were buzzed on the fumes of forbidden lust. Give them thirty years of togetherness, Old Giff always said, and Juliet would be plunging the dagger into Romeo.

"I was in love with her, too. That was the problem." The lie, once offered, felt true.

After all, why had he let Kat torture him so long when there were so many willing girls? He must have cared about her.

"How is that a problem, loving someone who loves you?"

"She was fifteen. I was nineteen. What were we going to do, get married? Start a long-distance relationship that would have had to last a minimum of three years before we could live in the same city? And that's assuming her dad would let her go to school in New York, when we all know he was pretty much pushing Stanford from the day she was born."

"She never dated in high school, not seriously. She had friends, guys she would go to dances with, but no true boyfriends."

"Friends with benefits?" His voice was casual, joking even, his use of the now passé term deliberately arch. Yet he cared more about the answer than he wished to let on.

"No, not like that. Kat wasn't into hooking up. If anyone got, like, serious, she shut them down. She said it was because of her parents' divorce, but I think it was you. Once burned, twice shy."

Peter, who had not thought about Kat Hartigan outside of occasional jerking-off sessions, when she usually morphed into someone riper and far more willing, couldn't help being flattered.

Josie's computer trilled.

"Someone's trying to IM you."

She shrugged, turning quickly and clicking her "away" message. "Just my mom. She messages me from the kitchen so I don't have to hop up and down the stairs. Probably wants to know what I want for dinner. Kat was the only person I really talked to on the computer. Kat and Perri."

"Yeah, you three used to be tight. What happened? How could Perri do what she did?"

The question was too direct, and Josie's face clouded over. Peter had always thought of her as monkeyish, but maybe she had changed, or was changing. Her skin was the color of pale tea, her features strong and compelling.

"I mean, that's something people *did* talk about. The Big Three, busted up. It's all I heard about when I came home last Christmas."

Another lie, but a plausible one. Hadn't Old Giff mentioned some sort of fallout over the school musical?

"What can I say? Perri got weird."

"Well, *yeah.* I always thought she was jealous of Kat." But he was being too obvious. He needed to be at once more provocative and subtle to get Josie talking. "Jealous of Kat's preference for you, actually."

"They were friends longer. . . ." Josie spoke in the wistful way of someone who wants to seize a compliment but can't quite believe she deserves it.

"They were friends first. But you and Kat were the ones who lasted. You were probably going to be friends for life. Be each other's bridesmaids, you know." He tried to think of other things that girls did for one another. "Be, like, godparents to each other's kids."

"I don't want to have kids." Said fiercely, as if he had insulted her. "Not everyone wants to be a mom."

"Kat did." He was bullshitting like crazy now. What did he really know about Kat Hartigan? That she was beautiful in a way that made him ache all over. That she had the tenderest heart, so soft and vulnerable that she wept at movies like *Meatballs* because she couldn't bear the early scenes where the kid was a misfit. He would tell her that it was part of the essential arc, that the kid had to be an outsider in order to make his triumph all the sweeter, but Kat still found it heartbreaking.

"It was really all she wanted," he insisted. "She said she'd go to Stanford because her dad cared so much, maybe even study architecture and take a job with his company, just to make him happy. But all she wanted to do was get married and have kids. Lots and lots of kids. Like, three or four."

"Yeah." Josie was starting to tear up. Peter worked up a few tears himself, using a sense-memory exercise, remembering how his dog had been killed by a hit-and-run driver when he was eight. Soon, however, his tears were as sincere as Josie's. How does someone like Kat disappear? A week ago, five days ago, she had existed, and now she didn't.

"I wish I could have saved her," Josie said. "If — But it happened so fast."

"I can imagine. Someone comes into the bathroom firing a gun. Who would have time to react?"

"It's, like, you're frozen. My legs wouldn't move."

"She just comes in, and bam, Kat's dead, and bam, you're hit."

"It was like a movie. I mean, it was like something happening outside me. All I could do was watch."

"You're lucky to be alive. Perri always

seemed wound a little tight to me."

"Not always. Just lately. I mean, going back to when we were kids, she wanted to have her way, but not like this."

This struck Peter as a hint, but he didn't want to pursue it too directly. "You have to be a nut to do what she did. Doesn't seem to be any point in looking for reasons, does there?"

"*Exactly.* What's the point? She's probably going to die anyway, so what does it matter what happened? She's dead and Kat's dead — and I wish I were dead."

It occurred to Peter that he could kiss Josie just now. People did things like that in the face of loss — made connections to show they were still alive. And if he kissed her, she might come to trust him and tell him more. How to do it? He should just swoop in fast, get down on his knees in front of her, do a real Hollywood kiss. But what about her foot, propped up on the footstool? How could he maneuver around the foot? It probably hurt her a lot if she had to have it elevated like that. Too bad, because suddenly he wanted to kiss her, and not just to win her confidence. He wanted to kiss her for the very reasons he had outlined to himself as reasonable pretexts for kissing. He was alive and she was alive, and that was worth remembering.

Instead he said, "I don't think Kat's dad is ever going to get over this."

"Why?" Josie's voice seemed shrill and fearful.

"Because parents don't. That's what my mom said. It goes against the natural order of things."

"I suppose so."

"I mean, it's like Mr. Hartigan needs to understand what happened to get past it. The why of it, you know? It's not enough for him to say Perri was crazy and just walk away. He needs to know the reason."

Her computer beeped again, but Josie didn't even turn her head toward the screen. She was staring at Peter, her eyes cold and hard again. He had lost her. The moment he had mentioned Mr. Hartigan, she had shut down.

Still, he persisted.

"So there wasn't, right?"

"What?"

"A reason. I mean, there's nothing more to say, right? Perri just came in and started shooting, and that's all there is to know."

"No reason."

"And it was just the three of you, the way it always was?"

"What do you mean?"

517

"It's just that there are these rumors. About maybe someone else being there."

It is a cliché that acting is reacting, that the best actors know how to listen, but Peter had been well trained over the past four years, his parents had gotten their money's worth from NYU, and he did know how to listen, pay attention. Josie was in turmoil, eaten up by whatever she knew, so close to wanting the relief of sharing it.

"People are saying that?" she asked at last. "Lots of people?"

"Some." One.

"But you don't even know people at Glendale anymore."

"I knew their older brothers and sisters."

"Like who? Who did you talk to, exactly?"

"Kevin — Shawn Weaver's little brother." He had talked to him at the funeral. But one name seemed a bit thin, so he pulled out the name that Kevin had whispered when he pointed out the girl in the low-cut top, the blow-job queen. "And Eve Muhly."

"She's, like, a pathological liar. She loves to say she knows stuff when she doesn't."

"Yeah, but she's not the only one, in this case." He was almost indignant, totally caught up in his stories as he spun them. Okay, so neither Kevin nor Eve had spoken about a fourth girl to him. Okay, so he had never actually spoken to this girl, Eve. But Mr. Hartigan said the police thought there might be a fourth girl or that Josie and Perri had conspired in some way. That's why Josie got nervous when Mr. Hartigan's name came up.

Josie's chin trembled, and she looked as if she might cry again. But her voice was measured when she spoke, exceedingly calm.

"I did lie."

"Yes?" Now she was going to tell him, now he was going to find out what she was hiding from the police and everyone else. Mr. Hartigan would be so pleased to learn that Peter Lasko had done so quickly and easily what no one else could do.

"You didn't really break Kat's heart," she said. "I mean, she dated Seth Raskin after you, and he was much handsomer. And then he died in that car crash last spring. He's the one that Kat can't get over."

He understood that this, too, was a lie, a punishment for his trying to get her to open up. The surprising part was how effective it was.

"Well, I guess I should go. You've got a

lot going on this week, with graduation and everything. Is Senior Ramble still a big deal?"

"Yes, but . . ." She indicated her bandaged foot. "Not for me. I'll be going to the ceremony, then coming straight home."

He left on that and she didn't even say good-bye.

From the hall, with its scarred walls and framed art posters, he could hear Josie typing furiously, pounding away at her computer without pausing, in a cadence that marked the rhythm of an IM conversation, or maybe e-mail. Whatever it was, Peter was pretty sure it wasn't a girl telling her mother what she wanted for dinner.

Dale Hartigan was in a meeting when his cell phone vibrated — he never had it on ring, a point of pride with him — and the caller ID showed it was Peter Lasko. Given how dreary the meeting was — the usual cranky homeowners, convinced that a mixed-retail space would be the death of their neighborhood, especially if the restaurant had a liquor license — he would have taken any call, even one from Chloe or his father. This interruption not only saved him, it filled him with hope. Certainly the boy wouldn't call unless he had something vital to report.

"Right back," he mouthed to Susannah, who was running the show, trying to make everyone happy. The great smoother-over, as Dale thought of her.

"Yes?" he snapped into the cell phone as soon as he cleared the room.

"Josie didn't have much to say."

"And I needed to know that right now because . . . ?"

"Because the *way* she didn't say it was kind of striking. Like she's hiding something."

If Peter had been his employee, Dale would have been sharp with him. Not unkind or abusive, for Dale did not ape his father in that way. But he disliked people who talked just to talk, the eager young ones — and they were almost always young — who manufactured excuses for face time with the boss, not realizing they were wasting the boss's time.

"That was always my supposition, Peter. And while it's nice to know you agree, it doesn't really seem to advance things."

"Yeah. Yeah. But it did give me an idea. You know the Senior Ramble?"

Dale did. He had one of his rare quarrels with Kat over this very subject not two weeks ago, saying he didn't care what other

Glendale parents did, he was not going to suspend Kat's curfew on graduation night just so she could increase her chances of dying in a traffic accident. When Kat had protested that the Ramble was zero tolerance, with students signing pledges to serve as designated drivers, parents agreeing to chaperone official parties in their homes, and public places staying open late so the graduates could congregate safely, Dale had not been moved. "Exhaustion alone is enough to get kids in trouble," he had said. "Your curfew stands, and I'm going to tell the Patels as much, so don't think you can get around it by spending the night with Josie, playing by their more lax rules."

How innocent Dale had been then, just two weeks ago, when he thought the worst thing that could happen to his daughter was a car accident caused by fatigue or youthful driving errors. Two weeks ago the Patels had been his allies in parenthood, and now they were on the other side, protecting their child, not caring about justice for his.

"What could the Ramble have to do with any of this?" he asked Peter.

"Kids are out, they're loose. I thought I would work it, you know. Assuming you think it's a good idea."

Dale was beginning to see how stupid this entire idea was, how worthless Peter Lasko was to him. But he had solicited the boy, sought him out. There was no reason to make him feel like the ineffectual failure he was.

"Sure," he said. "Why not? Knock yourself out."

Peter Lasko had called Dale from the Dairy Queen, and he was so undone by the man's obvious lack of faith in him that he ordered a Snickers Blizzard. After all, he wasn't trying to lose weight — he just had to make sure he didn't gain any. He'd do an extra-long workout tonight to make up for it.

Of course, Mr. Hartigan had always made him feel small and stupid. They had sat here, not even three years ago, at this very same Dairy Queen, as Mr. Hartigan had flattered Peter, asked about his aspirations, wondered if there was anything he could do to help him.

"Given the business my family is in," he had said, "we go way back with the Rouses."

Peter had bobbed his head politely. Back then he hadn't worried about what he ate, and he had let Mr. Hartigan buy him the works — two chili dogs, a shake, onion rings, a Peanut Buster Parfait.

"We know the Rouses quite well."

"Uh-huh."

"In fact, I hear Jim Rouse's grandson may make a movie in Baltimore next year."

"Is he, like, a director?"

"He has directed, I think. But he's primarily an actor. He's done quite well for himself."

"Never heard of anyone famous named Rouse, except that DJ on the local oldies station."

Mr. Hartigan had smiled. "The actor I'm speaking of is Ed Norton. His mother was a Rouse."

Even now Peter could remember how he had blushed at his ignorance. Of course, he had been more of a theater snob then, not easily impressed by movie types, but still — Ed Norton. Oscar nominee, serious guy, total cred.

"You know him?"

"Well, my father knew his grandfather. After all, they were in the same business, more or less, although my father's vision was far less utopian. In fact, he started buying the land out here because he thought he could imitate Rouse's success in Columbia. I could introduce you. I think he's coming home in August for a visit — his uncle told me the Maryland Film Commission got use of the governor's box and was going to have a little thing for him. He's a big Orioles fan, but aren't we all?"

Mr. Hartigan was not so crass as to make it an offer or a case of quid pro quo. And Peter was not so stupid that he didn't recognize it as such. At first he told himself he wasn't interested. But even as he congratulated himself for not falling for Dale Hartigan's unspoken bribe, one summer day slipped into another, and before he knew it, a week had gone by, then another, and finally all of August was gone, and he had simply stopped calling Kat Hartigan. The shock was that she didn't call him or e-mail him. She was fifteen years old, and she had more innate dignity than the college girls he would later know. You didn't want Kat Hartigan in your life? Then she didn't want you.

Unless — he paused in midslurp, the milk shake blasting his sinuses — unless her father had told Kat his version of the story, made it seem as if Peter had agreed to stop seeing her in exchange for a chance to meet Norton. After all, Peter hadn't turned down the ticket when it arrived in the mail, the governor's box being the governor's box. And even though Peter hadn't ended up meeting Norton, the Maryland Film Commission had snagged the production of *Red Dragon.* Peter could have gone after a part, but he didn't. He had his pride, even if you couldn't prove it by Dale Hartigan. Besides, he didn't really approve of the remake, the original version, *Manhunter,* being one of his favorites.

Yet Dale Hartigan still thought he was foolish and weak. Dale Hartigan thought Peter was someone who would drop a girl for the slenderest advantage. Dale Hartigan thought Peter was a fool, and maybe he had been. But he didn't have to remain one.

32

Alexa liked the bar — "No, really," she found herself saying over and over. "It's so real." Oh, Lord, she was being condescending, silly, but it confused her, seeing this man and being reminded how middle-aged he was, how much older than she, almost old enough to be her father, which should make the racing feeling in her stomach dissipate. Only it didn't.

"It's a place," Lenhardt said. "Baltimore County doesn't have a real cop bar per se. But then, Baltimore City doesn't have one anymore either. The place we went back in the day, it's" — he leaned across the table, lowering his voice — "a lesbian bar now."

"Oh."

"Not that I'm prejudiced. I worked a murder at a lesbian joint once. Cleared it, too. This was back in the city, and the bar was kind of a secret, this place down in Little Italy before Flag came down."

"Before . . . ?" Had he said *flag* or *fag*?

Maybe she didn't like him as much as she thought.

"Before Flag came down. Flag House, one of the last high-rise projects. Two kids approached this woman about a block from the place, shot her, took her purse, disappeared into Flag. No witnesses, of course. But the people who cared the most about it — the women who went to the bar, the residents of Little Italy — they made a big stink, but they didn't want any publicity."

"Why?"

"The women were . . . uh, discreet about their private lives. And Little Italy traded on this rep as a place where crime never happened. You know — wink, wink, nudge, nudge, crime doesn't happen here because we take care of our own? Totally hypocritical because they're the first ones to bitch about ethnic stereotypes. Not to mention apocryphal."

"What?"

"You surprised that a police knows a big word?"

"No, no, I just didn't follow," she lied. "*Who* takes care of their own?"

"The Italians. Everybody. Now, what was it you wanted to meet about?"

"Is it okay if I order something to eat?"

528

"Go ahead. Nothing here will kill you."

She ordered a turkey club with fries and a Coors Light draft, because that's what he was drinking.

"I think I've stumbled on something pretty vital," she began.

"Yeah?"

She had his attention now.

"Earlier this week the principal — Barbara Paulson — told us that Perri's diploma could not be awarded. No one expected it to be announced at the ceremony, of course. But she says that Perri will never be recognized as a graduate of the school — even though her work might be complete."

"Well, that's a matter for the school board and her parents to hash out. It's not really a police matter."

"Yes, but — Barbara ordered Perri's teachers to destroy any work that turned up, to say she hadn't done the work. Isn't that wrong? I mean, obstruction of justice and all that?"

"Still sounds more like a civil matter. Unless Perri's work included a confession."

"I'm pretty sure that Perri did submit her final paper to me that Friday morning, only it's missing."

He didn't say anything, but his look

was clearly an "And?"

"Here's the thing: What kind of a girl turns in her final work when she's planning to kill her friend, then kill herself?"

"Well, there are two ways to look at that. One, she's unstable. So she does things that don't make sense." His eyes were on the television set above the bar.

"And the other way?"

"What?"

"You said there were two ways to look at it."

"The other way is . . . probably not something I should be talking about."

"You mean, someone other than Perri might have done this."

"I *didn't* say that. In fact, I'm now more sure than ever that the Kahn girl brought the gun onto school property."

"Well, I think I know a student who might have been there. Another student. A fourth girl."

His attention was complete now, unwavering. "Tell me her name."

"I don't think I should. If the police were to visit her . . . She wouldn't tell you anything, and she'd never trust me again. It's better if I keep trying to get through to her."

"With all due respect, there's been a

murder, Ms. Cunningham —"

"Alexa. Even my students call me Alexa."

"There's a way to talk to people, to get information that's not prejudicial."

"I was a communications major at American. My field is actually rhetoric. I got the teaching credential so I could work in public schools, but I'm more of an ethnographer than anything else."

"That word I don't know."

She was charmed. Men so seldom admitted not knowing something.

"I study teen culture."

"Isn't that an oxymoron?"

"What do you do, the *Reader's Digest* Build Your Word Power?"

"Yes, in fact. That and lots of crossword puzzles. I hear they stave off memory loss."

She was looking at his mouth. Alexa had never cared if men were handsome — she liked to think it was because she was confident enough in her own looks not to need the ego boost of gorgeous guys. But she liked mouths, and Lenhardt had a nice one. Full, but not too full. A little too old for her, but she liked older men, and don't tell her that it was daddy shit. Older men were so kind. Older men were grateful.

"Look, Ms. Ethnicographer —"

"Ethnographer."

He smiled, letting her know he had gotten it wrong as a joke. Or that he didn't mind being corrected by her. She couldn't quite read him, and that guarded quality was part of what made him so interesting.

"I'm sure you're good at what you do," he said. "But I'm good at what I do, and I'm the person who should be interviewing anyone who has information about this homicide, no matter how tangential."

"But in your view it's all straightforward, right? You said you're sure that Perri brought the gun to school. Maybe this other girl's information is . . . apocryphal."

He didn't smile at what she thought would be a nice shared moment, their first private joke. "If you keep talking to this girl, she's going to get rehearsed. Or scared. Or she may actually come to believe whatever version she's giving you. If you tell me her name, I won't say how we know about her. I'll just say we developed it from our investigation."

"Teenagers aren't stupid. She'd know it was me. And that's one thing I won't do, compromise a student's faith in me. It's essential to my work. These girls have to trust me. They've been betrayed and bullied, often by those who were once their

dearest friends. I teach them how to survive."

"They give credit for that?"

She knew he was trying to make a joke,
but she couldn't help being a little of-
fended. "Yes. And they should."

Her sandwich arrived, along with his
second beer. He drank off half of it in a
few gulps, looked at his watch. "I really
should be getting along."

"Don't," she said, then wished she could
take it back. "I mean . . . stay with me.
Until I finish my sandwich. I'm a quick
eater."

"Until you finish your sandwich. But
don't get indigestion on my account."

"I never do."

In the parking lot, she asked him,
"Which way do you go?"

"North. Toward Freeland."

"Oh, I'm south. Beverly Hills."

"That's a nice neighborhood."

"I'm renovating my own house. I bought
this amazing buffet at a yard sale, but then
I put a new floor down over the weekend."
She waited to see if he would have anything admiring to say about this. "So it's
ridiculous, but I can't move it back by myself. My brother says he'll help me when

he visits from New York, but that's not until later this summer."

The moment yawned. He looked at her thoughtfully, then took a step backward, jangling his keys. "You drive carefully, now. Someone little as you could be over the legal limit, drinking two beers in an hour."

But Harold Lenhardt did not drive straight home that night. There was no rush, now that it was clear he would never make Jessica's meet. He still went north but took a slight detour, stopping at a town house in White Marsh, a place he had visited only once before, for a Christmas party.

Andy Porter — the big blond giant, as Lenhardt thought of him, half amused, half intimidated — opened the door.

"Nancy know you're coming?" he asked, clearly surprised. As close as Lenhardt and Nancy were at work, they didn't socialize much outside the office.

"No, but I was in the neighborhood and thought I should check on her."

"I've fixed her up a place in the sunroom. Less moving around that way. A few steps to the bathroom, a few steps to the fridge."

The family room was a den on the other

side of the kitchen, separated by the now ubiquitous breakfast bar. *Hey, there's another word I know,* Lenhardt said to the woman who lingered in his head. *"Ubiquitous."*

"Sergeant!" Nancy's voice squeaked with surprise. She was lying on a flowery sofa, a thin, summer-weight blanket covering her substantial bulk, the television on mute, a stack of paperbacks within easy reach.

"How you doing?"

"They say okay. It is what it is."

What it was was toxemia, a potentially fatal condition for mother and unborn child, and Lenhardt was pretty sure that Nancy was scared to death, but there didn't seem to be any reason to call her on her attitude. If she wanted to play strong for him, he was okay with that. A police should front for the boss.

"I can't help feeling cheated. I counted on you working until the moment your water broke. I was looking forward to seeing how a pregnant woman functioned in interrogations."

"You know they would have put me on desk work the moment I started showing."

"Probably." Lenhardt was tactful enough not to mention that Nancy, a big-boned girl, could have gone longer than most before that happened. "But you're okay for now? And the kid's okay?"

She nodded. "As far as we know."

"And it's a boy?"

"It's a boy."

"That's good. Boys are . . . easier. Maybe because I'm a guy, but our boy seems awfully simple next to our girl."

"Infante told me what you're working on — murder in the girls' room. You feeling kind of blue about teenage girls?"

Lenhardt hadn't realized he was feeling blue, much less that someone might notice. "I don't think I understand women of any age. I just talked to this teacher — young, younger than you. Swear to God, Nancy, I think she was coming on to me."

"Ladies like you, Triple L." That was Nancy's nickname for him, Triple L — Living Legend Lenhardt. "Did she touch your hand?"

"No."

"Because if a woman touches you in any way — on the hand or arm — she definitely wants to sleep with you. That's what women do."

"Where do you learn this stuff? I mean, not just you. Women in general."

"I could tell you —"

"But then you'd have to kill me, I know."

"No. But if you knew all our secrets, you'd be even more irresistible, have more women chasing you. That's not what you want." A pause. "Right, Sarge? That's not what you want?"

"I can barely handle the two I have."

"Two?" She furrowed her brow, worried for him.

"Marcia and Jessica."

They shared a laugh, but then Nancy started to hiccup, and Andy came in, a bottle of water clutched in his giant hands. Lenhardt let himself out, embarrassed that he had imposed on Nancy at such a time. She had too much on her mind to tend to his conscience.

But he had really wanted to know — not just where women learn such things but what he should do about his own daughter, how he could prepare her for this world without sheltering her from it. He didn't want to think of his daughter in her twenties all but propositioning a married man old enough to be her father. He didn't want to think about the man who might say yes.

What Lenhardt *didn't* want to know was the truth about himself: If he could have gotten away with it, he would have. Under the right circumstances, if he could have had a fling with a girl like that and be assured he could never, ever get caught, he would have done it in a second. But Infante, with his two broken marriages — and, yes, marriage two was to the woman who broke marriage one — was proof that men did get caught.

And Infante wasn't the only one who could smell crazy on a woman. There was more than a whiff of it on that teacher — not crazy-crazy, but romantic-crazy, the kind of girl who went in saying she knew the rules, and then, next thing you knew, she was calling your house, indifferent to caller ID. A woman like that claimed to be free and easy, but you paid in the end.

Still, if he could have gotten away with it — if there was some parallel universe where actions had no consequences — he would have. Wouldn't anyone?

His phone rang, and he almost didn't grab it. Probably Marcia, busting his balls for not making the swim meet. But he weakened and flipped it open, and the female voice that greeted his was refreshingly businesslike — Holly Varitek, the lab tech.

"Tell me something good," he said.

"Can't," she said. "I'm sorry. I can't tell you anything definitive. There are at least three sets of fingerprints on the gun, but

I've only identified two."

"Perri Kahn and Josie Patel," he guessed.

"Yup. And not Kat Hartigan. We'll have to bring the owner in, I guess."

"What about —"

"Blood type on the tampon doesn't match Perri, Josie, or Kat. But, fresh as it appeared to be, I can't place it within a time frame that eliminates the very real possibility that someone else came in, did her business, and left. Sorry, Lenhardt, but it's not like that damn television show, where a single pubic hair unlocks all the mysteries of the world."

"I know. Problem is, juries expect it to be that way. So as long as that . . . that *thing* is floating around, it raises all sorts of questions without answering any. What do you think, Holly?"

"Sorry, you don't pay me enough to think. And if you put me in front of a grand jury, all I could swear is that someone changed her tampon that morning."

If I'd slept with that teacher, he thought, she would have told me the name. *Maybe not the first time, but eventually.*

When he got home, both Jessica and

Marcia were giving him the silent treatment, which was infuriating. So he had missed the swim meet. It had been for work — at least, he thought it was for work when he headed out. And he hadn't slept with her, had he? A young blonde had all but offered herself up, asking nothing more from him than help in moving a piece of furniture, and he had sent her on her way. A man was always getting in trouble for things he didn't do, but he never got rewarded for the gauntlets he ran every day. Marcia might have him firmly in the debit column, but Lenhardt knew he had a million credits on his balance sheet.

twelfth grade

33

Old Giff, as theater teacher Ted Gifford was known throughout the school, was not old, and his name was not Gifford. He had changed it legally at twenty-two, aware that the Polish surname he carried out of the western hills of Pennsylvania — Stolcyarcz — would never work for an actor. So he became Ted Gifford, a name designed to be so bland that casting directors would have no fixed idea of who he was or what he could play.

But the name change was not enough to transform him. Giff landed a few cop roles, playing middle-aged men while still in his twenties. Playing old made him feel old, which he did not enjoy. Meanwhile he was still too callow to play the parts he felt he was born to play, Falstaff and Lear. So he went back to school and got a teaching certificate. A thirty-something man could feel old or young surrounded by teenagers, and Old Giff felt young.

Or so he told his students every new school year when he launched into his long-winded explanation of why Glendale staged its musical in the fall instead of the spring, as other high schools did.

"Tradition is merely habit hardened into ritual," he began. "We assume there must be a rational basis, but often there is none. Or if there was a reason, it disappeared long ago, became obsolete."

There was simply no basis for the schedule used by most other public schools in the state, Gifford told his students, and many arguments to be made for its inversion. Students were fresher in the fall, energetic and more capable of concentration, especially those who had spent the summer in Sylvia Archer-Bliss's theater program. The end of the year had too many competing interests, particularly for seniors. England had a long history of Christmastime extravaganzas, and a fall musical was a good substitution, as it provided a secular entertainment and bypassed the increasingly contentious debates over holiday programs.

"In England these productions were known as pantomimes," he said.

Here, every year, every time, some budding class clown did his rendition of Marcel

Marceau and the wall, or walking-into-wind. Griff would wait patiently for the laughter to die down, then explain that it wasn't the same thing. A pantomime was actually a pageant, something bright and *gay* — he always let this word linger a little longer than necessary, as if testing his students.

"As the days grow shorter and darker, we need something bright and festive," he continued. "So why not create a tradition with meaning, one tied to the calendar, to the earth's natural cycles? At Glendale High School, we do our musical in the fall — and we let the students have a hand in choosing it."

He didn't bother to disguise his amusement at the debate that followed, with students trying not to reveal their self-interest as they lobbied for this or that play. They all attempted to sound altruistic, to pretend that their only interest was what was best for the drama department. The most vociferous were often the most deluded when it came to their own abilities. Some short, skinny boy with a merely decent voice was always pushing to be Don Quixote in *Man of La Mancha*, while terribly plain girls yearned to play the Gwen Verdon sexpots — *Sweet Charity* and

Damn Yankees. If they could see me now indeed.

The fall of Perri's senior year, she clearly was bursting with an idea, but she was shrewd and strategic, waiting for everyone else to speak first. Josie watched her, curious, for Perri had not confided in her or Kat what her plan was. Come to think of it, Perri had not spent much time with them since the school year began.

Man of La Mancha was touted, as it was almost every year, and Giff undercut it. "It's not the right climate to have a gang rape onstage." A new girl, a junior transfer, April something, had a *Cats* fixation, which was unfortunate for her, as everyone else knew that Giff hated, hated, hated Andrew Lloyd Webber. Still, he listed them all on the board — *Man of La Mancha, Cats, West Side Story, Gypsy.* (The last was clearly Giff's preferred choice, and Giff's favorite somehow always won, despite his seemingly democratic method.)

Then, just as he was about to close the discussion, Perri raised her hand, confident of being recognized despite the already full slate. She was Giff's star student — not just talented but hardworking, too, willing to do all the grubby, behind-the-scenes tasks.

"*Anyone Can Whistle*," she said. Naturally someone did — whistled, that is — but the boy, a freshman, was silenced by Perri's withering look.

"Interesting," Giff said. "Of course, if it's Sondheim you like, he was the lyricist for *Gypsy.*" He ran his chalk beneath that title. "And it has such good roles for girls — Louise, June, the strippers. Mama Rose."

He seemed to be trying, with his emphasis on the last, to remind Perri that she would be the obvious choice for that role.

"But you also need at least four boys who can dance behind Dainty June, and our guys are weak on dancing." The males grumbled, indignant, but Perri seldom spared anyone's feelings. "It's true. We couldn't let the chorus do the Charleston in *The Boyfriend* because our guys are so left-footed."

"Make your case on the strength of your choice, not on the weakness of —" Giff almost said *mine,* then caught himself just in time. "Of Jill's."

"Well, given that three of the show's original stars were not trained singers, its score is clearly within the range of what we can do. It has a large number of parts — within the mayoress's cabinet, and the residents of the Cookie Jar — that can be played by either gender, which is always a plus for us. And it hasn't been staged by any school in the state."

"There might be a reason for that, Perri. The show was a spectacular failure on Broadway."

"Yes, but that was the early 1960s," Dannon Estes put in. "It was ahead of its time."

"And a little behind now, don't you think?"

"There are a few dated bits, but some of the satire is more relevant than ever," Perri said. "A city that relies on one 'miracle' to draw tourists — that's like all those cities that think ballparks are going to be their salvation, right?"

Everyone could tell that Giff was impressed by the last point. Perri had clearly prepared her case well.

"What about its attitude toward the mentally ill?"

"It argues that they should be assimilated. Is that so wrong?"

Giff could not resist needling Perri. "And I suppose you think you could play Cora, the mayoress."

"Actually, I'd prefer Nurse Fay Apple, although I think I could do the speech *and* the song. I have the wind."

Giff had created this monster. He had encouraged Perri in her love of Stephen Sondheim, and now, like every good Stephen Sondheim fan, Perri was steeped in all the backstage lore and trivia. Josie herself had been forced to listen to the original cast album over and over again, with Perri pointing out the highlights. *Anyone Can Whistle* had originally included a lovely ballad, "There Won't Be Trumpets," but it followed a long speech. The song had to be cut because the original actress couldn't do both. Perri had always longed to sing "There Won't Be Trumpets," with its call for an ordinary hero who would arrive without fanfare.

"It depends on rights, you know. It could be very expensive."

"It's not," Perri said. "I checked."

The students knew that the decision, ultimately, was Giff's. If he wanted *Gypsy*, he would somehow get the votes he needed. But perhaps he was swayed by Perri's passion. Or maybe he was enchanted with the idea of staging a show that no Baltimore-area high school had ever attempted. Perri was a senior, and this would be her last musical. She had earned her star turn.

But he could not give her quite everything she wanted. He told her at callbacks that the part she longed for, the starchy Nurse Fay Apple, was not right for her. Perri was good at the starchy side, much less persuasive when she had to play the character's alter ego, a sexy French actress. He gave Perri the part of Mayoress Cora, while making Kat Hartigan the nurse.

Under Giff's usual rules, Kat Hartigan should not have gotten a lead at all. She had not tried out for a single show during her years at Glendale, despite repeated encouragement from the chorus teacher, who admired her pure soprano voice. It was clear to everyone that Kat's sudden interest in the fall musical was all about sweetening her college applications, adding yet one more extracurricular to her résumé.

But Kat's voice was strong and she was fetching, as Old Giff was heard to say to the band director. She wasn't quite as fiery as she needed to be in the angry scenes, but Giff worked to bring that side out of her in rehearsals. Certainly her seduction of Dr. Hapgood was almost too credible. The only thing that was hard to believe was that someone as womanly as Kat Hartigan would really be drawn to the reedy, immature junior cast opposite her. That was the perennial problem with high-school shows. Most of the girls looked grown-up, while the boys were still skinny and unformed.

They were three weeks into rehearsals when the complaints started. Several parents found the show unsuitable, saying it was much too dark for high-school students. And what was the bit about communism, not to mention the exchange about taxes and nuclear weapons? It didn't seem quite patriotic, did it, given that the United States had thousands of troops in Iraq? The show encouraged a disdain for authority and a distrust of government. Were those values they wanted to endorse?

No one suspected Dale Hartigan of making these arguments. After all, his daughter had the second lead. But Josie heard from Perri that it was Mr. Hartigan, working quietly behind the scenes, who was determined the show would not go on. The rumor was that Mr. Hartigan's real beef was the mildly suggestive lyrics that Kat had to sing, "Come Play Wiz Me." Old Giff argued that she did it so freshly and prettily that it worked for the show in a wholly unanticipated way, underscoring the fact that the sexy French actress was

Nurse Fay Apple in disguise. Still, when it was learned that an Equity company in Harrisburg was invoking the 150-mile radius and forcing Glendale to cancel its production of *Anyone Can Whistle*, gossip continued to blame Dale Hartigan.

Instead of canceling the fall musical, Giff chose *Oklahoma!*, because he could stage it in his sleep, and he gave Kat the lead. And all the drama students could see that the part of a sweet-but-stubborn Oklahoma farm girl suited her far better than did a two-sided temptress.

They all assumed that Perri would play Ado Annie, every girl's dream role. But while a dozen girls had been called back for the part in the rushed-up audition process necessitated by the switch, Perri was not among them. She simply refused, and the absence of the obvious favorite stirred up a froth of longing and yearning that verged on hysteria. By the end of the audition, girls were weeping, on crying jags so intense that they had to bring in the guidance counselor, Alexa Cunningham, to calm them down. One girl cried and vomited until blood vessels burst at the bottom of her eyes, leaving her with the red-rimmed pout of a lesser monster on *Buffy the Vampire Slayer*. She got the part, too, although it was hard not to wonder what Perri might have done with it.

Choosing the male leads should have been blissfully anticlimactic after that sob-fest, but Perri threw Giff another curveball by showing up, breasts bound, and demanding a chance to try out for the part of Jud, the lovelorn ranch hand who turns violent at the play's end.

"C'mon, Perri," Old Giff said, treating Perri as if she were playing a practical joke. "That just can't be."

"But you're the one who's always talking about how unusual casting can make people see an old play in a new way, remember? You loved it when the Shakespeare Theater in Washington did *Othello* with a white actor as the lead and a black actor as Iago."

"This is different."

"I don't see how. There needs to be something truly forbidden about Jud's love for Laurey. When the play was first produced, they got that over with his love for dirty postcards. But those things seem pretty innocuous now. I wouldn't play him as a girl, but the fact that I *am* a girl would inject that sense of menace that Jud's character has lost over the years."

"The songs are written for a baritone."

"We perform with a piano, not an orchestra. It wouldn't be hard to transpose the songs to a suitable key for me."

As it turned out, there was something chilling about Perri's version of "Lonely Room," and a comic poignancy in her version of "Pore Jud Is Daid." All the students who saw that audition knew that no boy in the school could touch her subtle performance. But even in the allegedly hate-free zones of Glendale High School, there were boundaries. If Dale Hartigan had been troubled by the idea of his daughter in a negligee, singing suggestively about her own body, how would he react to a girl — even a girl disguised as a boy — singing a love song to Kat?

Old Giff told Perri that she simply wasn't large enough to create the physical threat that Jud needed to convey. She settled for the part of Gertie, a small but showy part, and Giff cast a wonderful baritone from the school chorus as Jud. This boy's mother also complained, accusing Giff of perpetrating old stereotypes by having an African-American boy pine for a blue-eyed blonde.

Given all this drama, it was several weeks before anyone noticed that Perri wasn't speaking to Kat, not outside their scenes together. She would deliver her lines with her usual professionalism but retreat between scenes, seeking as much distance as she could from Kat, giggling with Dannon, the wardrobe manager. And if Kat spoke to her offstage, Perri openly snubbed her.

Old Giff summoned Josie, who had signed up for dance troupe as she always did. It meant spending more time with Kat and Perri, and the dancers always needed someone little to throw around in the dance numbers.

"What gives?" he asked. "Is Perri mad at Kat because *Whistle* got canceled? Because it really had nothing to do with Dale Hartigan, no matter what everyone thinks."

"I don't think that's it," said Josie, who had asked Kat and Perri the same thing. But she asked them again, only to receive the same nonanswers.

"Ask Kat," Perri said. "If she'll tell you."

"Perri's just moody," Kat said. "I didn't do anything."

Part Six

commencement

34

Graduation day started with a yellow-red haze on the horizon, the kind of sky that promised a long, sticky day and thunderstorms late in the afternoon. Eve, walking with Claude and Billy, thought about what she should wear — not to school but tonight, when she planned to meet Val and Lila for the Senior Ramble. Because she would have to slide quietly along the porch roof beneath her bedroom window, she definitely had to wear pants, dark ones. But perhaps a halter beneath her flannel shirt, and her new sandals, which were adorable. She would have to carry them in her hand, given their height, but she could change into them once she was in Val's car.

The Ramble was supposed to be for seniors only, of course. The other students at Glendale were expected to be in class tomorrow, fresh and rested. The perquisites of graduation — the curfew-free night, the specials at the restaurants and ice cream shops that stayed open late, the chain of supervised parties across the valley — were not theirs to sample. But every official celebration eventually ends up with an unofficial partner, and while the seniors of north Baltimore County had been granted this night of controlled, alcohol-free partying, the other classes felt free to hold their own shadow party, one with fewer rules and controls. "Which means we get to have more fun," Val said, "because we didn't have to sign any stupid pledges."

Eve's mother remembered the Ramble in its earliest incarnation, when it began as a spontaneous car rally, the newly minted seniors driving around and around because there was no place to go, other than the Dairy Queen, and even that closed at ten back then. Over the years, as proms had migrated to downtown hotels, the Ramble had become the all-night prowl of choice, with parents volunteering to hold open houses and students agreeing to accept designated-driver status. Last year, after Seth, Chip, and Kenny had died in the car accident on Old Town Road, the Ramble had almost been canceled. But then it was decided that the student drivers would register and agree to wear red wristbands, so if one appeared under the influence in any way — which they shouldn't, being eighteen, but alcohol had a way of sneaking into such things — he or she would be sent home, along with those who had signed up to ride in that particular car. Student drivers may risk many things, but their parents believed that the wrath of their peers would achieve what nothing else could.

Last year Eve had not been sufficiently bold to try to sneak out for the entire night. She had made excuses to Val and Lila, who accepted them with their usual nonjudgmental nonchalance. But she felt it was important to join them tonight, to prove herself worthy of their friendship.

Dannon was going to run the lighting board for the graduation ceremony, costuming not being much of an issue. He had helped distribute the caps and gowns earlier in the week, and he would have the unenviable job of collecting them at the end of the evening, tracking down the crying girls and the high-fiving boys, who threw their caps in the air despite repeated admonitions.

The lighting scheme was relatively simple, at least — no split-second blackouts, no spots, no special filters — but Old Giff was a perfectionist about anything produced on his stage, and he had insisted on this tech run-through.

"At this point the senior members of the chorale society will come center and sing the 'Desiderata,' so we'll need to bring the lights up on the apron, but I don't want the rest of the stage completely dark," he told Dannon, looking at his typed rundown. "Then they return to their seats, and we have the presentation of the Hartigan scholarship, boom, diplomas, boom, recessional, and *out*."

"Three hundred seventy-five names," Dannon said. "It's going to take forever. Especially if people clap for individual students, and they always do, no matter how many times they're told not to."

Not that he had anywhere to go or anyone to go there with. He just couldn't imagine anything more boring than listening to a list of names.

"Three hundred seventy-*seven*."

"So if each student takes five seconds, which makes twelve students per minute, a hundred twenty students per ten minutes . . ." Dannon's voice trailed off, math not being his strong suit. "Well, more than half an hour."

"I'm counting on Principal Paulson to

make it brisker than that. Even she gets bored around the *J*'s, starts speeding up without realizing it."

The phone in the lighting booth rang, the short, staccato rings of an in-house call. "Gifford, speak!" Old Giff commanded in his usual tone of bored impatience. But his imperiousness instantly faded.

"Yes? *Yes.* He's right here. No. Of course, right away."

The face that Giff turned toward Dannon was pitying. No, not pitying, and maybe not pitiful either, as pity was a cheap emotion, distant and uninvolved. Giff was as affected by whatever he had heard as he expected Dannon to be. That could mean only one thing.

"She's dead. Perri's dead."

"She will be. Her parents have decided to turn off all the life-support machines, but they will wait for you to get there. Once everything is off — they don't know, Dannon. It's not like turning off a light switch, and there's always a chance — although not much of a chance — that a person might surprise doctors, start breathing on her own. But I'll take you down, and I'll wait there with you."

"Will we be back in time for graduation?"

"Who gives a shit? They can just turn on the stage lights and let it go, for all I care. I don't get paid extra for supervising this crap."

"No chance of a dying declaration, I suppose?" Infante asked Lenhardt after they were informed by the police officer posted in the Kahn girl's room that she was to be taken off life support.

"Doesn't seem likely."

"It could end here," Infante said, but his statement was a question, the kind of question asked when someone knows the answer but wishes it could be otherwise. "If we say it was her, just her, we're done. The extra fingerprints could be from anyone, anytime. The tampon could be from some girl who ducked in there earlier and got out, never knowing what a close call she had."

"Such a girl would call a press conference in this day and age, sell her story to the networks. 'A timely bathroom break saved my life.' I'm surprised we don't have forty girls claiming to have been in that bathroom just before it happened."

"Yeah, I know. I just hate being in a lose-lose, where whatever we do is gonna end up pissing people off. So why not say,

'Dead girl did it, go on with your lives.' "

"You mean, other than the fact that we know that's not the whole story?"

"It wouldn't be the first time we made a square case fit into a round hole."

"It would be the first time we did it consciously."

Lenhardt looked at the notes and files and photographs spread across his desk. Sometimes police work reminded him of algebra, not that he could do algebra for shit anymore, as he had discovered when Jason asked for help with his homework this past school year. Back in the day, however, he had been good at math, had even enjoyed it. The facts in front of him were like one of those long problems — $x + y + z = 2 (x + y) - z$. You simply had to isolate the variable. Well, they had isolated her again and again, and Josie Patel had proved to be all too consistent.

And once Perri Kahn was dead, Josie Patel would be untouchable. No one could contradict her, except the phantom fourth girl, and even Lenhardt was beginning to doubt she existed.

Infante was right: It would all go away if they decided things had happened as Josie said, and everyone would be happier for it. Hang it all on the dead girl, get their clearance, move on. The Kahns might squawk a little, but Mrs. Delacorte's photographs put the gun in the girl's hand just a few weeks out. He didn't doubt that Perri was the one who had brought the weapon to school. The only question was who else had known about it. Someone had taken that photo, and Lenhardt was reasonably sure it wasn't Mr. Delacorte. *Was that you, Josie, on the other side of the camera? Is that what you're not telling us? Why?*

Perhaps even Dale Hartigan would be satisfied with this outcome. It was an answer, neat and contained. The girl who had killed his daughter would be dead, and he wouldn't even have to go through a trial, much less risk seeing the girl acquitted on an insanity defense. All of Glendale would be happy to see this end, so it could go back to being known for its high-achieving graduates and its intermittently successful soccer team.

Yes, everyone would be happy — except Lenhardt and Infante, and their bosses if the day ever came that the fourth girl surfaced for some other reason. Putting down a bad case was much worse than keeping one open.

"We've got to talk to Josie Patel one

more time," he said. "Right now, before *she* knows that Perri Kahn is dying. It may be our last chance to get the truth out of her."

"But how do we nudge her forward? We can bluff the girl about the physical evidence, but we can't get anything past her lawyer."

"We get a search warrant."

"For . . . ?"

"For a pair of missing shoes."

"We've been over that. If we ask her for the shoes and she doesn't have them, she'll just say they got thrown away by accident or something."

"I don't care about the shoes. I just want another excuse to talk to her, let her think that we know more than we do."

Peter slept late, slept in the heavy, dreamless way that he hadn't known since he was in his teens and his body was perpetually exhausted by the demands of his late growth spurt. Still in his pajama bottoms, he padded barefoot around his mother's kitchen, looking for something healthy to eat, preferably low-carb. The refrigerator had plenty of nutritious options, but they were so much effort. Egg-white omelets required separating eggs, a process that Peter understood only theoretically. Salads meant washing and endless chopping.

He nuked one of his mom's Lean Cuisines, daydreaming while it turned lazy circles inside the microwave. On set, the food — you called it "craft services," according to Simone, based on her experience as a day player in *Good Will Hunting* — was constant, a cornucopia. There was always one sit-down hot meal and then, if the day went late enough, a second meal brought in. He would be able to save a lot of his paycheck.

Absentmindedly, he braced himself against the counter and did a few pushups. He didn't feel quite as fervent about going out for the Senior Ramble tonight. Chasing gossip seemed less important today than yesterday. But it was something to do, and he was so restless.

Dannon was terrified of being in the room while Perri's life ebbed out of her, but he did not see how he could refuse the Kahns' offer. They clearly considered the invitation a great honor, proof that he was like family to them. *One of us, one of us,* he chanted in his head, then realized it was the litany from Tod Browning's *Freaks*. He was no longer so sure that he wanted to be one of the Kahns.

He told himself that the person in the bed was a stranger, someone he didn't know. But there was no comfort in that.

"Do you want to hold her hand?" Eloise Kahn asked. "Or have a private moment?"

"No." It was all he could do to keep the panic out of his voice. In *The Three Faces of Eve*, another one of the old movies that he and Perri had gobbled up during their long afternoons at Dannon's house, an encounter with a dead grandmother was enough to explain multiple personality disorder. Kiss a corpse, go bonkers. People knew better now. Dannon knew better, but he still did not want to be left alone with Perri, for fear that she would suddenly snap into consciousness, fix those fierce blue eyes on him, and announce, *I know what you did, Dannon. I know how you tried to betray me.*

"I mean, no, please don't leave," he said. "I couldn't bear it if . . ."

Everyone in the room knew what could not be borne, or thought they did. Dannon took Perri's hand. It felt loose and floppy, boneless.

"Talk to her, Dannon," Eloise encouraged him. "She might hear you."

"Hey, Perri." God, that was lame. "So . . . remember Fatty Arbuckle and Kevin Bacon? I finally figured out how to do it. You go Fatty Arbuckle to Buster Keaton — they made a lot of shorts together. Then Buster Keaton to Zero Mostel, in *A Funny Thing Happened on the Way to the Forum*. Zero Mostel to Woody Allen, *The Front*. Woody Allen to Elizabeth Shue, *Deconstructing Harry*. Shue to Bacon, *The Hollow Man*. Done!"

There was no response. If Perri could talk, she would probably tell Dannon that she didn't want to spend her last minutes on the planet thinking about a stupid movie game.

"The thing is . . ." He lowered his voice, leaning closer to her. "The thing is, I cheated, Perri. Just a little. I used the Internet Movie Database to find out if Keaton and Arbuckle were in anything together. I mean, I thought they might be, but I'm not strong on the early stuff, but I knew if I could get the two of them together, I could complete on my own. I wasn't thinking of *Forum*, but I knew that Keaton was in *How to Stuff a Wild Bikini*, which meant I could do Annette Funicello or Frankie Avalon, and he's in *Grease*, so I could have done Buster Keaton–Frankie

Avalon–John Travolta. And Travolta was in *Phenomenon* with Kyra Sedgwick, and she's been in a ton of stuff with Bacon since she's his wife. But I knew you'd like it better if I went through *Forum*, it being Stephen Sondheim and all. Still, it was cheating. You were always adamant that we shouldn't use IMDb to figure out Fatty Arbuckle."

And you wouldn't approve if you knew I didn't erase that photo, the one with you in Mrs. Delacorte's underwear, holding the gun. But I didn't know what else to do. I had promised you I wouldn't tell, and I saw what you could do to people who don't take your side. You had cut off Kat and Josie because they had displeased you in some way, and they were your for-ever friends, whereas we had just been hanging out the past year. So I left the one photo in there, thinking someone might find it and call the police or tell your par-ents. It was so half-assed, so typically me. I should have told or not told. If I had been willing to risk losing your friendship, you might be alive. Jesus, Perri, what were you thinking?

But Perri's thoughts were long gone, shut off to him, lost to everyone, forever.

Josie knew the car by now. Not by

sound, not like her mother's chugging Accord, but she knew it by sight, the generic Ford Taurus that the detectives drove. She had seen them leaving Kat's funeral in this car, the older one staring her down from the passenger seat. And just as the detectives had been out of place in her hospital room, their car did not look right in a Glendale driveway. Too boxy, too plain.

Now the detectives were on her doorstep, ringing the bell, and she was balanced on her crutches three inches, four inches away — she really wasn't good with distances, as she had told the detectives that very first day — wondering if they could tell she was on the other side of her door, holding her breath.

"Josie?" the older one said. "Josie, are you there? Is someone there?"

Marta had left to run an errand and then pick up her brothers at school, which meant she wouldn't be home for an hour. Her parents were still at work. If Josie stood very still, if she didn't breathe or make any noise, the detectives couldn't know she was here. And even if they knew, they couldn't force her to open the door. Could they?

"We have a search warrant, Josie."

Search warrant? The shoes, the damn

shoes. Well, she had taken care of that. They wouldn't find the sandals here. It had broken her heart, but they were gone now, gone as the cell phones. She had taken care to get rid of them right after the funeral. Another piece of improvisation.

"Josie, just let us in. We won't try to talk to you until your lawyer shows up. Unless you want to talk, of course. But we're entitled to execute this search without your lawyer being here."

It was getting hard balancing on one foot. She gave a little hop, and a crutch bumped against the door.

"Josie — we *hear* you."

She opened the door but said nothing, absolutely nothing. Her parents and her lawyer had been adamant in their instructions: Do not talk to anyone without us present. She had been happy to follow their advice to the letter and had taken it even further, refusing to speak to her parents and her lawyer as well. She let the police in, pretended to read the paper that they thrust at her, then tilted her head toward the stairs, knowing it was her room they wished to search. She hopped back to the sofa in the family room and continued watching *Judge Joe Brown.* Her parents would be home early for the graduation ceremonies. In less than an hour, her father would come through the door and take care of these detectives. Until then all she had to do was stay quiet.

Quiet was something at which she excelled, Josie was finding out, a skill that she had acquired from Kat without even realizing what she was learning. For while she had often envied Perri and her endless, inventive rush of words, there were advantages to keeping still, saying no more than strictly necessary. In gymnastics the ability to hold a pose, to defy momentum or at least manipulate it, had been as essential as the movements themselves. It didn't matter how beautifully you tumbled and flipped if you couldn't nail the landing. Perhaps Josie had more of a game-day mentality than anyone had ever known, herself included.

She just hoped the detectives finished before she had to start getting ready for the evening. Her dress was laid out on the bed, a yellow-and-green sundress. Oh, her sandals would have been perfect with that dress, not that she could wear anything with a heel just now, even kitten heels. She was going to have to wear her clashing pink Pumas.

Puma, she corrected herself. Just the one.

35

Dale Hartigan remembered exactly one thing about his own graduation from Hereford High School: The speaker had predicted that the students wouldn't be able to recall his name, much less what he said. The guy had pretty much nailed it. The only thing Dale remembered from graduation night was that Cathleen Selden, a rather plain girl who had gone through high school in flannel shirts and work boots, had shown up in a black-print halter dress. Cathleen Selden's reinvention had fired Dale's imagination, in ways large and small, reminding him that there really was a reason the ceremony was known as commencement. He might not be going to his college of choice, he might still be yoked to his brother, but College Park was big enough to allow a fresh start. After the ceremony he had tracked Cathleen through the looser, less organized gatherings that made up the Senior Ramble in his day, and while they never got further than sharing a Miller Lite on the hood of his car, it had been a most satisfying night.

Yet Dale was certain that every detail of his daughter's graduation ceremony would have remained vivid. Not because she was first in her class — Glendale, following the cowardly example of other schools, had dropped valedictorian and salutatorian from its ceremony, denying Kat that recognition. Nor did he care that she was slated to recite that strange poem, "Dover Beach." His daughter could have been just one of the crowd, an ordinary student with no special role in the ceremonies, and every moment would have been etched in his memory as long as he lived. When it came to his own achievements, Dale felt vaguely shameful. But he had been able to glory in everything Kat did.

Of course, it hadn't quite worked that way in Dale's family, where his parents had been keen not to emphasize the differences between the brothers. Everything must be equal for twins, his father insisted. Dale remembered his parents' consternation when they finally left the house on Frederick Road and moved into the old Meeker farm, whose odd-shaped rooms made it impossible to give their sons identical bedrooms. So, rather than let one boy have what was clearly a superior room — even by random drawing of straws or flipping a coin — they had made them continue to double up. Dale had not minded, not until the issue of college came up and his father said each boy would get the same amount of money, no more. So if Dale wanted to go to Stanford, which was offering no financial aid, it was up to him to pay the difference in tuition. And not just the college costs but the difference in expenses, including the travel back and forth to California. It was probably a bluff, but Dale hadn't called it.

Wait — he did have another memory from his own graduation night: His father had arrived late. Dale had been third in his class, winning prizes for math and history, but his father had managed to miss that part of the ceremony. Yet he was there when the diplomas were awarded, clapping first for Dale Hartigan, then Glen. He knew that his father hadn't meant to teach him to be ambivalent about his achievements, and yet Dale always felt a little desperate whenever he received any public recognition.

So Dale had tried to do things differently with Kat, and he hadn't lacked opportunities to celebrate her. Number one in her class, a cheerleader yet, and popular too, the kind of girl who was elected prom queen not just because she was beautiful but because she was beloved. Early admission to Stanford. All that, and then the bonus of her lovely soprano voice, to which Kat seemed utterly indifferent. He remembered feeling a little startled when she said Perri had been given a solo while Kat was to recite.

"It's what I *want*," she insisted. "I specifically asked for a speaking part. Dad — don't interfere again."

"I never interfere."

"Dad." Kat could say a thousand things with that one word. In this instance she was saying he was full of shit. She knew him, his daughter. Her love for him was not blind, but it was constant, unwavering. Married people never knew this kind of love. A lasting marriage was full of rough spots and angry times; the only real victory was hanging on. But it was possible, with a child, to have a pure relationship.

"That was different, what happened last spring. You deserved the number one ranking in the class. It was silly of them to try to deny it, sillier still to just drop the valedictorian rather than sort out their own contradictory policy —"

"Dad." This time her tone signaled: End of topic. If Dale had been frustrated by his own father's refusal to brag about him loud and long, Kat squirmed a little at her father's obvious pride, which just made her more adorable. What would Kat have been like as a mother? What lessons would she have absorbed, what models would she have rebelled against? Her even temper, her dislike of arguments — were those inborn or the result of the fractious years in the Hartigan marriage?

Kat was Kat, her own person. He had looked forward to celebrating every milestone in her life, had cherished the idea of seeing her graduate, high school and college, find her way into the professional world, marry — but not too soon. Have children. Again, not too soon. He had envisioned her winning prizes first — he wasn't sure for what, just that there would be prizes, endless prizes, and he would always be there.

Alexa was one of the teachers assigned to keep the seniors in the cafeteria, where they were corralled like wild horses. After all, there were almost four hundred of them, and, understandably, their spirits were high verging on insane. Alexa tried not to find them annoying, but her own mood was gloomy. Perri was dead, so all her efforts on the girl's behalf were meaningless. And Perri had been her primary focus, she assured herself now. She had not used her concern over the girl as a pretext to spend time with the sergeant. He was much too old for her, and stocky.

Even Josie Patel, allowed to perch on a bench while the others stood, seemed happy, if not as gleeful as her fellow students. When the signal finally came, via walkie-talkie — Barbara Paulson had no intention of any unplanned contingencies in the graduation — Josie's fellow *P*'s helped her stand and accommodated her off-kilter gait as they began to march out to the recorded strains of "Pomp and Circumstance." Yes, Josie was smiling — wanly, to be sure, but smiling.

As the procession reached the door of the cafeteria, Alexa saw that strange little gay boy, Dannon something, appear at the threshold and fall into step alongside Josie, whispering urgently. Josie shook her head, trying to pick up her pace, but there was no place to go, and Dannon continued to dog her down the long corridor. Finally another teacher put a hand on his shoulder, told him to step back and stop slowing down the processional, which had to cover a lot of ground through the cavernous school.

Perhaps, Alexa thought, Dannon had last-minute instructions for Josie, whose participation in that night's ceremony had been carefully scripted so she could accept her scholarship, then wait in the wings for her diploma, instead of going up and down the stage stairs.

The last line of the "Desiderata" echoed in Josie's mind, more crystalline in Toni Singleton's soprano than it would have been in Perri's. *Peace in silence.* Perri had never been as good a singer as she yearned to be, so she had worked extra hard at chorus, winning solos through sheer determination. It had been difficult for her, when Kat's golden voice had emerged, although she had never admitted it.

How could she be dead? Until the moment that Dannon had grabbed Josie — hissing at her, as if it were her fault — Josie had believed that Perri would recover. Perri had to recover. Perri was the talker. Perri was the one who needed to explain what happened.

The speaker droned on and on, but Josie heard none of it, although her mind registered the relieved applause signaling that the speech was over. Only two more items on the program, the Hartigan Scholarship and the diplomas. She barely heard her own name when Mr. Hartigan called her forward, although each mention of Kat's name was like a low-level electrical shock. Kat! Hartigan! Kat! Hartigan! Kat! Hartigan!

Then there was a huge silence, and Rose Padgett nudged Josie, reminding her to rise and go up the stairs to the stage. It was hard to maneuver, even though they had arranged for Josie to be on the aisle, and she lurched a bit, rolling from side to side as if drunk. She hopped up the steps — they had offered to put in a ramp, but Josie had said she could manage the short flight of stairs, and made her way toward Mr. Hartigan. He had a handheld mike, and he tilted it toward her so she would not have to let go of her crutches while making her brief remarks.

Peace in silence. Josie would know peace, if only she could keep her silence. No, that was wrong. She would be miserable if she kept on this way. It was everyone else who would be happy. Her parents, Mr. Hartigan, the Kahns. The scholarship was a bribe, even if they didn't realize it.

Take the money, go to college, and stick to the version that made everyone comfortable. With Perri dead it would be easy. Even if they found her sandals, even when they retrieved the text messages from Perri's and Kat's phones, they couldn't *prove* anything. If Josie had learned anything from her mathematically inclined father, it was how hard it was to create a proof from a few scanty facts.

"Mr. Hartigan, parents, my fellow students," she said, stalling as she gathered her thoughts, trying to figure out if she really wanted to say the words forming in her head. All she had to say was thank you, according to her mother. A simple thank-you and she would be free. Or not.

"You are very kind, but I can't accept this scholarship. Kat would have wanted it to go to someone who truly needed it — and someone who deserved it."

It had been planned that the diplomas would be awarded next on the program and that Josie could wait in the wings for her name to be called, rather than make her laborious way back to her seat. The band played, covering the confused silence, and parents applauded as if the scholarship presentation had gone as planned. Josie stayed, making it through the *G*'s, but she simply could not take it anymore, and escaped through the stage door, following the curving paths around the school to her parents' car.

When they showed up twenty minutes later, they did not berate her for what she had done or pester her with questions, although Josie could see a thousand questions in their faces.

"Perri died," she told them. "This afternoon. Dannon Estes told me while I was in the processional. The police kept it from me."

"Oh, Josie," her mother said. "No wonder you're so upset."

"I want to talk to the police."

She was scaring them, she knew she was scaring them, but she couldn't help it. She had been protecting them for a week, and she was exhausted.

"Why don't you sleep on it?" her father suggested. "Go home, get a good night's sleep, and we'll call Ms. Bustamante."

"I'm not going to be able to sleep until this is settled."

Just as Josie had gone reeling, in her own fashion, from the auditorium, Dale had slipped away, too, leaving as soon as the principal began handing out diplomas.

What was the girl thinking? Why had she embarrassed him that way? True, he may have had ulterior motives when he offered Josie the scholarship, but it was, above all else, a sincere memorial to Kat, and she had been Kat's best friend. Angry, distracted, he drove blindly through the streets of Glendale, unsure of where he was going until he ended up at his old house.

"Dale," Chloe said. It wasn't even nine-thirty, but she was wearing a silk robe, which she had thrown over a decidedly odd outfit, even for Chloe — yoga pants and a tailored shirt. It was as if she couldn't decide what part of the day she was inhabiting. She held a glass of wine in her hand, and Chloe had never much cared for wine. "What in . . . ?"

"Can I have a drink?"

"Sure." She closed the door on him, returning to the porch with a second glass and the bottle of Vigonier in which she had already made a considerable dent. "Let's sit out here. It's a nice night."

She doesn't want me in the house, Dale thought. *She'll never let me in this house again if she can help it.*

"It will be loud," he said. "All those kids driving around, the night of the Senior

Ramble and all. The traffic on Old Town Road will be bumper to bumper."

"I don't mind noise these days," Chloe said. "In fact, I find I need a constant wall of sound. I've started sleeping with the television set on."

"I don't sleep at all." They were being competitive. Lord help them, they were competing to see who was suffering more.

"I don't really sleep. I lie in bed, and I listen to CNN. There's so much death in the world. Every day people die. Soldiers and civilians. Ex-presidents. A busful of people on their way to a riverboat casino in Mississippi."

"But none of them matter. Not like Kat."

"You only say that because she was your daughter, Dale. *Our* daughter. But everyone who dies is someone's child. Or a parent, or a sibling. This is our grief. But we're not alone. Every day someone in the world is grieving."

"No, Kat matters more. She was extraordinary. She would have done important things."

"Like you? Like me? What have we done with our lives that makes us so vital, so much more important than others?"

"Chloe —"

"We lost our daughter, Dale. You don't need to make it bigger than it is. It's big enough."

Oh, Lord, the world really was upside down. Chloe was wise and calm, while Dale was the hysterical one, scattered and out of control.

From Old Town Road, they heard the first slow rumble of cars, the honking horns, the blasts of hip-hop music, and, over it all, the loud, exuberant voices of eighteen-year-olds flush with the success of surviving their education. The Senior Ramble was under way.

36

Senior Ramble sucked sober, Peter Lasko was realizing. Or maybe it sucked because he was so much older than these kids. All he knew was that he was bored out of his mind, going from party to party, restaurant to restaurant, all in the hopes of finding some fresh gossip on Josie, Kat, and Perri. Someone had to know something, but the only news was that Perri had been taken off life support this afternoon and Josie Patel had shocked everyone by refusing the Hartigan Scholarship and then ditching graduation altogether.

"I can't imagine doing what she did." The girl was Lauren something, a bright-eyed brunette who was going to Beloit, a fact she felt the need to interject in the conversation about every sixty seconds. Peter had semi-tuned her out early on and had no idea what the girl was referencing, but he thought it had something to do with Josie.

"Turning down a scholarship?"

She rolled her eyes. "No, Perri. *Killing* someone. Josie just had some sort of breakdown. Oh, Janie just came in — she's going to Beloit, too." The girl eeled away from him, as if he were less desirable than some high-school senior bound for a second-tier school in Wisconsin.

It was time to move on anyway. This party was dead, a chaperoned event in one of the newer houses. Peter decided to head out to the fringes, the places where the sophomores and juniors gathered for their unofficial parties. There was an old parking lot near the Prettyboy Reservoir, a somewhat risky spot, as the county police would know to check it throughout the night, but it was irresistible — hidden, with a dramatic view and lots of dark places that afforded privacy, or the illusion of privacy.

Yes, a small circle of kids was here, skeezers and skateboarders, drinking beer. It was a mellow scene, in some ways more tolerable than the giddy senior gatherings, where everyone was acting as if they'd just split the atom. Boy, Peter would like to see those self-important seniors in a few months, when they'd been broken down, reduced to freshmen again. He'd been cocky, too, heading into NYU, but he had never been as cocky as those kids. Beloit! Imagine being full of yourself because you had gotten into Beloit.

A boy offered him a beer — a PBR, which was pretty much ten minutes ago as a trend, but cheap as ever — and Peter tried to ease into the conversation as nonchalantly as he pulled the tab on the can.

"I hear Perri Kahn was taken off life support today. So I guess that's it."

The boy shrugged. "Saves the county the cost of a trial."

"Unless there's another person who was involved. You hear anything about that?"

No one picked up the cue. That was the problem with the skeezer crowd — they were almost too mellow. It was one thing to be nonjudgmental, another to have no opinions, no initiative, no ambition whatever.

A short, dark-haired girl emerged from the shadows, standing just a little too close to Peter, especially given how humid the evening was.

"I've heard that, too," she said.

"Yeah?"

"In fact —" She stopped.

"What?"

"Nothing."

"What's your name?"

"Eve."

The girl that Kevin Weaver had pointed out at the funeral, the girl whose very name had made Josie so heated. A slut and a liar, Josie had said.

"You want to take a walk or something?"

"I came with my friends, in their car."

"I've got a car."

She hesitated, but he knew she wanted to go with him. He just needed to give her an excuse to ditch her friends.

"I'm . . . I'm so sad tonight, Eve. You know? Kat and I dated, way back. She was my girlfriend, and I knew Perri from doing theater stuff, and I'm just so sad and lonely. I need someone to talk to."

"Let me find my friends."

It had been a long time since Dale had unhooked anyone's bra one-handed and apparently just as long since anyone had tried this maneuver on Chloe, who was laughing hysterically. That is, she was laughing when she wasn't letting him kiss her, sloppy and uncoordinated as he was.

He was not sure just when they had ended up on the sofa in the alcove off the kitchen, although he thought it was some-where between killing the first bottle of wine and starting the second. Yes, that was it. He had followed Chloe into the house when she went to get more wine, and although she had ordered him back to the porch, he realized it was because she knew how susceptible she was to him. But she had started it, being so nice and tender, reminding him of the woman he had fallen in love with so many years ago. It had not been a mistake, after all, loving Chloe, marrying her. Lord, she had given him Kat. The only mistake was in not realizing that the woman he loved had always been here, buried beneath her disappointments and confusion and shame. He didn't need to award a scholarship to honor his daughter's memory. All he had to do was love her mother again. They would reconcile, make a new baby. Nothing would have made Kat happier.

"This is crazy," Chloe kept saying, but if she wasn't exactly helping him, she wasn't fighting him either. It was like a test, a quest. He was a knight, and he just had to get past all these barriers — the bra, the yoga pants, which had an unusual side fastening, something with laces. Their history, which was more complicated still. He should have done this four years ago, just planted himself here when Chloe ordered him out of the house and refused to leave.

But it was never too late. Nothing was truly over, as long as you were alive.

"We'll start when my partner gets here," Lenhardt said.

"Okay," Josie said.

"We're going to record it, on a little microcassette recorder that he's bringing."

"Okay." Her voice was low, but even and sure.

"And you'll need to read this statement, indicating this is voluntary —"

"It's not a confession," her lawyer put in. "I want to be very clear on this. My client is not confessing and is not going to be held liable for any charges."

"Gloria, if you want to make a deal, make a deal. Tell me what you want up front, and I'll call an ADA, and we'll see what we can do. But until then, if your client cops to a felony, I'm not going to promise what charges she's going to face. She called us, remember?"

"Is it a felony to shoot yourself?" Josie asked.

"Josie!" her lawyer all but yelped.

"Depends," Lenhardt said.

Her parents, sitting side by side on the sofa, were wide-eyed.

"Because I did, you know. I shot myself in the foot. But you knew that, from the very beginning. How did you know that? Was it because of the angle or because it was my right foot? If I had shot my left foot, would you have been fooled? Or because you couldn't find my sandals. I took them off, right before, because I didn't want to ruin them. That was stupid, wasn't it? But they were brand new."

"Josie," her lawyer repeated in that same yelping-warning tone.

"Josie," her father said sorrowfully. "What have you done?"

"Please," Lenhardt said. "Let's wait until my partner gets here with the recorder."

Several old paths wound through the underbrush along the reservoir, and Peter led Eve by the hand down one of these until they found a small clearing with a felled tree where they could sit and drink their beers. At least, he was drinking. Eve, gulping nervously, had finished hers in a matter of seconds, but she continued to bring the can to her lips. It gave her something to do with her hands. She wished she had a cigarette with her, but they were back in Val's car. Along with her regular shoes. It was going to be a bitch shimmying barefoot up the drainpipe and back into her room. And she couldn't throw the shoes up on the roof, because they would make an enormous clatter. She really hadn't thought this through. But what did you do when Peter Lasko asked you to go for a walk? Even Val, who took a dim view of ditching girls when a boy crooked his little finger — that was Val's expression, "crooked his little finger" — could not object to such a monumental opportunity.

"So did you know Kat and her friends?"

"I was a grade behind them. But my father's farm — it's between the Hartigans' property and that new development, Sweetwater. So I used to see her sometimes. Around."

"She was great."

Eve lifted a shoulder, wanting to be agreeable but not wanting to lie out and out. "Great" was not the word she would use to describe Kat Hartigan.

"I mean, she was such a sweetheart. She never hurt anyone."

"Not directly."

"What does that mean?"

"Nothing. Just . . . well, you don't have to hurt people if other people will do it for you, right?"

"You mean Perri? The way she used to

talk shit? You can't blame Kat for Perri."

"Look, it's not important. She's dead, and that's sad, and I don't want to say anything bad about someone who's dead."

"They're both dead now. So I guess we'll never know what happened."

She pressed the can against her mouth again, pretending to drink. It was no longer truly cold, but the metal felt good on her mouth. Above them cars were pulling out of the gravel lot, trying to stay ahead of the patrols. Evading the police was the only real excitement of the night. Eve wondered if the Ramble was always so anticlimactic. So far the best part had been sliding down the roof, running silently down the drive to where Val and Lila waited.

You're here with Peter Lasko, she reminded herself. *An almost movie star.* But he didn't seem particularly interested in her. Abruptly, she dropped her empty can, letting it roll down the hill, and knelt between Peter's legs, reaching for the fly of his jeans.

"What — ?"

"Don't you want to?" It was amazing, how he moved beneath her hand — not hard yet but already twitching a little. She thought of those gliding airplanes sold from the mall kiosks, the ones that seemed to fly by magic. It was almost as if she had that kind of control over him, as if her lightest touch could make him respond. She could be with him now, and years later, when he was a famous movie star, she would have that memory. Or if she was good enough, if she did it well, maybe he would want to see her again. Maybe he would want her for his girlfriend. That would be worth anything.

But before she could get started, he pulled her up by the armpits, so they were face-to-face.

"How old are you?" he asked.

"Eighteen," she lied reflexively.

"No you're not. You said you were a year behind Kat in school."

"I'm old enough. I've done it lots of times. Come on, it's just sex. It doesn't have to mean anything."

She reached for him again, plunging her hand down into his open fly, hoping she was doing it right. Hadn't Graham liked what she had done? It had seemed so at the time. And she hadn't wanted to be with him, whereas she would give anything, absolutely anything, to get with Peter Lasko.

He took her hand away, gently yet firmly,

and zipped himself up. "Actually," he said, "sex is a big deal. Kat and I never did it."

"Really?"

"Really. I never told anyone that, but it's true. I dated her all summer, and we never did it."

"Don't you wish you did? Now that she's dead?"

"I hadn't really thought about it that way."

"Well, I bet she wishes she had. If I were your girlfriend, I wouldn't be like that." Adding hurriedly, "Not that I want to be your girlfriend. I'm just saying I'm not a cocktease." Hadn't Lila said that was the worst thing a girl could be?

He finished off his beer, crumpling the aluminum can in his hand. "That's what I told people that Kat was. I wish I hadn't."

"It doesn't really matter what you say or don't say. People think what they want to think. You can tell them the truth, but it doesn't make a difference. Everyone's saying Perri shot Kat because she was jealous of her for some reason. That's not the way it was, but that's what people want to believe."

"How do you know?"

She studied his face, as handsome as any movie star's. But then, he was one, or

about to be. She wanted to give him something, anything, to remember her by. She
had thought sex would be the best way, but
any girl could give him sex. All Eve had
was a secret, but it seemed to be a secret
he would value.

"Because I know someone else who was
there."

"Binnie Snyder," Josie said. "Binnie
Snyder was there, hiding in a stall. There
was a struggle for a gun — no one meant
for anything to happen — and we were so
scared, and it was so stupid. I could have
run — Binnie told me to run — but I
couldn't leave them."

"Start at the beginning," Lenhardt
coaxed the girl. "Start at the very beginning."

He had no way of knowing that the beginning, as Josie defined it, was her first
day of third grade, ten years ago. He was
used to more straightforward confessions
— *Tater shot Peanut over drugs, I cut my
wife to shut her up.* Sometimes, for variety,
the wife cut the husband.

He was a murder police, well into his
third decade, and he thought there was
nothing new under the sun, no motivation
unknown to him, no scenario he had yet to

document. And he was right. The story Josie told, haltingly yet determinedly, had the usual elements. Jealousy, covetousness, anger over slights so tiny that it was hard to believe they had resonated for even a moment, much less years.

He let the girl go, allowed her all the extraneous details she thought so essential to her story. It seemed only fair, his having pressured her for the past week, to let her speak to her heart's content.

It was past midnight when Peter, at Eve's instruction, stopped at the end of her father's outlaw driveway, the one he had created at the edge of Sweetwater Estates.

"I was going to stay out all night," she said. "But there doesn't seem to be any point."

Was she still leaving the door open for some kind of sexual encounter? Peter was tempted. But he also wanted to go home, call Mr. Hartigan, tell him what he had learned.

"You know what? Nobody ever does. They say they're going to, but even the seniors are home by two. It's just so boring around here. Now, New York — New York is a city where you can do some damage, no matter what time it is."

"I'd like to go there," she said. "Not to do tourist stuff. But, like, go to clubs."

"It's a great city."

"Can I call you, if I go there?"

No. "Sure." He wasn't going to be there anyway. He and his agent had mapped out the strategy. After *Susquehanna Falls* wrapped, he was going to go to L.A. for pilot season and meet a lot of people but not commit to anything until they had a sense of what the gathering buzz was on the movie.

"Cool," she said.

"Is that where Binnie lives?" he asked, pointing to the dark house in the distance, a house where no lights burned, not even a porch light.

"Yes, but you *promised* —" Her voice was shrill, almost hysterical.

"I know. I promised I wouldn't tell. And I won't." Actually, he had been very precise, promising Eve he wouldn't tell the *police*. "But you should think about it, Eve. If she's telling you the truth, she doesn't have any reason not to come forward."

"Binnie always tells the truth — which is more than I can say for Kat and her friends."

"Okay, okay." He was going for a big-brother vibe with her. Should he have fucked her? No, discretion really was the better part of valor sometimes. "Just think about it. Promise me? Think about it. Turn in those cell phones, the ones you said you hid in the compost pile. You can do it anonymously, I'm sure. It could be bad for you if it's not as Binnie said. You could be an accessory."

"I'll think about it."

He wasn't fooled. She would think about it, but she wouldn't do anything. That was okay. He didn't need her to, and he wouldn't tell anyone of her involvement. All Dale Hartigan needed to know was that a fourth girl was there, a girl who could explain, once and for all, what had happened.

It was so dark here, with no streetlamps, yet Eve's eyes were bright, wet, and hungry. She seemed to want a kiss, so he gave her one. He was surprised at how tentative she was, how reserved, as if she had never been kissed.

He watched her run lightly up the drive, sandals in hand. She wasn't going to talk to her friend, and even if she did, she would be tentative, unwilling to press for the right thing. The loyalties, whatever the reason, ran too deep. Maybe it was the legacy of being redneck girls, growing up among these pricey houses. Or maybe it was some kind of deeper girl shit, the kind he never got.

What if he went to the Snyders' house, just knocked on the door, told them what he knew? Okay, so it was after midnight and her parents would probably freak. But if he just walked over there, announced himself, and told them what he knew and that their daughter had to come forward, he could put the whole thing to bed tonight and no one, not even Dale Hartigan, would be able to deny his part in it.

The road was rougher, far rougher than he realized, and he heard his mother's car make an ominous noise. Shit, something beneath the car had popped a bolt and was now dragging, making a huge amount of noise. He hadn't felt drunk, but now he realized that the beer was catching up with him. He was definitely buzzed. This was stupid. This was way stupid.

He pulled up to the gated driveway, intent on backing out and turning around, but it was dark and he heard a hard thunk. Shit, he had hit the fence or something, but when he tried to turn the car on again, nothing happened. His mom's distributor cap might have come loose on that road.

He was going to have to call in all his charm points when his mother saw what he had done to her Mazda.

He got out, trying to walk around the car to inspect the damage, but the car was angled weirdly, so he had to climb out the passenger side. Maybe he should raise the hood, check the distributor cap, then assess the damage to the rear end. He stumbled forward, falling to his knees. He hadn't eaten enough today. That's why the beer was making him light-headed. He had been drinking on an empty stomach.

"Who's there?" The question came from a shape, a huge, dark shape, almost like a bear, although Peter knew that bears cannot speak. He froze, trying to think what he should say. In his mind he was invisible as long as he didn't speak. He would just wait for the shape to go away and —

The pain seemed to come before the sound. Was that possible? Did sound travel slowly enough that the shotgun blast that tore through him really had a chance to announce itself? His middle seemed to be on fire, and Peter clutched himself as if he had a stomachache. His arms came away slick and red, his knees buckled beneath him. Was he fainting, or was he dying?

Now he was on the ground, and he suddenly felt cold, as cold as he ever had.

Not good, he thought. *Definitely not good.*

How far do sounds travel on a summer night? A shotgun, for example. Does the damp air slow it down, hold it close? Does it matter if those within its range recognize the sound for what it is or if they assume it's something more familiar — a fire-cracker, a car backfiring? Those in the Sweetwater Estates certainly heard Cyrus Snyder's shotgun, but it was only the sirens, then the whirring of another Shock Trauma helicopter over the valley, the second in a week, that alerted them to the fact that something had happened. In their pen, Claude and Billy nattered, and Eve's mother poked Eve's slumbering father. But Dale Hartigan, eight acres away, slept on.

How far does a girl's voice travel? Josie Patel was barely audible to the five adults gathered around her in the Patels' family room. The detectives kept glancing worriedly at the microcassette recorder, making sure that the voice-activated microphone was picking up her words. If Dale Hartigan had been in the next room, he might not have heard the girl's voice. But he was in his old bed, asleep in his ex-wife's arms.

Later, when he pieced together the events of that night, he would remember that dreamless sleep as a blessing of sorts. For while it could not be said that this June evening was the last happy night that Dale Hartigan would ever know, it was the last innocent sleep of his life. When he had passed out next to Chloe, he was a victim of circumstance, undeserving of his fate. He was still a man who believed he could afford to know the why of things, and that those explanations would then lead to solutions he could effect. He had gone to sleep feeling that his life was still open, that he was not as thoroughly destroyed as he feared.

By morning he would wake to a world where five young people's deaths, including his daughter's, had been traced back to him. Six, if one counted Peter Lasko, and Dale did. He had not meant any of this to happen. All he had wanted was the very best for his daughter. Wasn't that what everyone wanted?

But in the end it was Josie's story, and Dale Hartigan never challenged her right to tell it, much less tried to contradict a word of it, unflattering and damaging as it was to him. Josie told it in her own ragged, discursive way, for there was no one else to shape her words. Not Perri, with her heightened sense of drama and narrative. Not Kat, with her tendency to edit out the problematic details, to gloss over anything unpleasant and unflattering. Not Eve, who had only Binnie's version and one page of a letter. In the end it was Josie's story, and she believed that every detail mattered — the cupcakes and the Ka-pe-jos, the jokes and the plays and the crushes.

There were three girls. For ten years they were best friends who did everything together. Then they weren't, and then they didn't. It was only in how their friendship ended that there was anything singular about them.

37

In April of junior year, Kat checked her SAT scores on the Internet and found that they were still stubbornly short of the 1400 mark. "Short" was a euphemism: At 1340 she was closer to 1300 than 1400, and even 1400 was a far cry from the 1500 that her father said would make her a "lead-pipe cinch" for Stanford.

"Lead-pipe cinch," Perri said when Kat repeated her father's phrase. "What does that mean? I mean, why does it denote a sure thing?"

They were all a bit obsessed with words and meanings and analogies at this point, having spent the past three years preparing for their college boards. They had taken practice tests freshman year, taken the PSATs twice, studied vocabulary lists in English this year, then taken the SATs twice. But of the three, no one had spent more time preparing than Kat.

"Some building term, I suppose," Kat

said. "Anyway, I'm not too worried. I think being ranked number one in the class balances my SATs."

Her confidence didn't seem a put-on. With help from her father's girlfriend — an accomplished Stanford alum in her own right — Kat did appear to have everything else she needed for a spot at the school: straight-A grades, a sheaf of recommendations, a list of extracurricular activities that signaled her breadth and diversity. Even the news that Binnie Snyder planned to apply there was of little concern, because Kat was going early decision and Binnie was spreading her applications out, targeting all the big math-and-science schools — Caltech, MIT, Berkeley. Besides, Binnie was a math nerd. She didn't have the all-around profile that Kat had cultivated.

But Kat's calm assurance shattered when she learned that Binnie had signed up to take an advanced calculus course at community college that summer — and that she would be given high-school credit. Under the byzantine system that Glendale used to calculate class ranking, this would make Binnie number one and drop Kat to number two. Again Kat insisted she was not worried, but she was far less convincing this time. Whenever the girls got together the spring of their junior year, the topic was sure to surface, with Kat seeking her friends' reassurances, then saying she didn't need them.

Her usually mild-mannered father was apoplectic, complaining that Kat was being cheated out of an honor for which she had been preparing since middle school. "We've been outscheduled," he told his daughter. Her father even met with the principal and tried to persuade her that no credit should be given for outside coursework. He offered to underwrite a scholarship at the school, in his family's name, and back it with a large donation. But while Barbara Paulson took Mr. Hartigan's money, the only thing he accomplished was getting the school to scuttle its traditional valedictorian/salutatorian roles. There would still be a number-one ranking as far as colleges were concerned; it just wouldn't be announced at graduation.

"You're still applying early decision," Perri told Kat after she confided in her friends, embarrassed by her father's interference, but also visibly disappointed that he hadn't been able to change the principal's mind. "They won't know Binnie is number one until long after they've accepted you."

"I know, but number one makes much more of an impression," Kat said. "Being number two just leads people to wonder how much better number one might be. It's the damn reading comprehension. I'm too nervous to concentrate. I can zip through the vocabulary, and I was fine in the timed trials I did with my tutor. But my brain locks up on test day."

Josie, whose board scores were a mediocre 1260, said nothing, but she understood Kat's dilemma. Her old choke mentality had resurfaced in these tests, although her parents insisted they didn't care. Perri, meanwhile, had scored an enviable 1550 but had the good taste not to mention it. If anyone was a lead-pipe cinch, it was Perri for Northwestern's theater program.

"It's not going to matter," Perri said staunchly. "You've got a stellar application. You'll be okay."

"I know." Kat sighed, stabbing her Frappuccino with her straw. "I just always thought I'd be number one."

They were in a new Starbucks several miles south of Glendale. Now that they had licenses and cars — well, Kat and Perri had cars, Josie had only a license — they no longer met at each other's homes or in the woods behind Kat's house. They drove to the mall, the good one with the upscale department stores, or to restaurants that treated the high-school crowd hospitably.

Driving had opened up the whole world to them in the past year, although they seldom traveled more than five or ten miles from Glendale. Once, just once, Josie had borrowed her father's car and taken the girls down to South Baltimore, the neighborhood of her pre-Glendale life. But the streets were narrow and all the parking was parallel, and the girls were a little stunned at the sight of homeless men slumped in doorways along Light Street. Josie could sense the energy and eccentricity that would have beguiled her parents when they were young, but she was thankful her family had left for Glendale. She would not have wanted to grow up here, with its no-name stores and littered streets.

"I'm telling you it doesn't matter," Perri said. "Besides, it's not a done deal. You could take summer classes, too."

"No, I can't. I've already signed up to work at a summer camp for disabled kids."

"She still hasn't taken the class," Perri said. "Anything can happen. She could drop out, or not get an A."

"Ever since middle school, Binnie's been a straight-A student," Kat said. "I only stayed ahead of her by taking so many AP courses. I liked her better when she was a math genius."

"We never actually liked her," Josie pointed out.

"Well, you know what I mean. Why couldn't Binnie be satisfied being this huge math brain and a National Merit Scholar? Why did she have to turn it into a competition?"

The girls sucked on their drinks. Josie's mom liked to joke that Starbucks was the malt shop of Josie's generation, but coffee drinks were so much more sophisticated.

"Well, it hasn't happened yet," Perri reiterated. "And there's nothing you can do about it."

"Nothing?" Kat, like Josie, believed that Perri had a plan for everything. In fact, Josie realized, Kat had been fishing, trying to get Perri to solve her problems, as Perri usually did.

"Not that I can see. Like I said, she might change her mind about taking the summer course if something better comes along, like a hot job. She might not get A's. She could fall in love with some guy or

613

have a nervous breakdown. But it's out of your hands."

The conversation had not seemed important at the time. Even a month later, after the pigs were killed at the Snyders' farm, it didn't seem notable to Josie. Summer came, and they went off in various directions — the camp job for Kat, a mother's-helper gig for Perri, a mall job for Josie, who was trying desperately to earn money now that she knew the story of her compromised college fund. Things seemed normal enough when school resumed, but then this strange iciness set in Perri. She stopped speaking to Kat altogether, and when Josie begged her to tell her what was wrong, she referred her back to Kat, who said she had no idea what Perri's problem was.

"Perri's crazy," Kat said. "There's no talking to her. She's probably still pissed that I got the part she wanted in the school musical."

"Kat's the one who won't talk to me," Perri said. "Ask *her* why. Make her tell why I've been banished from her life."

But Josie did not dare ask, fearful that Kat would freeze her out in the same way she had exiled Perri. And while neither girl pressed Josie to take sides, it was natural for her to gravitate toward Kat. They were on the cheerleading squad together. Kat picked her up for school each day. Perri's silences grew colder, more noticeable. If Josie had believed she could put the three of them back together again, she would have interceded. But if Kat could drop Perri, then she could drop Josie, too.

On the morning of June 4, Kat had picked up Josie for school as usual. They needed to be there early, for a run-through of a cheer routine that would be performed at the last-day-for-seniors rally. They were in Kat's car — a used Mercedes that her father had justified on the grounds that it was safe — when her cell phone buzzed. Dutiful Kat, however, had promised her father she would never dial and drive, so she asked Josie to grab it.

"It's a text message," Josie said. "From Perri. She wants us to meet her in the north wing girls, second floor."

The "us" was a little presumptuous. The text message had been for Kat alone. Josie tried to rationalize that Perri had to know that Josie and Kat would arrive at school together.

"Perri," Kat said, "can go fuck herself."

Josie had never heard Kat say anything

so blunt, so naked. Oh, sometimes late at night — sitting by the reservoir, allowing themselves a beer or two just to be companionable with their jock friends — Kat might have let a profanity fly. But it was unusual.

"What if it's important?"

"Believe me, it's not. Just more drama from the drama queen."

"Please, Kat." Josie seldom argued with Kat, but she missed Perri, missed the three of them. It would be so sweet if they could reconcile before graduation. "Please go see her?"

"No."

"Then I'll go. I want to hear what she has to say."

"*No.*" Kat sounded almost panicky at the thought. "Okay, we'll both go. But I'm telling you, she's crazy. You can't believe anything she says."

The bathroom was empty when they arrived, with no sign of Perri.

"See?" Kat said, brushing her hair and then applying lipstick. "Just more Perri drama."

Josie tried one of the stalls. The door was locked, but when she glanced beneath the door, she didn't see any feet. The one next to it had an out-of-service sign taped to it. She was moving down the row, to the third and final stall, when Perri came into the bathroom.

This part happened just as Josie had said. Perri locked the door and removed a gun from her knapsack, an orange-and-black JanSport she hadn't carried all year. And yes, Josie knew what knapsack Perri carried, noticed what she wore, even what she had for lunch as she hunkered in a corner of the cafeteria with Dannon Estes. Her eyes had been following Perri all year, she realized. Perri came in, and she locked the door. This much was true.

But she never pointed the gun at Kat, not on purpose. She held it to her own head.

"I'm going to kill myself, Kat. If you won't admit what you did, I'm going to kill myself right here in front of you and Josie and leave you to explain it. I've decided I'm willing to sacrifice myself rather than let you go on pretending you're so innocent and pure."

Kat had tried, for a moment, to keep her back to Perri, to maintain eye contact only with her own reflection. But when Perri placed the gun against her own temple, Kat turned and faced her.

"Perri . . ." Her voice was — But Josie could not put her finger on what Kat's voice conveyed. Concern? Yes. Fear? No. Kat was never scared. Perhaps she thought it was a prop gun, stolen from the drama department. The thought had occurred to Josie, too. This was not real. It could not be. Perri was playacting.

"Go ahead. Tell Josie. Tell her how you tried, for once, to concoct your own scheme. You told Seth Raskin to go to the Snyders' farm. You told him to do something that would scare Binnie, but in an indirect way so no one could ever connect you to it. You took what I said about Binnie having a nervous breakdown and you tried to make it happen."

"I *didn't*. I told you that I had nothing to do with it."

Perri had been carrying her knapsack over her left shoulder. She put it down now but continued to hold the gun to her temple. "No, I can't prove anything. Which is why you need to confess once and for all."

"I never asked them to do anything. Seth asked me why I was upset one day, and I told him. That was all. I didn't ask him to do anything about it."

"You never *ask* anyone for anything. You don't have to. You never did. Ever since we

618

were kids, people have tried to guess what you wanted and do it before you asked. Everyone thinks it's such a goddamn privilege, taking care of Kat Hartigan."

"You're crazy."

Josie, almost without noticing, had backed herself against the stall in the corner. She was at once fascinated and repelled, incapable of breaking her gaze, desperate to disappear.

"If crazy is being willing to die for something you believe in, for a principle, then I'm that crazy, Kat. Agree to apologize to Binnie, or I'll shoot myself, right here. Explain yourself to Binnie — or explain my death to everyone else."

"I didn't do anything to Binnie," Kat said. "Her parents sent her away to spend the summer with relatives after the pigs were killed, so she didn't take the summer course. But she still got into MIT, with practically a free ride."

"It's a good thing she got financial aid, given that those pigs were going to be auctioned for her college fund. Who was the anonymous donor who stepped forward and made restitution for the animals anyway? Your father?"

"Leave my father out of this." Kat had always been hard to anger, but any mention of her parents brought this edge to her voice.

"Why? Your father's always inserting himself into your life. Making sure you don't get zoned into the bad middle school. Practically bribing Mrs. Paulson to change the class-ranking system for your benefit. Mr. Delacorte even offered Binnie an internship last summer, out of the blue, but she turned it down. Mr. Delacorte, your father's friend, offering Binnie a job that would keep her from going to summer school — was that a coincidence?"

"Shut up," Kat said. *My dad didn't do anything.*

"Your dad didn't do anything. You didn't do anything. No one in your family ever does anything. Unless it's noble and visionary, of course. Well, *I'm* going to do something, Kat. I'm going to pull this trigger and leave you and Josie to answer all the questions. Do you think Josie will take your side now, now that she knows? Let's see."

Perri and Kat turned to Josie, who was struck dumb. She did not want to be the referee in this ugly fight. She did not want to believe what Perri said, yet she could see that it explained so much. The Delacortes — Perri had gone to work for them this fall, and it was this fall that she had become so cold and odd toward Kat.

Even as she tried to process all Perri had said, the third stall banged open and Binnie Snyder emerged, face paler than ever, red hair bristling. Had Binnie been there all the time? She must have been, yet Josie had not seen her feet when she checked under the stalls. Binnie had been there waiting for them, part of Perri's last big production at Glendale High School. Who needed *Our Town* when you could stage your own drama?

"Stop it," Binnie screamed at Perri. "This is insane. You didn't say anything about a gun. You could get us all expelled. You told me that Kat wanted to come here today to confess and apologize. This is stupid."

She had a cell phone in one hand, which she threw to the tiled floor with such force that its battery pack fell off. The body of the phone skidded on the bathroom's slick tiles, and Binnie, her long, pale arms windmilling wildly, reached for the gun in Perri's hand even as Josie thought, but could not find the voice to say, *No, Binnie. It's a game, a play, an act. Don't, Binnie. Perri is just staging a big moment. It's probably not even a real gun. Where would Perri get a real gun? No one we know has guns.*

Perri tried to hold the gun away from Binnie, but Binnie managed to grab her wrist and then the gun itself, her hand closing over Perri's as they struggled. Josie could tell that Perri was trying to hold the weapon as far away from her own body as possible, and that was the only reason her arm was pointing straight out, toward Kat, when the gun went off. A second or two passed, seconds in which hope abounded, for Kat looked more puzzled and surprised than anything else. Then she sank to the floor and, in her very Kat-like way — polite, silent, asking for nothing — died.

Was there a scream? If so, whose was it? All Josie could remember was feeling as if her green-and-yellow sandals were made out of concrete, or stuck to the floor with some invisible glue. Just a few feet away, Perri was making odd, strangled moans, quite unlike any sound that Josie had ever heard. Josie knew she should go to her, help her, but she was frozen. Perri pressed the gun against her temple, even as Binnie swatted at it, screaming *"No."* But all Binnie achieved was moving the gun a few inches, so the bullet entered closer to Perri's cheekbone, transforming that dear, sharp face into something horrible.

Through all of this, from the moment that Perri had entered the room, Josie had not moved, had not spoken.

"We were never here," Binnie said, breathing so hard her chest heaved up and down, as if she had just been in a race, and her features were tight and ugly. Her thinking face.

"But —"

"We have to leave now. They'll find them, and it will look like what it is. Perri shot Kat, then killed herself. That's all anyone needs to know."

"But —"

"Josie, there's no time. Let's *go*." Binnie gathered up the cell phones — the broken one she had dropped, the one that Kat had placed next to her lipstick, the one from Perri's knapsack.

"We don't want them to see the call logs. Now, let's go."

"I can't go," Josie said. "They're hurt."

"They're *dead,* Josie. And if you're smart, you'll leave yourself out of it. As for me, I was never here. You owe me that much."

She left with her armful of cell phones, running in her strange, loping style, and it was only when she was gone that Josie thought of objections, arguments, counter-points. She owed Binnie no loyalty. She wasn't going to lie for Binnie. But if she told why Binnie was there, she would have to tell the other whys, and Kat would never want that. Even with Perri holding a gun, Kat had tried to hold on to this secret.

So what should Josie tell the police when they arrived? Why was she here? Why hadn't she left and gone to get help for her friends? Binnie was right; she should have run, but it was too late now. Rescuers could arrive at any moment, catch her trying to slip away. But if they found her here, then there should be a reason she couldn't leave, right? She should be injured, too. If she were injured, she would not be questioned. And no one would have to know that she had simply stood there, incapable of doing anything, as her friends died.

The gun had fallen next to Perri's body. Josie picked it up, examined it. How hard could it be to fire a gun? This one had gone off by accident, after all, and gone off again even as Binnie tried to prevent Perri from firing it. She hadn't wanted to live, Josie realized. With Kat dead, Perri didn't want to live. Should she make the same choice? Did she owe her friends that much? She placed the gun to her head, as

624

Perri had. But the fact was, she did not want to die. Stranger still was the shame she felt at this thought. A good person, a true friend, should want to die.

Instead Josie sat, extended her legs, and braced her feet against the wall, aiming the gun at the place where the thong, topped off with a lovely tulle flower, separated her big toe from the others. The sandals cost $125, an amazing extravagance for Josie, but her mother had agreed they went so beautifully with her graduation dress that they were worth the splurge. She took them off, put them in her knapsack. Then she aimed again, and fired.

Fuck. It hurt, it really hurt. And there was more blood than she thought there would be. Kat had hardly bled at all, although Perri's blood was still flowing, terrifyingly constant. Shit, it hurt, it hurt, it hurt.

The door. She had forgotten to lock the door. Perri had locked the door, so the door should be locked, right? She did not stop to think this through but forced herself to hop to the door, turn the lock, and then hop back again. And the gun. She had touched the gun. What if they took fingerprints? She would explain that she tried to take the gun away from Perri, tried to keep her from shooting herself. Shooting herself or Kat. And Perri shot Josie in the foot, then shot herself. Yes, that was it. Josie had grabbed for the gun, trying to take it away from Perri, but Perri had shot Kat, then shot Josie and shot herself. That all worked. That would make everyone happy. Binnie wouldn't be here. And Josie wouldn't be a coward who had failed to save one friend, then failed to die with another.

If she had to do it over again, she would have told the truth from the very beginning. She wouldn't have let Binnie leave. She wouldn't have gotten up to lock that bathroom door, leaving those drips of blood that had showed she was lying almost from the very start. She wouldn't have removed her sandals and hidden them in her knapsack, much less arranged for Binnie to come get them later on, hiding them wherever she had tossed the cell phones. If she had to do it over again — but she did, Josie realized. That was the epiphany that had come to her onstage at graduation. She had to tell the truth, because Perri wasn't going to do it for her. Until the moment she had heard of Perri's death, she had been counting on just that. Perri was the talker. Perri was the one who was supposed to explain things. Let Perri tell.

"And you wouldn't have shot yourself," the sergeant put in.

"No," Josie said. "I think I still might have done that." Then she flushed, as if she hadn't meant to say that last part out loud.

"How can you say such a thing?" her father demanded. "The risk you took, picking up a gun, shooting yourself. You could have hit a major artery in your leg and ended up bleeding to death. How can you not see how foolish it was?"

"We made a vow," Josie said. "I told you — we made a vow."

August

38

Every August in Maryland, there comes a moment when the wind shifts and, although the days remain hot and the nights humid, it is clear that something has changed. Summer is giving up, preparing to leave. It may linger for another few weeks, but its back has been broken, and everyone knows it. People suddenly have more energy, and only the youngest children mourn the passing of summer and the coming of school. Everyone else is eager for fall to arrive.

It was on such a day that Sergeant Harold Lenhardt asked Vik and Susie Patel if he could talk to their daughter, just one more time. They gave their permission reluctantly. They knew, intellectually, that the homicide sergeant had not caused them any harm; he was nothing more than a messenger, one who had no way of knowing what he was delivering. Still, they didn't like him much and couldn't help feeling he was somehow at fault for what they had been through.

Josie, however, didn't mind Lenhardt at all. Her only grudge against him was that he had provoked her into ruining her best sandals, the very ones that she had been trying to save. She had given them to Binnie, who arranged for them to follow the cell phones — into the Muhlys' compost pile.

"We're releasing all the evidence, since the grand jury wrapped up," he told Josie. They were in her room, at her insistence. Even when her parents were at work, she preferred the privacy of her room. "We don't really have much of your stuff, but I thought you might want to see this."

He handed her a piece of paper with just two lines: *"I ask only that the truth be told. Love, Perri."* The word "only" had been crossed out. Josie studied the familiar handwriting, unsure what was expected of her.

"What does this have to do with me?"

"Well, nothing." The sergeant perched on Josie's bed almost gingerly, as if he feared mussing the spread. "We didn't even present it to the grand jury, because it didn't seem to have any bearing on anything. The thing is, Josie — why would Perri write something like this? It was addressed to Kat Hartigan, mailed that morning. But what was the point? She was already planning on confronting her at school. Why mail the letter?"

"Could there be more to it, another page?" Josie asked. "It seems kind of . . . truncated for Perri."

"If there was another page, it never surfaced. Her parents looked, even checked her computer, but as you can see, she wrote it by hand, and there's no evidence of an earlier draft. And, well, I can't help wondering — what if this was a suicide note? What if Perri really did mean to kill herself and sent this just to torment Kat?"

"No." Josie shook her head, resolute. "You'd have to know her. To have known her." She was still having trouble with tenses.

"I'll have to take your word for it. I'm just glad that Binnie Snyder's testimony cleared up that locked stall door. That never did stop nagging at me."

"Well, she was hiding, right? She was standing on the toilet and waiting for us to come in, because Perri had promised her she was going to get Kat to confess."

"Right, but she unlocked the door to her stall. And I understand why the out-of-order stall was locked. It was the other one, the one that wasn't in use — the one where I found — Anyway, I never did understand that. Binnie explained that Perri told her to lock all three and hide in one, so that if anyone came in, they would end up leaving."

"See, that was Perri," Josie said. "She had it all planned out."

"Yeah, Binnie went into the first stall and . . . um, used it but realized she didn't have a good sight line from there. So she crawled under the partitions to the one on the end. And when you and Kat came in, she text-messaged Perri. That's why she had to take the phones. She didn't know we could have gotten the transcripts, in time."

Josie shook her head. Poor clumsy Binnie, forever so smart about big things, forever so dumb about small ones.

"Why did Binnie and I even have to go talk to those people, the grand jury?" Josie's parents had tried to conceal their worry from her, but she knew they were upset about the legal fees that Ms. Bustamante had charged them.

"When someone is shot, no matter what the circumstances, it's up to a jury to decide if he — she — should face any charges. Now it's official — what happened was an accident."

"Binnie's father shot Peter on purpose, though. Right? He didn't know it was Peter, but he aimed his gun right at him."

"He'll be no-billed, too." Josie frowned, not sure what bills had to do with any of this, and the sergeant clarified: "It's a way of saying no indictment will be handed up. It was unfortunate, what he did, and a young man died. But there's a tradition in the law of letting people protect their property from intruders. And Mr. Snyder was a little jumpy, understandably. Given the events of a year ago."

The events of a year ago. What a lovely, say-nothing phrase, Josie thought. She could use some phrases like that. *The events of a year ago. The accident with my foot. Just a little rumpus,* as Perri herself might have said.

"Anyway, you can have it if you like. The Hartigans and the Kahns don't want it, I can tell you that much."

"I'm not sure what I would do with it," Josie said, even as she refolded it into thirds and slid it beneath her keyboard.

"They were lucky, those girls," the sergeant said, looking over her shoulder at Josie's screen saver, a photograph of the three on the night of their junior prom.

"To have you as a friend."

"I always thought I was the lucky one."

"You're that, too, Josie. You're alive, and you've got your whole future ahead of you."

"Yeah, well, where else would your future be?"

The sergeant laughed and wished her well. His laughter pleased Josie, even though she had not been trying to make a joke. There had been so little laughter in her house this summer. Josie had found herself in the strange position of consoling her parents, repeatedly assuring them that nothing was their fault, and it wasn't. The thing that seemed to bother them the most was her blurted revelation that she didn't regret shooting herself. *Did she not want to go to College Park? Did she subconsciously resent the fact that she needed an athletic scholarship?*

Actually, Josie was quite keen to go away to school. College Park's hugeness, which had once frightened her a little, was now its chief asset. If anyone there remembered the shooting in Glendale, all Josie had to say was that it was tragic and she knew the girls.

Luckily, the latest doctor's visit had been promising, with all signs pointing to a full recovery. Her right foot still cramped suddenly sometimes, as if it, too, had vivid memories from that day. Her foot had needed some coaxing to touch the ground again, once the wound was healed and she stopped using crutches. For a couple of days, it curled against her calf, shy and tentative. But eventually it found the floor.

Her computer trilled, probably her mother checking in from work. No one else IM'ed her much, although Binnie had touched base off and on until the grand jury was through with them, and Dannon Estes e-mailed from time to time, wanting to rehash memories of Perri. But Dannon's Perri wasn't really Josie's Perri, and she didn't know how to explain that to Dannon.

Kat was here, too, at least in name. She lived on in Josie's IM box, although the icon showed that she was never signed on. Josie kept waiting for the Hartigans to realize that Kat's screen name remained active, but so far no one had seemed to notice. Every day Josie clicked on Kat's name, just to see the self-deprecating away message Kat had left there two months ago: "Trying to graduate. Be back in cap and gown." Josie supposed she should tell Mrs. Hartigan about the lingering account.

Her own parents would be horrified by such waste, paying for a service no one was using. But it was comforting, seeing Kat's message, to think of her as merely being away, not gone. And now she had this little scrap of Perri, too, this last fragment.

It did not bother Josie that Perri hadn't tried to write her. She was grateful, in fact. She understood now that Perri had been trying, in her own fashion, to keep the three of them intact. Kat would have been devastated if she thought the two of them had joined forces to confront her, or ganged up on her. In her own inimitable way, Perri was trying to put the three of them back together again.

There had to be more to that letter. How Josie wished she could read it.

Dear Kat:

When we were eight years old, we joined hands in a circle and promised to be true to each other and to do good in the world at large. Kid stuff, you might say, and maybe it was. But it was also a vow worth making and a pledge worth keeping. Tomorrow I will try to hold you to it.

Tonight I am putting a few things in writing because, for all my careful planning, I can't be sure you won't find a way around taking responsibility for your own actions, for continuing to deny the enormity of what you've done. You've always been very good, in your sweet way, at not doing what you don't want to do. How do you do it, Kat? How do you stop talking to your oldest friend and persuade the school that I'm the one who turned my back on you? All these months, I could have gone to Josie, told her what was going on, but I didn't want to put her in the middle. I didn't want to be the one to break the news to her that even Kat Hartigan isn't perfect. Is, in fact, a killer of sorts, responsible for the deaths of three of our classmates.

But even if you never speak to me again, you still have the option of admitting what happened. Not to your parents and the world at large, but TO YOURSELF! I'm not saying it's all your fault — you didn't tell them to speed or to let Kenny drive — just that you can't ignore the part you played in it. I know I'm asking you to do something hard, but I also believe it will liberate you in a way you never imagined. Stand up, Kat. For once do something that doesn't come easy. Earn your place in heaven. Earn all that love the world heaps on you.

Eve sat at the end of her family's driveway — the real one, off Old Town Road, not the fake one her father had cut into Sweetwater Estates — keeping company with two bushels of tomatoes, several ears of white corn, and endless zucchini. But it was a slow afternoon, with few people stopping to buy. She had only sixteen dollars to show for her two hours out here, and she was expected to split that with her father.

Bored, she had taken the creased letter from the back pocket of her cutoffs, a letter she had read many times over the past two months. It changed, according to Eve's mood, just as some movies changed when you watched them over and over again. But it never failed to fascinate her, this glimpse into another girl's life on the day before she died. So that's what they had been doing in the woods, all those years ago. Of course Eve knew the story about what had happened in the bathroom — Binnie had finally confessed all when she came to get the cell phones she had asked Eve to stash someplace safe. But the shooting was far less interesting to Eve than the emotion in the letter, as close to a love letter as anything she had ever read.

From time to time, Eve thought about destroying the letter or telling someone she had it. But, as with most of her secrets, Eve didn't think it was information that anyone wanted.

She admired her sandals, the green-and-yellow ones that Binnie had brought her a few days after the shooting and asked her to hide. They were really too nice to be wearing out here, at the end of the dusty driveway, but she loved them so much that she put them on at every opportunity. That's why she couldn't bear to put them in the compost pile with the cell phones, which Binnie had given her in those first frantic moments, when she found Eve waiting in the trees for Val and Lila. It seemed such a waste and the fact that they fit — well, that was a sign, wasn't it? It had never occurred to her that Josie might want them back. Eve wouldn't, in Josie's place.

A Volvo station wagon stopped, and Eve put on her friendly, helpful face, but it was Val and Lila, who were not likely to be in the market for vegetables. She faced them defiantly, not sure how they would react to seeing her behind the stand.

"You sell, like, vegetables?" Lila asked.

"My dad splits the take with me fifty-fifty," Eve said. "It's good money on weekends."

"Cool," Val said. "Want to go to the pool?"

"I'm not a member," Eve said.

"We can take you as a guest," Lila said.

"I have to ask my parents."

"You *ask* now?" But Val grinned, so Eve knew she was being teased.

"Yeah." Peter Lasko's death had shaken Eve's parents hard — not because he was killed by the Muhlys' neighbor and friend but because it quickly came to light that Peter had brought Eve home just a few minutes before he was shot. They had promised Eve they would be more lenient if she would be more honest with them. So far they were keeping their side of the bargain.

Val and Lila helped her load the produce, the sign, and the table into Val's Volvo, then drove her up the long, dusty driveway to the barn, where she stored the items in a freestanding shed and received her father's permission to take the rest of the afternoon off.

"It's so slow," Eve said. "I don't think

you'll lose a single sale."

"It must be slow," he said, looking at the five dollars in the cigar box Eve handed him.

"Weekdays," Eve said with a shrug.

Lenhardt ended up spending the rest of the day baby-sitting a jury in Towson, curious to see if he was going to get the first-degree conviction he deserved on the last of the suspects in the Woodlawn case. The jury was trying to claim it was deadlocked, which was a bad sign, but the judge decided to press them, make them spend the night in a motel and return for another day of deliberations. It would be a bitch trying this guy all over again.

Marcia was in the side vegetable garden clipping basil. Lenhardt happened to hate basil, but he wouldn't mention that, not tonight. He and Marcia were in a good place lately, one of those serene lulls that long-married couples learn not to take for granted.

He watched his wife bending over, scissors in hand. The black-and-white checked pants did her ass no favors, but the extra pounds she carried suited the rest of her, especially her face. With her full cheeks and blond ponytail, Marcia looked as young as she had when he married her, and no one would say the same of Lenhardt. He should take pains not to fall asleep in front of the television tonight and not to let her have the extra glass of wine that caused her to nod off over whatever she was reading for her book club.

In the house, shut up from the beautiful summer day in the bubble of central air-conditioning, Jason was at the computer in the family room.

"Mom fed us burgers already," Jason said, "but she's making a second dinner for the two of you. Something more grown-up, she said."

"That's nice." So he and Marcia were on the same wavelength, other than the basil.

"What are you reading on the Internet, Jase?"

"Porn."

"That's my boy. No, seriously, Jase."

"*Seriously*, I'm downloading a few songs. *Legally*."

"I appreciate that. Would be kind of embarrassing for me, having the feds raid the house because my son was a music pirate."

"Aaaaaaargh," Jason said in his old-salt croak, a voice picked up from some cartoon. "I sail the seas of the Internet, looking for musical booty to plunder."

"Where's your sister?"

"In her room."

"Doing what?"

"Who cares?"

"Jason."

Jessica was lying on her bed, plugged in to her digital mini — not an iPod but a lesser MP3 player, a faux pas for which her parents had not quite been forgiven even now, eight months after Christmas.

"Dad." She gave the word almost eight syllables. "You're supposed to knock."

"I did, but you didn't hear me. What are you doing?"

"Listening to music." Melodramatic eye roll and a huge, heaving sigh, but for whose benefit? He already knew that his daughter thought he was an idiot, and no one else was in the room.

"You blue because summer's almost over?"

"What?"

"Jesus, turn it down for a second." She dialed down the volume but wouldn't pull the little clips from her ears. Lenhardt remembered when the Walkman had been the big thing, the modern wonder. What was next? What technology, ten or twenty years in the future, would make his jaded daughter feel nostalgic for this little box on her belt while *her* kid sighed and heaved and rolled her eyes? God, he hoped he lived long enough to see Jessica being driven crazy by her children.

"How you doing?"

"Fine."

"Your mom mentioned that you might want to quit swim team."

Another eloquent shrug.

"I mean, the whole world is in love with an Olympic swimmer from Baltimore County, and you want to quit. That strikes me as kind of funny timing."

"Well, I'm not going to make the Olympics, so what's the point?"

"If you enjoy it, you should do it. If you don't, you shouldn't. It's that simple."

Jessica looked at the ceiling, as if amazed that someone could be ignorant enough to proclaim her problems simple.

"Honey, do you even know what makes you happy?"

"Daaaaaaaaaaaaaaaaaaaaaaaaaaaaaaaad."

"Because I want to know, okay? Your mom and I both do."

"I'm happy." Her voice was stormy, as if she had been falsely accused of some infraction.

"Okay. But you'd tell me if you weren't, right? You'd tell us if something was bothering you, no matter how hard it was? It's important that you know you can talk to us about anything. About parties and boys" — he choked a little on the last word — "and . . . well, pressure. Anything that's upsetting you. You'll tell us, right?"

"O-*kay*." This was exhaled from a clenched jaw as if a huge concession had been made, and perhaps it had. Lenhardt patted his daughter's hand and stood to leave, but he was stopped at the door by her voice — her real voice, as he thought of it, the voice of the little girl who just a year ago had let him take her in his lap, a voice without those drawn-out vowels and curlicues of sarcasm.

"Dad . . . what if I have a problem that you and Mom can't fix?"

From the mouth of babes — but while he would concede this point to himself, almost, there was no way he would admit it to his daughter. Lenhardt liked to tell himself that was the difference between him and a guy like Hartigan. He knew he couldn't do everything for his kids, that he couldn't keep them from disappointment and heartache. Lenhardt liked to tell himself that, but he also knew he was full of shit. His first daughter, Tally, was as lost to him as Kat Hartigan was to her father, and for less fathomable reasons. He couldn't stand in judgment of anyone.

"You just come and talk to us, Jessie, and we'll take it from there."

Dale Hartigan could see the red-and-white Long & Foster sign outside the Snyders' property even in the encroaching dusk. That made sense, with Binnie going away to school and feelings still running high over Peter Lasko's death. It was so odd. Because the grand jury met in secret, the circumstances of Kat's death — and life — were still largely unknown in the community at large. Yet everyone was aware that Cyrus Snyder had killed Peter Lasko. Now Snyder felt that he had to leave, while Dale Hartigan continued to receive sympathetic looks and warm hand-shakes on the rare days he ventured into Glendale. Even Chloe was kind to him. Too kind. Earning Chloe's ready forgive-ness only convinced Dale that he was be-yond hope.

Look at her now, he thought as she opened the door to him. It was almost un-bearable, the way she gazed at him, the gentle voice she employed, as if Dale were a wounded animal.

"The deed was in my safe-deposit box,"

he said, handing her a manila envelope. "An oversight. You know how papers flew back and forth in the divorce."

"I never would have sold if Kat — Well, you know how much she loved our little patch of woods. But there's a buyer for the Snyder farm, and he offered so much for my acres. Enough for me to move wherever I like, maybe even go back to school. It seems like fate."

"Sort of the opposite, if you think about it." Inviting her to castigate him, to connect the dots, to articulate how he had brought them here. But Chloe had completely lost interest in punishing Dale now that he was doing such a good job.

"Let's just say it's meant to be. How's Susannah?"

"Fine. I told her, you know. Made a clean breast."

"About what?"

"Us. That night."

"Oh, *Dale*." Just hearing the pity in her voice was like fingering a bruise, for it reminded him that Chloe had never entertained the same rosy hopes of reconciliation, not even while making love to him. He was the only one who had imagined starting over.

"I'm simply trying to be honest."

"It's possible to be too honest, Dale. Just because you need to say it doesn't mean anyone else needs to hear it."

"Well, she forgave me. She took me back. Susannah says that everyone deserves a second chance."

Yes, he was reproaching Chloe in his own way, reminding her that some women were capable of forgiveness. He didn't mention his sneaking suspicion that Susannah was delighted to have something so dire to hold over him, a card he could never trump. For Susannah Goode to be good, Dale was realizing, she needed the contrast of someone else's badness. For years that person had been tempestuous, unpredictable Chloe. Now it would be Dale.

"I have plans tonight, so if there's nothing else . . ."

"Plans? Like a date?"

"Dale."

"Okay. None of my business. Just make sure he's not after your money." It was a pathetic attempt at a joke, and it fell flat, as it deserved to. "Chloe . . . when you're getting ready to move, I'd like first crack at anything you get rid of. Especially Kat's things, of course."

"Even the painting?" She raised an eyebrow, capable now of making jokes at her own expense.

"Actually, I would love to have that painting. More than anything."

"It was always yours, Dale. Remember? I gave it to you for Christmas, the year Kat was eleven."

"Ten." But they smiled at the old disagreement. Their fractiousness was a memory now, a reminder of a time when they could afford such petty irritations.

Heading down the drive a few minutes later, Dale saw three small figures cutting across his land. Chloe's land, he corrected himself, and soon to pass out of the Hartigan name altogether. *Enjoy it now,* he wanted to yell out. If Snyder's property was already in escrow, bulldozers would probably be here by Labor Day, grading the land for the forty or so houses the site would accommodate. Would Muhly sell as well? No, he was too stubborn, too proud of being able to say he worked a farm that had been in his family for five generations. The old Meeker farmstead had stayed in Dale's family for three — which, as it turned out, was the end of the Hartigan line.

From this distance the children were

dim shadows in the twilight, and it was difficult to tell if they were boys or girls, especially as they moved single file through the grass, which was waist-high to their small frames. They had to raise their knees to right angles to find their footing. How had it gotten so overgrown? Chloe must have forgotten that she was responsible for maintaining this part of the property, or thought it no longer mattered with a sale imminent. Didn't she know that high grass like that attracted rats and other vermin? It almost made him happy, this evidence of Chloe's characteristic carelessness, his reflexive self-righteousness. Seemed like old times.

As the three children reached the tree line, they re-formed so they were walking abreast and reached for one another's hands. Swinging their arms between them, they ran toward the elms and maples and ailanthus. *Girls,* Dale thought, only girls hold hands. Boys, no matter how young and unself-conscious, would never be caught doing such a thing.

Then, just like that, the girls were gone, disappearing so suddenly in the gray-green dusk that Dale was forced to wonder if they had ever really been there at all.

Author's Note

Because of the odd nature of Maryland in general and Baltimore County in particular, it is possible that there is a Glendale somewhere within the county's strange and ragged boundaries. But the area described in this book is wholly fictional, as are the circumstances of its creation. Those who know the state will find a clue or two to Glendale's whereabouts, but they'll never find Glendale.

A fictional setting, as it turns out, requires just as much research and outside expertise as a real one. For myriad details on police work, farm work, high school, musical theater, fathers, daughters, mothers, sons, etc., I am grateful to: George Pelecanos, Anthony Neil Smith, Bill Toohey, Gary Childs, David Simon, Beth Tindall, Toby Hessenauer, Linda Perlstein, Denise Stybr, the Coles family (Charles, Mary Jeanne, Beth, Charlie, and Katie), the Russell family (Adam, Stacey, Rebecca, and

Harrison), Ann Watson and daughter Whit (and everyone else at Viva House), Joan Jacobson, and, finally, Haranders everywhere, to use Uncle Byron's phrasing. I wish I hadn't lost the name of my correspondent from Television Without Pity, the bright and articulate young woman from Norfolk, but I'll keep looking for you on the boards devoted to BMP shows. A special thanks to Maureen Sugden, who copyedited this book with extraordinary care. If any errors survived her scrutiny, it's clearly my fault.

Although I've always been quick to credit my editor, Carrie Feron, and agent, Vicky Bijur, I've never publicly tried to thank everyone at my publishing house because it's inevitable that someone will be overlooked and I'll feel rotten. But this time out I would like to essay at least a partial list: Selina McLemore, Michael Morrison, Lisa Gallagher, George Bick, Debbie Stier, Sharyn Rosenblum, Samantha Hagerbaumer, all the sales reps (but especially Ian Doherty), and, last but never least, Jane Friedman.

About the Author

Laura Lippman was a reporter at the Baltimore *Sun* for twelve years. Her Tess Monaghan books — *By a Spider's Thread*, *The Last Place*, *The Sugar House*, *Baltimore Blues*, *Charm City*, *Butchers Hill*, and *In Big Trouble* — have won the Edgar, Agatha, Shamus, Anthony, and Nero Wolfe awards, and her novel *In a Strange City* was named a *New York Times* Notable Book of the Year. She is also the author of the critically acclaimed stand-alone novel *Every Secret Thing*. She lives in Baltimore, Maryland.

The employees of Thorndike Press hope you have enjoyed this Large Print book. All our Thorndike and Wheeler Large Print titles are designed for easy reading, and all our books are made to last. Other Thorndike Press Large Print books are available at your library, through selected bookstores, or directly from us.

For information about titles, please call:

(800) 223-1244

or visit our Web site at:

www.gale.com/thorndike
www.gale.com/wheeler

To share your comments, please write:

Publisher
Thorndike Press
295 Kennedy Memorial Drive
Waterville, ME   04901